Silent Extras

Silent Extras

A NOVEL

Arnon Grunberg

Translated from the Dutch
by
Sam Garrett

F
GRUN

ST. MARTIN'S PRESS   NEW YORK

6/01   Brodart $23.95

www.stmartins.com

ISBN 0-312-20477-9

First published in Holland under the title *Figuranten*
by Nijgh & Van Ditmar

First U.S. Edition: April 2001

10 9 8 7 6 5 4 3 2 1

Contents

For Ewa
who tried to make a man out of me
who tried to make a writer out of me
who tried to make a better person out of me
and with warm memories of her beet soup.

'Too bad the only way to get to paradise is in the back of a hearse.'

Stanislaw Jerzy Lec

MONEYGRUBBER

I am the moneygrubber, dealer in tenements. It was in the winter of 1995 that I first began to think of myself as a moneygrubber. I had already thought of myself as a Latin lover, and as a tango dancer. I took tango lessons for a couple of months. Then they offered me a full refund if I promised never to come to tango lessons again. I took them up on it.

I've also thought of myself as an office boy pulling himself up by his bootstraps, as a movie star, as a publisher, as a vintner who drinks all his own wine, as a stockjobber, as a whore, as a comedian, as a film director married to an actress twenty years his junior, as a conman, as a writer, as a Don Juan, as a potential suicide, as four-eyes, as the lover of Frederika Steinman, as world champion table soccer, as Broccoli's friend, as secretary of the Association for Geniuses, as a covert member of Operation Brando, as the lover of Elvira Lopez, as a bumbling masseur to Elvira Lopez, as father to the children of Elvira Lopez – and then, in the winter of 1995, for the first time, as the moneygrubber.

You name it, no matter how crazy, and I've thought of myself that way. At the end of your life you probably start thinking of yourself as a walking corpse, but I haven't gotten to that point yet. Although, when it comes, I have the feeling it won't be a pretty sight.

Someone called me up once and said: 'God, you're such a moneygrubber.' It was a movie producer. I thought, yeah, that's exactly what I am, a moneygrubber. 'You're right,' I said, 'you're absolutely right.' Later, I wrote to him and said: 'Nothing inspires me like money. My leitmotif is my bank account number, my song a paean to money, and when I want to be sung to sleep I listen to the exchange rates on the radio. When you think of me, then think a little of money too, because when I think of you, I think of money as well.' When I'd finished the letter I opened the window and screamed out into the street: 'I am the moneygrubber, the moneygrubber's back in town.' Not that anyone noticed; from six in the morning to eight in the evening, trucks go roaring through my street and drown out every sound. Even if you hung out the window with a megaphone, no one would hear you.

Those trucks give off a black smut that gets into my apartment, even when the windows are closed. At first I tried to scrub it off the walls with a sponge. But I stopped doing that. Sometimes I talk about it with the man from the roach service, who comes to my door every Wednesday morning at eleven. He's very punctual. A nice man. We always talk a little. He says: 'You're the only normal person in this building.' He should know, he goes into all the apartments. In the rental agreement, it says: 'You are legally obliged to grant the roach service access to your apartment.'

A friend of mine recommended that I go into group therapy, so I did, even though I didn't feel sick. On the contrary. But he said: 'It's normal in America, it's not just for sick people. Everyone does it: managers, professors, performers, very successful people, it's nothing to be ashamed of. Besides,' he added, 'someday people are going to start saying you're crazy because you claim that your bank account number is your leitmotif, and because you think you're the moneygrubber. They don't like that kind of stuff. You'll end up in the gutter, or in a nuthouse where you can scream out the window all you want about being the moneygrubber. And believe me, American nuthouses are no laughing matter.'

'That last bit has me convinced,' I told him. Of course it didn't convince me at all. I'd managed to stay out of the nuthouse for the first twenty-five years of my life. Something pretty bizarre would have to happen for me to end up in one in the next twenty-five.

I spent four Wednesday afternoons in group therapy. In a beautiful old building on a street where trucks don't go barrelling through fourteen hours a day. During those sessions I found out about the collective subconscious. The woman who led the group told us we should think of the collective subconscious as a giant apple pie, a piece of which existed in the mind of every human being.

The week after that we had to relate a dream we'd had. I hadn't dreamed at all – I can't remember ever having dreamed – but I told them that I'd dreamed I was a general at the head of an army. An army of my own making. It was the Legion of Ridiculous People. We paraded down Fifth Avenue every weekday between six and eight, with me out in front. I had a megaphone in my hand and I shouted: 'This is the Legion of Ridiculous People. We summon all the ridiculous to join our ranks. Men and women, young and old, cute and ugly, regardless of your religious persuasion, everyone can join the Legion of Ridiculous People. Every weekday evening from six to eight we parade down Fifth Avenue, waving our umbrellas at other ridiculous people. That's all we're after. To greet the ridiculous with a wave of our umbrellas. Every weekday from six to eight, on Fifth Avenue.'

The group spent the next hour analysing my dream. They were like a starving mob pouncing on a bone. The collective subconscious in the form of an apple pie came up again, and I thought of Broccoli. If anyone had ever made short work of the collective subconscious, it was him. Still, it's strange that I thought of him. What I really wanted was to think about anything but him and Elvira.

Elvira probably has a husband by now, with a motorcycle. She wanted a husband with a motorcycle so she could sit on the back. She was wild about motorcycles, especially ones with sidecars. Elvira said: 'Of course it's not an absolute must, but it would make things a lot easier.'

'What?' I asked.

'Well,' she said, 'if my husband had a motorcycle with a sidecar.'

Moneygrubber is something you can be all your life. I mean, lover of Elvira Lopez or world champion table soccer or sex maniac you can't, that's clear enough.

Three days after the movie producer called me a moneygrubber, I had business cards printed with the text: '*I am the moneygrubber. I'm hollow inside.*' I passed them out, especially in bars. Broccoli had taught me that. Whenever people asked: 'What do you mean by that?', I told them: 'You know what a piggy bank is, don't you? That's me, a hollow piggy bank.' And then I made oinking sounds. That's the kind of thing that keeps me going. I almost never make oinking sounds any more. When I used to hang around with Broccoli and Elvira, I made oinking sounds all the time. In fact, all three of us did. That cheered us up.

I once made a deal that got me four, five hundred thousand. Let's round it off to five. People thought I had a rich father or was dealing drugs, or that I was real good with computers.

That five hundred thousand is gone now. I didn't do anything special with it. I mean, I didn't buy houses or boats, not even a stereo. I ate in restaurants a lot, it's true, and I slept in hotels, always in the bridal suite, even when I was alone, and I bought a few pairs of silk underwear and treated some people to bottles of wine and tiramisu and crêpes flambée and things like that. For a while there, I also drank a lot of champagne, especially in hotel bars, which adds up really fast. If I had a son I'd tell him: 'Take that champagne and drink it in the park, drink it in the subway as far as I'm concerned, but don't let me catch you with champagne in a hotel bar.'

During group therapy I had to talk about why I sometimes opened the window and yelled: 'I am the moneygrubber, the moneygrubber's back in town,' even though I knew no one could hear me.

'Sometimes it's all a bit too much for me,' I whispered.

'What's that?' the counsellor asked.

I didn't know what to say.

'Do you have the feeling that you are stingy?' a Swiss boy asked. He was extremely kind to me. He wanted to pet me all the time. 'I'm not a dog,' I'd hiss. But it didn't help. 'Easy, boy, take it easy,' the Swiss boy said, and just went on petting.

'No,' I said, 'I don't have the feeling that I'm stingy, I just have the feeling that money is the most important thing in my life. Everything I have to say can be expressed in money, my whole life can be expressed in money, the nine digits of my bank account are an adequate summary of everything I've ever done or thought, of everything I've prayed for, everything I've longed for, of everything I've ever worried about, everything I've written. Mallarmé thought that, in the end, everything would become a book. I used to think that too. Now I think that everything will become a bankbook. And if you've got smarts, you'll make sure it's a numbered account.'

The Swiss boy started petting me again.

'Günther,' I said, 'please.'

'I understand you,' he whispered. 'I understand your people so well.'

The next week I had to come in with a list of things that were too much for me. When we weren't talking about the collective subconscious in the form of apple pies, we had to bring in lists. I still remember what was on mine. Trucks. People who ask things that allow no sensible answer. Whether money can buy love, for example, questions like that. People who pet me like I'm a dog or a cat. My neighbour's music. My neighbour's boots. They go clomp, clomp, clomp, all day long. My neighbour practises clog dancing every day. Clomp, clomp, clomp, until it's time for him to go to bed. People like that should be put under psychiatric detention. The cockroach man feels the same way. ('Very good,' the therapist whispered, 'let the aggression flow.') Men who want to take women on kitchen tables. There are a lot of men walking around in this world who want to take women on kitchen tables. Millions of them, from all walks of life.

The therapist reacted to my list by bringing up the collective subconscious again. There may actually be something like a collective subconscious, it's just that I have the feeling it passed me by. Broccoli used to say that sometimes: 'The collective subconscious passed me by.' Then he'd shake his fist at passers-by. Elvira would laugh and say: 'I don't understand men at all, especially not married men.' Then she'd add: 'I don't understand women either.'

In March I became a real estate man. I figured my life had to change. I had to start viewing the future with confidence, instead of thinking that the future was a crocodile that wanted to eat me. I barely passed my exam. By the skin of my teeth, said the man who taught the course, who was also an estate agent. He had grey hair and glasses and wore tennis shoes all the time. He claimed to be one of the most successful real estate men in New York, but I thought: if you're really such a hotshot real estate man, what are you doing teaching a course on Sunday morning? I never laughed at his jokes. Maybe that's why he gave me a 'C', which is not really a grade to be proud of. There was a boy from Boston on our real estate course, a shy boy with black hair. He stank a little, because he didn't have a house where he could wash himself. That's pretty strange, of course, a real estate agent with no place to live. That's probably why no one wanted to talk to him. They didn't talk to me either. The first day we had to tell why we were taking this course, and I said: 'Because I'd like to get to know people.' Then I added quickly: 'To understand people.' That's not what you're supposed to say, of course, but it was out before I knew it. I just said whatever came up. In fact, I've never done the same thing for more than three years.

The boy from Boston who stank a little always sat beside me. One day, when we'd sent out for Chinese lunch, he lost a filling in his chop suey. As soon as class started again – we were going to talk about mortgages – he put up his hand and said: 'Could I leave early? I have to go to the dentist, I lost my filling in the Chinese.' We never saw him again after that.

My theory is that the more people you know, the greater the chance that you'll become an alcoholic. Talking to people is OK, of course, but taking them home with you is a big risk. For a variety of reasons. I had a girl over once who didn't want to leave any more. Right before I felt I was going to throw up, I said: 'I think it would be better for you to leave.' I fell asleep on the couch, and when I woke up she was still sitting beside me. Then I said again: 'I really think you'd better go home now, because I can't handle it any more.' Some people just don't care. No matter what you say to them, they stay in your house. They probably figure: once you're in, you're in.

I now have three diplomas: a swimming diploma, a bicycling diploma and a real estate diploma. In fact, I've misplaced the diplomas for swimming and bicycling, but I'm not planning to do either of them again anyway.

In a couple of years I'm going to open my own real estate office, and I'm going to call it: Moneygrubber, Inc. Let me explain the philosophy behind this. People will think: Hey, a real estate agent called Moneygrubber, that must be one honest real estate agent. And they'll come to me. When the office opens, I'm going to place an ad with the following text: '*Open for business: Moneygrubber. Agent in Real Estate.*' Nothing else. Broccoli and Elvira would definitely think that was a good idea, Moneygrubber, Inc. Maybe they've become real estate agents too.

I met Elvira through Broccoli, and back when I met Broccoli

and Elvira I hadn't become a moneygrubber yet. On the contrary, Operation Brando was still in full swing. I'd promised Broccoli I'd write a film script for Elvira, because he wanted to make her a big star. We wanted to make her a big star, I should say. Marilyn Monroe, that kind of big. Marlene Dietrich. That's why they went to New York too, to make her big.

There was a time there when I thought I had AIDS. Or something worse, if anything like that even exists. I had these lacerations on my wiener that just wouldn't go away. Three in total. Not really bad lacerations, just like when you get scratched by a cat. More like when you've been bitten by a little insect, actually. But they wouldn't go away. At least twenty doctors looked at them. And they all touched them, some of them without washing their hands first. I also thought I felt a burning sensation whenever I peed. Especially for a couple of days after having intercourse. I went to a doctor and he said: 'No, sir, you don't have a burning sensation when you pee.' Of course, I should have asked him: 'How would you know?' But I didn't dare. At a certain point I thought I couldn't pee at all any more. That was the worst. Nothing came out for two days. Then a sort of fountain.

I didn't go to a doctor's office, I went to a clinic. One of those clinics where you can remain anonymous. But if you go to a clinic like that every week, you don't remain anonymous for long. I always told them: 'Just call me David, at least that's a name I don't have to spell out.' Sometimes people ask me: 'If you had to do it all over again, what would you do differently?' And I always say: 'I'd give myself a name I don't have to spell out.' A stage name, in other words. Even if you're not on the stage, a stage name can come in handy.

I've been to bed with a lot of seedy individuals. In fact, I'm a seedy individual myself. Even though I put on clean socks when the man from the roach service is coming by. If I had to describe myself for an aptitude test or a psychologist, I'd just say: 'seedy individual'. And under 'further comments', I might add: 'moneygrubber'. Not that I'm ever planning to take an aptitude test or go to a psychologist.

There are plenty of people I've tried to imitate. Too many to mention. I've studied people in order that I might resemble them. Some people say I was Broccoli and Elvira's shadow. Elvira wasn't interested in God. At least, she never talked about him. After Elvira, I worshipped a woman who was Dutch Reformed and talked about God and other Old Testament figures all the time. Her name was Frederika Steinman. I have lusted after women who revealed nothing of themselves to me, so there is a chance that some of them were Dutch Reformed too, but Frederika Steinman was so Reformed that to worship her was to worship Reformed at the same time.

People with cultivated taste don't talk about money or sex. I've spent some time around people with cultivated taste. People like that made me feel I was right up there facing enemy lines, but then people often make me feel like I'm in the front trenches. To set the record straight, I've never been to the front trenches. Because when you're all on your own, there is no front. Even when you're armed to the teeth, you still need at least two people to form a front. For sex, all you need is yourself. That's an important difference between sex and the trenches.

I've drawn up a Top Three of fantasies that must *not* come true. If you ask me, one must do everything in one's power to make sure these fantasies do not become reality. About once a day I run through the charts on the Top Three. When I do that, I do a little drum roll with my fingers on an English-Dutch dictionary, because that resonates so nicely. Coming in at number three: sex with plants and animals. Number two: skydiving. And still up there at number one: suicide in all its variations, including auto-strangulation and putting yourself out with the garbage.

Relax, people say to me. I don't relax. In my grave I will relax. As long as you're alive, you have to stay on your toes, because before you know it another fantasy could come true, and that might be the very one that proves fatal.

Part One

BROCCOLI

*W*e'd been walking around Amsterdam all day, looking for the right place to take each other's picture. Something was always just a bit wrong. The light, or the background, or my nose was shiny.

'A shiny nose definitely doesn't make it,' Broccoli said. 'The world isn't waiting for people with shiny noses.'

I'd discovered that by now. We'd been traipsing around for six hours. It was hot. Our lives depended on those photos. Lives depend on the strangest things: on photos, on money, on a traffic jam, a watch that's running slow.

'We have to find a drugstore,' Broccoli said. 'We have to powder your nose.'

I trotted along behind him. He took big steps. His camera was dangling around his neck. I was eighteen and I wanted to be someone else, preferably in front of hundreds, thousands of people. In fact, most preferably in front of a rolling camera. Broccoli also wanted to be someone else in front of a rolling

camera. After all, if no one can see that you've become someone else, what good is it? Now and then Broccoli threw his arm
around my shoulder and said: 'We're going to be stars of the silver
screen, there's no two ways about it.'

Now Broccoli stopped suddenly and said: 'You have a really
strange head, you know that?'

'I know that,' I said.

He looked at me for a long time and said: 'You have the
strangest head I've ever seen.' And then: 'It's important to always
be aware of your own shortcomings.'

He was brilliant. I haven't met many brilliant people in my
life, so I know what I'm talking about when I call him brilliant.

Broccoli went on: 'You should buy a tape, one of those tailor's
measuring tapes, and then you should wrap it around it your
head. It's always handy to know the dimensions of your own head.
I carry the dimensions of my head with me wherever I go.' And
he actually pulled a little diary out of his pants pocket. It was
empty, except for the first page where he'd written down the
dimensions of his own head.

'Broccoli,' I said, 'your nose is shiny too.'

He stopped in his tracks.

'Is it really?' he said.

'It really is.' I squinted a little to get a better look at his nose.
I needed stronger lenses. 'And there are little black dots on it too.'

He swore. 'Then we have to powder my nose too. Otherwise
this will all have been for nothing. Otherwise they'll put us in a
drawer with all the other shiny noses.'

Broccoli had this idea that talent scouts had all kinds of
pictures in drawers they used to sort people according to their
physical shortcomings. He was running out in front of me again.
I'd never seen him walk as much as he did that day. He usually
moved around in taxis. When we finally found a drugstore,
Broccoli stopped at the door. 'Don't forget,' he said, 'everyone
has black dots on their nose. Otherwise the nose can't breathe,
and it dies off.'

The young woman at the counter had blonde hair and rosy cheeks. It looked like she'd slapped a bunch of red powder on them.

In those days I was highly inflammable. Like gasoline. I struggled against inflammability with every means at my disposal. Broccoli said I should do that. He also said you should always jerk off before trying to seduce a woman. Otherwise you were too nervous. The world wasn't waiting for the nervous, Broccoli said. People had enough trouble handling their own nerves. He also wanted to write a book about that. And then dedicate it to me.

'We need some powder,' Broccoli said.

'Excuse me?' the girl asked.

'It's for our noses,' Broccoli said. 'That's fairly obvious, I take it.' He wiped the sweat from his forehead with a handkerchief. Nothing seemed to embarrass Broccoli.

'It's for a photo session,' I heard him say.

'Oh, like that,' the girl said.

I stared at the floor, then I peered off at the section with the rheumatic bandages. Those bandages you stick on your back and the rheumatism goes away. I could see the girl holding her face right up to Broccoli's nose. I felt myself flaming up again, so I concentrated on the rheumatic bandages. Back then I used to get spontaneous erections all the time, especially in cafés. I was afraid people would see it, so I wouldn't get up. I'd just sit there until it went away. I even started wearing these huge pleated trousers. I thought people were looking at my crotch all the time. We had a rabbi who used to say that God saw everything, including your crotch, so you had to be sure to wash yourself well. And also arrange to be circumcised, if you weren't already. I'd rather have my crotch looked at by God than by people on the street. Broccoli said my pleated trousers made me look like an old Dutch farmer. So I started wearing normal pants again.

'Come here,' Broccoli shouted, 'she wants to look at you too.'

Before I could even get to the counter, she stuck her face up so close to my nose that I could see the wrinkles around her lips. I held my breath, just to be safe.

'You two don't have the same skin tone,' she said. 'I'll have to give you two different kinds of powder.'

'That's OK,' Broccoli said.

Before we left, she said she'd remember our visit for a long time, and Broccoli replied: 'I won't forget you either.'

Broccoli wanted to powder my nose right out in front of the store.

'Do we have to do that here?' I asked. 'Everyone's looking at us. I can't concentrate like this.'

'It's now or never,' he said. He took my face in his hands and smeared the brush all over my nose. I pinched my eyes shut to keep from seeing how people were staring at us.

'Now you.' He handed me the brush and opened the other box of powder. A gust of wind came along and blew half the powder into my mouth and on to my glasses, but Broccoli didn't care. He was obsessed. I saw more and more people stopping and pointing at us. The girl from the drugstore came outside with one of her customers, they were looking at us too.

'We're drawing a crowd,' I whispered. 'Let's go to the park.' Broccoli wasn't wearing his glasses, so he couldn't see much. Without glasses he couldn't see a thing.

'When you get to Hollywood,' he shouted, 'crowds will gather all the time when you go out on the street. All trying to get an autograph. If you can't handle a little crowd, you'll never make it in Hollywood.'

'But I'm not a make-up artist,' I complained.

'Powder my nose,' Broccoli barked, 'or I'll break your glasses, pizza face.'

Broccoli meant well by it. That's why I was willing to take that that kind of thing from him. It was actually pretty funny when he said that. He wanted to make people aware of their short-comings. Not everyone, of course, but I was his friend. I powdered his nose, just like he'd powdered mine.

We knew that, in this world, the man inside was manifestly reflected on the outside, and we were willing to submit to the rules this world had drawn up. Because Hollywood was calling us. Maybe it was calling Broccoli a little louder, but I was being called by Broccoli, which boiled down to the same thing.

When I was finished, Broccoli said: 'Now we won't end up in the drawer with the shiny noses.'

At a news-stand he bought a can of beer. I had the feeling that all that powder was making the sweat stick to my nose and form crusts, but I didn't dare to say anything about it.

Broccoli drank the way other people smoke. More from nerves than because he was thirsty or wanted to get drunk. In fact, he never got drunk. He just fell asleep.

'Not so fast, Broccoli,' I shouted. He stopped at a traffic light. The foam was stuck to his lips, and his face was covered with powder.

We'd heard Hollywood calling, the way other people heard the call of the monastery, or of their adulterous neighbour, or of big money or God. In the still of the evening, the call meant for us was especially clear. It drove us completely crazy.

Sometimes in the middle of the night Broccoli would dial a telephone number in Hollywood. Then he'd lie down on the bed and look at his stomach. He'd say: 'If I ever get a beer belly, it'll be the best-looking beer belly in the world.'

How he could get up at eight every morning and feel like a beer, was one of the things I never understood about Broccoli, and probably never will.

'Here,' Broccoli said, 'the light's good here.' We'd stopped in front of a house on the Realengracht. I couldn't see anything special about the light. Maybe he just liked the house, or maybe he had some business to arrange with the people who lived there.

'For the two of us, there are twelve more actors waiting in line,' he said. 'A hundred, make that a thousand.' Then he grabbed my ear, pulled me up close and whispered: 'All they do is look at the pictures, so give it everything you've got.'

It was hot, but Broccoli still had on a raincoat. He was four years older than me. At least that's what he said. He'd also said that, at the age of six, his entire family had pronounced him a wunderkind. It was in the living room, he said, he was playing his violin and suddenly the whole family started shouting: 'He's a wunderkind, he's a wunderkind.' Someone even fainted. An aunt of his cried: 'Oh my God, another wunderkind in the family!'

From then on his parents made him play the violin up on the rooftop patio. The neighbouring kids threw tennis balls at him and rotten apples from the tree in their garden. But his mother kept shouting out the window: 'He's a wunderkind, he's a wunderkind.'

After he'd told me all this, he took a few steps back and said: 'A wunderkind appears on an average of once every hundred years. What you see before you is a very rare phenomenon. Never forget that.'

He pulled one the handkerchiefs he used to cut from old dishtowels out of his pocket, and wiped the sweat from his face. He'd tried to get me to cut handkerchiefs from old dishtowels too. He said it was a good way to save money, but Broccoli wasn't the kind who saved money. If you ask me, he cut handkerchiefs from old dishtowels because he was too lazy to buy handkerchiefs. My family had plenty of handkerchiefs; to be precise, we had enough handkerchiefs to supply an orphanage. I told Broccoli that. Besides, my mother would have killed me if I'd started cutting handkerchiefs out of her dishtowels.

'Do I look right for a western?' Broccoli asked. That was the genre he wanted to specialise in. His favourite line was: 'I kill for money. But you are my friend, so I kill you for nothing.'

I didn't think he looked like he was cut out for a western, more like someone who'd audition for a role in *Death of a Salesman*. But I didn't tell him that, of course. I shot all twelve exposures, one after the other, without paying any attention to the light.

When it was his turn, he said: 'Brush that hair away, otherwise they won't be able to see your face.' He danced around in front of me with the camera. I felt like I had a puddle of powder stuck to my nose. But Broccoli said I looked like a little rat that was about to bite someone's balls off.

Right after he said that, he threw his arm around my shoulders and said: 'Maybe they're looking for a little rat. I bet they are; little rats are always in demand.'

He knew a cheap photo shop on the Munt where we could have the photos developed.

TECHNICALLY UNFIT

On my seventeenth birthday I went to Maastricht to audition for the theatre school. I'd heard that the best theatre school was the one in Maastricht.

I stayed at the Hotel de la Bourse. The place was full of travelling salesmen. At eight o'clock in the morning, the chambermaid knocked on the door and yelled in three languages that she was coming in to mop the floor. Even if you shouted: 'No, I'm naked', she still came in.

It was June, and it was hot. I was wearing some shorts I'd bought at Sissy-Boy just before I left. I remembered that the mod girls at school always bought their clothes there. The shorts were three sizes too big for me, but the salesman told me it was the fashion that summer to walk around in oversized shorts.

'So, young man, I see you're also wearing *It-Ain't-Half-Hot-Mum* pants?' was the first thing the drama teacher in Maastricht said to me. The term '*It-Ain't-Half-Hot-Mum* pants' didn't say much to me, so I just smiled amiably.

The second day in Maastricht they locked up all the boys in a little classroom and made us undress. The only thing we were allowed to keep on was our underpants. The girls were locked in another classroom. The teachers came and took us away one by one.

When it was my turn, a man came and led me to the gym. I walked along beside him, through the halls of the Maastricht theatre school, in my underpants. I realised then that people with clothes on have a giant edge on the naked or partly nude.

Two women and a man were sitting at a table in the gym. The man was in the middle. He was wearing glasses and had bristly white hair. He stared at me for a minute. He didn't say a word. I started thinking maybe something weird was stuck to my body, so I looked at myself as inconspicuously as possible, but I couldn't see anything. Fortunately, the two women weren't staring at me. They were looking out the window and yawning. Finally, I had to walk up to the table and say my name loud and clear.

'Ewald Stanislas Krieg,' I said.

'Stanislas-Krieg, is that a compound surname?' the man asked.

'No,' I said, 'Ewald Stanislas is a compound first name.'

The man wrote something down. Then he came out from behind the table and started pinching my Achilles' tendons. I told him it tickled. He didn't seem to be listening. After a couple of minutes he must have figured he'd messed with my legs long enough.

'Jump, Ewald Stanislas,' he said.

'Ewald, just Ewald, that's plenty.'

'Jump,' he said.

I jumped.

'Higher,' the man said.

I jumped higher.

'Higher than that,' the man said.

I jumped even higher. I was starting to feel like some kind of frog. But the man just kept shouting: 'Higher, higher.' I wondered why you had to break the high-jump record when all you wanted was to be an actor.

When the man figured I'd jumped enough, he said: 'Now walk a diagonal line.'

I walked diagonally.

He made me walk three more diagonals.

Finally, one of the women at the table said: 'T.U.'

I asked what that meant, and she told me: 'Technically unfit.'

'Well, thanks for all your time,' I said.

'Thank you for your time,' said the man who'd pinched my Achilles' tendons. I left the gym. The next candidate was already waiting in his underpants.

The next day was the singing test. I had to sing part of an opera with a lady, tête-à-tête. The lady was in her late eighties and had curly red hair.

'Stanislas,' the lady said, 'that's an unusual name; it sounds like Stanislavsky. You know Stanislavsky, I take it?'

'Vaguely,' I said, 'vaguely, we never actually met.'

'Stanislavsky, the great dramatic innovator,' the lady said.

I didn't know any opera songs. So she sang something for me. I had to sing along with her. That was hard. I kept thinking about how my breath smelled.

'No,' she said, 'if you're going to sing you have to open your mouth. Open your mouth, open it. There are more than two hundred candidates waiting for me.'

The lady put her ear to my lips and I had to make all kinds of sounds. An 'ooh' and an 'aaay' and a 'hoo-hoo' and a 'low ooo' and 'one from the diaphragm' and an 'ooo' that caught in my throat.

At one point, she wanted to look down my throat.

A few minutes later she said: 'T.U.'

I kept going to classes for the rest of the week, even though I knew my chances of being accepted were minimal. The organisers urged us to get to know other aspiring actors and actresses, but I couldn't even keep up a conversation with them.

I lived in great fear of all the people walking around at the

Maastricht Theatre School. A fear so great that I had to hurl myself through the gates of the school every morning with total disregard for life and limb. It was a huge struggle for me not to stay in the dark at the Hotel de la Bourse, where at least I didn't have to jump up and down in my underpants like a frog. I probably only stuck it out for that week because my father had said: 'Doing your best isn't enough. When you die, you have to be able to say: "I didn't succeed, but God knows I did all I could. It wasn't my fault."'

In the evening I wandered around Maastricht and, at my father's expense, ate in fancy restaurants where I sometimes pretended to be of poor but noble lineage. My fellow aspiring actors ate in the cafeteria and hung around in bars I didn't dare to enter. After dinner I'd lock myself in my hotel room and spend wildly passionate nights with myself. I even made love to myself in the bathtub. By way of experiment, I resolved to have an underwater orgasm every night. Sometimes my fingers still smelled of my own seed the next morning, but since I was the only one who smelled my fingers, that didn't seem like much of a problem.

Once, in the cafeteria of the Maastricht Theatre School, I told an aspiring actor: 'You know, my sperm's been black for the last couple of weeks. Everything that comes out looks like tar. Do you think I should see a doctor?'

All right, maybe it wasn't such a great joke, but at least I was trying. From that day on, the aspiring actor and his friends gave me a wide berth. I've never told anyone that my sperm is black ever again.

The younger, healthier and happier they were, the more I feared them. The Maastricht Theatre School was crawling with the young, healthy and happy. All Maastricht was crawling with young, healthy and happy people, with the exception of the cleaning lady who burst into my room every morning at eight.

On the last day we had to recite a monologue and a poem in

the school auditorium. I recited a completely incomprehensible poem by Boudewijn Büch. I'd come across it in an issue of *Avenue*, and I thought it was very deep. After that I did a monologue from a Greek tragedy. Halfway through the monologue, I got very bad stomach cramps.

During that week in Maastricht, I'd had my first experience with shrimp: king prawns, to be exact. I'd been raised in the conviction that I should only eat fish if it had fins and scales, things like cod, flounder, halibut and carp to name a few. Squid, shrimp, mussels and oysters were off-limits. My family stuck pretty strictly to the dietary laws. Not that anyone at our house believed in God. We clung to the laws because our ancestors had.

I was convinced that these stomach cramps were the hand of God, wreaking vengeance for the prawns I'd eaten the night before. During the monologue, my thoughts were pretty much fixed on prawns, but no one seemed to notice.

Later that same summer, I went on a one-week diet of mussels and king prawns, until I couldn't stand the sight of another shell-fish. It was like I was shaking my fist at the Almighty and saying: 'I quit, Your laws are no longer my laws; if You've got something against prawns, OK, but leave me out of it. I'm heading into the sophisticated world where they devour entire clam beds without batting an eyelid. I am no longer one of the prematurely afflicted, I'm shaking off the odour of the voluntary ghetto, I'm heading into the world of prawns. Monte Carlo, Las Vegas, Hollywood, the Italian Riviera; if You're looking for me, that's where You'll find me.' That was more or less my regular harangue against the Almighty.

The week I was on that prawn diet, someone from the Maastricht Theatre School called to say that I hadn't been accepted, and that there was no real reason for me to apply again. I wasn't home, so my father took the call. I had my whole life ahead of me, and there was nothing to do about it.

■ ■ ■

I didn't do anything. Early in the morning I'd sneak out of my parents' house on the Prinses Margrietstraat and come back late, sometimes in the middle of the night. I made sure no one from the Prinses Margrietstraat saw me. It usually worked, but sometimes I'd run into one of the neighbours with her dog. She walked that dog at the most impossible hours. Whenever I saw her, I crossed the street and walked along with my eyes glued to the pavement.

No one chooses to move to a ghetto, but everyone on the Prinses Margrietstraat lived there voluntarily. More than voluntarily. People saved all their money for years to be able to live there. One time I applied for a job at a company and the man said: 'Oh, you live on the Prinses Margrietstraat, sometimes I take walks there on Sunday. Ooh-la-la, the Prinses Margrietstraat.'

At the end of that summer, my mother received a visit from a hefty Jewish woman and her two marriageable daughters. The weather was nice, so my mother invited the woman and her daughters into our garden.

'Your son will turn eighteen soon,' the woman said. 'He doesn't have any papers and he doesn't go to the synagogue, but I still have a lot of confidence in him. Have I introduced you to my daughters?'

My mother pulled me out of the bathroom and put a yarmulke on my head. I shook hands with the daughters. One of them had a mouth like a mail slot. The other one looked like she was from outer space. She kept staring at the ground and had to be nudged a few times before she'd shake my hand. Maybe it was my imagination, but it looked like little drops of spittle were sticking to her lips.

After we'd all been given a cup of coffee, the girls' mother said: 'We're not wealthy, but our family is fruitful, which is also a kind of wealth.' I stared at the daughters, but they didn't stare back at me.

'Oh, of course,' my mother said, 'that's also a kind of wealth.'
'I have a lot of faith in young Ewald,' the mother said. She'd
suddenly stopped saying 'your son'. I took that as a warning. Then
she hugged me and said: 'You're my sweetheart, I already love you
like a son.' She pressed my face almost flat against her huge bosom.
'You don't have to do that,' I said.
'Yes I do,' she said, 'oh, yes I do.'

It was then that I had a flash of inspiration which, for some
time, created a breach between me and my parents, and between
my parents – particularly my mother – and the Jewish community
in general. I started jumping up and down like a frog, the way I
had at the Maastricht Theatre School. And while I jumped, I
started taking off my clothes. At first, the girls' mother laughed
and said: 'Oh, isn't he a cheerful boy.' But when she realised that
I wasn't going to stop at my underpants, she covered her daughters'
eyes. A few moments later she fled the house. The daughter I'd
figured wasn't all there turned at the sliding glass doors and stared
at me with big, bulging eyes. My mother ran after them, but it was
no use. I stayed behind in the garden, naked and jumping up and
down like a frog.

After that, my mother was offered no more marriageable
daughters. That's why I'm still single to this day.

The next spring I met Broccoli. He wasn't young and healthy,
and thank God, he was no happier than me. That's why I wasn't
afraid of him.

MRS MEERSCHWAM

*I*t was in the corridor at the Amsterdam Theatre School. Broccoli was standing in front of a pillar, holding a tirade again theatre schools in general and the Amsterdam Theatre School in particular. I'd never seen him before that.

Suddenly he turned to me and asked: 'What are you staring at, lummox?'

The last person I'd heard use the word 'lummox' was my mother, and even coming from her it had sounded pretty ridiculous. I was wearing my pleated trousers. They kept falling down, so I had to pull them up all the time.

'Did they take you, or did you get the boot?'

'The boot,' I said.

'Me too,' he said. 'So now we're going to drink some fish soup.'

He was wearing shorts. Broccoli explained to me later that his legs needed lots of fresh air. Much later still, he told me that the world wasn't waiting for people with pale legs. Especially not if those legs were really thin, too. There were all kinds of people the world wasn't waiting for, and to hear Broccoli tell it, the thing was to not be one of them.

And I believed Broccoli. Back then, if people had told me: 'He's the son of God', I would have taken a good look at him and thought: Yeah, now that you mention it.

We went to Café Walem. When we'd finished our fish soup, he told me that Broccoli was what his friends called him.

'And what about other people?' I asked.

'To everyone else, I'm *Mister* Broccoli,' he said. Then he pulled a credit card out of his pocket and waved it above his head. 'In places like this, rudeness is the only way to command respect,' he explained. Then he leaned over and whispered in my ear: 'And what goes for places like this, goes for most of the world. Sad but true.'

Then he kissed me on the earlobe. I'd never been kissed on the earlobe before by a man, not by a woman either. I wasn't sure how to react. So finally I just asked him: 'How do you get a credit card like that?' But he didn't tell me.

Later, as we were walking down the Leidsestraat, he said: 'You should come over to my place. I'd like to measure your head.'

'Excuse me?' I said.

'It's always a good idea to measure things,' Broccoli replied, 'take it from me. Especially heads. I've measured my own head on a few occasions. You learn a lot from it.'

Sometimes he spoke almost too quietly to hear, and then he would start screaming, right out in the middle of the street: 'I'm so sensitive, I'm so terribly sensitive.' At first, that embarrassed me. But he didn't like people who were embarrassed by him. No, in fact that was one thing he detested.

Broccoli lived in his parents' house on the Bernard Zweerskade, but they weren't there. As far as I could tell, they were never there. They had withdrawn to the Swiss mountains for some peace and quiet.

The first thing that struck me about the house was the way it smelled. A mixture of mothballs and that sweet perfume old ladies wear. The couches in the living room were covered in plastic. A pile of wood was drying in front of the fireplace. It looked like that was all the room was used for.

A lady with a big knot of grey hair was drinking tea in the kitchen. When she saw Broccoli, she stood up. 'There was a pan of sausages on the stove, it must have been there for at least three weeks. They were covered in mould.'

Broccoli kissed her hand.

'Bah,' the grey-haired woman shouted. 'Bah, you degenerate!'

'This is Mrs Meerschwam,' Broccoli told me. 'She comes in and cleans once a month.'

'But I don't come in to clean up your mouldy sausages,' she barked. 'Can I help it that you can't take care of yourself?'

Broccoli whispered: 'She's addicted to bonbons.'

'Aren't you going to introduce me?' Mrs Meerschwam asked, pointing at me.

'This is Ewald,' Broccoli said, opening the refrigerator. It was empty.

Mrs Meerschwam looked at me dubiously. Then she said quietly: 'He used to bring all kinds of things home with him.'

'Oh,' I said.

'Animals, people, missing items. But we put a stop to that.'

She seemed to be waiting for a reaction. I stepped back, afraid Mrs Meerschwam would think I stank. She gave off a strong odour of candy store herself.

'I've been coming here for thirty years, and I've seen a few things in my day,' she said, staring at me the whole time. She shook her head. I understood that she had learned to accept an awful lot in those thirty years.

Suddenly she hissed: 'What's your last name?'

'Krieg,' I said, 'Krieg, you spell it just the way it sounds.'

Broccoli's room was in the attic. It looked out over the canal and the Beatrixpark. There were clothes and shoes lying everywhere, three fishing rods were leaning against the wall. Stuck to the door was a movie poster from *Once Upon a Time in the West*.

We sat on the bed. Mrs Meerschwam came in and began mopping the floor loudly. She commented on everything she found, then threw it into the part of the room she'd just mopped.

'She follows me around,' Broccoli whispered in my ear. I nodded.

'Fishing doesn't interest me any more,' Broccoli said loudly. 'Besides, it reminds me too much of my father.'

'Did he tell you that I sewed the curtains for his crib?' Mrs Meerschwam said. 'That's how long I've been coming here.' She was kneeling on the floor. She was wearing knee-pads.

Broccoli pulled me out the door. When I turned to close it, I saw that Mrs Meerschwam was staring at us.

We went into the garden. It was a big garden, with a pond and a hedge of rhododendrons blooming in one corner. Broccoli said a lot of people thought that was romantic, blooming rhododendrons. He said: 'If you're ever planning to kiss a woman, be sure to do it under the blooming rhododendrons.'

I promised to keep that in mind.

'Keeping it in mind isn't enough,' he said. Then he added: 'What's important for you to know is that I'm a genius.' He looked at me earnestly. I didn't know what to say.

'That's right,' he said 'I'm a genius.' Then he started laughing. He laughed until I couldn't help laughing along with him. All kinds of stuff came flying out of his mouth and on to my face, and he said: 'Etiquette has never been my strong suit.'

I sensed he was telling the truth. Broccoli had set up an association, the Association of Geniuses. He wanted me to join. Broccoli said: 'It's for those who stand out so far above the crowd that their teeth sometimes start chattering spontaneously.' Then he pinched my cheek hard and said: 'Don't your teeth ever chatter?'

'Not very often,' I said. My teeth almost never chatter. They used to chatter when I went swimming, but I never do that any more.

Broccoli grabbed me by the arm and whispered: 'Stick around long enough, and you'll become a genius too.'

We crossed the yard.

'My father used to have a new lawn put in after every garden party,' Broccoli said. 'He couldn't stand the sight of trampled grass.'

Mrs Meerschwam came out on the second-floor balcony. She started pounding rugs, and while she was pounding, she shouted: 'I can't keep this up much longer, I swear to you, I can't keep this up. Look at this filth!'

Broccoli paid no attention to her. 'At the age of twelve, I was already an accomplished plumber,' he said solemnly, pacing back and forth.

'Oh yeah?' I said. He stopped.

'Aren't you interested in hearing how someone becomes an accomplished plumber by the age of twelve?' From the way he looked at me, I could tell he didn't think much of people who didn't want to know why some twelve-year-olds were already accomplished plumbers.

'Sure,' I said, 'in fact, I'm all ears.'

'Listen,' Broccoli said. 'If you want to go home, just tell me. I've got plenty of things to do. Pretty Face Bo is coming over, he's a friend of mine, a business acquaintance. So it's not like I don't have anything else to do.'

'OK,' I said. 'But I don't want to go home.'

'Our toilet was always clogged,' Broccoli told me. 'That's because my father produced the biggest turds in the world. Some of them were forty-five centimetres long. I bet your father never pinched a forty-five centimetre turd; I bet you never did either.'

I had to admit he was right. I told him twenty centimetres was my personal record, but that most of them never got past four or five centimetres.

'My point exactly,' Broccoli said excitedly, 'you're not very big, so if you averaged eight centimetres you could already thank your lucky stars. But my father's turds were too much for the toilet to handle, that's how big they were. And we had the best toilet money could buy. They just wouldn't fit through. Whenever my father came out of the toilet, my mother would shout: "Quick, unplug it before it's too late!"

'We had one of those big electric coils that could drill its way through anything. I was the only one in the house who knew how to use it. When we had visitors I had to do it on the sly, because my father didn't want other people to know he produced the world's biggest turds. That's how I became an accomplished plumber by the age of twelve.'

'You're a real wunderkind,' I said. I thought about what it would be like to actually meet the man who produced the biggest turds in the world.

Broccoli stood there beaming.

'My point exactly,' he said. 'Which is why I set up the Association for Geniuses; I'm not one of those people who think they're too good to share their knowledge with those less intelligent than themselves.' He looked at me searchingly. 'So now we're going to treat Mrs Meerschwam to bonbons.'

He took me to the cellar. It was a huge cellar, with thousands of cans on the walls. I'd never seen so many cans in one place. Even the supermarket didn't have cans like that. Cans of beef soup, cans of chicken soup, cans of wieners, cans of diced pineapple, cans of fish stock, cans of peas, cans of carrots. There were enough cans there to feed an orphanage. Somewhere under a pile of old newspapers, Broccoli found a box of bonbons. He took two of them and carried them up to Mrs Meerschwam, who was drinking tea in the kitchen again.

'Look at what I've got for our good girl,' Broccoli said, holding the bonbons under Mrs Meerschwam's nose.

'I'm not your good girl,' Mrs Meerschwam said. 'Spending all your father's money, that's all you're good for.'

Broccoli pulled me out the door again.

'He never was any good,' Mrs Meerschwam shouted after us. 'I've known him since he was born.'

'Once the bonbons hit the tummy,' Broccoli said, 'she becomes a good deal more pleasant.' Then he looked at me earnestly and said: 'True seduction starts with bonbons.'

He insisted that I repeat that after him.

'Beer, bonbons and bad jokes: those are the seducer's three most important tools, take it from me,' Broccoli said. 'And if you happen to have a way with clogged toilets, then you've got another ace up your sleeve.'

Broccoli invited me to play a game of badminton, but I refused. Our neighbour lady always wanted me to play badminton too. Playing badminton was her greatest joy in life. But she didn't have anyone to play with any more. All her badminton partners had died off, or were confined to wheelchairs. So she kept calling my parents' house every other day. 'Ewald Krieg,' she'd say, 'what would you say to a nice game of badminton in my garden?'

Broccoli pulled a toothpick from his inside pocket.

'I need to buy a beeper,' he said suddenly. 'I need a beeper real bad.'

I followed him down the street. Wherever he went, Broccoli always trotted along like he was trying to catch a tram. At a telecom shop, he went in and bought himself a beeper.

A NEW KIND OF SNACK

*W*e met at the De Oranjerie café to look at the pictures we'd taken. Broccoli was wearing a raincoat and sunglasses. He wore sunglasses almost all the time. Sometimes he didn't take off his sunglasses for days. At least not when I was around. 'I don't want them to recognise me,' he said.

He was sitting at a table in the corner. When I came over, he handed me a manila envelope and said: 'Later on, when you're earning lots of money, you can pay me back.'

For someone who said they'd been a professional photographer, the pictures were horrible. In fact, they were horrible even for someone who didn't say that. Broccoli claimed he'd spent a year working as a fashion photographer when he was sixteen.

Most of the pictures were blurry or underexposed. The only one that was any good had the top of my face missing.

'These are the people I had in mind,' Broccoli said. He reached into his inside pocket and pulled out a notebook with the addresses of film companies and casting agencies written in it.

At a liquor store on the Haarlemmerstraat, he bought a bottle of champagne to drink in the tram.

'We've got something to celebrate,' he told the man behind the counter. I'd never seen him so excited. Only later did I discover that his excitement could fade as fast as it came, and that when it did he would sometimes stay in his room for days on end. When I'd come to visit him then, he'd grab my hand and say: 'I'm suffering from ennui, I've got ennui so bad.' Back then I had no idea what ennui was; it sounded like some kind of kidney ailment.

'We have to write a good cover letter,' Broccoli said, once we got off the tram, 'a letter they can't ignore.' And when the champagne was finished, he added: 'Even if all we do is walk across the screen, once we're in they'll never get rid of us.'

Broccoli had arranged a screen test for us. He didn't want to tell me how he'd done that. The screen test was being held in a converted warehouse, not far from the Bijlmer Prison. When we came into the waiting room, there were ten guys sitting there, learning their lines by heart. The atmosphere was tense, like what you sometimes feel in a dentist's waiting room. Especially when people know they'll be walking out with a whole new set of teeth.

Broccoli was wearing a scarf and his sunglasses. 'Did any of you get the boot at the theatre school?' That was the first thing he said once we were inside. No one answered.

'Quiet!' the girl doing the organisation yelled.

The screen test was for a TV commercial for a new kind of snack made from ham and cheese: they were called 'Hamchies'. We waited for more than an hour. The boys coming out of the studio looked defeated. They told us you had to eat Hamchies while you were saying your lines. You had to remember to drink a lot before you went in.

I panicked, because I didn't eat ham back then. I ate everything but ham. It was the last trace of obscurantism left in my mind. At least that's what I told people.

'They're going to make us eat Hamchies too,' I whispered to Broccoli, but he didn't say anything. He was staring at his script as if it had been written by Schopenhauer.

I wanted to talk about my problem to the girl doing the organisation, but she'd been on the phone for a long time. We could hear her talking about a rendezvous she'd had. It must have been a pretty romantic rendezvous. It sounded like she'd been lying under a blooming rhododendron all night. And she talked so loudly that it seemed like she was speaking for our benefit.

Most of the rendezvousing I'd done had been with myself. That was my specialty. On late summer afternoons, I'd go to a little sidewalk café. 'Are you waiting for someone?' the waitresses would ask me. 'No,' I'd say, 'not just now.' I thought about what it would be like to have a rendezvous with a real person, but it was somehow comforting that it never got beyond just imagining. I'd resolved to expect nothing from people, and even less from animals. The problem is that someone always comes into your life who you secretly expect something from. Expecting nothing from animals isn't too hard, you can easily keep that up for the rest of your life.

'Do you think I could eat some nuts instead of Hamchies?' I asked the girl, once she was phoned out.

'Everyone can eat whatever they like,' she said. 'This is a free country, isn't it?' She picked up the phone again.

By the time our turn came, Broccoli had already asked three times for a cold beer. He kept yelling: 'Where's the cold beer?' But no one reacted. They all looked like you could knock them down with a feather. The girl doing the organisation looked especially perturbed.

'You have to go in one at a time,' she said.

'No,' Broccoli said, 'we're here together.'

The studio was lit by three spotlights: a man with a beard introduced himself as the director.

'Go stand on the "x",' he said to Broccoli, 'and say your name loud and clear.'

Broccoli raised his sunglasses and looked around for the 'x' on the floor. It took him a long time to find it; without his glasses, he was as near-sighted as I am. He said his lines about Hamchies the way the old thespians used to do 'Romeo, my Romeo' a hundred years ago. And he ate almost the whole bag. He must have been hungry.

'OK, that's enough,' the man with the beard said. 'That was just great. We'll call you.'

Broccoli went to the door. 'Yeah, do that,' he said before walking out. A couple of seconds later he came back: 'At the age of twelve I was already an accomplished plumber!' he shouted at the director. 'Put that in your pipe and smoke it!'

'You're on,' the director said to me, paying no attention to Broccoli.

They handed me a new bag of Hamchies. I had to hold it in my hand, up where the camera could see it.

'Give us your name, loud and clear,' the director said.

'Ewald Stanislas Krieg.'

'That name's not on the list,' another man barked.

'Would you please spell your last name?' the director asked.

'Krieg,' I said, 'as in "*Totale Krieg*".'

'That name's not on the list,' the other man said.

'Well, put it on the list,' the director ordered.

'Could you please give me the first letter of your last name again?' the man with the list asked.

'Oh, please,' the director said, 'please. Give us your name afterwards, otherwise we'll never get out of here.'

'That's fine,' I said. 'Who should I give my name to afterwards?'

'Action,' the director shouted. 'Action, action, come on, people, action.'

I really went through those Hamchies. They stuck to the roof of my mouth, they stuck in my throat and under my tongue, I thought I was choking, but I just kept eating, because this was about my career. I did my best to eat greedily, as if I'd never wolfed down anything so delicious. Because that's what it was all about. Getting people to buy and eat lots of Hamchies.

Everything seemed to be going well, until the director interrupted me halfway through. 'Could you try talking with your mouth just a little less full?'

Broccoli was waiting outside. 'What do they know?' he said.

HENRY FROHLICH

*'T*hese headshots aren't really usable,' Henry Frohlich said. It was the first time I'd ever heard anyone use the word 'headshot'. I'd always thought it meant a shot in the head. That in a movie you could say: 'One more step and it's a headshot for you.' But, Henry Frohlich explained to us, headshots were pictures of people's faces.

Broccoli and I were sitting on the couch; Frohlich was sitting in a black leather chair that could rock.

'Good headshots are indispensable for the aspiring actor,' he said, ticking his index finger against the pictures we'd taken.

Under his desk was a German shepherd that had jumped up on us a few times when we came in, until Frohlich told it to lie down. I wasn't very fond of dogs, not of cats or turtles either, actually. Maybe that's because I used to wake up every morning to the barking of hysterical dogs. All the old ladies on our street had hysterical dogs. Some of them even had kennels. They were supposed to be there to guard the house. When I told Broccoli about that, he grabbed my hand and said, without letting go, that I should take comfort in the thought that on death's far shore there were probably no hysterical dogs.

'Bastiaan!' Henry Frohlich shouted whenever the dog tried to come out from under the desk. Then he'd look at us and say: 'He doesn't bite. In fact, he loves children.' Frohlich looked about as nasty as his dog.

The walls were hung with pictures of actors and actresses. Some of them looked vaguely like people I'd seen in commercials or TV series.

'I don't know if I can really be of much help to the two of you,' Frohlich said. He had short prickly hair, and every once in a while he wagged his eyebrows. Like there were flies on them he was trying to shoo away.

Henry Frohlich was very well known, Broccoli assured me, and essential to our careers.

'I want to make one thing perfectly clear; we're not just any old casting agency. We have an A-list, a B-list and a C-list. The big actors are on the A-list, like the people who played in *Three Women and a Hot-Dog Stand*. But OK, you two aren't anywhere near that yet, so first we'll put you on the C-list.'

'We don't want to be on a list,' Broccoli said quietly, 'we want to work.'

'Yes, of course,' Frohlich said, and he started giggling. The German shepherd tried to get out again, but this time Frohlich yanked him back with both hands. A pained yelp came from under the desk, but Frohlich kept laughing.

'What does this C-list involve?' I asked.

'As soon as the two of you find work, we act as your agent. That's what we are: agents.' He stressed both syllables. Maybe he thought it was a word we needed to learn.

'And we get the usual fifteen per cent.'

He pulled a sandwich out from under a pile of papers and began eating it. The dog got some of his sandwich too. It didn't look like the first time they'd had lunch together.

'I'd like to see the two of you from the side,' Frohlich said, once he and the dog were finished eating.

We didn't understand what he meant.

'Look to the left,' Frohlich said.

We looked to the left.

'OK, that's fine,' he said after a few seconds.

'Mr Frohlich,' Broccoli said.

'Henry,' he said. 'To you guys I'm Henry.' He had a round head and his skin was the colour of browned butter.

'Henry,' Broccoli said.

The telephone rang. When Frohlich was finished talking, he grinned at us happily and said: 'I think I might have something for the two of you. Can you guys do animal imitations? It's for a voice-over.'

Broccoli and I looked at each other. I didn't know about him, but I definitely could not do animals. In my mind I tried to bark and miaow, but even in my mind it didn't sound like an animal. More like someone who belongs in an insane asylum.

'What kind of animals do we have to do?' Broccoli asked.

'How am I supposed to know?' Frohlich said irritatedly. 'You think I'm clairvoyant? Animals in general. Tell me what kind of animals you do, and I'll write it down.'

'I can't do any animals,' I said. 'My parents wouldn't let me.'

But Frohlich didn't want to hear about it. 'What about you?' he said to Broccoli.

'Cows and birds,' Broccoli said.

'Cows and birds,' Frohlich repeated, 'I'll make a note of that right away.'

His secretary came in with coffee. 'Put that down right here, sweetheart,' he said.

When we'd finished our coffee, Frohlich clapped his hands and said: 'Don't want to seem rushed, but I've got another appointment.'

He stood up. 'First of all, you two are going to need new head-shots. I'll give you the number of a professional photographer, and when your headshots are in we'll take a good look at them.'

He brought his face up close to mine. As if there was something unusual to see there. I stepped back, but Frohlich just took another step forward. I finally ended up with my back to the wall.

'You've got an unusual face,' Henry Frohlich whispered. 'But you should do something about the way you roll your "r"s. You sound like you're cooking up a little Yiddish.'

'Cooking up?' I asked. 'What do you mean?' It made me think of soup.

'The way you talk,' Frohlich said. 'That's what I mean.'

'What can I do about it?'

'I've got a tip for you,' he said. 'Spend twenty minutes every day saying "ring, rang, rung", over and over.' While he was talking to me, he stuck his hand in the dog's mouth.

'Ring, rang, rung?'

'Sounds wrong.'

'Twenty minutes, every day?' Broccoli asked.

Frohlich nodded. 'Miracles don't happen overnight.' Then he sighed deeply. On a scrap of paper he jotted down the name and telephone number of the photographer he wanted us to see.

He walked us to the door. In the hallway he patted me on the shoulder and whispered: 'You've got something special, kiddo, you're going to be all right.' Then he ran his hand over my cheek and said: 'Soft.' He sounded like he was deep in thought, so I didn't know whether he meant my cheek or something else that was soft too.

Henry Frohlich stuck out his hand, and you could still see the dog's saliva glistening on it.

COAL ALLOWANCE

One evening, Broccoli invited me to dinner at Henry Smith's, on the Beethovenstraat.

The first thing the waiter said when we came in was: 'The usual?'

Broccoli nodded. The waiter showed us to a table by the window. Most of the other people in the restaurant were old ladies, accompanied by even older men. There were also a few men on their own. Old, too.

I never used to go out to dinner with my parents. Only when we were on vacation, but then we weren't allowed to order anything to drink. My mother handed out glasses of apple juice under the table, from a thermos bottle she'd snuck in. After all, at the supermarket you could buy two bottles of juice for what they charged for one glass in a restaurant. A few times we got caught and had to leave. I'd always run out in front, holding the rest of my food. That's how I learned to run fast, and eat fast too. That way at least you got a piece of meat before you had to grab everything and get out.

'Hear anything from your parents?' the waiter asked.

'They're fine,' Broccoli said, 'the mountain air is doing them good.'

'I can still see your father sitting right over there,' the waiter said. He pointed to a little table behind us. 'At the end of every day. A generous man. An extremely generous man.' The way he said it made it sound as if the generous men had all died out.

Suddenly, the waiter pulled up a chair and sat down with us. 'I used to be a swimming instructor,' he said. Then he jumped to his feet and went back to work.

We ordered Bloody Marys. When the waiter put the glasses on the table, he said: 'This is like eating salad.'

During dinner, Broccoli showed me a picture postcard from a place called Lenzerheide. On the back, in very regular handwriting, it said: 'We're doing fine. We're thinking of you. Kisses. Pop & Mom.'

'Do you collect stamps?' Broccoli asked. I shook my head. The man at the table next to us had been joined by an elderly lady. He'd ordered an enormous steak. You could order small, medium-sized or enormous. He'd ordered enormous. A two-pounder, from the looks of it. There was a little flag stuck in the steak, and the chef had written the weight on it, so you knew exactly how much you were eating.

'Don't stare,' Broccoli whispered.

I turned back to him.

'My father sends me a money order every month,' Broccoli said, 'and the space for comments on the stub always says "coal allowance".' He lit a cigarette. I didn't know what to say, so I just sat there. I couldn't stop looking at the old man, who had now burst into tears over his steak.

We stayed until we were the only ones left in the restaurant. When the waiter came with the bill, he said: 'Drinks on the house. What'll it be?'

We ordered espresso and grappa. At least, that's what Broccoli ordered, I just said: 'Same here.' It was the first time I'd ever had grappa.

The waiter stood at our table. 'Entire generations have received their swimming diplomas at my hands,' he said. Then he walked slowly, almost solemnly, back to the kitchen.

'To the Association for Geniuses,' Broccoli whispered.

'To the Association for Geniuses,' I whispered back.

'So why exactly do they call you Broccoli?'

He stared at me for what seemed like a minute.

'You'll find out,' he said. 'I can't tell you everything.' His voice kept getting quieter. 'These days they're even up in the neighbours' apple tree.'

'Who?'

'The enemy.'

'Do you have enemies?'

'A whole phonebook full,' Broccoli said.

'But why?'

'I'm a genius, and geniuses have phonebooks full of enemies.' He leaned across the table and whispered: 'I take it you don't have a phonebook full of enemies?'

I shook my head.

'Exactly,' Broccoli said. 'That's my point.'

When he laid his credit card on the table, I saw the name on it for the first time: Michaël Eckstein.

'My father pays for the credit card,' Broccoli said, juggling a cigarette. 'I've never earned a cent in my life. That's not an accomplishment, but it's not necessarily a shortcoming either.' It sounded like a line he'd used before. A ready answer to bothersome questions.

'Shall I call you Michaël then?' I enquired.

Broccoli slammed his hand down on the table. He almost spat in indignation.

'If you want to make sure I never look at you again, just be sure to do that. The chairman of the Association for Geniuses is called Broccoli, and nothing but Broccoli. *Mister* Broccoli to the uninitiated.'

'Let's go to Oblomow,' he said, once we were outside. It was one of those evenings you don't need a jacket.

Oblomow was crowded. We had to stand. Every once in a while, Broccoli shouted things in my ear I could only half understand. But I just kept nodding in agreement. The way people do in crowded bars and discos.

When I came back from the men's room, Broccoli was talking to a girl with brown hair. She was a little taller than him. We shook hands, but I couldn't make out her name, and I don't think she heard mine. A lot of people were looking at her, but she wasn't looking at them.

'I'll be right back,' Broccoli said. He walked out the door with her.

I waited for half an hour. Then I went home. Oblomow didn't seem like the kind of place to have a rendezvous with yourself.

LA GAZZETTA DELLO SPORT

*B*roccoli called the next morning. 'Meet me at the news-stand in half an hour.'

In the summer, the news-stand on the bridge where the Beethovenstraat crosses the Stadionkade also sold ice cream. The man who ran it had a beard, and he also had a lot of customers who bought foreign magazines. He knew exactly which magazine each customer came for. Groaning slightly, he would bend over and pull the magazine they wanted from under the cash register. Conversation was not one of his favourite pastimes. But sometimes he complained about customers who would disappear from one day to the next, leaving him with magazines no one else wanted to read. That's probably why he gave me an American gun magazine once. He'd been robbed a few times, so he kept his banknotes in his back pocket, instead of in the cash register. One time a robber had given him a black eye. He was real proud of that. He showed it to everyone, even if they'd only come to buy a paper. 'Have you seen this?' he'd ask. Most of them had no idea what he was talking about.

Every summer he went for a two-week cycling holiday in Drenthe. He was a cyclomaniac. Whenever he was on holiday, a woman worked at his stand who looked like the daughter of Ti-Ta-Tovenaar. In fact, I think she didn't just look like her, she really was her. The actress, I mean. I always wanted to ask her. 'Did you play the daughter of the magician on that old kid's programme?' Even just to make contact. But I never did.

Broccoli and I used to meet there all the time. We were both very fond of Popsicles. Broccoli claimed that a Popsicle was an essential part of any nutritious breakfast. His parents had never let him eat Popsicles. Mine didn't either. 'It'll give you diarrhoea,' they'd told us, 'and then you'll dehydrate. Next thing you know, you'll wake up in the hospital.'

When Broccoli was waiting for me on the bridge, you could see him from far away. He always stood in the middle of the bridge, and he almost always had an Italian sporting journal in his hand. At first, I thought he knew Italian, and that he was keen on sports. But he couldn't read Italian at all, and he didn't care a whit about sports. He was convinced that carrying around the *Gazzetta dello Sport* could give you a major jump on certain situations.

One time he said: 'A burglar you should hit in the face with a rolled-up newspaper.' And another time: 'Italian men are the best men.' And then he whispered something that sounded sort of like 'machissimo'.

I bought four Raspberry Rockets. There were days when we lived on almost nothing but Raspberry Rockets. Broccoli also lived on beer, of course.

'We're going to the photographer,' Broccoli said. 'I called him. He can see us this afternoon.'

He was awfully excited that day. He said: 'Once we've got good pictures, they'll ask us to do a walk-on. And that'll be the start. The start of something very big.'

'Take the *Hörzu* along for your parents,' the newspaper man shouted after me, but I acted like I hadn't heard him. I wouldn't have been caught dead walking down the street with the *Hörzu*.

Broccoli popped into the Amro Bank on the corner of the Stadionweg to make a withdrawal. He didn't go to the teller's window, he just asked for a Mr Tuinier. I heard them whispering behind the counter: 'Young Eckstein has come in again.'

Broccoli pulled two bottles of perfume out of his coat pocket and gave them to the tellers. The tellers started laughing.

'We want to smell good for you, Michaël,' they said. When they saw me, they stopped laughing right away.

'I wish I could smell good too,' I said. It was out before I knew it.

At first, I thought Broccoli was sweet on the tellers, but when Mr Tuinier came out of his office Broccoli handed him a box of cigars too.

'Your favourite smoke,' Broccoli said.

'Oh, isn't that thoughtful of you,' Tuinier gushed.

Tuinier took Broccoli into the back office. I waited for them at the counter. The tellers were staring at me.

Outside, I asked Broccoli why he loaded down the bank personnel with presents.

'My father taught me that,' he said. 'It's one of the only things that was really worth learning.'

He didn't say anything for a few minutes, but when we got to Museumplein, he said: 'A cigar every now and then works wonders. Of course, I'm not saying you should hand out presents to *your* bank's employees. In fact, I'd strongly advise against it.'

The photographer lived on the Keizersgracht, close to Centraal Station. His name was Vink. He was short, and he paced back and forth nervously the whole time, complaining about the filth. We never found out whether he was talking about the filth on the street, or filth in general, or whether he thought we were filthy.

He led us into his studio and said: 'Have a seat, I'll get us some coffee.'

'Don't bother,' Broccoli said. He pulled a wad of banknotes out of his pants pocket. 'I'm paying for all three of us.'

'So who's the third party?'

'She'll be here any minute.'

Vink started with me. He took his time setting up the lights, and as he did he talked about how he had once photographed Margaret Thatcher. He was on the verge of telling us about other famous people he'd photographed when Broccoli said: 'We're in sort of a hurry.'

During the photo session, Broccoli kept telling me how to look. He warned me not to squint too much, because otherwise I'd look like a little rat again. After a while, Vink said to him: 'Please sit down, I've been taking photographs for twenty years and no one's asked for a refund yet.'

When Broccoli was finally seated and had combed his hair, the bell rang. Vink was already on his way to the door, but Broccoli raced right past him. He came back with the girl with brown curls he'd met the night before at Oblomow. This time I was able to make out her name.

'This is Elvira,' Broccoli said.

'Are you planning a career on the stage as well?' Vink asked.

'In the movies,' Elvira said.

'She's already famous,' Broccoli said.

Vink groaned. Vink made all kinds of noises with his mouth when things got a bit too much for him.

Elvira went next. She acted like she'd had her picture taken pretty often. In any case, Vink didn't make her nervous.

When Broccoli's turn came, he didn't say a thing.

'Try to relax,' Vink said, 'this isn't an operating room.'

'That's what you say,' Broccoli replied.

Elvira was sitting in a chair to one side. She asked me how long I'd known Broccoli.

'A couple of weeks,' I said. 'What about you?'

'Something like that.'

The day was warm, and it seemed like we could have stayed

for ever in the coolness of Vink's studio. Broccoli gnawing on his cigarette, waiting for the next photo; Elvira handing out pistachios; Vink getting more nervous all the time. It would have been nice if we'd never had to leave, but finally Vink said: 'Well, that's it. You can come by tomorrow to pick them up.'

Broccoli laid a twenty-five guilder note on the table and said: 'Drink a beer tonight to my health.'

We walked along the Brouwersgracht to Centraal Station. We ate pistachios. I've never eaten pistachios the way I did in those days.

ELVIRA

*W*e were lying on Broccoli's bed, looking at the photos. Elvira's had turned out the best.

'How well do you know her?' I asked.

'Well enough,' Broccoli said.

He was resting his head on a raincoat. Sunlight was coming through the little window. It was awfully warm in the attic.

'How long have your parents been gone?'

'Oh, a while,' Broccoli said. He opened a can of beer. There were empty bottles in the corners of the room. Some of them were already covered in dust.

'Are they coming back?'

'That depends,' Broccoli said. 'That depends entirely.' He was holding Elvira's photos, peering at them through a magnifying glass.

'In a minute we'll go and take her the pictures,' he said. 'I told her to meet us in front of Centraal Station.'

I went to the news-stand on the bridge for Popsicles. When I came back, Broccoli was asleep. There was a ten-guilder note sticking out of the pocket of his jeans. He always stuffed his money in his pants pockets like it was a handkerchief.

I put the Popsicles in the freezer and waited for him to wake up. I sat on the floor and hoped I'd find a money order with 'coal allowance' written on the stub. But there weren't any money orders. The room looked like someone had knocked over a trash can. There were dozens of Douwe Egberts coffee coupons in one corner. Broccoli didn't seem like the type to save Douwe Egberts coupons. Just when I was getting ready to open the cupboard next to the window and see what was in there, I heard Broccoli say: 'Human beings spend a third of their lives sleeping, but as far as I'm concerned you could make it two-thirds.'

Once we were in the tram, he said: 'Three-thirds, that might be even better.'

We'd been waiting for her in front of Centraal Station for half an hour. Broccoli was pacing back and forth. He seemed worried about her being so late. Whenever a tram pulled up, he waved the *Gazzetto dello Sport* in the air. 'That's the signal,' he said. My job was to carry the photos.

That signalling didn't really work. The only thing that happened was that a few boys came up to him and started speaking Italian. 'Take over from me here, would you?' Broccoli said.

I explained to the boys that just because we were waving an Italian sports sheet didn't mean we could speak Italian or even understand it. I had to explain it three times, until the oldest boy finally understood. He tapped his finger against his forehead. Then he said something to his friends in Italian, and they all tapped their fingers against their foreheads too.

Elvira finally showed up. She hadn't taken the tram. She was sitting on the back of someone's bike. She jumped off the bike, waved to the guy and he just kept on going. Like a taxi.

'Look,' Broccoli said, 'bicycling, that's not good for you.'

Elvira shook hands with us.

'This is going to be our first working meeting,' Broccoli said. 'Fix this date in your memories. It's a historic day.'

We went to the first-class restaurant. Elvira was wearing a long dress and these sort of espadrilles, like she was going to the beach.

There was a man playing piano in the restaurant. Every fifteen minutes he stood up and bowed, but the waiters were the only ones who clapped.

'Well?' Broccoli asked.

'They're good,' she said. 'They're very good.'

She had a red-checkered notepad with her, and a pencil she kept twisting in one of her curls. Her hair wasn't really that curly, it was more like wavy.

'Elvira is a star,' Broccoli said, 'a movie star.'

She laughed.

'She played the lead in an Argentine movie,' Broccoli said. 'She's from Argentina.'

She laughed again.

Elvira told us that the first part of the movie had been set in Buenos Aires, the second part on an island in the Caribbean. Somehow the shooting on the island had never taken place. I couldn't make out whether there had been a fight between the producer and the director, or whether the money ran out. Whatever it was, she'd spent four months in her room in Buenos Aires, waiting to be called to the Caribbean. The producer rang her up almost every day. 'Keep those bags packed, Elvira, we're leaving tomorrow.' But they never left. After three months, the cameraman, Elvira and a couple of other actors went to the offices of the producer, a Mr Galani. An elderly housekeeper opened the door and told them Mr Galani wasn't in, he was out doing some shopping. They came back a few hours later, but Mr Galani was still out shopping. And when they rang the bell the next day, the housekeeper said: 'Mr Galani has gone out to do a little shopping.' When they came back the week after that, the housekeeper didn't even open the door. Elvira waited a month, then left for Europe. Apparently, they finally edited the first half of the movie, and it even ran for a few days at a little art theatre in Buenos Aires.

The sunlight through the tall windows of the lounge blinded me. The people sitting with their backs to the windows were nothing but silhouettes. Our table was covered with pistachio shells.

Elvira was almost a head taller than me, and her eyes had this way of shining, like she'd just heard that she'd been given a leading role in a major motion picture. But how do eyes shine? And if people would ask: 'And her mouth then, what did her mouth look like?' then I could only tell them: 'I don't know.' Her teeth I know about. She had really white teeth, like she enamelled them. I always paid attention to teeth in those days, because people had told me: 'If your teeth turn out like your father's, you'll be single for the rest of your life.'

'I have contacts,' Broccoli said. He said it very seriously, almost too seriously.

Then Elvira said: 'I have contacts too,' and cracked a pistachio. At first, it seemed like that annoyed Broccoli. But then he looked at me and said: 'Do you have contacts too?'

I hesitated. 'No, not any more.'

'Excellent,' Broccoli said, 'just leave the contacts to me. My father has boxes of cigars piled in the cellar, and that works wonders when it comes to contacts.'

'Are you sure about that?' Elvira asked. Then she took her notepad and wrote down the time and place of our next appointment. It seemed like she was looking forward to it. She said: 'I'll bring a box of cigars. I'm crazy about wonders.'

Before she went away she kissed us both on the cheek and left a few pistachios on the table. When she walked it looked like she was dancing.

We were pretty much the only ones left in the place. The pianist stopped playing and came over to stand next to our table.

Broccoli was euphoric. 'You've got talent, you've got an incredible amount of talent,' he said.

When Broccoli had left to go to the toilet, the pianist asked me: 'Is he a friend of yours?'

I didn't want to talk about Broccoli with him, so I just nodded.

When Broccoli came back, he pulled a business card out of his pocket and handed it to the pianist. The pianist looked at it, shook his head slowly and laid the card on the table. He walked back to his piano without saying a word.

Broccoli smiled and watched the pianist go. Then he stuck three sugar cubes in his mouth and said: 'People who talk too much give me a headache.' He showed me what was on his business card. '*Mr Broccoli has the honour of offering you a drink.*'

'I used one of these cards to pick up Elvira,' he said, 'and there are two thousand of them lying in my cellar.'

He told me he'd met Elvira at Café Schiller. He'd been sitting at a table, reading the paper. It was still early, but Schiller was already crowded. A group of people came in and asked if he'd mind them sitting at his table. 'Not at all,' Broccoli had said. When one of the women in the other party ordered hot chocolate and the waitress claimed that they didn't serve hot chocolate at this time of year, Broccoli went into action. Somehow that didn't surprise me at all. Broccoli handed the woman who wanted hot chocolate one of his business cards. On the back of the card, the woman had written 'plese'. Without the 'a'; she hadn't been in the country that long.

He'd had two thousand of them printed, so he got a discount. His strategy was to hand out as many as he could, because that made it more likely that someone would take him up on it. When he handed one of those cards to a lady, he'd often tell her: 'Everything I have to say to you is on this card.'

Broccoli stared into space, stuck a few more sugar cubes in his mouth, then said: 'I'm not some piece of dirt, and I don't wish to be treated that way either.'

'So what about Elvira?'

'That same evening she told me her name was Elvira Lopez, and that she was an actress, a movie star.'

I've never heard anyone since then use the term 'movie star' with such obvious relish.

He smiled. But a little later he started shaking his fist at the pianist. 'No one treats me like dirt,' he muttered.

I wondered where Elvira lived, but I didn't dare to ask him. She probably got money orders every month with 'coal allowance' on them too.

'T HAANTJE

*E*lvira's flat was on the Tweede Tuindwarsstraat. Sooner or later, all walks with Broccoli ended up in the vicinity of the Tweede Tuindwarsstraat. 'Let's wait for her here,' he'd say. Or: 'Let's give her a call.'

The two of us were waiting for calls from agents and film companies. Broccoli had bought an answering machine specially for that purpose, so we could be reached day and night. It was one of those machines you could listen to on remote. At first, Broccoli called his own number every fifteen minutes, to listen for messages. Later on, he calmed down a bit.

I don't think Broccoli had friends. Sometimes he said hello to people he met on the street, but you probably can't call that having friends. But perhaps I should make an exception for Lopatin.

Like Broccoli, Lopatin had lunch every day at 't Haantje, on the Leidsekruisstraat. Lopatin had a beard and moustache, but he was starting to go bald way up on top of his head, and he had a pretty big belly. He always wore suspenders, preferably red ones. I figured he must be somewhere in his thirties.

Lopatin had quite an appetite. He'd order soup, a sandwich, then pie and coffee afterwards. He didn't stutter, but he seemed to have some kind of impediment. That's why he kept his conversation down to the most crucial utterances. When he wasn't eating, he made noises that sounded most like growling. The sort of growling bears do in cartoons. When the growling got too bad, the owner of 't Haantje would shout: 'Down, Lopatin.' Actually, Lopatin was supposed to be living in one of those projects they call 'halfway houses'. But he said they'd overlooked him because of a computer malfunction, or some other common calamity.

After he'd eaten, Lopatin would wipe his hands with a paper napkin, then roll the napkin between his palms until it was nothing but a little ball. His beard and moustache would still be full of food residue. Then Lopatin would get up and walk to the men's room. Along the way he'd try to make contact with 't Haantje's other customers. But whenever the owner saw him doing that, he'd shout: 'Keep moving, Lopatin, the men's room is right in front of you.'

Most people didn't want to sit too close to Lopatin, but Broccoli didn't mind. On the contrary: he treated him regularly to chocolate cake. Lopatin's face would be all brown when he was finished.

And Lopatin brought presents for Broccoli. A blank pocket diary from 1974, an opened carton of coffee creamer, body lotion, that kind of thing. Broccoli was overjoyed with them, and Lopatin always said: 'I saved this for you out of my own mouth.'

Mimi worked the register in 't Haantje. When things weren't too busy, she also helped cut onions and cucumbers. Lopatin loved Mimi, but Mimi didn't love Lopatin. Whenever he'd approach the cash register, the growling would pick up. Sometimes it got so bad that the owner had to take him outside. Sometimes

Lopatin would try to start a conversation with Mimi, but the owner would yell: 'Mimi's already married, Lopatin.' On rare occasions, Lopatin would try to touch Mimi's breasts. When he did that, she'd smack him on the hand with the ladle that was always next to the register. After a while, I realised that the ladle was only there for smacking Lopatin on the hand.

Lopatin called Broccoli 'buddy'. He never liked me much. Maybe he saw me as an interloper, maybe he thought I was trying to take Broccoli away from him.

One afternoon, a man was shot in front of 't Haantje. He fell right there in the doorway and started bleeding like a stuck pig. Everyone went out and stood around him, except for Mimi. She couldn't stand the sight of blood. The owner shouted: 'I just had the place painted.' Lopatin stayed inside, close to Mimi. She was so shocked, I think it was the only time he was able to touch her breasts without getting whacked with the ladle.

We were at 't Haantje the time Broccoli said he'd found work for us. In a promotional film. The film was being commissioned by the FNV trade union, and it was meant to stimulate young people to join up. I don't know how Broccoli arranged that one. Maybe he'd made a big donation to the FNV. I wouldn't rule anything out. Elvira had started taking acting lessons, and I'm pretty sure Broccoli was paying for those too. 'You see,' he said, 'you're finally going to make your first buck in the movies.'

Elvira invited us over to the Tweede Tuindwarsstraat to celebrate.

Elvira's apartment was small, but nice and neat. Maybe she'd tidied up especially for us. The place was so tidy that it looked like a waiting room, or a romantic rendezvous. We sat on the couch and drank artichoke liqueur. It was disgusting, but Elvira had bought it for us, so we didn't say that. We acted like it was divine elixir, and every time we acted like it was divine elixir she'd give us a refill. According to her, it was an Argentine delicacy.

She'd made soup for us, and she was wearing the same long dress she'd had on when we showed her the photos. Her feet were bare.

'Do you do a lot of cooking?' I asked her.

'Only soup,' she said.

The little red notepad was lying on the table. I'd noticed that she used it to write down words she didn't know, so she could look them up later.

She put the bowls on the table.

'To the FNV,' Broccoli said. He raised his glass of artichoke liqueur.

'To the FNV,' we said.

'This is where it starts,' Broccoli said. 'Mark my words, this is where it all starts.'

Elvira went into the kitchen.

'Wait a minute, I'll help you,' Broccoli said.

I went and stood at the window and watched a couple of boys playing soccer. I remembered how Broccoli and I had stood at his attic window and vowed to become philanderers the likes of which were rarely seen. To be honest, we'd used the word 'philan-thropists'. Maybe we'd misunderstood the term. A few weeks later a bartender was kind enough to ask us if what we meant was 'philanderers'.

When I finally went into the kitchen to see what was going on, it was exactly as I'd thought. The lid was off the pan, and the little kitchen looked like a steam bath. And in the midst of all that steam were Broccoli and Elvira. I turned my back. Some things you don't want to see. Actually, there are a lot of things you don't want to see.

'Wait,' Elvira said, 'we're tasting the soup.'

We had to drink even more artichoke liqueur; the divine-elixir act must have been pretty convincing. Broccoli was leaning against the wall. I thought about the amazing way people's lives become entangled, and about the amazing way that entangle-ment comes untangled.

'You kissed her,' I whispered, once we were back in the living room. We'd both been planning to kiss her. But the agreement was that, if she gave one of us permission, we'd inform the other one before the actual kissing began. 'A gentlemen's agreement' is what Broccoli called it. He liked the word 'gentlemen'. I bet he used it ten times a day.

There was a fan blowing full-force, but none of us were cold. We sat at the table and stirred our soup.

'Do you guys want dill in your soup?' she asked.

We both shook our heads.

'How long have you been in Holland?' I asked.

'A year and a half,' Elvira said. 'I came here and never left.' Then she said: 'I love you guys.' And she laughed real loudly. Like it was a joke. Maybe it *was* a joke. Yeah, it must have been a joke.

It happened awfully fast, and then there was this sudden silence without much to hear except for the ticking of our spoons. There are a thousand reasons to say something like that, but I couldn't put my finger on why Elvira had said it.

'Come on, let's go to 't Haantje,' Broccoli said. ''t Haantje awaits.'

'I'm going to get a sweater,' Elvira said. 'You two go ahead.'

'She's embarrassed to open her closet with us around,' Broccoli whispered on the stairs.

In 't Haantje he ordered three cans of beer, because that was the only thing they served. The owner was standing behind the counter. Whenever you said to him: 'We'd like to settle up,' he'd say: 'OK, let's step outside.'

'Tonight is party time,' Broccoli said. 'We've got parts in an FNV movie.' The owner grumbled something about how the FNV had never gotten a foot on the ground in his place, and never would as long as he was around. One time I'd also heard him say: 'So, no fresh-squeezed orange juice today? Not turning stingy, are we?'

Elvira kissed me and Broccoli, to congratulate us. A Pakistani rose vendor took a Polaroid picture of us. Elvira in the middle, Broccoli on the left, me on the right. We all look as if we hadn't slept for days, and the heat and the glow from the sun make my face look like a red blotch. Elvira is laughing, and right behind her you can see the back of the owner of 't Haantje.

THE FNV SHOW

They'd sent us the script for the FNV movie. You could tell it was supposed to make young people – especially ethnic young people – join the FNV.

We were sitting at Elvira's table; except for a bed, three chairs and couch, that was all the furniture she had. Elvira asked whether we minded if she lit some candles. Broccoli said candle-light reminded him of a few dinner parties his parents had organised; if she insisted, though, it was all right by him.

We all agreed that the FNV script was one of the worst things ever written.

'This is the work of some dangerous psycho,' Broccoli kept saying after he'd read out bits of dialogue we'd be doing.

'Watch where you're going, asshole,' Broccoli was supposed to say. And then I had to answer. 'You watch where *you're* going, dickhead.' That went on for pages and pages.

'What does this have to do with the FNV?' Elvira asked. We couldn't tell her.

We smoked cigars. Broccoli had taught us to bite off the tip of the cigar. But when I bit my cigar, Broccoli said: 'You're not supposed to chew on it like a hot dog.'

There was nothing else in the house, so we'd finished off another bottle of artichoke liqueur. None of us felt like going to the all-night deli. The light from a street lamp and the Chinese takeaway sign was coming through the window of her room. The disc jockey on the radio was playing requests, and Broccoli said he'd like to call up and request a record for us, but he didn't have the strength.

When the only thing in the house left to drink was olive oil, Broccoli and Elvira started kissing. Then she kissed me too. On my forehead. I didn't mind. I thought it was pretty special, being kissed on the forehead.

When she was finished doing that, she said her first kiss had been at the age of fifteen, and that after that she hadn't done it for four years because she found it so disgusting.

Bram Jongevos was the director's name. He'd written the script himself. He had white hair and the eyes of a cornered animal. The warehouse we met in had been converted into a theatre and movie studio.

'How did you guys like it?' he kept asking. We just nodded. What else could we do? We couldn't really say we thought the script had been written by a dangerous psycho. Besides Elvira, Broccoli and myself, there was another actor playing in the FNV movie. He'd just made a big splash in a feature film. He called himself Roberto, and in the dressing room he told us he fucked everything that came his way. The make-up girl, who'd run a catering firm until just a few months before, told him: 'Things are pretty tough in the restaurant business, too.'

Her catering firm had taken a dive when it turned out that the chef – who was also her boyfriend – had not only taken off with all the smoked salmon, but also with the till.

The part about the smoked salmon really seemed to get to

Broccoli. While she was powdering his nose, he said: 'Brigitte, I have friends in smoked salmon.' But she said: 'It's too late now. My future is in make-up.'

The oldest person on the set was the cameraman. He told us he'd almost died of cancer. But now he was missing three teeth. 'Riding a bicycle drunk, and I hit a lamp-post. I was too drunk to find them again, and when I went back the next morning they were gone,' he said gloomily. He walked as though every step he took was a struggle. During the coffee break he started in about cancer again. He was like a soldier who'd come back from the front and couldn't stop talking about it. He didn't have much good to say about the FNV either. And we were supposed to be promoting the trade union movement. His only comment was: 'You can take the whole FNV and stick it up my woo-woo.'

One time, Roberto said: 'But you don't even have a woo-woo.'

'How would you know?' the cameraman said. That made Broccoli think the cameraman had lost his manhood, which Broccoli thought was sufficient explanation for the sadness that permeated his every move.

We were supposed to be playing a group of young people who are so enthusiastic about the FNV that they decide to go out to a bunch of schools and put on *The FNV Show*. During the tour, all kinds of irritations arise. Bram Jongevos had come up with that angle himself. '*The FNV Show* should be like life,' Bram Jongevos said, 'and in life all kinds of irritations arise between people.'

That's what the film was called, *The FNV Show*. There were motorcycles and choruses and a machine that made smoke, because the glories of the FNV were to be set to music as well.

The shooting was supposed to last a week, but by the third day things were so tense that Jongevos walked off the set in tears. It had apparently started when Roberto said to Elvira: 'You've got a sweet little butt.' But maybe he didn't say that at all, maybe he'd just touched her. Or maybe he'd whispered in her ear: 'I'm going to come by later on and steal a kiss.' That's what he whispered in almost every woman's ear. Once he even bit me on the ear. I still don't know why he did that. Elvira said: 'He did it to make you look like a fool. Real machos bite the ears of boys they think are sissies.' I wasn't familiar with that custom. In my view, I gave absolutely no cause for others to think of me as a sissy. Although I have to admit that back then, when I walked into a café and ordered a beer, the barman would often say: 'A beer for the young lady?' Of course, I never said: 'I'm not a young lady.' There are some things you simply don't quibble over.

Whatever happened that afternoon, what's sure is that when Roberto bothered Elvira, Broccoli boxed his ears. He boxed his ears so hard that Roberto's sunglasses flew across the set. And all this happened at the very moment Bram Jongevos shouted: 'OK, everybody, quiet on the set.' Next thing we knew, Roberto was sitting on top of Broccoli.

'Hey, cut it out,' Jongevos shouted. 'Kids, cut it out.' I hid behind a pillar. Roberto was swinging hard, and Bram Jongevos danced around and shouted: 'Let's stay professional, guys, for Chrissake, let's keep it professional.' Jongevos started crying, and then, because he didn't want us to see that, he ran away. Like a rabbit, that's how fast he went.

When Roberto was finished beating up Broccoli, Bram Jongevos came back. Broccoli's eyebrow was split open. Brigitte came running up with a bag of ice. 'When you work in the restaurant business, you see it all,' she said.

'No kidding,' Broccoli replied. He was bleeding, but Brigitte said it was nothing serious.

The cameraman came over and took a look. He asked whether we needed him to help look for any teeth.

'Now shake hands,' Jongevos shouted. 'Come on, you two, shake hands.' But he kept his distance.

Elvira was standing at the door of her dressing room. She already had her coat on. 'What are we doing here?' she asked.

'Damned if I know,' I said.

She hugged me and held me tight. I didn't try to get away,

but I was afraid to make it any easier for her either. I could feel her breasts and smell her perfume mingled with sweat. When she let go of me, I went to get her something to drink. But when I came back she was sitting in a chair in her dressing room, with that absent-minded smile on her face. She told me she'd been on nicotine gum for a long time. More than a year and a half.

I have no idea whether the FNV movie was ever really shown at schools. I only know that, seven days after the shooting started, Jongevos shouted: 'That was it, guys, that was it.'

He shook everyone's hand, and he even kissed some of us. His wife was there waiting for him. They were going on vacation to recover. When he hugged Elvira, his wife called out: 'Bram!' But he didn't let go.

'It was wonderful,' he said, 'it was wonderful.' He looked deep into Elvira's eyes, like he was trying to hypnotise her.

'Bram,' his wife shouted again. 'Bram!' I felt sorry for him. His wife was tall and spindly, like some overgrown bird.

'I have to go,' Bram said, 'but we'll stay in touch.' He was still holding Elvira's hand.

At the door he turned around again. 'You were all fantastic.' Then his wife pulled him away.

In the dressing room, Brigitte and Roberto were kissing. They'd been doing that all week. She was wearing one of those shirts that left her navel sticking out. There were two rings in her navel.

'See you, guys,' she said. She gave us a kiss. Her lips were still wet from his saliva.

She said she wasn't so sure she wanted to stay in make-up any more, not after that week. The restaurant business was calling her. She was thinking about a restaurant of her own. 'When I read the paper,' she whispered, 'I think: What's gotten into everyone?'

Broccoli patted her hand reassuringly.

Two months later, Broccoli and I ran into her in a café. She told us she was going to become a belly dancer.

When we came out of the warehouse, the cameraman was still waiting for a cab.

'Good luck,' he shouted after us. We turned and looked. That was the last time we saw his mouth with the three teeth missing.

Roberto and I ran into each other a few years later, at a crosswalk. He recognised me right away. I didn't recognise him. Jesus Christ had come into his life and he'd sworn off the violence and the fucking. Now he was using his acting talent in a gospel show. Before he walked away he hugged me, like an old friend. And somehow he found a way to slip me an invitation to a revival meeting.

GARE DU NORD

*T*he Wednesday after we'd finished the FNV movie, we went to Paris. Elvira had heard that her Argentine movie would be playing in a little theatre there. We were only going for the day, otherwise she'd miss her acting lessons.

Broccoli was wearing a suit. He must have been expecting a gala premiere or something.

'Why are you wearing that?' Elvira asked when she saw him at the station.

'You wouldn't get married in your pyjamas, would you?' Broccoli said.

We took the seven a.m. train. Elvira had made a tortilla for us. Broccoli had brought a bottle of wine and a corkscrew. Right after we pulled out of Brussels, he said: 'That FNV movie, that's going to be our breakthrough. All we need is for one director to see it and say: "Yes."' Then he sank back in his reverie.

'What ever made you come to Holland?' I asked Elvira.

'I wanted to see Europe,' she said. 'Besides, I had to get out of Buenos Aires.'

'You have that many enemies?'

She laughed. 'No, I just had to get out. When you live somewhere all your life, at a certain point you've pretty much seen it all.'

Broccoli had put his head in her lap and fallen asleep. He'd handed the Belgian conductor one of his famous cards. '*Mr Broccoli has the honour of offering you a drink.*' The Belgian conductor wasn't honoured at all; in fact, he was insulted.

We'd forgotten the glasses, so we had to drink from the bottle. The conductor didn't want anything to drink, and he didn't accept Broccoli's card either. He referred to us as 'the scum of the earth' in French. I told Broccoli and Elvira: 'No, no, that means something different, it doesn't mean "the scum of the earth".' I was afraid Broccoli would run after the conductor and make a scene. But Broccoli wasn't convinced. 'He called us the scum of the earth,' he said. Then he fell asleep again.

Elvira wrote something on her red notepad.

We stared out the window at the monotonous landscape of northern France.

'The cameraman will be in Paris too,' she said.

Maybe it was the wine, or maybe it was the way we were sitting there with Broccoli lying half across us, or maybe it was the heat in the train. I kissed her right below the ear. Like it was something I did every day. The wine must have helped. The wine and Broccoli lying there.

Then Elvira said: 'I'm twenty-eight.' In a way that made it sound like she'd forgotten and it had suddenly come back to her. She seemed surprised about it herself. Maybe she'd never been kissed by anyone ten years her junior.

It was then that I first noticed that Elvira had a faint moustache. A minuscule moustache. The word 'moustache' is actually too much to describe the little brown hairs on her light-brown skin.

'In Argentina, I had a waterbed,' Elvira said, looking out the window.

'Funny,' I said. 'I had a Murphy bed. My parents bought it for me when I was eight.'

'My mother bought the waterbed for me, but I had to get rid of it because it started leaking.'

'Electric blankets are pretty dangerous too,' I said.

She was still staring out the window.

'It's nice talking to you,' Elvira said.

'Yeah, I think so too, very nice.'

'But I don't like pleasant conversation, just so you know. At my acting lessons there's this girl who sometimes says: "What I could use tonight is a good conversation." Weird, huh?'

'Absurd,' I said. 'She must be sick.'

'Conversations don't mean that much to me, I'd rather dance.'

'I can't dance, but conversations don't mean much to me either.'

It was quiet for a while. Finally, I asked: 'Is Buenos Aires a nice place?'

'The restaurants are wonderful,' she said, 'everyone dines late and stays out late. In Amsterdam, everything closes so early.'

I agreed with her. I told her I'd once walked around town for an hour, looking for a kebab place that was open at six in the morning.

'What a bunch of barbarians,' Elvira said. 'Don't they care about making money?'

I was pretty sure we'd never get off this train. We'd become club-car regulars, travelling back and forth for ever between Amsterdam and Paris. 'Oh, them,' the steward would say, 'they're always in here.' Then he would lean over to the man who'd enquired about us and say: 'To tell you the truth, they live here.'

We took a taxi from Gare du Nord to the movie theatre. It was my first time in Paris. Broccoli was still very groggy. Once we were out on the platform, he grabbed my arm.

'One of us has to become a star,' he whispered. And he looked at me so strangely that for a moment I thought I was dealing with a lunatic. 'The FNV movie will help,' he murmured. 'If people ask us "What kind of work have you done?", we can always show them the FNV movie.'

It was hot in Paris. My clothes stuck to my body. I didn't look like the friend of a movie star, but then I never did. Still, I would have given my eye-teeth to look like that. Maybe that's what they call the folly of youth, but then, what isn't? Some people's lives can be summarised in four words: 'the folly of youth'. But does that tell us anything? Does that do justice to those lives?

Maybe Elvira wasn't really a movie star, maybe only for Broccoli, and maybe that made her one for me as well.

The taxi driver asked Elvira if she was from Morocco, like him. When we got out he called her his 'little pretty one'.

I have no idea what neighbourhood the theatre was in. In any case, it was one with lots of huge tower blocks. There was a South American film festival going on. This was the first time Elvira's movie had ever been shown. It was also the first time she'd see it. She didn't seem particularly nervous. More like resigned. She said: 'At first, we looked at the rushes every day, but after a while we stopped doing that.'

Only a few people had showed up for the film. About six. One was a girl with two toddlers, who looked like an au pair. She kept peering around nervously, as if the movie theatre was actually a peep show.

We met the cameraman in the theatre lounge. He was tall and slim and had a heavy growth of beard. One of those beards where you can't tell if someone's trying to let it grow or if they've just been lost in the jungle for two weeks. His name was David, and he seemed very fond of Elvira. He lifted her in the air in any case. Broccoli was wide awake when he saw that. 'We'll never be able to do that,' he said. I had to admit he was right. Even if we started working out every day from then on, there wasn't much chance of our ever getting her that far off the ground.

David acted as if we were long-lost buddies too. 'Friends of Elvira's are friends of mine,' he said. Broccoli wanted to give him one of his cards, but Elvira explained that David couldn't read a word of Dutch, and that it wasn't such a great idea anyway to start passing them out now. The movie was about to begin.

The inside of the theatre reminded me of the 'Du Midi' on the Apollolaan, where my father and I used to be almost the only people in the audience. It usually took us about ten minutes to find a seat with no gum stuck to it. 'Going late to the Du Midi is taking your life in your hands,' my father used to say. 'I've already ruined three suits there.' I'm pretty sure the ultimate demise of the Du Midi was partly his fault. He always made them pay his dry-cleaning bills.

The film was in black and white, with French subtitles, so I couldn't make head or tail of it. I couldn't even tell if Elvira played her part well. Whenever she was on camera, the shots were long and pensive. There was one scene where she was sitting on the toilet, taking a pee and holding her lover's hand. That's the only thing I remember about the movie. Except that the story took place in a village where nothing ever happened. The funny thing was, you couldn't tell that part of the film was missing. When it was over, the cameraman said: 'You were fantastic.' He said it in English, then repeated it in French.

The lights in the theatre went on. No one recognised Elvira. The girl with the two children bumped into her on the way out and mumbled: 'Stupid cow.'

One old man had fallen asleep. Broccoli woke him up. 'It's over,' he said.

The lady who ran the box office was working on her knitting. 'Was it as bad as the other ones?' she asked the old man. He shrugged. Then he saw Elvira. For a moment I thought he recognised her, but all he did was make a noise with his tongue.

'She was in the movie,' the cameraman said, 'she was that girl.' The old man put on his glasses.

'Oh yeah,' he said, 'now I see it. Good job, good job.' He shook her hand. At the door, he turned around again. He looked like he thought we'd been pulling his leg.

'It was really bad, wasn't it?' Elvira said. We told her it wasn't bad at all, that the movie actually had something.

At a café two doors down from the theatre, we drank a bottle of wine. We sat in the back garden.

'Argentina has no film industry, that's why I left,' David said. He smoked Gauloises. Every now and then he touched Elvira on the shoulder. He had this way of touching people when he talked to them. He even touched the waiter, to the man's obvious displeasure.

When the bottle was empty, Elvira said again: 'It was really bad, wasn't it?'

We tried to convince her she was wrong, but with a little less fervour than before. When David went off to the toilet for a moment, Broccoli gave her a quick kiss on the cheek. There wasn't anything particularly funny about it, but still we had to laugh. The waiter even came out to see what was going on. Maybe we were actually laughing about a film where no one could tell that half of it was missing, or about the café owner who had just tossed his garbage bags next to us in the garden.

David had them bring another bottle of wine. He told us that the producer of the film, Galani, had died recently. They'd called it an accident, but everyone knew it had been suicide. 'The police had to fish him out,' David said, 'he'd been in the water for a week.'

Elvira seemed very upset. I wondered how well she'd known Galani. She wrote something in her red notepad again.

When we said goodbye, David lifted Elvira up in the air for the last time, and promised he'd come to Amsterdam soon.

In the taxi, Broccoli said: 'Give him a little more time and he would have lifted us off the ground too. That guy wants to pick up everyone. It's a perversion.'

This taxi driver called Elvira his 'little pretty one' too. He raced at top speed through the industrial area. No one said a thing, only Broccoli whispered: 'He does it to show off.' We didn't ask him whether he meant the cameraman or the taxi driver.

We were much too early for the train. At a café right across from Gare du Nord, we ordered another bottle of wine. The café looked like it was there specially for travelling salesmen, and for commuters who got gassed before leaving for the suburbs.

'How well do you know this David?' Broccoli asked. We were sitting at the sidewalk café, watching people run by on their way to the trains.

'Oh, pretty well,' Elvira said. 'His parents are from Montevideo. He invited me a few times to come to Uruguay, he had a house on the beach there. After a while I decided I would. He picked me up at the airport. He had a big balloon that said "*I love you*".

'David looked like a little giant. Head and shoulders above everyone and everything. I saw him there at the airport in Montevideo, with that big balloon above his head. He had a two-week beard then too.

'We spent a month at his beach house. Whenever we came back from the beach, I'd say: "Let's take a nap."

'A couple of hours before my plane left we went to bed again. Afterwards, I told him: "That was the last time."'

It was the first time I'd ever heard Elvira talk so much.

At the kerb in front of the café, an old lady was threatening to run a taxi driver through with her umbrella. All kinds of people were standing around, egging her on. But what I was seeing was Elvira, sitting on a bed in a house on a beach somewhere in Uruguay. It's afternoon, and she's putting on her shoes. She's saying: 'That was the last time.' I should have been like the cameraman, I thought, because then I could have received Elvira at my beach house too. But I wasn't like the cameraman, and I had a hard time imagining I ever would be. A big, boisterous guy with a two-week beard who lifts people off the ground and smokes Gauloises. Someone who turns brown in the sun, instead of red.

Maybe even then I sensed that I would become the money-grubber, maybe I've always known that.

Meanwhile, the police had arrived. The lady with the umbrella shouted in a shrill voice: 'Bastard!'

'We met at Galani's,' Elvira said.

'Was Galani your boyfriend?'

Broccoli looked at her with his mocking, yet still extremely charming smile. Maybe we shouldn't have worn her out with questions, maybe we should have just taken her to the disco, because she wanted to dance so badly.

'Sort of,' Elvira said. She told us that Galani had dealt in leather and hides and fur, and that at the age of forty-eight he'd decided there was more to life than leather alone. So he'd started producing movies.

In the train we went straight to the club car, because there was nowhere else to sit. We ordered something to drink, but the waiter didn't understand us very well. We got rabbit and soup for starters, cheese for dessert. And two bottles of wine.

THE BUTCHER'S WIFE

*M*r Frohlich had a part for me. In a major Dutch motion picture. I had to play someone who was being thrown down the stairs. My lines consisted of the words: 'Friggin' hell, man.' How someone being thrown down the stairs could come up with the words 'friggin' hell, man' on the way down was a mystery to me. Fortunately, it wasn't my problem. It all had to happen real fast, within a couple of days after we got back from Paris. 'You can do it, sweetheart,' Mr Frohlich said, 'I know you can.'

And Broccoli said: 'This is your big break. It's like I always said. All they have to do is let us walk across the screen, and we're in like flint.'

The shooting took place at night in Rotterdam. A little woman in a woollen hat picked me up at the station. The hat was decorated with things that looked sort of like raspberries and blackberries. If you looked closely you could see a whole fruit salad on her head.

I shouldn't go thinking she was the driver, she said. She was the photographer, she was just nice enough to give other people a lift. 'And you,' she said, looking at the script, 'you must be the pimply punk.'

'Oh yeah?' I said. I didn't know what they called me in the script. It turned out she was right. In the script, the character I played was called the 'Pimply Punk'. That's what they called me in the credits too.

The famous actor Klaus Zwaagstra was in the car: he played one of the leading roles in the movie, the title of which was *The Butcher's Wife*. Klaus Zwaagstra was a hunk. At least, that's what some of the girls in the class called him, back when I was still at school. *Yes* magazine held a survey among young women, which showed that Klaus Zwaagstra was by far the best-looking man in Holland.

I said hello when I got in the car, but Zwaagstra didn't say anything. The hair on the back of Klaus Zwaagstra's neck was still wet, like he'd just come out of the shower.

Klaus and the photographer with the hat were talking about cocaine. I sat in the back seat and thought: This is it, this is the life, Klaus Zwaagstra, cocaine, the Dutch motion picture *The Butcher's Wife* – Hollywood, here I come.

The set was in an apartment building that was only halfway built. Or halfway torn down. The director, Danny Brummelkamp, greeted me by giving me a little pinch on the cheek and saying: 'This is the eighteenth night, but it feels like three years. And a year in the movie business is a donkey's years, let me tell you, a donkey's years.'

Then he plopped down in his folding chair and lit a cigarette. Brummelkamp reminded me more of a retired veterinarian than a film director, but that was probably because I hadn't met very many directors in my life.

The make-up lady led me over to a mirror. 'Well, we won't have to do anything about the pimples,' she said. 'That should save a lot of time.'

'Right,' I said.

They threw me down the stairs twenty times that night. A whore threw me down the stairs, to be precise, because I couldn't pay. That was the scene. That's why I had to be thrown down the stairs with my pants around my ankles. And while that was happening, I shouted: 'Friggin' hell, man.' Then she threw my clothes down after me.

Twenty times that night I shouted 'Friggin' hell, man' while flying through the air. I wasn't allowed to wear my glasses, so a couple of times I landed in the wrong place, I knocked down a script girl and one of the other people standing around. Whenever that happened, they kicked me away as quietly as they could, because the camera was still rolling. One time, someone yelled: 'That dickhead bumped the camera again.' But Danny Brummelkamp shouted: 'Quiet on the set.' Then everyone shut up.

After each take they put a blanket around the shoulders of the woman who played the whore. It was cold. No one put a blanket around my shoulders, which was especially bad because I was standing there half-naked. Once in a while I snuck off to warm up in the dressing room, where two make-up ladies were reading the paper. 'They really did some serious casting on this one,' I heard one of them say. And the other one said: 'Yeah, you can say that again, they really went overboard.'

In the middle of the night, we all went up to the top floor to eat. They'd set up wooden benches and tables, and an older woman in a black shawl was standing at a big pot of mashed potatoes and endives. You had to take a plastic plate and walk past her to have it filled.

'That's what I love about making movies,' Klaus Zwaagstra shouted, 'eating together, that unity, that solidarity.' Then he pushed a few people out of the way to get to the mashed potatoes.

When I finally got to the front of the line, the woman with the shawl asked: 'So, you work here too?' Without waiting for an answer, she tossed a big splat of potatoes and endives on my plate. Half of it missed and landed on my shoe, but she didn't bat an eyelid. I couldn't say anything about it either, because just then Danny Brummelkamp got up.

'OK, people, dig in,' he shouted. He didn't seem to notice that most of them had already finished eating. There were a lot of things he didn't notice. He looked like he was heavily under the influence of narcotics. Maybe the producers had decided halfway through to put Brummelkamp on a narcotics diet, just to save the movie. Or maybe Brummelkamp himself had realised that taking lots of narcotics was the only way to survive this movie.

There was one place left, next to Brummelkamp, so I took it. He'd already spoken to me three times, by a different name each time, but that didn't stop him from calling me something else the fourth time. I let it go; it's fine by me when people don't call me by my right name.

'The Polish philosopher Kamelakowski,' Brummelkamp said with his mouth full, 'has a fascinating theory about identity. In a blue room, you have a completely different identity than in a red or a green one.'

He took another big mouthful of mashed potatoes. He didn't seem to like it much, because after every bite he took a swig of mineral water to wash it down.

I leaned over to wipe the endives off my shoe with a napkin. When I sat up again, I said: 'So what you're saying is, in a blue room you have a blue identity, and in a green room you have a green one?'

'Exactly,' Brummelkamp said excitedly, 'that's the crux of Kamelakowski's theory. And that's been my policy in making this movie.' He was about to say something else when the producer stood up and shouted: 'Another great meal, Auntie Sjaak!'

'Yeah,' Klaus Zwaagstra yelled, 'long live Auntie Sjaak!' Then everyone cheered: 'Long live Auntie Sjaak!' Auntie Sjaak stood beaming behind the pot of mashed potatoes and endives. Brummelkamp had his mouth full again, so he couldn't shout 'Long live Auntie Sjaak'. He just pounded on the table a few times with the flat of his hand. Then he rinsed with mineral water and said: 'Back to work, people.'

He was already a few steps away when he turned around as if he'd forgotten something, and said: 'Nice talking to you. Kamelakowski, remember that name.'

I wasn't in the next scene. I had to wait in the dressing room until they were done, so someone could take me home. Auntie Sjaak was in there too. She kept saying: 'That Klaus Zwaagstra, so famous, but so nice.'

At six in the morning, the shooting was finally over. Brummelkamp was the first one into the dressing room. He looked more like a strung-out phantom than ever. He poured some effervescent powder into a glass of water and gulped it down. 'My stomach,' he said, 'these late dinners.' But no one was listening. They were all standing around Klaus Zwaagstra, who was relating anecdotes from his own life while one of the make-up girls pulled off his shoes. Zwaagstra put on his glasses. He had gold-rimmed glasses. He talked real softly, so everyone had to be real quiet to hear him.

'I think I'm going to direct a film myself one of these days,' I heard him whisper. 'I mean, you have to have something to say if you're going to make a movie. I want to do something with Genet. That underworld of Genet's, that rawness, that pain of Genet's, that's no private pain any more, that's metaphysical.'

Auntie Sjaak almost fell into a swoon. 'Oh my God,' she shouted, 'can't you people be quiet, I can barely hear him.'

When Brummelkamp saw me sitting there, something seemed to occur to him. 'Kamelakowski,' he said pantingly, 'has already said everything I want to say, all I have to do is turn it into cinema.' Then, like a pathetic drunkard, he grabbed the hand of the actress who'd been throwing me down the stairs and said it again: 'All I have to do is turn it into cinema.'

'Oh yeah,' she said, 'life is hell.' But you could tell from the way she looked that she thought hell was a pretty nifty place to be.

Part Two

MR BERK

*E*lvira wanted to play a few scenes from *Macbeth*.

Broccoli started rehearsals in her little apartment. She read Lady Macbeth's monologues and he sat on the couch. Every once in a while he shouted: 'Beautiful!' He had nothing else to do anyway. That's how he came up with the idea of turning the house on the Bernard Zweerskade into a theatre, so Elvira would have a stage on which to shine. I asked him if he didn't need his parents' permission. But he said: 'If Mr Berk says yes, then everything's OK.'

I must have met Mr Berk a couple of days after we came back from Paris. It was at Henry Smith's. Broccoli had taken me there again. He had a tab. Actually, it was more like his father's tab.

Mr Berk was introduced to me as a friend of Broccoli's father. He kept looking at his shoes the whole time he was shaking my hand. Mr Berk said the Ecksteins had asked him to keep an eye on things. He didn't want anything to eat, but he did have a few whiskies. His head was big and bald as a cue ball. He said his parents came from Romania, and that their name had originally been Bercowicz. But they'd written a letter to the Queen, and she'd given them permission to change it to Berk. He, in turn, was now planning to shorten it to B. He'd written the letter already, all he had to do was send it to the Queen. Broccoli and I had serious doubts about whether the Queen would allow surnames consisting of only one letter. But Mr Berk was obsessed with the idea.

After his third whisky, Berk asked: 'How are your plans coming along?'

'Good,' Broccoli said. He told him about meeting Elvira, that she was an actress and that we were also planning to become actors. Not just any actors, no, world-famous ones.

Mr Berk was quite excited to hear that. 'World-famous actors,' he said, 'that's a capital idea. Always make plans in life, even if they don't work out, it doesn't matter.' Then he announced that he was going to sing a song about spring, but because it was in Romanian we wouldn't be able to understand it. When he was finished singing he insisted on paying for our dinner. He walked to the kitchen, then he sang of spring in Romanian for some total strangers as well.

As he was getting ready to leave, he told us: 'I've already informed my business contacts and acquaintances of the fact that the last three letters of my name will soon be eliminated.' Then he raised his glass to his lips, but it was empty.

'Berk,' he whispered, barely able to contain his laughter, 'what kind of name is that, I ask you, what kind of name is that?'

It was raining softly; even when he'd almost rounded the corner of the Gerrit van der Veenstraat, we could still see Mr Berk's big, bald head glistening in the dark.

The next time we saw Mr Berk he had, by his own account, become Mr B. He spent all day at Henry Smith's. His greatest joy in life seemed to come from singing songs of spring. Whether

the house on the Bernard Zweerskade could be turned into a
theatre was a matter he refused to address.

'Mr B, please,' Broccoli shouted, 'Elvira needs a stage to shine
on.' Mr B answered Broccoli's cry for help by launching into
another song in Romanian.

Between verses, he said: 'Athletics: have you boys ever thought
about that? World-famous athletes are always in short supply, and
you get to be on TV a lot. Never put all your eggs in one basket.
I've been using two baskets all my life.' Then he started singing
again.

The manager of Henry Smith's looked at us and shook his
head. 'If I didn't know your father so well, what a rascal,' he said.

I couldn't tell which Eckstein he thought was a rascal, the
young one or the old one. What I do know is that, half an hour
later, Mr B was removed from the restaurant, still singing. He
must have stood in front of the window singing for ten minutes,
but Broccoli had stopped listening. He was deep in thought about
where Elvira would play Lady Macbeth. I was embarrassed to sit
there eating while old Mr B sang outside the window. So I nodded
to him now and then, just to indicate that, in my own way, I
appreciated his musical talent.

I went to rehearsals at Elvira's place a few times. Not very often
though. They were too boring for that.

Once, in the middle of a rehearsal, Elvira suddenly said: 'I
prefer to eat on my feet.' So we went outside to walk around and
eat something. She felt like rice pudding. We had to eat it on
our feet, so we left a trail of rice pudding wherever we went.

'Why do you prefer to eat on your feet?' I asked, seeing how
difficult it was to eat rice pudding and walk at the same time.

'I just do,' Elvira said. 'When I'm by myself, I always eat on
my feet.'

All three of us were in an extremely good mood, so I didn't
go on questioning her. The life we yearned for was within arm's
reach.

'Could you two help me out?' Elvira asked, once we were finished eating on our feet. We nodded. 'My mother's coming to visit soon, but my apartment's awfully small.'

'The Bernard Zweerskade,' Broccoli said. He was beaming. 'I'll make of it a veritable palace for her. Mr Berk has nothing to say about that. I'll ask Mrs Meerschwam to fix up the rooms.'

'She's not an easy person,' Elvira said.

It was strange, but suddenly I had a vision of Broccoli and Elvira's mother playing badminton in the garden at the Bernard Zweerskade.

Broccoli said: 'I know how to handle mothers. I'm a match for the best of them. I spent half my childhood playing violin on the rooftop patio. With rotten apples flying past my ears. That makes you tough. And that's what I became, I'm one of the toughest guys in Amsterdam, which is why I'm where I am today. I don't let anyone get in my way, that's why I'm chairman of the Association for Geniuses.'

Elvira laughed really hard when she heard that. Broccoli stepped up to a news-stand and came back with a copy of the *Gazzetta dello Sport*.

'You know what I like about you?' I told Broccoli. 'You're a very sick man.'

'No, I'm redolent with health,' Broccoli replied. 'I can actually figure skate. My mother saw me as a figure skater. "You're my prince on ice," she used to tell me; I bet your mother never said that to you.'

'No,' I said, 'my mother never said that to me.'

That afternoon Broccoli wanted to go out shopping for clothes for Elvira. We raced through department stores and boutiques while Broccoli bought one dress after another. Sometimes Elvira didn't even have time to try them on.

At De Bonneterie we locked ourselves in a changing room while Elvira tried on a summer dress.

'What am I supposed to do with all these dresses?' she asked.

'You're a femme fatale,' Broccoli said, and a femme fatale

wears a different dress every day. And now we have to take the oath.'

'What oath?' I asked.

'We have to vow that Elvira is a femme fatale.'

'A femme fatale,' Elvira said, 'I'm not so sure.'

But Broccoli would not be moved. We had to lay our hands on Elvira's dress and swear that she was a femme fatale, and always would be. Even when her ashes had long been scattered over the Atlantic, when our ashes were scattered and everyone in the world owned their own helicopter, still she would remain a femme fatale. The Association for Geniuses would see to that. Said Broccoli.

THE ADOLF HITLER CAFÉ

*E*lvira had an admirer. A little Jewish doctor who sent her flowers all the time. She laughed about it. They'd met at a nightclub. More than anything else in the world, Elvira loved sleeping and dancing.

I only knew his first name. Wolf. He was a neurologist at a hospital, but his true interest lay not in neurology, but in women who were at least twenty years younger than him.

He'd told Elvira he was thirty-five, but she said you could tell he was pushing fifty. She wondered how someone could hang around in nightclubs till four in the morning, then saw open someone's head at ten.

I finally met him, at 't Haantje. After a great deal of urging, Elvira had consented to have lunch with him, but at the last moment she asked us if we wouldn't mind coming along.

He was already waiting when we got there. He was wearing an expensive suit, or at least a suit that was supposed to look expensive. Broccoli and Elvira were walking arm-in-arm. Without letting go of her arm, he introduced himself to the neurologist. 'Broccoli,' he said, 'events organiser.'

The doctor stood up. His head came to Elvira's shoulder. 'Wolf,' I heard him say, 'a friend.' Then he kissed Elvira three times on the cheek and we all sat down. Lopatin was sitting two tables away from us, but he didn't dare to come any closer. Broccoli was nervous. Wolf didn't notice, he was completely absorbed in Elvira. He showered her with compliments, even about the way she ate her cheese sandwich. That made Broccoli even more nervous, so he started complimenting Wolf on the way he ate his cheese sandwiches too.

'Do you have a waterbed?' Broccoli enquired.

Wolf shook his head in annoyance.

'Elvira's wild about waterbeds. I just ordered a new one. Those things leak like hell.'

'Fascinating,' Wolf said.

Broccoli pointed to me. 'His father's in waterbeds. He's got a big showroom, close to the yacht harbour at Loosdrecht.'

'No,' I said.

'Oh yes,' Broccoli said. 'Krieg, the waterbed baron of the Low Countries, that's his father, and this is Krieg, Jr.'

'I think you've mistaken me for another Krieg.'

Whatever my father was in, it wasn't waterbeds. This Wolf was the kind who might show up at my parents' door some morning and try to buy a waterbed. I didn't much like that idea.

The neurologist was determined not to let us spoil his lunch date. In the end, he was almost sitting on Elvira's lap, and he kept saying: 'Divine, simply divine.' Elvira just laughed, without saying anything. But when he said 'divine' yet again, she said: 'OK, enough's enough.' And Broccoli said: 'Yeah, we've heard that one already.'

Wolf didn't seem put off; he took Elvira's chin in his hand and said: 'You're the kind of girl I'd like to marry.'

The fact that he was already married must have slipped his mind. He'd told Elvira, after they'd kissed once – 'Just once,' she'd warned him – that his wife was sickly and hadn't left their bedroom for the first ten years of their marriage, and that she was now in a sort of sanatorium.

'How can you kiss someone like that?' Broccoli had shouted. 'How can you do that?'

Elvira answered: 'You can. Someday you'll understand.'

Now Wolf turned to us. 'And you two will be my best men.' His glasses were almost falling off his nose. The sunlight was making him sweat. Maybe being so close to Elvira was making him sweat too.

'Let's have another sandwich,' Wolf said. 'I don't have to be back at the hospital till four.'

'But what about your wife, Wolf?' Elvira said.

If someone had heaped burning coals on his head, he couldn't have looked more stricken. He let go of Elvira.

'Bedridden,' he said, sounding subdued, 'bedridden, for quite some time now.' Then he picked up the sugar bowl and brought it down on the table with a crash. 'She sees ghosts,' he said. As if that was what we'd been waiting to hear the whole time. Then he carefully wiped the grains of sugar from the table, and I wondered whether he wasn't the ghost she saw.

Ever since he'd decided to produce *Macbeth* for Elvira, Broccoli had started going to De Smoeshaan. He said a lot of theatre people went there. A lot of actors especially. He said: 'I have to start mingling with theatre people, and you two should be doing the same.'

I didn't want to mingle with theatre people. Theatre people made me uneasy. In fact, there weren't many people I did feel easy around. But I didn't tell Broccoli that.

He'd had new calling cards made. The new ones said:

M.J. Broccoli
producer, events organiser

He'd bought a boa for Elvira to drape around her neck. Actually, it was one of those shawls that just looks like a boa constrictor.

Broccoli said: 'Everyone knows me at De Smoeshaan, and they all want to talk to me. That's how it goes when you're a wunder-kind.'

I went with him once. No one wanted to talk to him that evening. But there were all kinds of people we had to push aside just to get to the bar. People give off a kind of muggy heat, especially when they've been pressed up against each other all evening in a bar.

'Let's get out of here,' I said to Broccoli. 'It's too crowded.'

'No,' he said, 'we still have to mingle with the theatre people. When we've mingled with them, the rest will come by itself.'

Once we'd finally reached the bar, we started talking to a man who told us that all men were hunters. He asked us if we were hunters too.

'Let us drink to the hunters,' Broccoli said.

That evening, for the first time in my life, I realised I had to become a hunter. It didn't matter what was being hunted, as long as a hunt went on.

'Yes,' I said, 'to the hunters.'

Later that evening, in that same café, we ran into Wolf. He was standing with a whole group of people. 'Come and join us, boys,' he shouted, 'come over and join us.'

Broccoli and Elvira used to spend entire evenings there, but the interest in Elvira and her boa constrictor, Broccoli and his calling cards was very limited.

After a few weeks Broccoli started calling De Smoeshaan the 'washed-up actors' café', and, not long after that, the 'Adolf Hitler café'. 'Adolf Hitler,' he said, 'was a washed-up actor, as we all know.'

After he'd mingled with theatre people every night for almost six weeks, Broccoli finally got into a conversation with a man with short black hair who claimed to be a backer.

'I don't know what he backs,' Broccoli told me, 'but he's a backer, and that's what we need for Elvira.'

The next evening, I went with Broccoli to meet the backer. He barely listened to what we said. 'You're so right,' was his reply to everything Broccoli said, and he kept looking around nervously, as though he was afraid he'd miss someone.

Half an hour later, I ran into him in the men's room. We were standing next to each other at the urinals. I noticed he was staring at me. 'Haven't we met before?' he whispered.

'That's right,' I said, 'we just met downstairs.'

For no good reason, he grabbed me by the face and kissed me. I could feel his stubbly cheeks, and I peed all over my shoes.

While he was straightening his clothes in front of the mirror, he said: 'Oh, to be young again, oh God, to be so young.'

I had no idea what to say to him. Situations like that were new to me. So I nodded amiably. Nodding amiably is often the best you can do.

Broccoli told us: 'Alcohol has made wrecks of the washed-up actors at the Adolf Hitler café. There's no reason for us to hang around here.' He left the pile of calling cards with '*producer, events organiser*' lying on the table.

'Isn't that a waste?' I asked him on the way out. 'You just had them printed.'

Broccoli shook his head.

When we passed the Hotel Americain, he stopped and talked to a doorman. He asked about the price of a suite.

'It's important to keep doormen on your side,' he whispered. And right after that: 'We're going to Bark. It's time to eat. Elvira likes to eat at night.'

'I thought she liked to eat on her feet,' I whispered. I looked at Elvira. She had her notepad in her hand. The boa constrictor too.

'It's warm out,' was all she said.

I wondered why she'd ever left Buenos Aires, and what she was looking for in Amsterdam, of all places.

We bought coloured marshmallows at a fruit stand. The marshmallows were so old that we couldn't bite through them, and they smelled like exhaust fumes.

I suddenly found it impossible to imagine that we would not always be together, Broccoli, Elvira and I.

We walked to Bark in the Van Baerlestraat. Elvira didn't say a word the whole way. When we got to the restaurant, though, she said she missed Galani, she missed Buenos Aires, and she never wanted to do anything like the FNV movie ever again.

'That was the FNV,' Broccoli said, once we were seated. 'Wait till they see you as Lady Macbeth. And you,' he said pointing at me, 'as Macbeth himself.'

Later, as we were getting ready to leave, we heard the waiter say to Broccoli: 'I'm sorry, Mr Eckstein, but your credit card has been refused.'

Broccoli went white as a sheet. 'There must be some mistake,' he shouted, 'that's impossible.'

Broccoli without money was like a man without clothes. I'd never seen him so upset. 'Call Mr Berk,' he kept shouting. 'Mr Berk is bound to know something about this.' But no one answered the phone at Mr Berk's.

Elvira paid the bill. She said Wolf had given her the money. That made Broccoli even more furious.

'Who does this Wolf think he is?' he shouted. 'What does that little pimp do for a living, anyway?'

'Wolf is one of my contacts,' Elvira said. 'When you get to know him better, I bet you'll like him.'

Broccoli raged against Wolf, against the waiters, he raged against this restaurant in particular and all restaurants in general. He raged against Elvira, who he called the lowest type of parasite. She didn't say anything, maybe because she didn't know the word 'parasite', or maybe she was acting like she didn't. He called me a parasite too. He raged against Mr Berk, who he said was good for nothing but singing songs about spring-time. He called him a traitor and demonstrated to everyone how badly he sang. When Broccoli started singing, we dragged him outside.

'A newspaper,' he mumbled while we were waiting for a cab. 'We should start our own newspaper. A daily, different from all other dailies.'

His mood only improved when we went to the Beatrixpark to play soccer in the middle of the night. Elvira was wearing shorts Broccoli had lent her.

'Maybe we'll get raped and murdered,' Elvira said.

'Yeah,' I said, 'who knows, maybe we'll get raped and murdered.'

MRS LOPEZ

*M*rs Meerschwam refused to prepare Broccoli's parents' bedroom for Elvira's mother. She shrieked like a banshee, even though I was there, and Broccoli said Mrs Meerschwam only shrieked when the two of them were alone. 'I won't do that to your parents!' she shrieked. 'I won't do this to them!'

'But they're in Lenzerheide,' Broccoli kept saying, 'they're never coming back. The bedroom isn't a museum, is it?'

It looked like she was going to have a heart attack. Suddenly she turned to me. 'You've never met Mr and Mrs Eckstein. They were very special people. Generous people. Extremely generous. And not only at Christmas.' I understood that the extraordinary thing about Mr and Mrs Eckstein lay in their singular open-handedness.

Broccoli finally decided that Mrs Lopez would sleep in the living room. Mrs Meerschwam reluctantly began setting up a bed there. 'I'm going to inform Mr Bercowicz about this,' she said.

She always called him Bercowicz, even though his name had been Berk since before we were born.

'He's called Mr B these days,' Broccoli said, 'and the only thing he cares about is singing.'

'Stop it,' she shouted. 'I don't want to hear any more.'

In the kitchen she told me: 'I've been coming to this house for thirty years. And I've seen some things here in my day. Parties. But I'll spare you the details.'

'Yes, spare him the details,' Broccoli shouted from the other room. 'For God's sake, spare him the details. They never spared me a detail, and look what's become of me.'

'Do you hear that?' Mrs Meerschwam said. 'And these are the people you hang around with.'

Elvira, Broccoli and I were waiting in the arrival hall at Schiphol. Broccoli had passed around chewing gum, so our breath would be fresh. He said there was a distinct possibility we would have to hug Elvira's mother, and Elvira said that, knowing her mother, that possibility was extremely distinct. She even warned us not to get crushed in the embrace.

After an hour and a half, Elvira said: 'There she is.'

Mrs Lopez took tiny little steps. That might have had something to do with all the clothes she had on, but it might also have been her shoes with the giant heels. She was wearing a fur coat and a hat with a bunch of feathers stuck to the top. A shiny red handbag swung from one arm. She looked like she could lose her balance any moment. When she finally got to Elvira, she hugged her passionately. Then she hugged Broccoli and me just as passionately. To do that, she first had to suspend her full weight from our shoulders. It was more like someone clamping hold of a lifebuoy than like someone saying hello.

'I've heard so much about the two of you,' she said to us in English. 'You must call me Helena.'

Then the man who'd been standing behind Mrs Lopez the

whole time stepped up to us. He had six suitcases with him, and a couple of plastic bags. We hadn't realised that Elvira's mother was going to bring her boyfriend along. We were amazed when this complete stranger started hugging us too.

'This is Emile,' Mrs Lopez cried, 'my turtle-dove.'

I don't think Elvira had ever heard of him, but she didn't let on.

All those suitcases he had to carry made Emile seem kind of awkward.

'That's no dove, that's more like a trained bear,' Broccoli whispered. Emile and Elvira began speaking Spanish, and Mrs Lopez opened her bag and began forcing all kinds of presents on us.

'Not here, Mama,' Elvira kept shouting. But there was no stopping her. We got three bottles of aftershave each.

'Maybe they run a perfume shop,' Broccoli said under his breath.

We walked out to the taxis. Emile was toting four of the suitcases now, and Broccoli had the other two. Mrs Lopez just tripped along gingerly. Her hat with the feathers kept blowing off, so Broccoli had to run after it. 'Get it,' she shouted, 'get it.' It was almost like a sporting event.

We took a taxi to the Bernard Zweerskade. No matter what she saw, Mrs Lopez cried: 'My God, isn't it beautiful?' In a tone that sounded like she'd had the wind knocked out of her. Like the Virgin Mary had appeared to her. What would have happened if the Virgin Mary actually *had* appeared to her?

They settled right down in Broccoli's living room. It was a good thing Mrs Meerschwam wasn't there to see it.

Elvira had to come and sit on Emile's lap while she unwrapped her presents, and Emile said: 'You don't look at all like your mother.'

Mrs Lopez was still walking around in high heels. Whenever she lost her balance she grabbed hold of the first thing she could find. The first day she broke two vases. Every time she broke something or knocked it over she'd cry: 'This is such a lovely house.'

Of course we didn't call her Helena. We called her Mrs Lopez. Even though she kept saying that there was nothing in the world she'd like more than to have us call her Helena.

Emile and Mrs Lopez had brought their complete wardrobes and an incredible number of perfume bottles. Broccoli's house started smelling like a beauty parlour. Mrs Lopez's breath, on the other hand, smelled like an old attic. Maybe that's why she went so heavy on the perfume. No one wants to smell like an old attic. I used to think that people wanted the impossible, the impossible dream. But people don't want the impossible dream. Good thing, too. People want their breath not to smell like an old attic, and they want a pair of clean shorts now and then, and on a hot summer day a nice peach is nothing to turn up your nose at either.

When the contents of the six suitcases had been dealt with, Mrs Lopez grabbed Broccoli's hands, pressed them to her bosom and said: 'You're such a sweet boy.'

Broccoli whispered: 'I'm a wunderkind. They found out about it when I was eight, and I had to spend the next four years playing violin on the rooftop patio. The neighbours turned the garden hose on me, but that only improved my playing.'

Fortunately, she wasn't listening to what Broccoli was saying. She didn't listen to anyone, only to herself. That's one way to get through life.

She pulled a little photo album out of her handbag. She was breathing hard. We were standing on each side of her, and she pressed us against her. Whether we wanted to or not, we had to look at those photos. Her big breasts heaved up and down. They were like living creatures. I felt the urge to stick a pin in them or bite them. I'd never bitten a woman's breasts. From what I'd been told, it was the thing to do. Almost every man I'd talked to had bitten a woman's breasts, and they were all enthusiastic about it. I'd talked to a woman once who told me that there was almost nothing she liked more than biting her baby's buns. To hear her tell it, biting her baby's buns was the greatest thing she'd ever done.

'And this,' Mrs Lopez said, 'is Elvira's husband.' She pointed to a man. A real man. Suddenly, I understood what they meant when they said men were hunters. We took a good look at Elvira's husband.

'Lovely,' Broccoli said at last, 'a lovely fellow.'

Early that evening, Mr Berk walked in. He had his own set of keys. Berk didn't seem surprised to see the guests: he just walked straight over to Broccoli.

'Turned down,' he said, 'I've been turned down.' His bald skull shone the way it always did. I've never seen a skull as nice and round as Mr Berk's. He showed us a letter. 'We see no reason to comply with your request for a change of name. Unfortunately, your dossier cannot be processed further.'

He was wearing the brown suit he always had on, and his big brown shoes. Mrs Lopez shook his hand, but he seemed not to notice. Mr Berk pulled a bag of liquorice drops from his inside pocket and began handing them out. Emile shook his hand too, but I believe the only thing Mr Berk could think about was the Queen's letter.

When everyone had a piece of liquorice, he put the bag away and said to Broccoli: 'I talked to your father. He'll be in Amsterdam for the day next Thursday. He wants to see you.'

When he left, he stepped on the beds we'd worked so hard to make. He didn't seem to notice, or maybe it was his way of protesting against the sacking of his friend's house.

Mr Berk never said much to me. Except for that one time in the tram when, for no apparent reason, he said: 'I knew your father when he was young. He was a real butt-pincher.'

He said it without a hint of disapproval. Maybe he'd been a butt-pincher too when he was young. Maybe he still was, although that was hard for me to imagine.

'Mr Berk,' Broccoli said, 'this is Elvira. I told you about her.'

At the kitchen door, Berk stopped and turned. He walked straight over to her. Long before he got there, he stuck out his hand. He looked at his shoes instead of at Elvira. Then they shook hands for a long time. I think that was mostly Mr Berk's doing, because he wouldn't let go.

'The pleasure is all mine,' he said before leaving.

SOCK PULLER-UPPER

'As old as God and as fresh as the morning,' Mrs Lopez said. She spoke English with a heavy accent, and she was still walking around in a cloud of perfume. Just like Emile.

They'd been living in Broccoli's house for two weeks already, and there was no indication that they'd be leaving soon. The house was slowly going to pot; Mrs Meerschwam refused to come as long as they were sleeping in the living room.

Wearing her tennis outfit, Mrs Lopez was sitting at the bar of the racquet club on the Karel Lotsylaan, knocking back one gin and tonic after the other. Emile was wearing shorts too; only now was his complete girth truly visible. He had heart problems, so he carried a gold pillbox wherever he went.

'If I keel over, I have to put a pill under my tongue,' he'd said to me, 'and if I can't do it, then you have to.' In my view, anyone who might have to put a pill under his tongue at any moment had no business playing tennis. So I just nodded. Broccoli was all too happy to have them out of the house.

After Emile and her mother came to town, Elvira had become increasingly withdrawn. Broccoli and I were often stuck with Mrs Lopez and Emile, because Elvira said she had no time, or she had acting lessons, or didn't feel good. According to Broccoli, she and the neurologist met on an almost daily basis. 'What does she see in that Wolf?' Broccoli would ask me at least twice a day. 'What does she see in that munchkin?'

'As old as God and as fresh as the morning,' Mrs Lopez said again. She was engaged in conversation with a young man, and for the last half-hour they'd been playing a game that boiled down to guessing each other's age. Emile was pacing back and forth at the window. Every once in a while he'd stop and jack up his shorts. The little box of pills was on the bar, next to his beer glass. 'Self-control,' he'd said, 'self-control, that's the alpha and the omega.'

'Isn't it about time you two went out and played?' Broccoli asked.

Mrs Lopez shook her head. 'We'll wait until the wind dies down a bit.' They'd been waiting all morning for the wind to die down.

'Every year I have myself examined,' I heard her say. 'From head to toe. In Miami. They've got the best doctors there. I don't want any hacks looking at me. My body is too precious for that. I told my doctor in Buenos Aires: "You're a hack. I wouldn't let you fix my bicycle."'

'You're right, you don't want any hacks working on your body,' the man beside her said. He ordered another gin and tonic for Mrs Lopez, and I heard her say: 'You don't look like a hack.'

Emile was still pacing at the window with the rental racket in his hand. He kept swinging the racket back and slicing it through the air. 'I'm in form,' he said quietly. 'I am in form.'

Approaching in the distance, I saw the lady who lived next door to my parents. It seemed she not only played badminton, but tennis as well. And she was also into power-walking. I'd heard her talking about it in the backyard. She'd said: 'If you want to lose weight, the only thing that helps is power-walking. Preferably power-walking with weights in your hands.'

That was exactly what she was doing now. She had a dumb-bell in each hand and a tennis racket slung over her shoulder. And she was heading towards the clubhouse, as fast as her old legs would carry her. Her bright-red training suit made her look like a tropical bird, but then one that's been badly mistreated.

'Come on, let's get out of here,' Broccoli said. 'They'll be all right by themselves.'

We went to Elvira's house, but she wasn't there.

'I bet she's off making out with that neurologist,' Broccoli shouted. He was completely hysterical. I'd never seen him like that.

'This is no way for the chairman of the Association of Geniuses to behave,' I tried, but it didn't work. He pushed me away and began kicking at the door, until someone upstairs opened the window and shouted: 'You want I should break both your legs?'

When we got back to Broccoli's house that evening, Mrs Lopez and Emile weren't back yet.

'Probably still waiting for the wind to die down,' Broccoli mumbled.

At eleven o'clock, the racquet club called and asked us to come and pick them up. They were the only ones left in the clubhouse. Emile's gold pillbox was still on the bar. Mrs Lopez was half-undressed, but only from the waist up.

'Let's go out to dinner,' she said when she saw us come in. Emile said nothing. He was still holding his tennis racket. When we got back to the house, Broccoli went straight to bed, without saying a word to Mrs Lopez. He swore to me that he wouldn't come out for the next twenty-four hours.

At eight o'clock the next morning, Elvira called me at my parents' house. She'd never done that before. In fact, I'd never even given her the number. I didn't want people calling me there. 'Could we meet somewhere?' she asked.

We met at a pancake house. She was wearing her boa constrictor. I knew she only wore it to please Broccoli. Everything in the pancake house was greasy. The waiter's hair, the tables, the chairs, even the toilet paper.

'The neurologist says he's going to commit suicide,' she said.

'Oh yeah?' I said.

'Yeah,' she said, 'if I don't keep seeing him. People are so pathetic.'

'Yeah,' I said, 'real pathetic.'

Then she looked up at me and said: 'I'm glad you're not pathetic.'

'Never have been,' I said.

Elvira bent down, disappeared under the table for a good two minutes, and when she came back up she said quietly: 'The elastic in my socks is shot, do you want to see?'

'Yeah, let's take a look,' I said. I crawled under the table. The elastic in her socks was definitely shot. They were both hanging down around her ankles.

'I just bought them,' Elvira said, 'two days ago.'

'What a gyp,' I said. And then I began caressing her legs softly, right on the spot where her socks should have been. I don't know what came over me. I'd never dared to do anything like that before, and now I was sitting there under the table, caressing her legs like I'd never done anything else but sit under tables and caress women's legs.

'Poor socks,' I murmured, 'poor socks, we'll have to give them a decent burial, somewhere close to the sea. Whatever happened to you, socks, to make your elastics go bad? You're only two days old, and you're already shot to hell. We'll have to bury you in the big sock cemetery beside the sea.'

I kept going on like that, like some kind of nut, while I caressed Elvira's legs. And feeling her hairs and the broken elastic and talking like a nut the whole time. No one around us seemed to notice, but the whole pancake house was actually watching us on the sly. Elvira told me that later, much later. Right then she didn't dare to say anything, because she was afraid I'd stop caressing her legs. She enjoyed having someone caress her legs, right at the spot where her socks should have been. No one had ever caressed her quite there before, and she was pleased to have it happen now.

'Today, I'll follow you everywhere and pull up your socks,' I said when I resurfaced, because my arm had gone numb.

She looked at me thoughtfully. 'It's a profession that suits you: sock puller-upper.'

I told her I couldn't agree with her more. That there was nothing I'd rather do than throw all my ambitions overboard and go through life as a sock puller-upper. But that I couldn't do that to my parents.

Elvira didn't seem particularly impressed by the neurologist's impending suicide. She was busy knocking back a big plate of Swedish pancakes. It was nine-thirty in the morning, but she called it her 'dinner'. I sat across from her and thought about ordering something myself.

'I had an affair with a rugby player once,' she said suddenly. 'I met him in a hotel in Argentina. There were lots of rugby players at that hotel. And my parents and me. He was very gallant. He started massaging my shoulders in the swimming pool. A bit brash, but also gallant, don't you think?'

'Yeah,' I said, 'a bit brash, but gallant.'

'That night I went to bed with him. I thought of it more as a practice session: I hadn't been to bed with anyone for a long time. But he thought it was more than that. He came looking for me in Buenos Aires, and he wrote a letter to my parents saying he would give up rugby for me.

'He had a motorcycle. He was crazy about rugby, and about that motorcycle. I liked to ride on the back. Maybe I liked the motorcycle more than the rugby player. Then I was offered that part in the movie. He came to the set every day on his motorcycle; he'd even had a sidecar made especially for me. But he thought I was messing around with other men. So he followed me everywhere with that sidecar of his. He worked for the post office, but they hadn't seen him for a long time because he was following me around everywhere.'

Her plate was empty. I wondered why she was telling me this. And whether she thought Broccoli and I were following her around too. I wanted to say something that would put her at ease, that would make it clear that I was glad she'd told me this, but I couldn't think of anything. So I just dove back under the table to pull up her socks.

WOLF'S BIRTHDAY

1 finally met Mr Eckstein, Sr. It was in the bar of the Victoria Hotel, across from the Centraal Station. Broccoli had insisted that I come along.

'That's my father,' he said. He pointed to a man talking to an organ grinder. Mr Eckstein was wearing a grey sports coat. He was badly shaven, there were whole patches he'd missed. There was nothing conspicuous about him. Not the kind of man you'd think produces the biggest turds in the world.

'You've turned my house into a camp site,' Mr Eckstein said, without introducing himself to me.

'It's not a camp site,' Broccoli said. 'Those are very nice people.'

'A camp site,' Mr Eckstein repeated. 'Bercowicz told me.'

Poor Mr Berk. Even Broccoli's father called him Bercowicz. It must have driven him crazy.

We were sitting at a table by the window.

'And you,' Mr Eckstein said to me suddenly, 'do you camp out there too?'

'No, I sleep at home,' I said.

Mr Eckstein ordered coffee for the three of us, without asking whether we wanted any, then he said quietly: 'You're ruining me.'

'I'm doing all kinds of things,' Broccoli said.

Mr Eckstein shook his head. He watched the endless stream of passers-by like he was searching for a familiar face.

'And what do you do?' he asked.

I hesitated for a moment.

'I work with Broccoli.' I didn't know whether I should say 'your son' or 'Broccoli'. I chose the latter. By now, he had to be used to his son calling himself 'Broccoli'.

Mr Eckstein started laughing. He put his head in his hands and mumbled: 'Heckle and Jeckle.'

Could this be the man who'd organised those terrible garden parties Mrs Meerschwam talked about?

Mr Eckstein dabbed at his lips with a rumpled handkerchief.

'I have to be getting back,' he said. We went with him to the station. He walked just like Broccoli. As if his legs were a pair of rhythm sticks going up and down. At the news-stand in the station hall we said goodbye.

'Your mother misses you,' he said to Broccoli. 'We all miss you.' He hugged Broccoli. He shook my hand. He wanted to know my name.

'Ewald Krieg,' I said. 'Ewald Stanislas Krieg, actually.' My name seemed to interest him. He wrote it on the back of a paper napkin.

He walked away, but then he came back again. 'How's it going with the girl? I heard about it from Bercowicz.'

'It's going fine,' Broccoli said.

Mr Eckstein started laughing again, like he had in the Victoria Hotel. But this time he didn't put his head in his hands. He just stood there for a moment, in the middle of the hall at Centraal Station. 'Take good care of her,' he said.

Then he gave us both a hundred-guilder note and whispered: 'Use it to buy something wholesome. Your body you can never get back.'

Then he turned and walked away as fast as he could, even though his train wouldn't be leaving for another twenty minutes.

We went outside. Broccoli didn't say a thing about the talk with his father, and I didn't dare to ask. I wondered whether I should keep the hundred guilders or give it to Broccoli.

'Let's get Elvira,' he said.

We found Wolf in front of the building where the acting classes were held. It was a private school where anyone could take lessons, as long as they paid. You didn't have to be able to do anything, all you had to do was pay.

Four girls were sitting on the verandah, smoking. They looked like they were ready to go out and hang themselves.

Wolf acted very pleased to see us. 'Hey, guys,' he shouted. We waved to him from a distance, but it didn't work, he came over anyway.

'Today's my birthday,' he said, 'I'm throwing a party tonight. If you two want to come . . .'

'That's awfully nice of you,' Broccoli said.

We shook Wolf's hand by way of congratulations, and Broccoli asked: 'So how old are you, actually?'

The party was in Wolf's attic room, right above his mother's apartment. But he had his own stairway. The attic consisted of two little rooms and a kitchen. Occasionally, there was this pounding from downstairs. That was Wolf's mother, knocking on the ceiling with her cane to tell us the music was too loud.

'My wife's in the hospital,' Wolf told us, 'so I moved back in with my mother. That empty house was driving me crazy.'

Three nurses from the hospital were sitting on the couch. For the rest, there was a male colleague of Wolf's, and a friend of his from the university. And us.

On the counter was a bowl of Wolf's mother's egg salad. No one wanted egg salad, but Wolf kept calling out: 'Plenty here for everyone, people.'

We'd given Wolf one of those pans with the no-stick surface. He seemed pleased.

One of the nurses, I think her name was Emmy, was very interested in Broccoli. Especially when he gave her one of his calling cards.

'I always wanted to be an actress,' she explained.

Wolf's colleague was called Professor Roos. 'Roos,' he said to Elvira, '*Professor* Roos, but you can call me Jimmy.' He kept talking at Elvira the whole time, he never stopped once.

'I've been to Buenos Aires,' we heard him say. 'That café, that famous café, I was there, the one that starts with an "H".'

Elvira said: 'I don't know any café that starts with an "H".'

She danced with Wolf for a while. It looked more like the way we used to slow-dance at the end of the evening in junior high school. At least, the way some of us did. Now that I think about it, I've never slow-danced. One of those things I'm saving for a following incarnation.

Emmy said to Broccoli: 'I think your work must be fascinating.'

'I do too,' Broccoli said. I thought about Elvira and those socks of hers, about whether she was wearing socks tonight that would have to be buried at the sock cemetery. You couldn't tell. She had on pants, not a skirt.

Halfway through the evening, when Professor Roos was dancing pretty sloppily with one of the nurses, Elvira suddenly disappeared. We found her in Wolf's bedroom. She was in bed. It was a good idea, actually, because Wolf's room was pretty cold. We climbed into bed beside her. The bed stank a little of Wolf, but there weren't any other beds to climb into.

Broccoli unbuttoned her blouse and kissed her breasts, which I now saw for the first time. Maybe I should have gone away, because you don't just lie next to something like that. But I was too tired and too drunk.

Suddenly, Elvira grabbed my head and pressed it against her shoulder. I kissed her breasts too, and I kissed her nipples. As though by reflex. I didn't even think about it. I was able to think about it later, though, and I have done so often. I've never considered it a waste of time, even though I've spent days thinking about it, without pause.

'I think you're sweet,' Broccoli whispered. It was the only time I've ever heard Broccoli say something like that. Maybe he'd taken a vow to say it only three times in his life, or twice.

I fell asleep, and woke up only when Elvira's body started shaking back and forth and this strange noise started coming out of her mouth. At first, I thought she was making love with Broccoli. Or that there was an earthquake, or worse, but she was crying.

'I don't want them to hear,' she whispered.

I've never heard anyone cry the way Elvira did that night. It was like all the sorrow in the world was coming out of her mouth and out of her eyes and her nose and her ears.

'I don't want them to hear,' she whispered again.

We had to hold Wolf's pillow pressed over her mouth, because she was screaming between the sobs.

'It's OK,' I kept saying, 'it's OK.' I didn't know what else to say.

There was nothing else for us to do but sit on the edge of the bed and watch her cry. Finally, all three of us fell asleep.

Wolf's mother woke us up. She came into the room, turned on the light and shouted: 'What do you people think you're doing, on my son's birthday, do you know what I call this?'

We never found out what she called it, because she started slamming her cane down on the blankets and the floor like a madwoman. That sound of it drowned out everything, including her own bellowing. She was awfully strong for such an old woman. We got up, grabbed our shoes and ran. The party had been over for a long time. Wolf was standing in a corner, pressed up against Emmy. His shirt was open to the navel. He'd cultivated a lot of chest hair through the years.

He waved to us as we ran past. We didn't have time to stop,

because his mother was coming after us. In the doorway, I caught a glimpse of her grabbing the bowl of egg salad off the counter, ready to pitch it at us. But she was too late.

Outside, Broccoli said: 'Let's go to my place.'

It was almost light. I never found out why Elvira cried so hard that night. And I never dared to ask about it.

I've also thought on numerous occasions about that half-hour when Elvira cried so hard, and I've never considered that a waste of time either. Even though there've been so many things I've considered a waste of time. There were days, in fact, when I thought almost everything was a waste of time.

FLYING FEMALES

*W*e went out to dinner one last time with Mrs Lopez and Emile. Elvira was with us. We had to convince her it was better if she went along. Her mother had on her five-inch heels again.

Emile was wearing a white suit. He was edgier than ever. He had the little gold box clenched in his hand. 'They didn't find a thing,' he whispered in the taxi, 'but they can't guarantee anything either.' A few minutes later he whispered: 'I could drop dead any moment.'

Elvira and Broccoli took a separate cab. He'd told Emile and Mrs Lopez that his father thought his hospitality was tantamount to opening a camp site.

Mr Berk had started coming by every day to check up. He pretended he was there to pick up the mail, but we knew old Eckstein had sent him to see if the camp site was still there. His stepping on the beds each time couldn't have been an accident either. After a lot of encouragement, Mrs Lopez and Emile had announced they'd be leaving for Rome and would fly back to Buenos Aires from there.

'I just hope I make it to Rome,' Emile had said a few times already. But to tell you the truth, he'd never looked better. He just seemed to get fatter all the time. According to Broccoli, in the middle of the night Emile would often say: 'I could sure stand a drumstick.' Then Broccoli would have to go to the all-night deli on the Beethovenstraat to buy him grilled drumsticks. The people at the deli knew Broccoli by now. They'd hand him the drumsticks before he could even say a word. Emile devoured at least four drumsticks a night.

'You're a fantastic driver,' I heard Mrs Lopez telling the taxi driver.

'She flirts with everyone,' Emile whispered. 'I'm sure you've noticed that already. But it is innocent flirting. Completely innocent.' Then he shook me by the shoulder and said: 'You're a good boy.'

Broccoli had made reservations at a restaurant on 't Spui. As soon as we walked in, Mrs Lopez threw her arms around the neck of the first waiter she saw. Two other waiters had to escort her to the table. Once she was seated, she started blowing kisses at everyone. Not only at the two waiters who'd brought her to the table, but to almost the whole staff.

'We'll come back,' Mrs Lopez said. 'We'll come and visit you again sometime.'

'Is that a threat?' Broccoli mumbled.

Elvira was toying with her rice. She had her boa constrictor on.

'Where did you get that horrible thing?' her mother asked. She didn't wait for an answer. She never waited for an answer. She just went on talking at Broccoli. 'I'm having an exhibition in Buenos Aires in November. Did I tell you I paint? Flying females and trees. I'll send you a painting. You've been so wonderful to us all these weeks.'

'That's awfully nice of you,' Broccoli said.

It seemed like Elvira wasn't following half the conversation. Every once in a while she'd look at me. Then she smiled. I didn't smile back, because Mrs Lopez was keeping an eye on everyone.

After dinner, Emile said: 'It was lovely, but there were no drumsticks.' He had dark bags under his eyes.

When they brought the coffee, he pulled a packet of sweeteners out of his pocket and dropped two tablets into his cup. 'I like sweet things,' he whispered. And a little later: 'I can feel it in my arm again.' He laid his left arm on the table, like it was a huge sausage. I was sitting next to him, but I didn't ask what it was he felt in his arm.

'I hope you come back to Buenos Aires soon, Elvira,' her mother said.

'I feel it in my arm again,' Emile yelped.

Mrs Lopez slammed her hand down on the table and shouted: 'Spare us the pain in your arms, please, for one evening. The doctors have looked at you and there's nothing wrong.' She took a big slug of coffee, then said: 'Your husband's waiting for you, Elvira. We all are.'

Elvira didn't say a word. No one said a word, except for Emile, who whispered in my ear: 'I can't take it any more.' I didn't know whether he was talking about the pain in his arm or about Mrs Lopez.

'You can't just leave someone who loves you,' Mrs Lopez said, 'especially not your husband.'

Elvira smiled. Maybe she felt like saying that you can leave anyone, whether they're your husband or not, whether they love you or not.

'It's better this way,' Elvira said finally.

'This is him,' her mother said, pointing to a photograph she'd pulled out of her bag. We had to look at the photo of Elvira's husband again. It must have been the rugby player, or maybe he was a bouncer.

'When Elvira turned eighteen I gave her a waterbed,' Mrs Lopez said. She was beaming. Broccoli took her hand, the way

I'd seen him take Mrs Meerschwam's hand before.

'I had arthritis by the time I was four, but do you think my parents bought me a waterbed? Wooden planks and an old mattress, that's what I slept on for fifteen years.'

We got up from the table. Broccoli and I had to help Mrs Lopez walk. Somehow she still succeeded in stumbling up against a waiter. When we said goodbye, Emile shook me till my teeth rattled. 'You're a good boy,' he said again.

Mrs Lopez was crying. The taxi was waiting at the kerb. She cried the way some women do when they have an orgasm. With huge gasps and heart-rending sobs.

'At least tell him yourself,' she said. 'He suffers so much. He loves you.'

When Mrs Lopez wasn't looking, Emile slipped Elvira some money. He gave me two ten-guilder notes as well. 'Put it away quick,' he said. 'I'll never make it back to Holland, and young people can always do with a little something extra.'

They climbed in the taxi; Mrs Lopez in front, Broccoli and Emile in the back. Mrs Lopez rolled down the window. 'Come back,' she yelled, 'please come back.' The only thing was, you couldn't tell who she was talking to. As they were pulling away, we heard her shout: 'Oh my God, I've got an appointment at the hairdresser's tomorrow.'

Emile stuck his arm out the window to shake hands with Elvira and me, but he was too late. The taxi shot off. Elvira and I just stood there in front of the restaurant. We remained standing there for quite some time.

I WANT TO FEEL YOU IN ME

*E*lvira didn't feel like going home. She was afraid Wolf would
be waiting at the door. 'Wolf won't be there,' I said a couple
of times. But she didn't believe me.

We walked along the Herengracht. She held my hand. We
were both sweating heavily. It wasn't that hot out, so maybe it
was from the spicy food. I noticed four young guys following along
behind us. I didn't want to say anything. I just started walking
faster.

'How much did he give you?'

'Two tens,' I said.

'That won't get us far,' she said.

We sat down on a bench next to a *pissoir*.

'Galani wanted to marry me,' she said. 'He always used to say:
"I'm sick, Elvira, I'm sick." He claimed he was sick with love.
Can you imagine that? But he already sagged all over the place.
I don't want a man who sags all over the place.'

'Of course not,' I said.

'"There's no way," I told him, "there's just no way." "But I'm sick, Elvira," he'd say, "I'm sick."

'He was good at cards. Whenever we finished shooting for the day, the men on the crew had to play cards with him. And he always won. At a certain point they'd had enough. But they depended on him for money. So they kept playing.

'In the end, Galani was more interested in playing cards than he was in the movie. Sometimes, even though it was only two o'clock, he'd shout: "OK, let's wrap it up." Then we had to play cards.

'Once, when I was sitting on Galani's lap, he said: "I worked in hides for twenty-five years, all for myself. Now I'm making this movie for you."

'One morning, he called the whole crew over. "Yesterday was the last shooting," he said. "The money's finished. And besides, no one has the patience to sit through long movies any more."

'"Marry me," he said to me once. He wanted to take me to the festival at Cannes. "A hide salesman at Cannes, that would show them," he said. Later, when it was all over, I dropped in on him once at his house. He was living in one little room. Everything else he'd had to sell. There were furs all over the place. He'd had to sell everything to make the movie, but he still had a lot of coats. You almost couldn't move around the room. "Just step over them," he said.

'I sat beside him for a while. He kept falling asleep. When I got ready to leave, he said: "Pick a coat for yourself. Then you can think of me when winter comes."

'I started looking around. There were fur coats everywhere. Even the bathtub was full of them. But he didn't have my size. He started swearing. He pulled a couple of furs out of the cupboard, but he still couldn't find my size. Finally, he said: "Well, you'll just have to think of me in winter without a fur coat."

'So I married the rugby player. I figured: at least then it's over and done.'

Once again I wondered why Elvira was telling me all this, and what I was supposed to say, what in God's name I was supposed to say. Later, I found out that people will tell you all kinds of things, as long as you keep your mouth shut.

That evening she was wearing socks that didn't fall down around her ankles. I'd already bent down a few times to check, but to no avail.

'Where do you actually live?' she asked.

'On the south side, but my parents don't like people staying over.'

I thought about Broccoli, who at that very moment was probably buying drumsticks at the all-night deli on the Beethovenstraat. I thought about Mrs Lopez, who painted flying females. In oil, only in oil, she'd hastened to add.

'I can't go on,' Elvira said. 'I'm tired.'

'Go with me to my place,' she said. 'Wolf might be there. You have no idea how crazy he is.'

We couldn't take a cab, because Broccoli wasn't there to pay for it. Emile had given Elvira a hundred guilders, but she wanted to spend it on something else.

When we finally got to her house, she said: 'My mother made a big party out of it, out of my wedding.'

'Oh yeah?' I said.

'Yeah,' she said. 'A really big party. But I didn't wear white, I refused. She thought that was really terrible. She went on about it for years.'

I missed Broccoli. Broccoli knew what to do in situations like this. He wouldn't have been afraid, and I'm sure he would have cracked a joke. Beer, bonbons and bad jokes, that's what Broccoli said it was all about. I didn't have any beer, no bonbons either, and the few bad jokes I knew I'd already told too often.

'So what colour did you get married in?'

'In blue,' Elvira said, 'almost purple. Just to get back at them.'

'Aha,' I murmured.

'Shall we have some artichoke liqueur?' Elvira asked. The thought of artichoke liqueur made me nauseous.

'That would be great,' I said.

As we were walking up the stairs, I said: 'See, no neurologists here.' I took the only chair in her apartment. 'I had to sell all the other ones,' she said.

She poured what was left of the artichoke liqueur into two espresso cups.

There was a carton next to her bed with half a pizza still in it. I'd already stepped in it twice. There were pieces of olive and anchovy stuck to my toes, and now there were bits of olive and anchovy in her bed too. She didn't mind.

She'd kissed me, right in the middle of a conversation. About *Macbeth*, I believe. Or maybe it was about the rugby player. Or flying females. On the cheek. That's where she kissed me. Just like that. Out of the blue. We hadn't been staring at each other romantically. If there's anything that makes me sick, it's people who stare at each other romantically. Don't even try that with me. Not with Elvira, either.

I kissed her back. On the lips. 'You started it,' she said.

'No,' I said, 'you're the one who started it. I'm positive.' Then we went on talking. About *Macbeth*, or flying females, or maybe even about Buenos Aires.

Suddenly, she said: 'I want to feel you in me.' I looked at her. At first I didn't say anything, but then I asked: 'You want to feel me in you?' It was the funniest thing I'd ever heard. I've never heard anything that funny since. I was laughing so hard I couldn't sit up straight. She couldn't either. 'I want to feel you in me,' she kept saying. I started saying it too, the tears running down my face. In one of Schierbeek's poems he says we must never forget how we've laughed. I never understood that poem as well as I did that evening. It's just so damn funny when someone says to you: 'I want to feel you in me.' While you're nauseous from the artichoke liqueur.

We couldn't stop laughing. I kept bending over to whisper in her ear: 'I want to feel you in me.' I laughed so hard that I was drooling. It got on her T-shirt.

The next day we found a green spot on her T-shirt, close to the left shoulder. Of course I didn't tell her it was my drool. By the way, I not only drool when I laugh, I also drool in my sleep.

Finally, we went over to the bed. That was the first time I stepped in the pizza.

'Whenever I like a girl a lot, I come too fast,' I said quietly. As far as I knew, I always came too fast. It was a hypothesis I hadn't yet been able to verify. I had to say something. 'But I can always do it again,' I said. I wasn't afraid to say that. Because someone who makes you laugh so hard that the tears run down your face and the drool out of your mouth, and that twenty minutes long, that is someone you don't have to be afraid of.

We did it all over again, and this time it wasn't over quite as fast. I lay next to her and said: 'I'm not wearing a condom any more.' That was strange, because I knew for sure I'd put one on. Elvira had given it to me. From a teacup. We'd laughed a lot about that too, about fishing condoms out of teacups.

We looked around in the bed first, but it wasn't there. Then we looked under the bed, but that was no use. We turned the pizza box upside-down, but we couldn't find anything there either.

'It stayed up inside me,' she said. For the third time that evening, we went limp with laughter. I'd never thought I'd ever laugh the way I did that evening. It was more than laughter, but I have no idea how to explain what was more about it.

'But I don't feel it,' she said. She wasn't laughing any more. She had her hand up inside herself, trying to find it, but she couldn't.

'You have to help me,' she said.

I climbed out of bed and stepped in the pizza again. 'Me?' I said. 'I'm not a doctor.'

'But we can't just leave it in there,' she yelled.

I started walking around the room. 'There's that free clinic, isn't there?' I yelled back. 'They do all kinds of things. I bet they pull out condoms, too.'

'I'm not going there,' she said. 'I'm not going to some free clinic. You can help me, can't you?'

She was crying.

'I'm not a gynaecologist,' I said. 'I've never done that kind of thing. And I'm not even sterilised.'

Her whole body was shaking. Just like that night in Wolf's bed. 'I'm not going to some free clinic,' she shouted. 'I'm never going back there again.'

I was still pacing around the room. I'd stepped in the pizza five times already. 'We could always go to the hospital,' I suggested. 'It can't just stay in there. It might start rotting. That's a lot worse.'

But she didn't want to go to a hospital either. She would rather have had the condom rot away inside her than go to a hospital.

'I can't get to it,' she said, 'otherwise I'd do it myself.'

'But I'm not a doctor,' I said. I held her head pressed against my chest. 'I've got pizza stuck all over my body. Have you ever seen a doctor whose body was covered with stale pizza?'

'You have to wash your hands real well,' she said. 'Please.'

I wanted her to stop crying, so I washed my hands.

'You're hurting me,' she said.

'I can't help it.' I had to put my whole hand up inside her. Finally, I felt something that seemed like a condom. But it was hard to get hold of. Everything inside there was very slippery. When I finally got the condom out, I tossed it on to the pizza. Then I smelled my hand. It smelled faintly of poop. I didn't think it was a bad smell.

We held each other tight. That's how we fell asleep.

Two days later she came down with a bladder infection.

'It's from your hand,' she said. And she laughed.

We never went to bed together after that, although I would have liked to, and even hinted at it once.

'My hand gave you a bladder infection,' I'd say to her now and then. And she'd say: 'Right, your hand.' Then we had to laugh. Not because what we were saying was so funny, but because we remembered how we'd laughed.

ONION SOUP AND CHURCHILL CIGARS

*T*here was one other time when Elvira and I laughed the way we had the night I had to pull the condom out of her. It was while she still had that bladder infection. Not that she cared much.

We hadn't seen Broccoli for a few days. He was busy making important contacts, he said. We left him to it. Late one afternoon, I picked her up from acting class. As always, she had her little red notepad with her. Sometimes she let me read what was in it. There were things like: '*The Meisner Method for Actors. Day One. Listening is the key.*' And: '*Day Two. Don't ask questions. Do nothing until you feel you have to do something.*' And: '*When the action stops, don't go back.*' Interspersed with the phone numbers of people I didn't know, and meeting times. And here and there a word in Spanish, with the Dutch translation next to it.

Broccoli wasn't there, so we couldn't go to the kinds of restaurants he took us to. We didn't have money for that. There were days when all Elvira ate was rice pudding. Sometimes we got hungry in the middle of the night. That's how we ended up one time at 't Kalfje. The sign on the door said '*Open 24 hours*'.

We ordered onion soup, which was the cheapest thing on the menu. There isn't an awful lot to say about that soup: it was simply the filthiest onion soup I'd ever tasted. To be frank, after my experience in 't Kalfje I didn't eat onion soup for two years.

'This soup tastes like they ladle it right out of the toilet,' Elvira said.

I climbed up on my chair and shouted: 'Folks, the onion soup's on me. Bartender, go back to the men's room and ladle us up some of that onion soup.' The place was full of people who were confident they were going to make it in life, or who already had. Elvira had to pull me down off my chair.

'They'll beat you up,' she said. 'And then I won't have a sock puller-upper any more.' When the place closed we were still sitting there with our onion soup in front of us, and we were still laughing. I'd drooled on her again. It went like this: I kept bending over to whisper things in her ear, but then I had to laugh so hard that I drooled and it dripped all over her shoulder.

'Could we have a doggy bag?' I asked the barman, pointing to the onion soup. 'Then we'll have something to savour when we get home.'

When Broccoli surfaced again, he'd been to the barber. We found him sitting in a white chair in his garden. The grass was up to his knees. No one ever mowed it. Mrs Meerschwam refused. One time I'd heard her shout: 'Listen, I'm not your gardener.'

Broccoli had a cigar in his mouth, and there were beer bottles lying all around his chair. 'I've fixed it,' he said when he saw Elvira and me at the garden gate. He was wearing his father's clothes. At least I assume he was. He looked like someone who'd lost his way in his own wardrobe.

Mr Berk was sitting next to him. Berk shook hands with us, and said he was pleased that the camp site in the living room had been dismantled. This time he didn't start singing songs about spring. Elvira had a restful influence on him.

Broccoli pulled a little wooden box from under his chair. There were big cigars in it. Those Winston Churchill cigars. Elvira and I had to light one up. The cigar barely fit in my mouth, that's how fat it was.

'This is a red-letter day,' Broccoli said. 'I've decided we're going to smoke Churchill cigars.'

Elvira asked: 'What did he decide?'

'When we're sixty,' Broccoli went on, 'we'll still smoke Churchill cigars, and we'll remember the day we decided to smoke Churchill cigars as a red-letter day. And on our deathbeds we'll say: "We did a lot of dumb things in our lives, but the day we decided to smoke Churchill cigars, that was a good day." Then he poked me in the chest with his finger and said: 'Write down what I'm saying, otherwise it will be lost to posterity.'

That was the first time he'd said that to me.

Mr Berk and Broccoli had been playing chess. Mr Berk was still peering at the chessboard.

'I've been in touch with Marlon Brando's agent,' Broccoli whispered. 'This is the start of something very big.' And again he whispered. 'Marlon Brando.' Like it was a magic formula.

Elvira didn't seem too impressed by Marlon Brando. She'd brought a box of tutti-frutti with her. Every once in a while she'd fish one out. I looked at her to see if she was thinking about the onion soup at 't Kalfje, but when I tried to ask her, she just said: 'Concentrate.'

'On what?' I asked.

'On Marlon Brando.'

We went inside to call Marlon Brando's agent. The living room was back to normal now. The couches had their plastic slip covers again. Broccoli spent an hour and a half calling all kinds of people. After a while, we stopped believing he would ever get hold of Marlon Brando. Elvira may not have believed it from the start.

Mr Berk was still in the garden, staring at the chessboard. He had that vacant look on his face again. I was expecting him to break into Romanian song any moment. Elvira was sitting on the couch next to Broccoli. She'd told me once that she didn't want children. But if Broccoli was prepared to be the father, she was willing to sleep on it.

'I'll call him tomorrow,' Broccoli said at last. 'I'm going to set up a meeting with Marlon Brando. Operation Brando starts now. Once we've met Marlon, the rest will be like rolling off a log.'

Elvira wanted to know what 'rolling off a log' meant. When Broccoli refused to tell her, she sat there moping for at least an hour. Finally, she asked me to write 'rolling off a log' in her notepad. Then she disappeared upstairs. Half an hour later we found her taking a bath. A bubble bath.

'In Buenos Aires I took a bath every day,' she said. Broccoli didn't seem impressed.

'Mrs Meerschwam takes a bath every day too, it's not such a big deal.'

'My mother was worse,' Elvira shouted after us, 'she used to go to the hairdresser's every day.'

Broccoli took me down to the cellar to help him find a can of fruit salad. He wanted to serve Elvira fruit salad while she was taking a bubble bath.

'Have you noticed?' he asked, puttering around amid what must have been a thousand cans.

'What?'

'At this very moment, a femme fatale is lying in my bathtub,' he said. 'This is the biggest day of my life.'

FRENCH BALLADS

*W*e were listening to French ballads. We were at Café Cox, and that morning they were playing French ballads back-to-back. Café Cox had just opened its doors, and Broccoli said it stood a good chance of becoming the next Adolf Hitler café. We were sitting there until we got to talk to someone who'd help us move up in the world.

'Cafés are the place to make contacts,' Broccoli said, 'take it from me.'

We used to spend days in cafés. But we never made any contacts. Sometimes people talked to Elvira, who always had a box of tutti-frutti with her or a can of fruit salad, or pistachios. Sometimes her role in the conversation consisted of nothing more than offering us something she'd brought along to eat. And Broccoli would say: 'Someone's going to come up and talk to us any moment now, I can feel it, it's about to happen. Today, we're on to major contacts.'

One time, someone actually did come over and talk to us, at

ten in the morning. A young man, who asked if he could join us at the table.

'It's going to happen,' Broccoli whispered in my ear, 'this is an actor, a real one.'

The first words the young man spoke were: 'It's all a matter of hormonal balance. In the long run, everything is a matter of hormonal balance.'

It looked like he'd shaved all the hair off the sides of his head. 'In the same way you can view reality as a collection of atoms, so you can view human beings as a collection of hormones,' the young man said. 'And what does this teach us?'

He looked at us penetratingly, especially Elvira, with piercing brown eyes.

'No idea,' Broccoli said. Elivra was looking out the window. She still hadn't said anything. She wasn't going to say anything either. Maybe she'd already reached the point in her life that I've reached today. I still go to bars once in a while, but not to be talked to. In fact, preferably not.

I thought about Broccoli and how we'd sat in his room and he'd promised me that, once we were actors, the world would never be the same. Our lives would take a dramatic turn. We would no longer be afraid of women and their men. Not of animals either. Or cars. When Broccoli played violin on the rooftop patio, no one would throw rotten apples at him any more. We would no longer need cards that said: 'M.J. Broccoli, producer, events organiser'. We would finally know where we belonged. We would belong with the actors and actresses, and with the make-up girls and the guys from the crew.

But sitting there in Café Cox, across from that boy, I suddenly knew that's where we'd never belong. Maybe it was the way Elvira stared out the window. Or maybe it was because, while we were talking to that boy, she suddenly whispered in my ear: 'Concentrate.' She smiled, one of those covert smiles of hers. You could only tell it was a smile if you knew her really well.

'Why?'

Broccoli and the boy just kept talking. They were discussing philosophy.

'When things aren't working out in bed, I tell them to concentrate too.' She said it real dreamily. And then, then she said: 'I like sperm between my legs.'

I looked at Broccoli, but he hadn't heard it, and fortunately the other guy hadn't either. We looked at each other, and we almost laughed. But we didn't. Maybe she really felt like crying, you never knew with Elvira.

'I like sperm in my ears,' I whispered.

She nodded. 'Yeah, me too, a lot, and I also like sperm in my hair. When it's so sticky you have to wash it three times to get it out.'

'I like sperm between my toes.'

She nodded. 'Yeah, and I like sperm in my intestines, where it burns like chilli peppers.'

'I like sperm in food.'

'And I,' she said, 'I like sperm in my eyes, where it stings like shampoo.'

'I like sperm on chocolate cake.'

'And I like sperm in my throat, litres of it, all swimming around in there until you think you're going to choke, that's what I like. Like you're trying to paddle across the ocean but can't go any further. That's what I like.'

She never talked about sex much, but when she did it was always very dreamy. In her sex, there was a grassy hillside, a rowboat and picnic baskets: that's right, picnic baskets. I couldn't believe it either at first. Then she started talking about picnic baskets, and we knew she was really talking about sex. About really rough sex. As rough as it gets. So rough it brings tears to your eyes.

I never said more than that, there at Café Cox, and I also never asked her: 'Why did you go to bed with me only once, and not ten times, or twice, or never, or sixty-three times, why only once?' Back then, I thought despair was something dead serious, the way it is in books and movies. Despair is extremely droll and humorous. Like Elvira, in fact, who could spend a whole morning eating tutti-frutti and then suddenly say: 'I like sperm between my legs.'

It was one of those mornings in early autumn. It was still foggy, but in a few hours the fog would lift and we could go to the beach again, or play soccer in the Beatrixpark.

'I'm a young god,' I suddenly heard the guy say. He was playing with a cookie and looking at us expectantly, as if he hoped we'd confirm that he was, indeed, a young god. He looked tired. Like anything but a young god, in other words.

'Yes,' Broccoli said, 'you're a young god all right.'

Years later, I ran into him again, early one morning on the Leidseplein. I was coming out of a café and he almost jumped on my back. 'They're making a movie about Indonesia, and I've got the lead. They still need a couple of indigenous people, are you interested?'

'I'll think about it,' I promised.

'You'd make a good indigenous person,' he shouted after me.

We got up from the table, because Broccoli had an appointment with Mr Kuilman from the theatre company. How he'd arranged that was beyond me. Back then I believed Broccoli could do anything.

'I've known so many young gods,' Elvira said in the lift. 'Old ones too.'

Broccoli had to say his name three times. The receptionist refused to understand him. Finally, she picked up the phone. 'Karel, there's a young man here who claims to have an appointment with you.

'Have a seat,' she said to us. There were no chairs anywhere. Obviously, she would rather have thrown us out right away. Or skinned us alive.

We leaned against the wall instead. Elvira had her eyes closed. It looked like she was asleep. The receptionist was reading a magazine. Occasionally, she answered the phone and said: 'Sorry, he's not in.' One time I heard her say: 'If you don't believe me, come by and see for yourself.'

After half an hour, Karel Kuilman came out of his office. His hair was standing straight up on his head, but it wasn't because he'd just gotten out of bed. That was his haircut. He looked at us in surprise, as if he'd actually expected someone completely different. When he saw Broccoli, he said: 'Come on in.'

He led us into a cubicle, sort of an overgrown broom closet. 'How can I help you?' Kuilman said.

'It's about her,' Broccoli said, pointing to Elvira. She looked at Kuilman.

'You promised me she could do an audition.'

Kuilman was cleaning his nails. 'I know, but that was more like a joke,' he said quietly. 'I think you didn't quite grasp the mood that evening.'

'You promised,' Broccoli said.

'All right, all right,' Kuilman said to Elvira, 'do something.'

'Right now?' Elvira asked.

'Yes, now,' Kuilman said. His nails were clean, so he started using them to pick his teeth.

'What should I do?' Elvira asked.

'What you usually do,' Kuilman said.

It was awfully warm in the cubicle. Elvira stood up. She began a monologue. After two minutes, Kuilman interrupted her. 'Just do it normally,' he said. Then he looked at Broccoli and me and said: 'That, by the way, is the art of play acting, just doing things normally.' Then he sort of tilted his head and looked at the ceiling. He probably thought he was some kind of Einstein. A little later, he went back to picking his teeth. Finally, he shook his head in despair.

'No,' he said, 'I'm afraid this just isn't working out.' He stood up.

'Are you disappointed?' he asked Broccoli. But he didn't wait for an answer.

We went back to Café Cox. Broccoli said: 'We have to drink vodka. The members of the Association for Geniuses have to drink vodka.' He'd bought a notebook to keep the Association's minutes. That was my job, to keep the minutes. I'd been appointed secretary.

At the first meeting, we had decided to smoke Churchill cigars; at the second, a motion was made and seconded to drink vodka, no ice, in shot glasses.

GERMAN MEASLES

*B*roccoli was throwing a party. We were there, and so was Lopatin. Mr Berk was downstairs. Pretty Face Bo, who Broccoli referred to as a 'business acquaintance', was there too.

Broccoli had bought a few cases of wine and a huge quantity of lychee nuts. There were enough lychees to feed an orphanage. 'I got a good deal on them,' Broccoli told us.

There was chocolate cake for Lopatin. Broccoli had spread a towel under his chair, but Lopatin didn't mind. Occasionally, he called Elvira 'Mimi'. Halfway through the party, Lopatin climbed up on his chair. He wanted to make a speech, he said, but the speech consisted of only three words: 'Mimi is nice.' Then he climbed back down off his chair.

Not long after that party, by the way, the real Mimi whacked Lopatin so hard on the hand with her ladle that it broke his metacarpus. He had to wear his hand in a cast for six weeks. 't Haantje sent him a cream cake, but he was afraid to come in any more. Strangely enough, he wasn't mad at Mimi for breaking his hand. From then on, he started hanging around at the window of 't Haantje, just to look at her.

Up in his attic room, Broccoli kept playing the same song. 'Nenanana,' sang the lady, whose name I forget. He kept playing the song over and over, because Broccoli liked to play songs over and over. The guests had all started in on the lychee nuts, except for Mr Berk, who was reading the newspaper. Every once in a while, he shouted: 'Why don't you let me sing something?'

'You slept with Elvira,' Broccoli whispered.

'That's right,' I said, 'didn't you?'

'That's not something you talk about,' Broccoli said. 'It's extremely vulgar to talk about things like that. Didn't anyone ever tell you that?'

I shook my head.

'Make her happy,' Broccoli said.

'Who?' I asked.

'You,' Broccoli said. 'Make her happy.' I'd never made anyone happy in my life. I'd never even made myself happy. According to my mother, I was a walking fount of misfortune.

'How am I supposed to do that?' I whispered, because Elvira had gotten up from her chair and was standing beside us.

'You know,' Broccoli said, 'the way you make people happy.'

Then the lychee fight broke out.

Lopatin started it. He threw a lychee nut down the attic stairs, and Mr Berk said it hit him on the head. So he threw one back. Then everyone started throwing lychees. First only the husks, but later they began throwing lychees that weren't even peeled. There were so many lychee nuts that the fight could have gone on all night. And it almost did. At three o'clock, when one of Pretty Face Bo's girlfriends came to pick him up, she was so horrified that she left again without a word.

When the guests went away, they all got a bag of lychees as a souvenir. But even after that there were enough left over to fill two garbage bags.

Mr Berk stayed to the bitter end. We had to tell him: 'Mr

Berk, the lychee fight is over, it's almost light out.' Only then did
he pick up his umbrella, thank us for the wonderful evening and
walk off into the night.

The next morning, there were lychee nuts in every corner of
the house. Even the bathtub was full of them. 'I'm not taking a
bath with a bunch of lychee husks in it,' Elvira said. Some of
them were still stuck to the walls. Broccoli brought in the garden
hose to wash them off. When he was finished, he said: 'Let's rent
a car and drive to the south of France.'

He started calling car rental places. He had four credit cards,
so one of them was bound to work.

'I'll probably think about Galani the whole time,' Elvira said.
Neither of us asked her why. No one asked Broccoli what we
were going to do in the south of France either. All Elvira said
was: 'I didn't know you could drive.'

Broccoli finally found a car. A convertible. We spent eight hours
in a traffic jam just north of Lyons. The only thing we had to
eat was chewing gum.

There were big signs along the road telling us we were on the
Route de Soleil and what the temperature was, but it wasn't
getting any warmer. While we were sitting in traffic, a thunder-
storm started. When it started pouring, the man who'd been walking around the whole time selling cola and toilet paper ran back
to his car too.

Elvira was lying on the back seat. She said: 'When I was little,
I used to dream of being kidnapped.'

'This isn't a kidnapping,' Broccoli said, 'this is a traffic jam.'

Elvira started laughing. 'It's so funny,' she said. But she wouldn't
tell us what was so funny.

It kept getting darker, and we watched the other cars turn into
houses. Some people even hung curtains in their windows. The
people in the car next to us were making love. They did it without curtains, but then they kept their clothes on too.

We watched them. It was sort of like an erotic movie without the sound. When they were finished, the man hopped out of the car and peed against the guard rail. Then he ran back. The girl went to sleep and the man started working on a crossword puzzle. He was very handsome, but he chewed on his pencil.

'My father and I used to go to the south of France all the time,' Broccoli said. 'He loved to drive at night.'

'What did you do there?' Elvira asked.

'Nothing,' Broccoli said. 'We'd stay for a day, sometimes less. My father liked to drive long distances. He liked expressways at night, when there was almost no traffic. He drove as fast as he could, and when he was about to fall asleep he'd stick his head out the window, but he wouldn't stop. It made him calm. We often got in early in the morning. He'd empty his post office box and we'd walk along the beach. He'd get a shave from a barber he'd known for twenty years, a fat man with a huge razor. I wanted to get a shave there too, but I had nothing to shave. Sometimes, when it was really early, he'd take a hotel room and we'd sleep for a few hours. It was only for a couple of hours, but my father always insisted on a room with a sea view.

'One time, I wasn't allowed to go up to the room. He said he had an appointment, and I had to wait in the lobby. I heard him order a lobster and two bottles of champagne from the lady at the desk. He never ate lobster.

'I waited in the lobby for five hours. When it was dark, I went upstairs. I knocked, but no one answered. Then I opened the door. My father was lying on the bed with his clothes on, just his shirt unbuttoned a little. The lobster and the champagne were still on a tray, untouched. He wasn't alseep, he had his hands clasped behind his head. "She couldn't come," he said, "her children have got the German measles."

'We locked the room behind us; in the corridor he said: "Wait a minute." He came back carrying the bottles of champagne. "No reason to leave them any presents."

'After a while, those long drives stopped calming him down, and he started taking the train.'

It was pitch black outside. The man in the car next to us was still working on his crossword puzzle.

'I'm cold,' Elvira said.

Broccoli put his sweater over her.

'I know a game,' Elvira said. 'Let's all tell each other a secret.'

Broccoli nodded, but I was afraid I didn't have a secret and that I'd have nothing to tell.

'OK, go ahead,' Elvira said. But Broccoli said: 'You go first.'

She was quiet for a bit, then she said: 'First, I have to pee.'

Broccoli walked her over to the grass behind the guard rail. She squatted down there and I watched them from the car. When they came back, they were soaked, and they had enough mud on their feet to fill a small truck.

'Tell up,' Broccoli said. His hair was dripping. He looked paler than ever, but that could also have been the fatigue. The car radio was turned off. It seemed like this traffic jam was all there was, as if we'd spend the rest of our lives in the rain, a little north of Lyons.

'I've already told you everything,' Elvira said. Her eyes were closed. She lay on the back seat like a little wet cat that wasn't planning to get up. 'All I want to do when we get there is dance, it's been so long since I've danced. It's too bad you two don't like to dance.

'When I was fifteen I danced all the time. I had a girlfriend who liked to dance, her name was Beatrice. She always wore long fake nails, this old woman made them for her. I thought those long fake nails were the greatest thing. I thought that was pretty much the most wonderful thing there was. My mother wouldn't let me have long fake nails. She said: "What's more beautiful than a young girl's nails, fresh as the driven snow?" But my nails weren't fresh as the driven snow, because I chewed them. One morning in art class, Beatrice raked open the teacher's arm with her fake nails. He'd turned down one of her drawings. We had to draw trees and he said: "This isn't a tree." So she scratched him. Her nails broke, so it was worse for her than it was for the drawing teacher. But he didn't see it that way. He was very religious. He said: "Go to confession, and when you've drawn me a tree that looks like a tree, you can come back in my class." She didn't want to go to confession, and she especially didn't want to draw a tree that looked like a tree. We were always friends after that.

'Her father drove a cab. During the weekend she'd get up at eleven o'clock at night, then I'd pick her up and we'd go out dancing. She put all her energy into dancing. I used to stay over at her place; her father always slept in his taxi. One Sunday afternoon, she said she wanted to paint a nude portrait of me. I said: "OK, but then I get to paint you too."

'The paintings turned out really nice. I still have mine. After that, we went to bed together. She said she was in love with me, and I was in love with her too. I had long fake nails made. After a while, I also started falling in love with men, but Beatrice stayed in love with me.

'She wanted to be a dancer. She ran away and started dancing in a club. I went there and saw her once. She didn't have those long nails any more, but she recognised me right away. And she danced for me. "You going to give me a good tip?" she said afterwards. I gave her a good tip, but I didn't stay long, I didn't feel comfortable with all those men around.'

Lyons was as far as we ever got. When we pulled into town it was early in the morning, so we waited on a park bench until the cafés opened. Then we drank coffee and cognac and ate crêpes. After that, we went back and sat on the bench. I can't remember a thing about the city. We were only there for a couple of hours.

At a certain point, Broccoli said: 'I feel like playing chess.' We went all over Lyons looking for a chessboard. I didn't mind, I would have followed them to the ends of the earth without asking myself what I was doing there, or where I'd live, or whether anyone had a good funeral policy for me or an accountant.

We finally found a chessboard and carried it back to the park. Broccoli and I played. Elvira watched. I lost. It was over pretty fast. Broccoli said he was going for a little walk, and Elvira and I fell asleep. When we woke up he was talking to a beggar.

After that, we drove home. Along the way we bought a big salami and a bottle of vodka, in case we got stuck in another traffic jam, but there was no traffic jam. Broccoli sat behind the wheel and didn't say a word. He smelled of manly sweat. Every once in a while he opened the window and stuck his head out.

A LOVELY SHED

*T*he man had a grey beard he kept rubbing with the back of his hand. He wanted to rent his shed to Broccoli so he could produce *Macbeth* there, with Elvira as Lady Macbeth. Broccoli was stuck on the idea. 'Once a few people have seen her as Lady Macbeth, the rest will come of its own accord,' he said.

The man with the beard lit a cigarette. 'Four hundred a night,' he said, 'and I'll do the lighting.' His name was Lebbing, Harry Lebbing.

We were sitting at a sidewalk café. Elvira was writing something in her notepad. Broccoli was smoking a cigar, and one of his calling cards was on the table. He was the only member of the Association who still smoked Churchill cigars. Elvira and I couldn't handle them any more. Try as we might, Churchill cigars made us nauseous.

'It's a lovely shed,' Lebbing said. 'I usually rent it out for small parties, but I actually like this idea a lot more.' Then he tapped the back of Elvira's hand and said: 'And I can tell: you've got what it takes. I've worked with plenty of performers, so I know it when I see it.'

Elvira nodded and went back to writing.

'Four hundred?' Broccoli asked.

'Four hundred,' Lebbing said, 'and then I'm doing you a favour. I used to do the lighting for fashion shows, and if I told you what I got for that, you'd fall off your chair.'

'We don't fall off our chairs that easily,' Broccoli said.

'So it's a deal,' Lebbing said. He picked a shred of tobacco off his lip and shook hands with Broccoli. 'Half now, the other half when it's over.'

Then he said to Elvira: 'It's great to have friends who do things like this for you.' He took her chin in his hand. 'Just great,' he said again. But more quietly. Then he started rubbing the back of his hand over his beard again.

Broccoli had to go by the Amro Bank on the Stadionweg. But first he bought a bottle of wine for Mr Tuinier.

As soon as he saw us coming, Tuinier shouted: 'Ah, Mr Eckstein, please do come in.'

He served us coffee. Mr Tuinier couldn't stop talking. About the weather, about Mr Eckstein Sr and about young Mr Eckstein. Elvira sat there without moving; she was probably off in Buenos Aires with Galani or Beatrice. Maybe she wasn't anywhere.

Finally, Tuinier asked: 'Are you ready to go to the vault?'

'Yes,' Broccoli said.

'I'll have one of my colleagues take you there.'

He smiled at us the whole time.

Someone came to get Broccoli.

'The two of you can stay here,' Tuinier said. We stayed in his office. He didn't know what to say to us, so he started leafing through some files. But he kept staring at us as he leafed.

'A very special person,' he said, pointing to the door. 'A very special family.' I believe his own words made him uncomfortable, because he coughed drily a few times. Then he went back to leafing.

I looked at Elvira. I wanted to kiss her, but just then she said: 'I have to go to acting class, and I need to take a bath first.' She stuck a few Amro Bank sugar cubes in her pocket.

When Broccoli came back, Tuinier walked us to the door.

That evening the three of us went to play billiards at the pool hall above the Hema on the Reguliersbreestraat. None of us was any good at billiards. Broccoli wasn't. I wasn't, and Elvira wasn't either.

Part Three

POINT AT US BEHIND OUR BACKS

*W*e had to pick up Mr Eckstein from the station. Broccoli had asked me to go along. Mr Berk was there too.

'There he is,' Mr Berk said. It sounded like he'd spotted some rare bird.

Broccoli's father had on the same suit he'd worn last time, but now he was walking with a cane. Tagging along was a little woman with black hair. She had a backpack. Was that his wife?

He barely said hello. Not even to Broccoli.

'Is the camp site still in business?' were his first words.

'No,' Mr Berk said quickly, 'the camp site has been dismantled.'

'Good, otherwise I would have booked a room,' Mr Eckstein said. The woman with the backpack came up behind him. She hugged Broccoli for so long I thought she was going to crush him. Like Elvira's mother, she tried to crush everyone too. Mr Eckstein went over to the platform elevator. He didn't seem to be paying attention to any of us.

'Where are we going?' asked Mr Berk.

'To the Victoria Hotel,' Eckstein said.

'What about your luggage?'

'There isn't any luggage. We won't be staying long.'

When the elevator doors opened, he said to me: 'So it's you again.' He nodded as though he'd expected nothing different.

We walked to the Victoria Hotel: Mr Eckstein and his cane out in front, then Mr Berk, then Broccoli and me. All the way at the rear was Mrs Eckstein with her backpack. At least, I assumed it was Mrs Eckstein.

The waiters at the Victoria Hotel seemed to know him. 'Good to see you again, Mr Eckstein,' they said. All Mr Eckstein did was nod.

We took a table. No one seemed to notice I was there, and they all started talking at once. I wasn't listening. I was thinking about Elvira. Her acting class was almost over. In a little while she'd be walking back alone through the city. I heard Mrs Eckstein repeating: 'We'll all end up in prison, I always knew we would.' I thought about Harry Lebbing and the *Macbeth* Broccoli would be staging in his shed. And in the midst of it all I heard Mr Eckstein say: 'Why didn't you keep a better eye on things?' And Mr Berk saying: 'I did my best.'

'Doing your best isn't good enough,' Mr Eckstein said. And then his wife's complaining voice again: 'We'll all end up in prison, I always knew we would. They'll point at us behind our backs.'

Mr Eckstein was drinking coffee with cognac. Another shift had come on. We must have been sitting there for more than two hours already, but I only realised that when I suddenly heard Broccoli's voice.

'Don't ask me,' he was saying. 'Really, don't ask me.' Mr Eckstein slammed his hand down on the table so hard that the coffee splattered all over the place. Two waiters came rushing up, ready to intervene. Even Mrs Eckstein stopped talking for a moment.

'I'm not asking you, I'm telling you,' Mr Eckstein said. He put his chin in his hands. I'd seen him do that before, but now it looked like he was going to cry. He didn't cry. Instead, he whispered: 'Where's my car?'

'Where it always is,' Mr Berk said. 'Remember, you gave me strict instructions to—'

Mr Eckstein slammed his hand down on the table for the second time. There was almost no coffee left in the cups now. Mrs Eckstein started shrieking: 'We'll all end up in prison.'

'Instructions,' Eckstein shouted. 'Don't make me laugh.' But he did laugh. He laughed like he'd just heard the joke of the century. And Mrs Eckstein said: 'Won't they love this at the bridge club? The Ecksteins have gone to prison, I can hear them already, we always knew that's where they were headed.'

'It's all bound to come out in the wash,' Berk said.

'That's right,' Broccoli said, 'maybe it will all come out in the wash.' It was the first time he'd actually gotten into the conversation.

'In this world, nothing every comes out in the wash,' Eckstein roared. 'Am I dealing with the mentally deficient here?' Then he whispered: 'Bring me to my car.'

'You can't drive in your condition.' Mr Berk turned to Eckstein's wife, but she didn't seem to see him. She was probably thinking about the ladies from the bridge club. In any case, she murmured: 'Oh, won't they be tickled? The Ecksteins in prison. And what kind of food do you think you get in prison? My stomach can never take that.'

'Bring me to my car,' Eckstein whispered. 'Or has that disappeared too?'

'No, of course not,' Mr Berk said.

'Then bring me to it.'

'You can't drive in your condition.' Then, right away: 'Maybe I should sing a song for you?' Mr Berk looked helpless. It wasn't hard to imagine him not following all kinds of instructions. They'd probably just gone right over his head. The way everything seemed to go right over his head.

'Ludwig, if you start singing here I'll break your neck.' Mr Eckstein stood up slowly. It seemed to take a lot of effort. 'Go to the house and get whatever you can't do without,' he said to his wife. 'And leave the rest to me.'

Mr Berk had to grab him to keep him from falling over.

'Are you forcing me to go back to that house?' Mrs Eckstein cried.

'I'm not forcing you to do anything,' Mr Eckstein said. 'And now I want to go to my car.' He turned to Broccoli and asked: 'What's he doing here, anyway?' And he pointed at me.

'He's a friend,' Broccoli said.

For the first time that afternoon, Mr Eckstein looked at me.

'Oh, sure,' he said. 'Nice friends you have.' And then, a bit more quietly: 'Nice friends I have, what a family.'

Suddenly, he began rummaging through his pockets. 'I wrote your name somewhere,' he said, 'I'm sure I did.' All kinds of things came out of his inside pocket: a lighter, a comb, four rolls of peppermint lozenges and a nail file. But not the note with my name on it.

'Ewald Stanislas Krieg,' I said.

'Ewald Stanislas Krieg,' Mr Eckstein repeated, and he wrote my name on a paper napkin again. When he walked past the waiter, he handed him a tip. Mr Berk was following along behind him. And Broccoli and I were following Mr Berk. We were already at the corner by the time Mrs Eckstein came running up behind us. 'Take good care of him, Ludwig,' she shouted. 'He hasn't been himself lately.'

Mr Eckstein waved his arm. 'Leave me alone for once,' he shouted.

Mrs Eckstein stopped following us. Standing there clutching her backpack, she looked like she was about to start handing out pamphlets.

ENJOY SUCH A RIPE OLD AGE

*W*e took a taxi to the Minervalaan. Mr Eckstein sat in the front. He didn't say a word the whole way. Broccoli didn't say anything either. It wasn't like the Broccoli I knew.

The taxi dropped us off in front of a garage. Mr Berk walked over to the chief mechanic, who led us to a car all the way at the back. It was a completely normal car. I don't even remember what make it was.

'Your car, Mr Eckstein,' the mechanic said. 'We've taken good care of it.'

'I should hope so, after what I pay you,' Eckstein said. He climbed in.

'Where do you think you're going?' Mr Berk asked him. 'What's this supposed to mean?'

'Leave me alone,' Eckstein said again. He was searching for something in his pockets. Maybe for the car keys, but Berk had them in his hand.

'Would you talk to him?' Berk said. But Broccoli just shook his head.

The mechanic was still standing next to us. 'How old is your father anyway?' he whispered in Broccoli's ear. 'Not many men get to enjoy such a ripe old age.'

'My father doesn't enjoy anything,' Broccoli said. 'He may once have given the impression that he enjoyed something, but that was a long time ago.'

The mechanic looked at me. He raised his eyebrows. 'Jewish humour, I take it?' he said quietly.

We watched Mr Eckstein trying to climb out of the car. His cane had fallen on the ground. He bent down to pick it up, but once he was bent over it seemed like he couldn't stand up straight again.

'A good customer,' the mechanic said, 'is hard to find these days.'

Mr Berk tried to help Eckstein stand up, but he pushed him away. 'Stop treating me like a child, Ludwig,' he shouted. His voice echoed through the garage. Hunched over on the floor in his grey suit, Mr Eckstein looked like some little animal.

'Going out for a nice little spin, Mr Eckstein?' the mechanic asked. He approached slowly, like he was staying on his guard.

Eckstein didn't answer. He'd found his cane. The mechanic had come up beside him now. He took Eckstein by the arm and lifted him to his feet. 'That's pretty much it,' he said.

'Yes,' Eckstein said, 'that's pretty much it.' There was a big black spot on his trousers.

'Give me the keys, Ludwig.'

Berk looked at the mechanic. 'It's a real crime,' he said softly.

'You know what's criminal? The banks,' Eckstein yelled, 'the banks, they're criminal!' He slapped his hand down on the roof of the car.

'Michaël,' Berk said, 'would you drive your father where he wants to go?' Broccoli had been leaning against a pillar the whole time. He took the keys out of Berk's hand and climbed in behind the wheel.

Mr Eckstein limped over to the mechanic and pulled out his wallet. It was the first time I noticed how badly his hands shook, especially the left one. 'I won't be coming back here again,' he said, 'so use this to buy some Christmas stuffing.' Then he climbed in and sat beside his son.

'What do you want me to do with the mail?' Berk asked.

'Eat it when you get hungry,' Mr Eckstein said. Then, to Broccoli: 'Go on, get going.'

From the other side of the garage the mechanic shouted: 'I don't deserve to be treated this way, Mr Eckstein.'

It seemed about time for me to be getting home. Mr Eckstein was growling. At least that's what it sounded like. 'What do they want from me, Ludwig?' I heard him say. 'What does everybody want from me?'

Berk didn't reply. He'd stuck his head in through the window.

'Twenty years I've been at your beck and call, Mr Eckstein, even on Sunday,' the mechanic shouted.

'Get in,' Broccoli said to me.

I climbed in. I would have gone anywhere with him. The car smelled of mothballs. Just like the house on the Bernard Zweerskade.

'Now the time has really come,' Eckstein said to Mr Berk. They shook hands. Berk opened his mouth a few times to say something, but no sound came out.

'No formalities, Ludwig,' Eckstein grumbled. 'Enough formalities.'

In the background the mechanic roared: 'You haven't seen the last of me yet, Mr Eckstein.'

Eckstein said: 'Drive.'

DON'T BOTHER WITH THE SHOES

*M*r Eckstein wanted to go to the beach. He was breathing heavily. At a gas station along the way I called Elvira, but she wasn't home. I thought about her, and again I imagined asking her: 'Why once? Why not twenty times, or eighty-four times, or never?' Back then, I thought you could give sensible answers to questions like that. Answers that explained everything. Answers everyone could live with.

'How's that girl?' Eckstein asked.

'Good,' Broccoli said.

'Am I going to meet her?'

'Maybe.'

Mr Eckstein was slouching in his seat. Every once in a while he took out his handkerchief and wiped his lips. He turned to me and said: 'I always used to invite my girlfriends up to my attic room and make them an omelette.'

I nodded.

'Oh, yeah,' Eckstein said, 'the omelette, that was my secret weapon.' It was quiet for a moment, until he went on: 'I always did my best on them. Only the best was good enough for those girls, even if I had to eat stale bread for three days afterwards.'

Broccoli said nothing.

'Actually, I liked the hungry ones best,' Eckstein went on. 'Not the ones who'd had enough after half an omelette. No, when they said: "Could you make me another one?", then I knew I was on a roll. Of course, I'd figured it out beforehand. I always tried to suss them out first. Was it going to be one omelette, or two? And I usually had them pegged.' He nodded, deeply content, as if those had been the best days of his life.

We drove into the dunes. What am I doing here? I asked myself.

The restaurant we stopped at was close to the sea. Broccoli took Mr Eckstein by the arm. I didn't know whether I should follow his example, so I just stuck close to them. Whenever it seemed like he was going to fall down, I'd grab his arm, but then Eckstein would twist away and say: 'Stop treating me like a child.'

They showed us to a table by the window. The restaurant was almost empty. A woman in a cocktail dress was sitting at the bar. For a moment there, I thought she knew Eckstein, but maybe she was just looking for company. She was old, and the cocktail dress had seen better days as well.

'We'll never come back here again,' Eckstein said. 'I'm going to miss the herring.'

It was the first time I noticed the grey hairs growing out of his nose.

'We have to find a house for you,' he said to Broccoli. 'Do you think you could stay with that girl for the time being?'

'I don't know,' Broccoli said. 'We'll see.' Broccoli didn't seem too interested in where he was going to sleep.

Mr Eckstein ordered a cognac. I wondered how many bottles he'd already had. 'To warm up a little,' he said quietly. But if the cognac hadn't made him warm by now, it never would.

I should really have stood up and told them it had been a lovely day, but that I really had to be going. I knew my parents would be wondering where I was, but I didn't care.

'What are you looking for?' I asked.

'My magnifying glass,' Mr Eckstein said. 'I can't read this menu.'

He called the waitress over. 'Do you have a magnifying glass?'

'No,' she said, 'I'm sorry. Perhaps one of your sons could read the menu for you.'

'First of all,' Mr Eckstein said, 'these aren't my sons. Secondly, if they have to read this menu out loud we'll still be here tomorrow morning. Thirdly, I'd like to ask what you'd recommend. You seem like a woman of taste. Anything would be fine, as long as it's not pork. Not that I'm religious, but pork gives me a rash.'

'Excuse me?' the waitress said.

'A rash,' Mr Eckstein said. 'Little red dots. Recommend some seafood for me, this is a fish restaurant, isn't it?' Then he stood up and said: 'And now I want to dance.'

Broccoli stood up too. 'Dad,' he said.

Everyone seemed to be standing up, so I got up too.

'And what would the rest of you like?'

'The same,' Broccoli said. He walked off after his father. 'Dad, please.'

Mr Eckstein stopped. 'Would you please knock off the "Dad this" and "Dad that"?' he said. 'You sound like your mother.' His cane slid out of his hands and fell to the floor. An elderly couple by the window further up were staring at us. Eckstein left his cane lying on the floor. He supported himself by leaning on chairs and tables. How he did it was a mystery to me, but he actually made it to the bar.

He said something to the woman in the cocktail dress. I couldn't make out what it was. Her shoulders were so fat that they hung over the seams like flaps of gristle. Her dress was also a little too tight in the hips, so the hem kept creeping up her legs. When she slid off the barstool she was almost standing there in her panties.

The two of them walked to the dance floor. Mr Eckstein was leaning heavily on the woman in the cocktail dress.

Broccoli had picked up his father's cane. 'There are at least three cans of spray in that hairdo,' he said.

'Is that your father?' the waitress asked.

'No,' Broccoli said, 'a distant relative.'

We went back to our table. The music started.

You couldn't really call it dancing, what they did. Mr Eckstein took a step forward, then a step back. The only thing keeping him from falling was the woman in the cocktail dress. She held him tight between her fat arms. Mr Eckstein looked like a lump of dough she was kneading.

Broccoli walked out on to the dance floor a few times to talk to his father. He probably whispered something like: 'Dad, please.' But Mr Eckstein didn't answer him. He just stood there, leaning on the woman in the cocktail dress. She was almost a foot and a half taller than he was.

Our soup arrived. 'Let's just start,' Broccoli said. He looked out the window, at the sea and the few people still walking along the beach.

When we'd finished our soup, Mr Eckstein finally stopped dancing. He came walking over to us slowly. His face had turned red.

'You two should really meet Sabine later on,' he said.

Broccoli didn't say anything, so I asked him: 'Have you known Sabine for a long time?'

Eckstein sat down and said: 'About twenty minutes.' Then he began crumbling a piece of French bread into his soup. It took him ten minutes. He crumbled with astounding precision.

'The soup is cold,' he announced loudly after a few spoonfuls, 'but cold soup is better than no soup at all.'

Every once in a while he nodded to Sabine at the bar. He called the waitress over and said he wanted to buy Sabine a drink. He himself took another cognac.

Later, I went to bars pretty often, and there were always men who seemed to be sitting there for the sole purpose of buying women drinks. I've always found it a peculiar ritual. Whenever I stayed in one of those bars for any length of time, I always expected Mr Eckstein to come walking in. And when he did, he would make this little gesture to indicate that the one over there in the corner should have a drink on him.

Eckstein wasn't even half finished with his soup, but he slid his bowl away. 'Maestro, music,' he shouted.

'Please, not again,' Broccoli said.

For a moment there I thought they were going to get into a fight.

Mr Eckstein leaned his full weight on the table to stand up. The table tipped, and Eckstein's soup bowl fell to the floor. He didn't seem to care about what had fallen on the floor, but he did pick up his glass.

'Michaël,' he said, taking a sip. He looked around. It was like he was standing at the head of a long table full of guests, about to hold a speech for the bride and groom. Maybe he'd always wanted to do that, but had never had the chance. And now he'd decided just to do it anyway.

'Michaël,' he said, 'you've been my son for quite some time now, and the moment has come for you to set out into the world on your own.' He seemed to have trouble remembering exactly how long Broccoli had been his son. He was casting about for words; it took a few seconds before anything else came out.

'You can't spend the rest of your life on the Bernard Zweerskade. Your mother and I . . .' Here he took another sip, a big one this time. It didn't all fit in his mouth. The waitress was down on the floor at his feet, mopping up the soup. 'Your mother and I would be very pleased to have you come with us, but I certainly understand your not wanting to do that. We won't be coming back here any more, however, and I'm sure you realise that. So if you wish to stay in Amsterdam, you'll have to find a way to support yourself.' He looked down at where the waitress was doing her mopping.

'Don't bother with the shoes,' he said. Then he put down his glass, because his hand was shaking too hard, and said: 'Let me be frank. I expected great things of you. It's taken a while, but now I realise that I was mistaken. Therefore, I will be pleased with any profession you choose to make your own. Even if you should become a cobbler. As long as you make a living at it, as long as it doesn't ruin your health and you don't need too many lawyers along the way. Because banks, insurance companies and lawyers are all criminals.'

The waitress had risen to her feet. Sabine waved to Mr Eckstein, but he didn't see her. Maybe she wanted another drink.

'I know,' he went on, 'that you hope to become an actor. Your mother thinks you have absolutely no talent for that. Usually she's wrong, but in this case I'm inclined to wonder.'

Then he sat down. Standing upright had probably proven too much for him. Still he acted like he was speaking to a fairly large crowd. He even nodded to an empty table every now and then.

'What did you say?' the waitress asked.

'Cognac,' Eckstein said. His manner of speech at that point lay somewhere between coughing and talking with his mouth full. His lips were purple and his face had turned an even deeper red.

When the glass was finally set in front of him, he mumbled: 'We're all going to pot, but not just yet.' He looked at the two of us and said, a little louder: 'Going to pot is something you should do when you're about my age.' He took a sip, set the glass back down and added: 'Or older still. That's even better.'

He stood up. Broccoli didn't move a muscle, so I grabbed hold of him. This time he didn't shake me off. Maybe he didn't even notice that someone had grabbed hold of him. I walked him over to Sabine. She gave me a moist, clammy hand. Then she laid her hand on the back of his neck.

'That does me good,' Mr Eckstein said. He was leaning on the bar. Fortunately, it couldn't tip over.

'Sugar,' I heard Sabine say. I'd never heard people their age call each other 'sugar', It made me uncomfortable. I didn't know whether to stay at the bar or go back to the table. I still had hold of Mr Eckstein's arm.

Then Sabine said it to me too: 'Sugar.'

She brought her face up close to mine, and for a moment there I thought she was going to kiss me, like she'd just kissed Eckstein. But all she did was wink.

Eckstein ordered another cognac. The next course was already on our table, but Broccoli hadn't touched a thing.

'Are you two family?' Sabine asked.

'Today we are,' Eckstein said.

You could tell Sabine had once been a pretty woman, but that was a long time ago.

'I think this is your last drink,' said the man behind the bar.

'I'll be the judge of that,' Eckstein said. He let go of the bar and threw his arms around Sabine. 'You're a real beauty,' he whispered.

'I know,' Sabine said softly.

'I want you to massage me,' he said, 'here, on my bald spot.' He lowered his head so we could get a good look at his bald spot. It had crusts on it. It must have been a while since anyone had massaged him there.

When Sabine started rubbing his scalp, I went back to our table.

ONE LAST DANCE, SUGAR

They were dancing again. Sabine was dragging Mr Eckstein around the floor, and he had no trouble letting himself be dragged.

'Go ahead and take what you want,' Broccoli said. 'He's not going to eat now anyway.'

I went downstairs to call Elvira, but she still wasn't home.

'She'll be back,' Broccoli said.

I wished I could talk to him about Elvira. I would have liked to know what he thought of her, and whether he planned to stay with her always, the way I did. I would have liked to ask him what Elvira had said to him before she went to bed with him. Whether she'd also said: 'I want to feel you in me.' And whether he'd had to laugh about that as wildly as I had. Maybe she said something different to everyone. I wanted to know that too. I would have liked to ask him if she walked around the house naked while he was there, and whether he also thought she smelled like French cheese when she woke up in the morning.

But we didn't talk about Elvira. We didn't talk about anything.

Broccoli watched his father the whole time. How he danced, and how he went downstairs to the men's room later on. Then he looked at Sabine. She was back at the bar, and she'd ordered another of those cocktails.

'You can clear the table,' Broccoli told the waitress. 'Nothing's happening here any more.'

After half an hour, when Mr Eckstein still hadn't come back, we went downstairs to find him.

There were six urinals and four toilets. Mr Eckstein was sitting on one of the toilets. The door to the cubicle was open; he was sitting there with his trousers up and his jacket still on, like he was just taking a breather in a deckchair.

'I thought you two would never show up,' Eckstein said.

Broccoli didn't say a thing.

There was no one else in the men's room. Folded up next to the sink were towels with the name of the restaurant on them.

'I couldn't get back up the stairs,' Mr Eckstein said.

'You need to go home,' Broccoli said.

'No,' Mr Eckstein said. 'We're little lost sheep and we've gone astray.' Then he slammed the door of the cubicle. At first, I didn't understand what was going on. I thought maybe he had to pee or throw up. But the sounds coming from the cubicle made me realise he was weeping.

Broccoli was leaning against the wall, like none of this had anything to do with him. I started washing my hands. I was hoping the sound of running water would drown out Mr Eckstein's sobs.

Ten minutes later, the door of the cubicle flew open. Mr Eckstein was sitting there, exactly as he'd been before.

'Men don't cry,' he said. Then he tried to pull himself to his feet on the toilet roll.

'Don't do that,' Broccoli shouted. But it was too late. The whole toilet-paper mechanism ripped right off the wall. Then Mr Eckstein slammed the door again and shouted: 'Leave me alone for once.'

We waited for a good fifteen minutes. I didn't dare to say anything to Broccoli. He was just standing there. Maybe he'd stood like that before and knew that you just had to be patient, that everything would turn out fine. One of the waiters came into the men's room. He looked at us a bit strangely, but didn't say anything. He just walked over to the mirror and began plucking his eyebrows.

Once he'd left, Broccoli knocked on the toilet door again. 'Do you think we can get out of here now?'

'I can't do anything any more,' Mr Eckstein said quietly. 'Just leave me alone, is that too much to ask?'

We could barely hear him.

Broccoli opened the door. Mr Eckstein was lying jammed in between the wall and the toilet bowl. But he wasn't on the floor. There wasn't enough space between the toilet and the wall for that. He just hung there, looking baleful.

Broccoli pulled Eckstein out of the cubicle. I heard the sound of tearing cloth, but Eckstein's suit had already been through a lot that day. Broccoli took his father back upstairs. I tagged along behind them. At a little table close to the bar he let go, and Eckstein dropped right on to a chair.

'Could we have the bill?' Broccoli asked, and the waitress laid it on the table right away. The waiter who'd been plucking his eyebrows downstairs asked: 'Did you enjoy your meal?'

No one said a thing. Sabine was still sitting at the bar. She was blowing us kisses.

Broccoli started rummaging through Eckstein's pockets. All kinds of things appeared again: newspaper clippings, pens, train tickets, a yellowed photograph, a paper napkin, a library card, a senior-citizen's pass.

'Where's your credit card?' Broccoli asked. He was almost shouting now.

'Don't ask stupid questions,' Eckstein mumbled. 'Where do you think my credit card is?' Then he saw Sabine and waved to her.

Broccoli finally found Mr Eckstein's card in his breast pocket and handed it to the waitress. Sabine had climbed down off her bar stool. Her dress was almost up to her navel.

The credit card came back. Broccoli pushed a pen into his father's hand. 'Just sign here,' he said.

Mr Eckstein held the pen and stared dully into space for a few seconds. Then he drew something that looked more like those swords the Saracens used to hack Christians to pieces. And it wasn't on the line where the signature was supposed to go. It was scrawled all over the bill.

'No,' the waitress said, 'I'm afraid we can't accept that. This isn't a signature.'

'What can't they accept?' Mr Eckstein asked.

The waiter came over too. The two of them were bent over Mr Eckstein's drawing.

'No,' the waiter said, 'this isn't your signature. Your signature looks very different. You'll have to sign again.'

Sabine was standing beside Mr Eckstein now. Her hand was resting on his shoulder.

'What do they want from me?' Eckstein mumbled. 'What do these people know about my signature?'

Broccoli pushed the pen back into his father's hand and shouted: 'Now sign that thing. I want to get out of here.'

Without looking, Mr Eckstein scribbled something. It could have passed for a signature, but it was on the tablecloth.

'You're not going to leave me, are you?' Sabine said.

'Mr Eckstein,' the waiter shouted, 'try to concentrate. This is the tablecloth.'

'No,' Mr Eckstein said, 'I'm not going to leave you.'

'Try to concentrate,' the waiter roared in Eckstein's ear. 'That was the tablecloth.'

'Oh, right,' Eckstein said. I don't think he had any idea what the waiter was talking about. The waitress walked away. Probably to get help.

'Now you're going to sign your name,' Broccoli yelled, 'or I'm going to beat your brains out.' That made a big impression on everyone, except Mr Eckstein. I'd never seen Broccoli like that.

'Take it easy, buster,' Sabine cried in a high voice, 'this isn't a wrestling match.' Then she added emphatically: 'This is a three-star restaurant.'

'What does it say?' Eckstein asked. 'I didn't bring my magnifying glass.'

No one replied.

'What's it say on the bill?' Mr Eckstein asked.

Broccoli read the amount out loud.

'What a bunch of crooks,' Eckstein mumbled.

Broccoli picked up the pen. He was about to sign it himself, but the waiter was too fast for him. 'Oh no,' he said, 'I'm afraid we can't accept that. Mr Eckstein has to sign it himself. Otherwise we'll get in trouble with the bank.'

'Damned if I will,' Eckstein roared. 'And would everyone please stop yelling at me. I'm not deaf.'

'Well,' the waiter said more quietly, 'as far as I'm concerned your son can sign for you. But you know how banks are these days. I'd get in trouble. With my boss, too. You know how it is; there are ten unemployed waiters standing in line to take my place.'

'Oh, man, go home,' Eckstein said.

The waitress came back with another waiter. He was probably the head waiter. I'd never heard anyone with diction as posh as his.

'Would you be so kind as to put your signature here?' he said. 'Then we won't keep you any longer.'

'I don't want to go home,' Eckstein said.

'Please don't be like that, Mr Eckstein,' the head waiter said. 'We've already been quite accommodating by not charging you for the tablecloth. The fountain pen will never come out of that.'

'Michaël,' Eckstein roared, 'pay this man for the tablecloth and take it home with you.'

'How much will that be?' Broccoli asked.

The head waiter hesitated. 'Twenty-five guilders,' he said. 'It's very special linen, you see.'

Broccoli paid. The head waiter put the money in his pocket.

'And now sign it!' Broccoli roared.

Mr Eckstein signed his name, but said right away: 'I'm never going to sign anything again.'

The head waiter and the waiter walked away. We were alone with Sabine.

'Come on, sugar, one last dance,' she said.

Mr Eckstein was still sitting there with the pen in his hand. 'Cognac,' he murmured.

Broccoli stuffed the papers and other rubbish back in his father's pockets, and Sabine said it again: 'One last dance, sugar.'

The only person left in the restaurant was the barman. I thought about Elvira, but I didn't have the nerve to call her again.

'I've known him such a long time,' Sabine said. 'He's such a sweetheart.'

She couldn't have known him more than a couple of hours. Something must have been wrong with her memory. I wondered why no one bothered to tell her she was standing there in her panties. Maybe it was up to me. But I was thinking about Elvira, and that's all I wanted to think about.

Mr Eckstein tried to put away the pen, but he couldn't find his inside pocket. Broccoli had to help him. Then Eckstein peered up at Sabine. A little trail of brown spittle was running from the corner of his mouth. Sabine didn't mind. She kissed him, just like she'd kissed him an hour ago.

'Dance with me,' she said. At first her accent had sounded posh too, but that was gone now.

'First we have a drink,' Eckstein said. He tried to flag the barman, but Broccoli yanked his arm back down. You could hear the bones crack. It was a wonder his arm stayed in its socket.

'*Verdammt nochmal*,' Eckstein shouted, 'this isn't a prison, is it?'

'I'm right here beside you,' Sabine said. She had pulled up a chair and was sitting next to him.

'Yes, I see that,' Eckstein said. This time it was Sabine who raised her arm. Broccoli didn't try to stop her. He could hardly pull her arm out of the socket too.

The barman came over to our table. 'Well,' he said, 'at least you've got yourself a nice tablecloth.'

Sabine whispered something in the barman's ear, and Eckstein said: '*Voilà, une femme.*' He looked at us to see if we'd heard. Then, just to be sure, he said it again: '*Voilà, une femme.*' He laughed loudly at that, but Broccoli pretended he hadn't heard. So I pretended I hadn't heard either.

'I'm longing for Elvira,' I told Broccoli. But he said: 'Shut up, just shut up for once.'

Still, I really was longing for Elvira. I don't think I've ever longed for her as badly as I did that night in that deserted restaurant. Almost nothing can be as thoroughly and abjectly ruinous as longing can. Not that it goes away. It just becomes more and more important, but what you're longing for becomes less important. Maybe it's because when you're drunk everyone starts looking the same. Whenever I think about Elvira I also see Mr Eckstein, and when I see Eckstein I see Sabine, and then I hear Eckstein saying '*Voilà, une femme*' while he waits for his hundredth cognac.

Sabine held his hand while he had another drink. Then they stood up. Broccoli didn't try to stop them any more. He didn't even say 'Dad, please'.

The music had stopped. There was only some song coming from the radio, or maybe it was one of the barman's tapes. They danced they way they had an hour ago, but now it was even a little worse. Suddenly Eckstein shouted: 'Michaël, where's my walking stick?'

Broccoli got up. He looked under the table, went over to the bartender, then downstairs to the men's room. I went after him. Eckstein's cane was in the cubicle. It had a wad of chewing gum stuck to it.

'Broccoli,' I said.

'Shut up,' he said, 'just shut up for once.'

When we got back upstairs, Sabine and Eckstein were sprawled on the dance floor. The music was still on and the barman was still rinsing the glasses. When he saw that Broccoli wasn't going to do anything, the barman said: 'They can't just lie there like that.'

'They love each other,' Broccoli said.

'Then they'll have to take a room.'

Broccoli walked out on to the dance floor. Sabine was crawling towards a chair. I think she was hoping to sit on it. She had an unbelievably huge backside.

'Everything's all right,' Eckstein said when he saw his son. 'I didn't break anything. And if I do break anything, they'll just take me to the hospital.' Then, pointing to Sabine as she crawled away, he whispered: 'What a woman, what a woman.'

'It just never quits, does it?' Broccoli said.

'No,' Eckstein said, 'it just won't quit.'

CAN YOU MAKE MY FATHER HAPPY?

*I*n the end, Sabine had to help us pull Eckstein to his feet. She took her shoes off first. Otherwise, she said, she might slip and fall.

Sabine walked us to the car. Mr Eckstein protested loudly when we left the restaurant, but no one paid him any attention. 'So where's my dinner, the food I paid for?' he shouted. No one bothered to tell him what had happened to his food. He probably wouldn't have believed it anyway.

The three of us were holding him upright. Every time his cane fell on the ground, I picked it up. Sabine was clutching Mr Eckstein's buttocks. There was no need for her to do that, but maybe it helped his balance a little.

By the time we got to the car, I thought Broccoli was ready to drop. He climbed in on the driver's side and leaned his head against the wheel. Mr Eckstein sat beside him. Eckstein rolled down the window and said to Sabine: 'At home, I always got the smallest piece of meat.' There was this strange tic at the corner of his mouth. Maybe it had always been there, but maybe it was the cognac.

'It'll be all right,' Sabine said. She held his hand.

'I don't believe that for a minute,' Eckstein said.

When I went to open the door and climb in the back, she let go of his hand and kissed me on the forehead. As she did, she whispered something that sounded a lot like 'God bless you'.

We drove off. Sabine stood there, waving to us with her shoes. After a while, all you could see of her was her cocktail dress.

'I always got the smallest piece of meat,' Mr Eckstein repeated. We didn't say a thing. Maybe it had had something to do with the food he'd missed that evening. If you always got the smallest piece of meat, of course, it's natural to assume that someday you won't get anything at all.

Broccoli drove in silence, and way too fast. I didn't know what to say to him, and it seemed better not to talk to Eckstein either. His white collar had turned grey, and he wasn't wearing his tie any more. Right before we got to Amsterdam, he sat up straight with more energy than I'd thought he had in him.

'We're not going home, are we?' he shouted.

'No,' Broccoli said, 'we're not going home quite yet.'

I know I should have said: 'Drop me off somewhere, I'll take a bus home.' I knew my parents were waiting for me. But I just sat there, probably because that was the easiest thing to do. When asked why people have done certain things in their lives, there's often only one possible answer: 'Because it was the easiest thing at the time.'

At a stoplight, Broccoli leaned over and buttoned the top buttons of Eckstein's shirt. 'Everything will be all right,' Broccoli said. Then he kissed him.

We started zigzagging back and forth through the centre of town.

'What are we doing?' Eckstein asked after a while.

'You don't want to go home, do you?' Broccoli said.

'No,' Eckstein said, 'I don't want to go home.'

Again I thought of Elvira and imagined her dancing with Wolf right then. Maybe I should have told her that not becoming an actress wasn't so bad, that it wasn't so bad to be satisfied with less, that it wasn't bad to change your plans, because everyone does that. One day you discover that you have to adapt your desires to fit reality. But Broccoli would never have forgiven me. He didn't want to be satisfied with less. He didn't want to adapt his desires to fit reality, he wanted reality to adapt to his desires. Even if I had said all those things to Elvira, the only thing she probably would have said back was: 'Try to concentrate.'

Broccoli picked up a bottle of perfume that had been in the car the whole time, maybe for years. He sprinkled some of it on Eckstein's cheeks. 'You have to smell good,' he said.

'Yes,' Eckstein said, 'that's important.' Then we drove on. It felt like we'd keep driving around for ever. Mr Eckstein said: 'I could use a cognac right now.' But Broccoli shook his head. Then no one said a word, not even Eckstein. About fifteen minutes later, Broccoli stopped the car. He rolled down the window.

'Can you make my father happy?' I heard him ask.

I couldn't make out the reply, but it must have been negative because we drove away. I looked out the window and said: 'You're mad, Broccoli.'

'Yes,' Broccoli said, 'I am mad. Stark raving.' He laughed. He had the same look on his face he'd had the night he said: 'We should start a paper. A daily. Different from all other dailies.'

He stopped again. He asked the same question. Mr Eckstein was staring straight ahead. Maybe he was remembering how they'd always given him the smallest piece of meat. Again the answer was negative, and again we drove on.

Broccoli stopped and asked that same question about six times before a girl finally climbed in. There was no room up in front, so she had to sit next to me. She leaned up to Broccoli and said: 'I've made so many fathers happy in my life.' Then she whispered something in his ear and Broccoli said: 'That's fine.'

She wasn't much older than me. She had black hair, probably dyed. Her face was thin and her lips were painted pink. She stank a bit of perfume, but then Mr Eckstein's perfume didn't smell so hot either.

We pulled away from the kerb. 'Oh, yeah,' the girl said again, 'I've made lots of fathers happy in my life.' She had to laugh at that. I did too, in fact. Probably more from shyness. But no one else was laughing.

'God will reward you,' Eckstein mumbled, 'but I could stand a cognac.'

We drove through the embarcadero district west of town. I wasn't familiar with the neighbourhood. In fact, I'm still not.

'What's your name?' the girl asked a little later. I told her. She had a little shoulder bag with her. It looked like the kind of doll's shoulder bag you'd buy at a toy store.

It was quiet for the next ten minutes, except when Mr Eckstein mumbled: 'Can't they just leave me alone for once?'

I tried to turn my thoughts back to Elvira. I would have liked to ask Broccoli why I should make her happy, and especially how. It was the first time I'd ever been afraid of him. He came from a world where I'd always be a stranger, no matter how much time I spent wandering around in it. My parents would never end up in prison, they'd never have to be afraid of that. They were already afraid of the conductor on the tram. And their son was a walking fount of misfortune.

We stopped, I had no idea where. The girl whispered in my ear: 'I'm carrying a weapon. Just so you know. There are a lot of crazies around.'

I looked at her and saw from the roots of her hair that it must once have been sandy-coloured. 'Yes,' I said, 'there are a lot of crazies around.'

Broccoli got out. So did the girl. When she slammed the door, she looked at me. I thought she was expecting me to do something. To get out of the car too, or maybe to tell Broccoli she was armed or should at least be considered so. But now I think she was just looking at me. She must have known that there's no more suitable victim for deception than he who hopes for salvation. In fact, the very earmark of the deceived may very well be their having hoped for salvation. If they hadn't done that they wouldn't have been so blind, and they would have seen what everyone else could see. These days I believe that there's no difference whatsoever between salvation and deception.

'They're negotiating,' Mr Eckstein said. He turned around, or at least he tried to.

'Are you really his friend?' Then he asked me that again, but the second time he didn't use the word 'friend', he used the word 'helper'. I remember that because it was such a strange word, it made me think of Santa Claus.

'I think so,' I said.

He rummaged around in his pockets. 'Ewald,' he mumbled, 'Ewald Krieg.'

'Ewald Stanislas Krieg,' I helped him.

He nodded. 'Any relation to the singer?'

'There are no singers in our family,' I said. 'We did have an animal impersonator in the family though. Maybe that's the one you're thinking of?'

He shook his head. Then he turned back to the window. They were still talking. 'They're negotiating,' he said again.

A couple of minutes later Broccoli opened the car door. 'Come on,' he said to his father.

Mr Eckstein gestured with his hand. The same gesture he'd made when he said he always got the smallest piece of meat.

'Help me here,' Broccoli said.

I climbed out. There wasn't much room to help.

'He's pretty old,' the girl said. Again I thought of Elvira, and I heard Broccoli say: 'You've got to work along with me a bit.'

Then Eckstein was finally out, leaning against his car.

'Pull his pants down,' the girl said. 'I'll never be able to do that alone.'

Broccoli began opening Mr Eckstein's trousers. They were the old-fashioned kind with buttons down the side. It was almost dark, but I could clearly see the black spot on the legs.

'I'm going to catch a cold,' Mr Eckstein grumbled. 'Can't we do this inside?'

'No,' Broccoli said, 'we can't do this inside. This is a good place.'

FAIRE PIPI

*T*he place where we'd stopped the car looked like a cross between a construction site and a park. Mr Eckstein's grey trousers and white underpants were down around his ankles, and his white buttocks reminded me of two cream cakes that had collapsed from old age. Mr Eckstein didn't seem too worried about his predicament. He said: 'What I could use right now is a cognac.' He was holding on to the rear-view mirror. I hoped it was one of the sturdy kind.

'Pay now please,' the girl said.

Broccoli pulled the money out of Eckstein's inside pocket. He'd hid it there himself, so he knew where it was.

'Now turn around,' she said.

'What?' Broccoli asked.

'Turn around, both of you,' she said. 'So I can put it away.'

We turned around.

'Let's stay like this,' Broccoli said. We heard Mr Eckstein say: 'I know I'm going to catch a cold. Can't we go inside somewhere?'

'No,' the girl said, 'you won't catch a cold. I'll see to that.' And then Eckstein: 'God will reward you for this.' And the girl: 'No, that's not necessary. As long as you do. Afterwards. A nice tip.'

We heard Mr Eckstein cough, then say: 'If God doesn't do it, I guess it'll all be up to me again.'

Then it was quiet. We stood there with our hands behind our backs, staring ahead without turning around even once. It was already dark, and there was nothing else to stare at but some trees that looked like shadows.

I thought that if there was something like salvation it would be sure to have Elvira's face, and her eyes and her mouth and her accent, even her artichoke liqueur. But no matter how I tried, I couldn't see Elvira; I saw the girl with the straggly black hair and the pink lipstick and Mr Eckstein, without looking at them even once. And I heard her say again: 'I'm armed, you know, there are so many crazies running around.' And then: 'I've made so many fathers happy in my life.'

Broccoli was next to me. He was staring straight ahead too, he didn't seem to hear what I was hearing. He made me think of a general viewing the bloodbath he's caused.

It took an awfully long time. It seemed like an eternity. Then we finally heard the girl say: 'It's finished.'

Broccoli was the first to turn around.

Mr Eckstein was standing against the car, exactly the way we'd left him. He had an erection, or at least something that passed for one. So that's what erections look like when you're really old, I thought.

The girl was fixing her lipstick. Broccoli was tugging up Eckstein's underpants and his grey trousers.

'So I get a nice tip now?' the girl asked.

'Oh, sure,' Eckstein said. I wondered whether he'd even heard what she said.

'It was quite a job,' the girl said quietly, 'I thought it was never going to end.'

Eckstein seemed to have snapped out of it, because suddenly he said: 'Everything happens twice in this life, that's what Marx said.'

'No,' the girl said. 'Once is plenty.'

Eckstein was half-draped over Broccoli's shoulder, but at least he had his clothes on. 'I have to,' Eckstein said. He hesitated. 'I have to – *faire pipi*,' he peeped. It came out real high, like he was a castrato.

'Why didn't you say so?' Broccoli shouted.

This hoarse noise was coming from Eckstein's mouth. We couldn't tell what he was saying. Broccoli led him over to a tree. They stayed there for at least fifteen minutes. I stood next to the car with the girl.

'*Faire pipi*,' she said.

'*Faire pipi*,' I repeated. I didn't know what else to say. Somehow it made me think of my old French teacher, and I wondered what she was doing right then.

When they finally came back, Mr Eckstein claimed he'd lost his cufflink. He was breathing hard, it was more like panting. 'Let's look for my cufflink.'

'No,' Broccoli said, 'we can't do that.'

'A nice tip,' the girl repeated.

'We agreed on a price,' Broccoli said as he lowered Eckstein into the car.

'He promised me,' she said. For the first time, I felt sorry for her.

That evening in that vacant lot or construction site or whatever it was, I looked at the girl and thought about Elvira and the salvation and deliverance her face would bring.

'You give her a tip,' Eckstein said. 'I've already caught a cold and lost my cufflink.'

Broccoli pulled a twenty-five-guilder note out of Eckstein's pocket. This time the girl didn't say: 'Turn around.' She put the money away right in front of us.

'Then I guess we'll be going,' Broccoli said.

'All right, here we go,' Eckstein said.

Broccoli led Eckstein around to the other side of the car. I walked along behind them, without really helping. The girl waited until we'd all gotten in, then she climbed in too. I was sitting next to her again.

'My cane,' Eckstein yelled.

'It's right here,' Broccoli said.

We drove along a sandy road, or at least one with lots of bumps.

Eckstein tried to turn around to look at me and the girl. Broccoli was chewing gum.

'You know what,' Eckstein said, 'I used to think there could be nothing worse than feeling like you have to pee, but it won't come. But in reality it's a lot worse. As usual.'

No one said anything. Only Broccoli asked: 'Are you happy now?'

Eckstein thought about it, then he said: 'Not unhappy. A little bit of cognac would do me good, but I'm not unhappy.' He started crying again. It was a kind of growling with big gasps. This time there was no toilet for him to lock himself in.

'What's your name?' I asked the girl, just like she'd asked me.

'Aw, forget it,' she said.

We weren't on the sandy road any more. Mr Eckstein's sobbing kept getting quieter until it stopped completely. He turned around. 'I wasn't crying,' he said.

'That's OK,' the girl said. 'I've seen lots of people cry before.'

Broccoli was driving like a madman. I think he was trying to get us all killed. I was afraid I was suddenly going to ask Eckstein: 'Are you really the guy who produces the biggest turds in the world?' I was so afraid I was going to blurt it out, I had to concentrate.

Broccoli stopped at the spot where we'd picked up the girl. But she said: 'No, go on, around the corner is better.'

Before she got out, she said: 'See you later.'

'See you later,' Eckstein said, 'and when we meet again, I hope it's not under the stars. I'm not much of an outdoorsman.'

We watched her walk away. She kind of blended in with the crowd. Broccoli started the car.

'I know I caught a cold,' Eckstein said. He turned around to look at me. 'At my age you could catch your death of cold, that's what that nutty Ludwig would say.' Then he started laughing.

A BANK ACCOUNT IN ZURICH

*W*e drove to the house on the Bernard Zweerskade. Mrs Eckstein was there. Broccoli's father sank down into an easy chair. In the bright light of the living room, I finally saw the way he looked. Like he'd spent a couple of nights under a bridge.

Mrs Eckstein had brought all kinds of suitcases up from the cellar and was busy packing. At the back of the living room sat Mr Berk. When he saw us, he raised his hand. He was reading the paper.

Mrs Eckstein was trotting back and forth with linen and candlesticks. 'I knew it,' she said, 'I always knew it would end like this.' No one asked whether it wasn't about time for me to go home. But now I didn't want to go home any more. If Broccoli had gone off with his parents, I would have gone with them too, because at that moment all I wanted was to go away. Away from where I'd been born, away from where people knew me and where that made them think they knew what would become of me. Away from Amsterdam-South, where every doorway, every traffic light had some memory or other attached to it. Wasn't that where I'd kissed so-and-so, wasn't that the shop where I'd stolen a pack of chewing gum, and wasn't that the ice-cream parlour where we hung out in the summer, so we wouldn't have to go home? We used to sit there for hours, until it started getting dark, and that often took till ten. What in God's name had we been waiting for?

Later, when people our age started getting married and I stood at the back of the church in my best suit, I would always try to drive away the boredom by thinking about that ice-cream parlour. What did we do there but eat ice cream and talk, to drive away the boredom of who was marrying whom, of how many children they'd have, the trips they'd take, the great deeds we'd perform?

'None of this is going,' Eckstein mumbled, pointing at the things his wife was loading into the suitcases.

'My mother embroidered this,' Mrs Eckstein said.

'That was awfully nice of her, but it's not going.' Then Eckstein turned to Mr Berk and said: 'All these years she hasn't had one good thing to say about her mother, and now we have to break our backs carrying that woman's tablecloths around.'

Mrs Eckstein threw the tablecloth on the floor and shouted: 'If this isn't going, then I'm not going either. Let them come and arrest me. This tablecloth is going with.'

'You'll have plenty of time for needlework when you get to prison,' Eckstein murmured. He looked at Mr Berk and said: 'Ludwig, get me a cognac; I've caught myself a cold.'

Mr Berk got up and headed for the cupboard, but Mrs Eckstein shouted: 'Have you caught a cold? That's all we need. Now I have to drag a sick husband along with me. We're all going to end up in prison, I've always known that. My aunt saw it coming. She said: "Marry that man, and you'll end up in prison." My parents would roll over in their grave.' Suddenly she looked at me and said: 'I come from such a good family.' I lowered my eyes.

'They don't have a grave, so they can't roll over in it,' Eckstein shouted. 'Now where's my cognac?'

Mr Berk opened the cupboard and took out a bottle of cognac. For a moment it looked like Mrs Eckstein was going to fly at him, but instead she walked over to Broccoli, pressed him against her and said: 'Be sure to eat lots of apples when we're gone. Fruit is the only thing that helps.'

'What?' Eckstein said.

'Fruit is the only thing that helps,' Mrs Eckstein repeated. 'You're our wunderkind aren't you? Our only wunderkind.'

And Broccoli said: 'That's right, I'm your wunderkind.'

'He's going to be a great professor some day,' she said to me. 'A very great professor. Do you know what they called him at school? They called him "The Professor", because he was so smart, a real wunderkind.' Then she let go of him. All the blood had left his face.

'No,' Broccoli said, 'that's a misunderstanding. They never called me "The Professor".'

His mother went into the next room and came back with her hands full of cutlery.

'What's that?' Eckstein shouted.

'Cutlery.'

'I see that, but it's not going with.'

Mrs Eckstein put the cutlery in the suitcase and said very calmly: 'I thought maybe we could start a hotel when we get there.'

Eckstein put his head in his hands, the way I'd seen him do before. He started laughing.

'A hotel,' he said. 'Did you all hear that? She's out of her mind. A hotel. She's getting crazier every day.'

'I called Mrs Meerschwam,' Mrs Eckstein went on. 'She's coming right over to help me pack. In the middle of the night, who else would do a thing like that? She's such a good woman. She also said a hotel was an excellent idea.'

'You called who?' Eckstein asked.

'Mrs Meerschwam, she's all we have left here. Thanks to you. At the butcher's they start whispering whenever I come in.'

A terrible yelp came from Mr Eckstein's mouth. 'Did you hear that, Ludwig?' he cried.

'I can't do all this packing on my own,' Mrs Eckstein said. 'Just look at what I still have to pack. And there's a whole cellar full.'

'Oh, no,' Eckstein interrupted her. 'We're not going to drag preserves along with us. We're not dragging any preserves along, do you hear me?'

Mr Berk was bent over his newspaper again.

'I wouldn't dream of throwing it all away, I wouldn't dream of it; besides, it's not all preserves, there's a lot more down there. A very expensive wine collection, chocolate-cake mixes.' She took a few steps away from the suitcases, in my direction. 'They're very special, those mixes, you can't get them any more. I'm not just leaving them here. At least I haven't lost my senses. Ludwig, that chocolate cake I make for your birthday, you always think it's delicious, don't you?'

'Delicious,' Berk said, 'delicious.'

Mr Eckstein had seized a candlestick from the table and was waving it in the air. 'If that shrew Meerschwam sets even one foot across the threshold here tonight,' he roared, 'I'll chase her away, by force if necessary.' Then Eckstein slammed the candlestick down on the table, picked up his glass of cognac and shattered it against the wall. It must not have been completely empty, because it left a yellow spot on the wallpaper. Then he said quietly: 'Ludwig, fix me another drink.'

'Don't,' Mrs Eckstein said. 'He'll just break it again.'

'Bubie,' Eckstein shouted. 'Bubie, I'm warning you.'

'He used to call her "Bubie",' Broccoli whispered. 'But sometimes he forgets and starts calling her "Bubie" again.'

'Bubie, that's a nice name,' I whispered back. Broccoli looked at me like I'd gone insane.

Berk came over with another glass. He filled it with cognac.

'Michaël,' Mr Eckstein said, 'now that we're about to leave, it's time you knew—' He came down with a coughing fit that must have lasted three minutes.

'Look at him spitting mucus all over the room,' Mrs Eckstein shouted. 'Do you see that? The animal.'

When his fit was over, Mr Eckstein said: 'You should know, Michaël, that your great-grandfather had a bank account in Zurich, your grandfather had a bank account in Zurich, and your father had a bank account in Zurich. But judging from the way you run your life, you'll be the last Eckstein with a bank account in Zurich. Think about that before you decide to have children.'

With the spots on his pants, his torn jacket and his shirt unbuttoned, he looked more like a tramp than someone with a bank account in Zurich. Mr Eckstein tried to get up to take the cutlery out of the suitcase, but he couldn't. Instead he shouted: 'Ludwig, that cutlery's not going with, unpack that stuff.'

Mr Berk made a move for the table, but Mrs Eckstein pulled a pair of shears out of one of the open suitcases, those shears you can use to cut a chicken into pieces. She had the look of a madwoman. Or maybe it was more the look of a wildcat that's been cornered.

'I'll cut both of you,' she shouted. 'If you touch my cutlery, I'll cut you.'

Mr Berk took a few steps back. 'That's overdoing it a bit,' he said. 'How long have we known each other?'

They all seemed to have forgotten I was there.

'Shit on your bank account in Zurich,' she shouted. 'Shit on your cognac. My cutlery's going with.'

'That woman is dangerous,' Eckstein mumbled. 'Wasting so much time on cutlery in a situation like this.'

'The cutlery is going with,' Mrs Eckstein shrieked. 'We have to leave so much behind as it is.'

Then I knew for sure that she would fight to the death for her cutlery. But suddenly she sank down in a chair. She still had the chicken shears in her hand, but she wasn't holding them very tightly.

'Our lives are finished,' she murmured.

'That's right,' Mr Eckstein said, 'finished. They've been finished for a long time, and now I want to go to bed. I'll sleep on the couch.'

Mr Berk walked over to the couch, as though he was planning to fix a bed for Mr Eckstein. He must have had second thoughts, though, because he stopped halfway and went back to his chair on the other side of the room. No one else moved.

'Could I use the phone?' I asked. Broccoli nodded. I dialled Elvira's number, but no one answered. When I came back, Mrs Eckstein was still filling a suitcase with cutlery. I guess Mr Eckstein had given up the fight. Berk was humming quietly to himself, and Broccoli was flipping distractedly through the *Yellow Pages*.

'Ludwig, help me take off my shirt,' Eckstein whispered.

'Can't you even do that for yourself any more?' Mrs Eckstein said as she closed the suitcase.

'Harpy,' Eckstein whispered. He kicked off his shoes. He had on black socks with holes in them. 'And bring me my bathrobe.'

Mr Berk unbuttoned Eckstein's shirt and used his handkerchief to wipe his face. Mrs Eckstein was filling one suitcase after the other. She was running back and forth with cutlery and candlesticks like it was an Olympic event.

Then the telephone rang. Mrs Eckstein froze. 'Who in the world could that be, in the middle of the night?' she cried.

Elvira, I felt like saying, that must be Elvira, let me get it.

No one answered it. They all stared at the phone as if they'd never heard one ring before. Berk had stopped unbuttoning Eckstein's shirt. He stared into space without moving. Broccoli finally picked it up.

'It's for you,' he said. He brought the phone over to Eckstein. When Eckstein took hold of the receiver, I was struck once again by how badly his hands shook. I thought the receiver would go clattering to the floor any moment.

'*Du Vollblutidiot*,' we heard him say. Then the receiver really did slip out of his hand. Mr Berk picked it up.

'Berk here,' he said. 'Hello?' And after a brief pause: 'No, everything's fine. Everything's under control. He'll get in contact with you as soon as he arrives.'

'Oh my God,' Mrs Eckstein moaned. She ran up to Broccoli and said: 'Eat lots of fruit, believe me, that's the most important thing.' She hugged him, but not as long as she had before. Then she ran over to her husband. She started shaking him and shouting: 'What have you done to us? What have you done to us?' Every time she yanked on him, Eckstein came up off his chair and then sank back again – it looked like he was on a trampoline. 'We can't stay in Lenzerheide for ever. They'll find us there eventually. They'll find us wherever we go. And they'll point at us. Six months ago they stopped talking at the butcher's whenever I came in.'

'They can't lay a finger on me,' Eckstein said. 'Trust me, they can't lay a finger on me. So, Ludwig, I'd like my robe now.' His shirt was still hanging from his shoulders. Mrs Eckstein had let go of him. With all that shaking back and forth, Eckstein's suspenders had shot loose. He stood up. 'They can't lay a finger on me,' he roared. 'I'm no *Vollblutidiot*, not like that one there, or that one there.' He pointed at Mr Berk first, then at his son. Then he let himself fall back in his chair and threw the second glass of cognac at the wall.

Berk didn't seem to mind being called a *Vollblutidiot*, or maybe he'd gotten used to it. He came over with a dark-red bathrobe.

'That's my wife's,' Eckstein mumbled.

'This marriage was a mistake, a big mistake,' Mrs Eckstein said, pulling a rope tight around the suitcase full of cutlery.

'Well, that's a bit late, after thirty years,' Eckstein whispered. 'But then better late than never.'

Berk came back with a blue bathrobe. 'Yes,' Eckstein said, 'that's mine.' He looked at Broccoli, who was still leafing through the *Yellow Pages*, and said: 'Never be afraid. I'm too old to care whether people like me. If I was you, I wouldn't care whether people liked me either. It's a waste of energy. As long as you've got money, just be sure you've got money. Then at least you can sleep in a good hotel.'

Broccoli had his nose in the *Yellow Pages* and didn't seem to hear a thing.

Once Berk had finally hoisted him into his blue bathrobe, Eckstein said: 'I'd like to take one last look around the house.'

'This house was our undoing,' Mrs Eckstein said. The fifth suitcase now had a rope around it as well. I think they were all filled with household articles.

'Harpy,' Eckstein whispered. To Broccoli, he said: 'When the families no longer stick together, it's all over. Then everything's lost. How do you think the first Eckstein ever ended up in Zurich? Never forget that we started out as trash.' He stepped over to Broccoli and took his chin in his hand. 'If the families had stuck together, we'd have ourselves a little empire by now. A little empire, believe you me.'

The two of them took Eckstein up to the second floor. Mr Berk pulled on him, and Broccoli pushed him from behind.

He paused in a doorway. The room behind it was empty, except for a cupboard and a table with a sewing machine on it.

'This is where you were born,' Eckstein said. He leaned against the doorpost and came down with another coughing fit. More brown stuff came out of his mouth. Mr Berk wiped Eckstein's lips.

'*Vollblutidiot,*' Eckstein hissed. He walked over to the cupboard and opened one of the drawers. It looked like Mrs Eckstein had already emptied them. 'Your crib was over there,' he said. 'After you were born, I had to take four weeks' vacation to recover. Those nine months were pure hell.'

I'd come along with them so I wouldn't have to stay downstairs with Mrs Eckstein and her cutlery. We went into another room. There was a big desk there with a plastic sheet over it.

'This was my office,' Eckstein said. 'You used to play on the floor. I bought you an omnibus. A red toy bus, from London.' He soiled his face again, and Mr Berk pulled out his handkerchief.

'*Vollblutidiot,*' Eckstein shouted once his mouth had been wiped for the umpteenth time. He went over to the desk. 'It must still be here somewhere.' He opened a few drawers, but couldn't seem to find the bus.

Mr Berk followed him around like a faithful retriever. Ready to step in if he stumbled. Eckstein leaned on his desk. 'What have you done with my money?' he said quietly.

'Who?' Berk asked.

'Him,' Eckstein said, pointing at Broccoli. 'What have you done with my money?'

Broccoli took a few steps towards the desk.

'Nothing special.'

From downstairs came the tinkling of glass.

'This isn't the moment to . . .' Mr Berk began.

'This is the moment for you to keep your mouth shut, Ludwig,' Eckstein said. 'You're a *Vollblutidiot*. You always were. There's nothing you can do about it.' He leaned on Mr Berk. 'Is that the phone?'

'No, that's the glassware,' Berk said.

'Oh my God,' Eckstein murmured. 'Oh dear God, not the glassware. Not that too.'

The tic at the corner of his mouth was even worse than it had been a few hours ago. 'If you can't trust your own son any more,' he said quietly, 'then there's nothing left. When the families no longer stick together, everything's lost.' He twisted out of Mr Berk's grip. He was swaying on his feet, but he stayed upright. Then he yelled: 'Stop that tinkling, you're driving me mad. That tinkling is driving me crazy. Do you hear me?'

'If I want to go on tinkling all night,' Mrs Eckstein shouted from downstairs, 'it's my business. If you don't like it, go hang yourself from a rafter.'

We went into the next room.

'This is where we slept,' Eckstein said. He pointed to the bed, which was also covered with a thick plastic sheet. 'But this is not where you were conceived. You were conceived in the Black Forest. She took her temperature every day to find out when she'd be most fertile. And when that day came we were in the Black Forest.'

He dropped on to the bed with a sigh and said: 'Leave me for a moment.'

'Don't you want me to take the plastic off?' Berk asked.

'No,' Eckstein said, 'there's no call for that.' We heard him mumble: 'Have Mrs Meerschwam clean up when I'm gone. And give her a good tip.'

The three of us went downstairs again. The glasses were still tinkling. Mr Berk made tea for us. He asked if we'd mind him singing a song about springtime.

'As long as you do it quietly,' Broccoli said.

We drank our tea in the kitchen.

THE CUTLERY'S GOING WITH

'*Y*ou might as well sleep here,' Broccoli said. 'We have to get up early anyway. Their train leaves at nine.'

I went to the phone again. This time Elvira answered.

'Where have you been the whole time?' I asked.

'Out,' she said.

'You sound so far away.'

'No I don't,' she said.

I knew she sounded far away, but this wasn't the right moment to argue about it. 'How about coming over to the Bernard Zweerskade?'

'When?'

'It's five o'clock now,' I said. 'In two hours?'

'OK.'

The tinkling of glassware didn't matter any more, Mr and Mrs Eckstein didn't matter either; even the way Broccoli was acting had become unimportant. For the second time that night, it occurred to me that what I wanted most was to go away. I wanted to leave town too, but not with a bunch of cutlery and chicken shears.

At five-thirty, Mrs Meerschwam arrived. She had a huge shopping bag with her. When she saw Mrs Eckstein she tried to throw her arms around her, but Mrs Eckstein pushed her away. 'We don't have time for that,' she shouted, 'there are at least three more bags to pack.'

'I wouldn't do this for anyone but you,' Mrs Meerschwam said, pulling an apron out of the shopping bag and tying it around her waist. 'You don't think I'd help anyone else pack at this hour, do you?' She went down to the cellar and began carrying up the entire food supply.

Berk, Broccoli and I spent the rest of the night in the kitchen while Mrs Eckstein and Mrs Meerschwam did the packing. Every once in a while we'd hear a loud 'boom-boom-boom'. Broccoli said it was only the sound of Mrs Meerschwam going down the cellar steps. One time we heard Mrs Eckstein scream: 'Those chocolate-cake mixes are no longer available, Frida, no longer available, do you hear me?'

'Is her name Frida?' I asked.

'Yes,' Broccoli said. 'Mrs Meerschwam's name is Frida. But we are not to call her Frida. I beg you, do not call her Frida; she'd have a fit.'

Mr Berk nodded. 'Only six people in the whole world are allowed to call her Frida. And two of them are dead.'

Occasionally, Mrs Eckstein came into the kitchen to check if the cupboards were really empty. 'The fruit is in that cabinet,' she said. 'Be sure to finish it before they impound it. I can't take everything with me.'

When Broccoli tried to light a cigarette, she snatched it from his lips and crumbled it above the bin. 'No,' she shouted, 'no, great God in heaven, no. Absolutely no, no, no.'

'She's even taking the tea bags with her,' Mr Berk said between songs. He was off on a singing jag again.

'I asked Elvira to come over,' I told Broccoli.

'That's great,' he mumbled. 'Wonderful. Elvira here, that's all we need.'

I remembered him kissing Elvira in her kitchen, and how I'd watched without them knowing. But maybe they'd known and just hadn't let on. I knew he longed for Elvira as much as I did, maybe even more, and I hoped some day he would tell me everything about her that she hadn't told me herself. 'What does she say to you when you two are alone?' I'd asked him a few times. 'Later,' he always said. Or: 'Some other time.' Or: 'You don't talk about things like that. Didn't anyone ever tell you that? Am I the first respectable human being you've ever met?'

We sat there like that until six-thirty came and Mr Berk said: 'We'd better wake him up.' Berk and Broccoli went upstairs. The living room had been transformed into a delicatessen. The tinkling of glassware had finally stopped. I trailed along behind them again, like a dog that keeps coming back to its old house.

He was lying on the plastic sheet, just as we'd left him, with his socks still on. The only thing different was that his bathrobe had fallen open.

'You're going on a trip today,' Mr Berk said.

Eckstein didn't react.

'Time to get dressed,' Mr Berk said, a little louder now. He grabbed Eckstein by the shoulders and shook him.

'Get me some cognac,' Eckstein roared.

'He's awake,' Berk said.

Eckstein looked at us without a word. He twisted his mouth a bit, then looked down at his socks and bathrobe.

'Who put me in this get-up?' he asked hoarsely.

'I did,' Berk said.

'*Vollblutidiot*,' he whispered.

Mr Berk pulled him upright. When he saw me standing in the doorway, he squinted like he was trying to focus. Like he didn't recognise me any more.

'What was that girl's name?' he asked.

'Do you mean me?' I said.

'Yes, you over there,' Eckstein said. 'What was that girl's name?'

'What girl?' Berk wanted to know.

Broccoli walked over to the bed. 'Why do you want to know?'

'That's my business,' Eckstein shouted. 'I want to know that girl's name.' He'd sat straight up in bed on his own. There was a little dried blood stuck to his lower lip. He looked like some kind of scarecrow. 'She told you,' he said, pointing at me.

I shook my head. 'No, really.'

'Who is this girl, anyway?' Berk said.

Broccoli laid his hand on Eckstein's head. 'She didn't introduce herself,' he said emphatically. 'We don't know what her name was.'

'Didn't she introduce herself?' Eckstein asked. 'Not at all?'

We heard rummaging coming from downstairs. The tinkling of glassware seemed to have started again.

'Is there any way I can help?' Berk said.

Eckstein pushed Berk away. 'You know nothing about it,' he mumbled. Then he came down with a coughing fit. Between coughs he kept saying he wanted to know the girl's name.

'But why?' Broccoli asked. Eckstein refused to explain.

When the coughing fit was over, Berk said: 'We really have to get you dressed now, otherwise you'll have to take a taxi in the nude.'

Eckstein was in a very nasty mood that morning. He pulled Berk down by his necktie and hissed: 'You'd like that, wouldn't you, Ludwig?'

'We need to be alone for a moment,' Broccoli said.

I went downstairs. The suitcases were lined up, at least as many as Mrs Lopez had had with her, and there were a couple of backpacks too. When the bell rang I ran to the door, but Mrs Eckstein beat me to it. 'I'm afraid you've come at a rather bad moment,' I heard her saying.

I wormed my way past her. 'Excuse me,' I said. 'This is Elvira. Your son asked her to come over.'

She looked at me. 'It's really not a very good moment,' she

said again. Then she turned to Elvira: 'You see, my husband and I are taking a trip.' She seemed completely shattered. She was holding a butter dish in her hand.

'She's only staying for a few minutes,' I said. I led Elvira to the kitchen.

'What's going on here?' she asked.

I wanted to hug her, but she didn't act like she wanted to be hugged. She didn't look like someone who's been up all night either. Maybe she'd slept very soundly. Maybe she had a new bed.

'They're going on a trip,' I said. 'I'll get Broccoli.' As I walked past, I touched her arm. It didn't necessarily mean anything, it could also have been by accident.

In the bedroom, they were hoisting Eckstein into a new suit. It looked like quite an operation. When I got closer, Eckstein pulled me down to him and whispered: 'You all know exactly what her name is, but none of you want to tell me. Do you, you jackanapes?'

I pulled myself loose. Everyone was going mad.

'Elvira's in the kitchen,' I said.

'Get her some tea,' Broccoli said, 'or something. Get her some cognac for all I care.' He went on tying his father's tie.

'Jackanapes,' Eckstein whispered.

When I got back to the kitchen, Elvira was eating a bun.

'They're lovely buns, aren't they?' said Mrs Eckstein. She already had the next one in her hand.

'Where have you been all night?'

'Let the girl eat,' Mrs Eckstein said.

I went to the living room. Practically everything that wasn't bolted down had been packed. From upstairs, I heard Mr Eckstein scream: 'If you don't tell me her name, I'm not going anywhere!' And then Mr Berk: 'Don't be so difficult, do me a favour just this once, don't be so difficult.'

The bedroom door flew open. Eckstein appeared on the landing. He was wearing a white suit. They'd put a straw hat on his head and given him a shave as well, from the looks of it.

He looked like a runaway circus horse. He had his cane in his hand.

'Don't go down those stairs by yourself,' Berk shouted.

'See how they treat me?' Eckstein said, waving his cane at me. 'Do you see this?'

They came down the stairs one at a time. Eckstein stared at each step as he went. Halfway down, his hat fell off. He kicked at it. 'See what they make me wear?' he said, pointing his cane at me again.

Berk picked up the hat. 'Come along now,' he said.

When he finally reached the bottom, he looked at all the suit-cases and backpacks and the enormous piles of cans. He shook his head a few times, then sat down beside me. 'What was her name?' he whispered. 'Please, just tell me her name.'

At that very moment, Mrs Meerschwam came up from the cellar with cans of concentrated lemon juice. I recognised those cans; my mother used to buy them too.

'Bubie,' Mr Eckstein shouted. 'Bubie, what did I say to you?'

Mrs Meerschwam said: 'I'm pleased we finally have a chance to talk, Mr Eckstein. Have you noticed the garden? Do you think I'm going to cut the grass, at my age? The neighbours say your garden is scandalous. I come here every month, so I hear these things. They say: "That man lives in a huge house like that, then he refuses to take proper care of his own garden." Well, I can't blame them.' She gave Mr Eckstein a defiant look.

'Bubie,' Mr Eckstein shouted with a tremor in his voice. 'Bubie, do something, or I won't be responsible for my actions.'

Mrs Eckstein came in from the kitchen.

'I told him,' Mrs Meerschwam said. 'I told him right to his face.' Then she laid the cans on the table one by one.

'Now you've heard it with your own ears,' Mrs Eckstein said. 'For years I've been telling you how they look at me because of that garden. And how do you suppose they'll look at us now? We're going to end up in prison. Oh my God, our names will be in the paper. We'll be in the paper, it will be the death of me.'

'No, no,' Mr Berk said, 'you have my solemn promise that neither of you will be in the paper.'

'The point is,' Mrs Meerschwam said, 'the point is that we never agreed that I would do the garden. That's why I don't do the garden, but the neighbours blame me because you don't hire a gardener. So I finally end up raking leaves anyway, and that with my back. And those twigs with the red berries on them that you planted in '85, did you know that I spend three days every fall picking those berries off the ground? And I warned you back in '85: don't do it, I said. Your whole garden will be covered in red berries. And who's going to pick them up?'

'Those aren't twigs with red berries,' Mr Eckstein shouted, 'those are Japanese shrubbery. Bubie, please tell her to go away and come back when I'm gone, otherwise I'm going to do something rash.'

Mr Eckstein was holding his cane out in front of him and shuffling towards Frida Meerschwam. 'Leave me alone,' he roared. 'leave me alone for once.'

Bubie screamed: 'I'm married to an old rapscallion, my family always said: "That man will be the death of you." And now they'll read all about it in the paper.'

Mr Eckstein was standing in front of Mrs Meerschwam now. He stared at her grimly for a few moments.

'*Raus*,' he shouted suddenly, '*raus*, before I do something irresponsible.'

'Shall I go?' Mrs Meerschwam asked.

She'd started coughing, and Mr Berk was pounding her on the back. 'You know how things are around here,' he whispered.

'Get out,' Mr Eckstein yelled, 'get out and take those preserves with you.' He brought his cane down on the cans.

'You'd better go,' Mrs Eckstein whispered, pushing three cans of lemon juice into Mrs Meerschwam's hands. 'And take these for your children. You can't get it any more, it's the best there is, believe me. I've had them tucked away all these years, but here, take them.'

'I warned you,' Mrs Meerschwam said. 'I warned you. Those twigs with the red berries on them, there'll be hell to pay. And they don't even look nice, if they looked nice that would be different. Do you know what the neighbours say? "Those twigs with the red berries on them keep multiplying and blocking out all our sun. And we get those red berries in the garden too. And we have children, and they put those red berries in their mouth. They think: oooh, nice!" And then they blame me for it, the neighbours. Because you're never around. You're off in Switzerland. "Oh," the neighbours say, "is he in Switzerland again? He has enough money to stay in Switzerland all year, but he doesn't have a gardener. No gardener." I've been meaning to tell you for years, but I never got the chance. They blame me for it. And I'm sick of it. Once you've left, I'm going to pull them out by the roots, all those twigs with the red berries on them.' Then she walked out with her shopping bag and the cans of lemon juice.

'Can that woman ever talk,' Berk said, once she was gone. 'Unbelievable.'

I got up and went to the kitchen. I was alone there with Elvira. She was staring at her bun. I didn't know what else to do but join her in staring at her half-eaten bun. 'You're sure quiet,' I said at last.

'I'm like that sometimes,' she said. Then she suddenly grabbed my head like it was a football and kissed me. I didn't mind her acting like my head was a football. If only she'd held my head like a football more often. But the timing was a little weird, and I realised then what people meant when they said they were afraid they were going crazy. I pulled away from her carefully. 'Maybe we should go in with the others.'

'Do you think I'm getting fat?' she asked.

'No,' I said, 'absolutely not. On the contrary.'

She looked at me thoughtfully, then wrote something in her notepad.

■ ■ ■

Broccoli was wearing a suit now too. He and Berk were combing Eckstein's hair, but they stopped when we came in. Everyone stared at us; actually, it was more like everyone was staring at Elvira. Especially Mr Eckstein. His eyes were really big. For the first time, they reminded me of the eyes of Derrick, that German detective on TV.

Elvira stared back at him with big eyes too. I'd never seen her stare at anyone like that before.

No one said a thing, until Mr Eckstein shouted: 'Aren't you going to introduce us?'

Broccoli brought Elvira over to Eckstein. She had to step over all the suitcases, which was almost impossible. 'This is Elvira,' he said.

Eckstein took Elvira's hand. Her hand shook in his grasp, but then everything shook in his grasp. 'What was the name again?' he said, and laughed.

'Elvira.' She said it herself now.

'That's a lovely name,' Eckstein said. He kissed her hand and let it go. There was still some dried blood on his lip.

'Ludwig, when will the taxi arrive?'

'In fifteen minutes,' Berk said.

'Then fetch us something from the *Keller*.'

'What do you want me to fetch from the *Keller*?'

'Champagne, *du Vollblutidiot*.'

'Is this really the right moment for that?' Berk asked.

'I'll throw the bottle at your head,' Mrs Eckstein said. 'I'm warning you, I'll throw it at your head.' But Mr Eckstein simply waved his cane and roared: 'A bottle from my *Keller*.'

All the excitement had made his lip split open again. Broccoli dabbed at it with his handkerchief. Berk went downstairs.

'This life offers little cause for celebration,' Eckstein said, 'so it's important to seize the slightest opportunity for a good drink, take it from me. I speak from experience. The slightest opportunity.' As he spoke, he stared at Elvira. And she stared back.

The cut on his lip was bleeding heavily. I was wondering whether they'd met somewhere before.

Berk came back with glasses and a huge bottle, one of those one-and-a-half-litre bottles of champagne.

'You do the honours,' Eckstein said, pointing to Broccoli.

Broccoli popped the cork. No one spoke, not even Mrs Eckstein. Eckstein raised his glass. All he said was: 'Champagne is completely harmless.' The next moment his glass was empty.

Broccoli turned on the radio. A man was singing: *'Ich bin so hässlich. Ich bin der Hass.'*

'Top up my glass,' Eckstein said.

'But you have a long journey ahead of you,' Berk said. It was a weak protest, though; Eckstein's glass was full before he'd finished saying it.

Now a woman was singing: *'Denn die Liebe, Liebe, Liebe, Liebe, die macht viel Spass, viel mehr Spass als irgendwas.'*

When the bottle was empty, Eckstein said: 'I hate emotional farewells at the station, so say goodbye to me right now.'

Mrs Eckstein had kept her mouth shut the whole time, but now she cried: 'The taxi will be here any moment. Are you trying to ruin us all? Do you want us to end up in prison?' Then she added: 'And the cutlery's going with.' As she said it, she slapped her three backpacks, like they were her horses.

'That's her new battle cry,' Broccoli whispered. '"The cutlery's going with."'

'Farewells at the station make me nervous,' Eckstein said.

Broccoli wasn't holding his handkerchief to Eckstein's lip any more; a thin trickle of blood was running down his chin. No one seemed to notice.

'Say something, Ludwig,' Mrs Eckstein cried.

Berk shrugged to show that he had nothing left to say, that it had been a long time since he'd had anything left to say.

'Go on,' Broccoli whispered, giving me a little shove. I almost tripped over a suitcase. I walked up to Eckstein and shook his hand. 'Have a good trip,' I said, but he wasn't paying much attention. Good thing too, because I didn't have much to say. He pounded me on the shoulder and said: 'I'm glad the camp site has been dismantled. If you ever need a woman, be sure to buy a good bed first. No one in their right mind would give themselves a hernia for the sake of love.'

They all looked at him like he was a prophet or a creature from outer space. Eckstein laughed loudly at his own joke. He raised his glass to Berk, but there was no champagne left. Berk filled it with cognac instead. Then Eckstein grabbed Berk by the necktie again and pulled him up close. But this time he hugged him, and whispered: '*Du Vollblutidiot.*'

We couldn't hear what he said to Broccoli. But we all saw him tug on Broccoli's ear when he was finished. He must have tugged pretty hard, because Broccoli's ear turned all red. I looked around to see if the others had noticed, but they were looking at the suitcases and backpacks. Mr Berk was humming. For the second time that night, I thought: They've all gone mad. Creatures from outer space landed last night and spread insanity throughout Amsterdam-South.

Once he'd let go of Broccoli, he turned to Elvira. Mr Berk had stopped humming; the only sound was the radio. Elvira walked over to him. Even before she got there, Eckstein grabbed her and pressed his forehead against hers. Then he just sat like that, without saying anything, for minutes it seemed. Broccoli was rubbing his ear and Mr Berk started humming again.

Mrs Eckstein broke the silence. 'But you don't even know her.'

Eckstein let Elvira go. 'That's irrelevant,' he said. 'Totally irrelevant.'

I looked at Elvira, but she was staring at the floor. There was blood on her chin, and I thought about how little it took to make someone look ridiculous.

Eckstein stood up and threw his champagne glass at the spot on the wall where he'd thrown two glasses of cognac the night before. 'Now you,' he shouted. After embracing Elvira like that, the blood was all over his face. To tell the truth, he seemed completely beside himself.

'My crystal,' Mrs Eckstein howled.

'We don't need it any more,' Mr Eckstein roared back. 'Smash them.' He glared at us like a general inspecting his troops.

Elvira was the first to step forward. She stood where Eckstein had been standing. There weren't many times that I'd found her as beautiful as I did at that moment. Not because of what she was wearing, or her lipstick, or the bloodstains or because she truly was beautiful. But because of the way she stood there, aloof and dignified. Precisely what we were not, but what we wanted to be most. All the rugby players and cameramen and film producers seemed to have rolled off her like water off a duck's back. That wasn't true, of course, but it seemed that way, and that was beautiful.

Mrs Eckstein jumped out in front of Elvira, between the glass and the wall. 'That's our best crystal,' she shouted. And then more quietly: 'Those glasses have almost never been used.' She looked at Elvira, but Elvira looked back at her as though she couldn't help it that she happened to be standing there, and that she was going to throw that glass against the wall.

Berk tried to pull Mrs Eckstein away. 'What's the point?' he said to Mrs Eckstein. 'We've known each other all these years, is this any way to say goodbye?'

The radio was playing one soppy German song after another.

'My crystal,' she said.

'You can buy new ones,' Berk said.

Then we heard something shatter. Broccoli had thrown his champagne glass against the wall. When we turned to look at him, we saw a little man with a moustache standing in the kitchen doorway, hat in hand.

THE LORELEI EXPRESS

*T*he little man cleared his throat a few times. Then he said: 'The back door was open.' He stepped into the room, still holding his hat.

'Good thing you showed up,' Mrs Eckstein said, 'finally.'

He nodded. Then he trundled up to Mr Eckstein, grabbed his hand and murmured: 'It's good to see you, I mean, in good health. Your wife told me about your sudden departure. I'm so sorry—'

'The less you say, the better,' Eckstein said.

'Don't mind him,' Mrs Eckstein said. 'He hasn't been himself lately.'

'That's understandable,' the little man said. He kept wiping the sweat off his forehead with the back of his hand. But it wasn't even that warm.

'That's Mrs Meerschwam's husband,' Broccoli whispered. 'He moonlights as a taxi driver. With the meter off, of course.'

'You smell like a rose and you are a rose,' we heard Mr Meerschwam say to Mrs Eckstein. She began weeping softly.

'My crystal,' she murmured. Was she really crying over her crystal? I didn't ask her. No one else did either.

'Here we go, Ludwig,' Eckstein said to Berk. 'Have Mrs Meerschwam clean it up, and give her a good tip. This place is a pigsty.' He pointed at the shards. 'And donate the preserves to a good cause.' The room was covered with cans Mrs Eckstein couldn't fit in her bags. In the corner, close to the fireplace, was a stack of at least fifty jars of apple sauce.

Then Eckstein said to us: 'Auspicious occasions should not go unmarked.'

Berk nodded. Elvira was leaning against the wall. She wrote something in her little red notepad.

'We really must be going,' the little man said. He'd picked up two suitcases. He was already wearing a backpack.

Berk put the hat back on Eckstein's head, but he knocked it off again right away. 'Keep in mind that I am not a clown,' he said quietly, 'and even if I am, then at least I'm still a clown with good taste.'

Berk picked up the hat. There were black smudges all over it from being kicked so often. 'But you'll catch a cold,' Berk said, and he tapped his head as if to point out that Eckstein had almost no hair.

'If I do, that's my own business,' Eckstein said.

Mr Meerschwam came back in. He picked up three more suitcases and trotted off with them. Like a skittish pack-mule.

'No hat then?' Berk said. He sounded rather sad. I realised he'd picked out the hat himself; maybe it had even been a present.

'No hat,' Eckstein said.

'And are all these people going with us?' Meerschwam asked. He pointed at us. The suitcases were in his car now.

'Yes, we're all going with,' Broccoli said.

'But they'll never fit in the car,' Meerschwam cried. 'And we're already running late.' He seemed like he was going to have a nervous collapse.

'Should I take my father's car?' Broccoli asked.

'No, no,' Berk said. 'Don't do that. Everything is to be sold.'

Mrs Eckstein came out of the bathroom. She was wearing a hat. It looked like an upside-down flowerpot. It had flowers stuck to it as well, but I think the moths had gotten to them.

'I got married in this,' she told me quietly, pointing at her headgear. I wondered whether anyone else had noticed what Mrs Eckstein had on her head, but no one was looking at her.

'We really have to go,' Meerschwam shouted. 'The train won't wait.'

Eckstein went to the front door. Berk followed him, but when he tried to take his arm, Eckstein turned around. He looked at the living room. 'So that was it,' he said. It sounded like he was talking to Elvira.

Berk led him out to the car. Mrs Eckstein came after them clutching four plastic bags from the Albert Heijn supermarket. 'This house never brought us anything but bad luck,' she murmured. Then came the skittish pack-mule, then us. Broccoli was bringing up the rear.

Eckstein sat in front, beside the driver. The same way he had the night before. Meerschwam held the back door open. As Mrs Eckstein was climbing in, he said: 'What a lovely hat you're wearing.' She started beaming. 'It's my wedding hat,' she said.

The pack-mule grinned. Then he slammed the door. Mr Berk was sitting next to Mrs Eckstein. He waved to us.

They drove off and left Elvira, Broccoli and me waiting for the cab Broccoli had ordered. There was still a little blood on Elvira's chin, but neither of us said anything about it. We waited for fifteen minutes. 'We're never going to make it,' Elvira said.

When the taxi finally arrived, Broccoli told me to get in front. Elvira laid her head in his lap, as though she wanted to catch some sleep.

'We're in a hurry,' Broccoli said.

'Who isn't?' the driver said.

■ ■ ■

They were still on the platform. The train hadn't come in yet. Mr Meerschwam was keeping an eye on the bags. He peered around nervously. Eckstein was handing out peppermints.

I noticed that Berk had brought the hat with him anyway, in a plastic bag. 'In case you should need it,' I heard him say. 'They say it's chilly in Zurich.'

There weren't many other passengers on the platform. A few old ladies for the cabin huts, obviously on their way to the mountains. The train to Zurich would not be crowded.

Mrs Eckstein paced the platform in her upside-down flowerpot. 'We arrived here like criminals, and that's how we're leaving. And it's all your fault,' she said, pointing at Eckstein. 'They'd roll over in their grave.'

'They don't have a grave,' Eckstein said calmly. 'Let that be of some comfort to you.' He put the last peppermint in his own mouth and said: 'And take off that bucket, otherwise I'm going to a separate compartment.'

But she wasn't listening to him any more. She walked over to the pack-mule and said: 'Be sure to give your wife my regards.' He nodded. Mrs Eckstein suddenly put down the four plastic bags she'd been clutching the whole time and said: 'I can't keep this up, I'm not fifteen any more. We're going to spend the rest of our lives in prison. We'll never have another moment's peace.'

'I'm sure it will all turn out fine,' the pack-mule said, 'and that hat of yours is absolutely stunning.' He wiped the sweat off his forehead again.

'Haute couture,' Mrs Eckstein said quietly, pointing at her hat. 'It's haute couture.'

Elvira was reading the timetables. Or pretending to. Every once in a while I looked at her, but she didn't look back. Eckstein shouted: 'I hurried for no good reason, that's the story of my life.'

Then the train pulled in. Mrs Eckstein yanked open the first door she saw and tried to climb in, but Berk yelled: 'Wait, I made reservations. First class. Car 176.'

Mr Meerschwam picked up the suitcases and started running,

without knowing where he was going. He ended up running in circles.

Berk stepped up to a conductor. 'Car 176?' he enquired.

The conductor pointed towards the locomotive. 'All the way at the front,' he said.

Mr Berk began running to the front of the train. The pack-mule ran behind him with the bags, followed by Mrs Eckstein. She'd taken off her hat.

Eckstein shouted: 'Ludwig, hold the door open, then the train can't leave.'

Elvira had been standing off to one side the whole time, but now she came up and walked beside Eckstein. She took his arm. They looked like they were attending a ceremony, that's how slowly they walked. Or going to a celebration. But Eckstein probably just couldn't walk any faster.

When we found car 176, Mrs Eckstein cried: 'The fifth suitcase, where's the fifth suitcase?'

Berk counted the suitcases. There were only four.

'We had five suitcases when we left,' Mrs Eckstein said. 'I'm sure. It's still on the platform.'

Mr Meerschwam ran back to where we'd been standing. 'Forget the suitcase,' Eckstein said. But Mrs Eckstein stepped out in front of a passing conductor. 'Please don't leave,' she said, 'my cutlery is still on the platform.' She tried to grab his hand, but the conductor walked on and said calmly: 'That's not my department.'

'My cutlery's still on the platform,' Mrs Eckstein shrieked.

Elvira was standing next to Mr Eckstein, and I saw him whisper something in her ear. No one was paying any attention, because they were all looking at the pack-mule running up with a Scottish tartan suitcase. 'It was still there,' he panted, 'it was still there.'

Mrs Eckstein tore the suitcase out of his hand.

They climbed aboard.

Mr Meerschwam seized Eckstein's hand and said: 'It's always

been an honour to work for you, you've done a great deal for our family—'

'All right already,' Eckstein said. Then he turned to Berk and said: 'Give him a good tip, Ludwig.'

We all went with them to the compartment, except for Mr Meerschwam. He stayed outside. There were seats for six people, but with all the suitcases, backpacks and plastic bags there was barely enough room for Mr and Mrs Eckstein.

Eckstein had settled down in a corner.

'Where are the passports?' he asked.

'Which passports?' Berk said.

'How many passports do we have?'

'I put all the papers in your inside pocket this morning,' Berk said.

Elvira was still standing in the passageway.

'They're going to arrest us at the border,' Mrs Eckstein shouted in a panic. 'They're going to arrest us at the border.'

'Please, trust me, everything is arranged,' Berk said, patting her on the shoulder. She laughed. 'Ha, that's right, all arranged for us to end up in prison.'

'Good luck,' Berk said, and he kissed her on the cheek. 'Good luck.'

She pulled some fruit out of a plastic bag.

'The families should have stuck together,' Eckstein said from his corner. 'If they had, we never would have wound up in Zurich. Never. And now go away, all of you.' He almost hugged Berk. Then he said to me: 'Michaël tells me you're friends. It was nice getting to know you, only a bit rushed.' Then he began rummaging in his inside pocket, without finding what he was looking for.

'Ewald Krieg,' he said finally. 'Ewald Krieg, wasn't it?'

I nodded.

'Give my regards to your family. Tell them "Eckstein sends his regards". They know who I am; tell them "Eckstein from the Bernard Zweerskade", then they'll know for sure.' He pulled two hundred-guilder notes out of his pocket and stuffed them in my hand, mumbling: 'Young people can always use some money.'

Then he turned to Broccoli. It looked like he wanted to lift Broccoli in his arms, but of course he couldn't. He said nothing to Elvira.

Berk said: 'The hat is in the baggage rack.'

Eckstein looked up. 'I can always give it to a passing itinerant,' he whispered.

We went and stood outside the open window of the compartment. Mrs Eckstein had found a washcloth and was busy dabbing at her husband's hands. 'You could get a disease here otherwise,' we heard her say.

The pack-mule whispered: 'Such sweet people.' But no one was paying any attention to him.

When his hands had been washed, Eckstein stood up and opened the window a little further.

'Call us when you get there,' Berk said.

Eckstein nodded. He looked at Elvira. Or did it only seem that way? Did I think everyone was looking at Elvira?

Mrs Eckstein was wearing her flowerpot again. She'd put a Thermos bottle on the little side table and was busy pumping coffee; the pump didn't work too well any more, so no coffee came out.

'I'll arrange everything,' Berk said. 'Don't worry.'

'*Vollblutidiot*,' was all Eckstein said. He turned to his wife. 'Bubie, take off that hat. I won't be seen with you like that.'

She'd eked a little coffee from out of the Thermos. 'Never,' she said. 'I'm keeping my hat on. It's haute couture, I have nothing to be ashamed of.'

'Take off the hat, Bubie,' Eckstein shouted.

Mrs Eckstein pulled an umbrella out of one of the plastic bags and opened it. It was red.

'I'm going to stay like this the whole trip,' she said.

We crowded closer to get a better look. Mrs Eckstein was sitting under the umbrella as though she expected rain in the train, or a little too much sun.

'I'm staying like this the whole trip,' she explained again. 'They can come and arrest me, I don't care.'

Berk pushed his way up to the window. 'That's taking things too far,' he said calmly. 'Now just close the umbrella.'

'I'm going to stay under it the whole time,' she stated, 'so I won't have to look at that man.' She pointed at Eckstein. He was still leaning out the window.

'The families should stick together,' he said, 'otherwise it's all over. Believe me, I could have built an empire if I'd been the only one doing the thinking. If no one else had stuck their noses into it, if I hadn't listened to those idiots' advice. Yes, Ludwig, that was great advice, thanks a million.'

He pointed at Broccoli. 'You'll be the last Eckstein with a bank account in Zurich. Don't forget that.'

Mrs Eckstein was still sitting under her umbrella. They say love has a face and a mouth and eyes, but then deceit must have a face and eyes and a mouth too. Deceit also exists only for those who are willing to see it, and there wasn't much I wanted to see, there was very little I wanted to see.

'Come on, close the umbrella,' Berk tried again. She actually did close the umbrella then, but not for long.

'Shit on your bald head, Ludwig,' she screamed. 'I shit on it.' Then the umbrella popped open.

Berk looked at us. 'She's joking,' he said, like he was apologising for her.

'Eat plenty of fresh fruit,' she yelled to Broccoli, 'otherwise your teeth will fall out. Apples. Apples are the best.'

'I don't like apples,' Broccoli said, but either she didn't hear him or she'd stopped listening. 'My wunderkind,' she cried, 'my wunderkind.' Then she looked at us. 'He's going to be a great professor.'

The train began moving. Very slowly, inch by inch. We stayed where we were. First, we saw Eckstein's head sticking out the window, then he pulled it back, and a few seconds later his cane appeared.

'Oh my God,' Berk said. But then the cane was pulled back and the Scottish tartan suitcase appeared. It balanced on the edge of the window for a few seconds, half in and half out of the compartment. Mr Berk started running after the train. The suitcase fell on to the platform. Right after that, Eckstein stuck his head out the window again. 'The cutlery stays here,' he roared. He roared more things too, but we couldn't hear him because the train was making too much noise. Finally, all we could see was his fist sticking out the window.

We walked over to Mr Berk. He was waiting for us with the suitcase in his hand. 'Let's go up to the end of the platform,' he said. 'Maybe he threw something else out of the train.'

And indeed, all the way at the end of the platform we found the red umbrella and four boxes of chocolate-cake mix.

'I hope they don't arrive in Zurich empty-handed,' Berk said. He picked up the umbrella.

We walked to the exit.

'What a woman,' Berk said quietly, 'what an impossible woman. But then, she's from the old Europe.' As if that explained everything, as if everyone from the old Europe was impossible.

'Could I offer you a ride home?' Meerschwam asked.

'No,' Berk said. 'We'll take the tram. We don't have much baggage.' He pressed a few banknotes in the man's hand.

'Tell your wife to come by soon,' Berk said. 'And tell her not to blame Mr Eckstein; a move like this can be rather taxing.'

The little man moved away, walking backwards, as if he was planning to bow before taking his leave.

'Where's Elvira?' Broccoli said.

We waited ten minutes for her to show up. I thought about how often I'd taken the same trip the Ecksteins were taking now. All the way down along the Rhine. And how we'd always waited at the window to see the Lorelei. 'We mustn't miss the Lorelei,' my father always said. But how were we supposed to tell the Lorelei from all those other mountains?

'Where were you?' Broccoli asked.

'I was looking for something,' Elvira said. She had a box of chocolate-cake mix in her hand.

Broccoli shook his head. 'Who goes scavenging on platform 7b? Can you figure that?'

'We deserve a cup of coffee,' Berk said.

We walked over to Smits Koffiehuis. It was nine-thirty in the morning, on a truly lovely autumn day.

Part Four

Q-TIP

'They're in Cologne now,' Berk said. We'd been sitting at a table by the window for the last two hours, not saying a word, just looking at the tour boats. It seemed to make him sad that they were already in Cologne. But maybe it was just the morning, the sun, the water or the coffee. The coffee was pretty awful.

Elvira was doodling in her notepad, and Broccoli still looked like he'd spent the night in the refrigerator.

'You can't go on staying at the Bernard Zweerskade,' Berk said. 'It all has to happen fast. We're in a hurry.'

'I know,' Broccoli said.

I thought about the people who had urged me to think about the future, especially my own. I hadn't thought about that for the last few months, and here at this table that seemed the only right way to go about it.

'I'll move to a hotel,' Broccoli said.

'That's craziness,' Berk said. 'Your father would never have approved.' He rattled the spoon around in his cup, but it was empty.

'You can sleep at my place,' Elvira said.

They looked at each other, but Broccoli didn't say anything. I didn't mind Broccoli going to live with her, in fact, I thought it would be convenient.

'When I was eight,' Elvira said, 'I wanted to be a saint. I went to church every day after school, even though my father hated it – he hated churches. There was a man at the church who said: "Come with me, I'll make you a saint. Come on and be a saint."'

'Why did you want to become a saint?' I asked.

'I thought saints were the most beautiful thing in the world,' Elvira said. 'The way they looked, the way they acted, how they lived their lives. They were the most beautiful thing there was.'

'I never wanted to be a saint,' Broccoli said. 'Never for a moment have I considered becoming a saint.'

Berk stood up. 'I have to get moving, it's going to be a busy day,' he said. He picked up the Scottish tartan suitcase.

We watched him walk to the tram. He was walking rather crookedly. I wondered what he was going to do with the cutlery.

'One of us has to become world-famous,' Broccoli said suddenly. 'One of us has to make it.' He looked at us as if he expected us to decide right then and there which of us that would be.

Elvira laughed. 'I don't understand men at all,' she said.

'What about women?' Broccoli asked.

'Probably not either. So, do you want to move in with me?' She asked it the way you'd ask someone if they'd like an ice-cream cone.

'Sure,' Broccoli said. 'See much of that neurologist these days?'

'Almost never,' she said. 'He's completely absorbed in his work.' She stood up, and I remembered how she'd stood in the Ecksteins' house a few hours earlier, the champagne glass in her hand, ready to smash it. When it's been a late night, I sometimes shatter a glass in the corner of my own living room. By way of salute. The way other people drink to absent friends.

Broccoli paid the bill. I resolved to pay for Broccoli some day, the way he'd paid for me. And if he wasn't around, I'd pay for someone else. It's better to pay for others than to have them pay for you. Deceit, I believe, works in just the opposite way. It's better to be deceived than to deceive. That probably also goes for murder.

We walked down the Damrak and along the Rokin, and on until we reached the Ceintuurbaan.

'Let's go for Chinese,' Broccoli said.

'Chinese?' Elvira asked.

'Chinese,' Broccoli said. 'Sin Ta Wah on the Scheldestraat: the best Chinese restaurant in Amsterdam. That's what the sign says. I should write a book about Chinese restaurants. My father is wild about Chinese food. He's wild about all things Chinese.'

'That may be overstating it a bit,' Elvira said.

We walked to the Scheldestraat. We ordered egg foo young to take away. Then we went by the Venice ice-cream parlour. They were still open. They closed at a certain point every autumn, and only opened again in the spring. I thought about how often I'd been here, but never with Broccoli and Elvira.

We took a table inside.

'Your father is a strange man,' Elvira said.

'Yes,' Broccoli said, 'he's a strange man.' Broccoli was still wearing that suit, the one I'd never seen before. He looked like he had to go to a party later on. I had just suggested to them that we go to Venice. The city, that is.

'What would we do in Venice?' Broccoli asked.

'The same thing we do here,' I said.

'Well then, that's OK,' Elvira said.

And it was, because everywhere we went we did the same thing we did in Amsterdam. And even when we were no longer together, I went on doing the same thing. It was a way of life that suited me just fine. Wandering around a city, in no hurry and with no particular goal, like a travelling salesman with nothing to sell.

We drank iced coffee, except for Elvira. She wanted something more complicated, with half a peach. We had to wait half an hour for it, and when she'd tasted it, she said: 'This peach has been lying around since the seventies.'

There was absolutely no reason to think about what had happened that morning. The ice cream was good, just like the afternoon. Later on, we'd go to her place. The only thing I wished for fervently was that she wouldn't serve us any more artichoke liqueur. But as wishes go, that was a minor, relatively easy one to make come true.

'So, are you happy now?' she asked.

I looked at her in amazement.

She smiled. 'Only kidding.'

'No,' I said. 'It's a good question.' She wiped her hands on her bare leg.

We hadn't drunk any artichoke liqueur, but we did get drunk. And at the bottom of the containers of egg foo young we'd found cat hair. Not one, no, whole clumps of it. When Broccoli called Sin Ta Wah to complain, a woman told him: 'Oh, please accept our apologies, but we have mice.'

After that, Elvira jerked us off. First Broccoli, then me. We'd wanted to go to bed with her, but she said that was impossible. That she was really sorry, but today there was no way. And then she started talking again about how we should buy a picnic basket, a big one with real silverware. And while she was going on about that picnic basket, she unbuttoned her blouse. That's how it went. We didn't understand at all, but that's how it went.

I wasn't embarrassed. Everything Elvira did was natural. Or seemed natural. To be embarrassed you have to have the feeling that something isn't completely natural. Elvira had the gift of making everything she did look like it was the most normal thing in the world, as if she'd been doing it for a hundred years. People have since told me that that is a dangerous gift.

I looked at Broccoli and at her hand. I found it breathtaking.

Not because she was so beautiful, or because love is so beautiful. The first time you see a cow being milked is probably breathtaking too. Even if you're a cow yourself. My friend, the chairman of the Association for Geniuses, was being jerked off by the girl I would have liked to love, if I'd only known how.

Then she came and sat on me. On my stomach, with her back to my face. I caressed her back, and later she turned around and I kissed her navel. I had never kissed a woman's navel before, but I'd never kissed a man's navel either. Navels are strange things. I clean my own navel once a week with a Q-tip. I'm afraid that otherwise it will start stinking; besides, you never know when someone's going to kiss your navel.

Broccoli was lying next to me, his hands clasped behind his head. He looked like he was dreaming. Maybe he was thinking about Elvira as Lady Macbeth. Or about his parents, or about the girl whose name his father had wanted to know so badly.

Maybe I admired Elvira too much. Apparently, it's not good to do that. Admiration usually ends up turning into contempt. I even signed a contract with someone once in which we agreed to do our best to disguise the contempt we felt for each other, for the last few months we had to spend together. It would have been better for me to hide my admiration for Elvira, but I couldn't do that very well. Not as well as I can now.

I was embarrassed that it took so long, so I pressed like I was having a baby. Finally, she wiped her hand on her bare leg and said: 'So, are you happy now?'

It was such a weird question that all three of us had to laugh. Not as hard as that one night, but still. 'I don't know,' I said.

Broccoli said: 'When you go to church to pray and you're finished, God doesn't ask: "Are you happy now?"'

'That's true,' I said. 'God never asks that.'

'So I should be able to ask it if I want,' Elvira said. She was lying between us.

'I don't understand men at all,' she said quietly.

'And what about women?' Broccoli asked.

She shook her head. She probably remembered having this conversation before.

Broccoli and I got up. We wanted to go to the all-night deli. We couldn't be sure she had a couple of bottles of artichoke liqueur tucked away somewhere, but we weren't taking any chances.

Elvira lay on the bed without moving. She said: 'There's a leak in the kitchen, but I think it's starting here too.'

At the deli Broccoli said to me: 'Pretty soon I'm going to take her to America. It's no good around here.' He had a bottle of wine in his hand.

I wondered whether Elvira wanted to be taken anywhere. I couldn't imagine it. Although, in the end, that's exactly what most of us do want, to be taken away by someone or something, even by God if necessary.

When we got back, Elvira was still lying on the bed. Staring at the ceiling, she said: 'We'd better hang some umbrellas above the bed, otherwise we're going to get wet.'

OPERATION BRANDO

*W*e climbed the steps to Mr Berk's house. The staircase smelled of cat piss. Elvira was carrying a bunch of flowers. 'Are we there yet?' she asked every time we came to a door.

Berk had invited us to dinner. 'To discuss the situation,' he'd apparently told Broccoli.

When we finally got to Berk's attic door, Elvira asked: 'Does he really live here?'

There was a handwritten sign on the door saying 'Berk'.

He seemed delighted to see us. He brought out the folding chairs. Berk must have been well into his seventies, but it looked like he'd never moved out of his student flat. The place had never been spruced up. There were newspapers lying everywhere, in one corner were shelves containing books and, strangely enough, also two chunks of cheese and a salami.

'They need a place to dry,' Berk said when he saw me staring.

Elvira gave him the flowers. He didn't know whether to kiss her or not, so he just kissed her hand. He went looking for a vase but couldn't find one, so he divided the flowers over three empty wine bottles. The Scottish tartan suitcase was standing by the door.

'Could I offer you a glass of wine?' he asked us. He pulled three glasses out of a cardboard box. It wouldn't have surprised me to come across textbooks that had been lying open at the same page for the last fifty years.

'Your parents arrived in one piece,' Berk said, 'and they send their regards.' He'd filled the glasses to the rim. Elvira looked at him attentively.

Three identical suits were hanging from a nail on the wall. Just back from the cleaner's, from the looks of it.

'They're in Zurich now, but your mother doesn't want to stay. She wants to go to Mexico.' Berk fell silent, as though he wanted this announcement to sink in properly. But what did we care about Mexico?

'Why Mexico?' Broccoli asked at last.

'She wants to start a hotel there.'

I looked at the suitcase full of cutlery. I noticed then that there were three mousetraps lined up under the radiator.

'I had her on the phone. She said Switzerland was crawling with hotels. She said: "They'd laugh at me with my hotel." Besides, she doesn't believe in the discretion of Swiss banks.'

'Why not?' Broccoli asked.

'She didn't say. She just doesn't believe in it, and nothing will change her mind. Your father is at his wits' end. He doesn't want to go to Mexico. He says Mexico will be the death of him.'

Broccoli chewed his gum. He didn't say a thing.

'I figured maybe you could talk to her,' Berk said. He pulled a telephone from under a pile of newspapers. It was one of those old-fashioned ones. He dialled a number. We heard him mention a room number. Then he handed the phone to Broccoli.

Elvira winked. I winked back.

'No, you're not going to end up in prison,' we heard Broccoli say, 'they won't find you there, so don't worry, no, don't worry.'

He kept repeating it, but it didn't help. From the sound of it, his mother was very worried.

Mr Berk began cutting salami. 'It's real Hungarian,' he said.

'Why does he keep sausage in his bookcase?' Elvira whispered.

'It seems that's the best place for it to dry,' I said.

'Oh, OK,' she whispered. Then Broccoli said: 'But there are already lots of hotels in Mexico. They don't need your hotel there either.'

Berk sighed. He handed out slices of salami. He said to Elvira: 'That's why I never got married. Allergic to marriage, from the age of two.'

She nodded. As though she agreed with him, as though she'd also been allergic to marriage from the age of two.

Broccoli said: 'Just stay put. It's a good place for you. You can always go to Mexico. Mexico isn't going anywhere.' Then he hung up.

'She won't listen, will she?' Berk said. He slid the telephone back under the pile of newspapers, as if he was afraid of it getting dusty.

'No,' Broccoli said, 'she won't listen.'

'Would you kids like to eat here, or shall we go somewhere else?' Berk asked.

'Somewhere else,' Elvira said.

Berk held the plate of sausage out to Broccoli. 'Real Hungarian,' he said proudly. 'Take a whiff.'

Broccoli took a whiff. Then Berk laid his hand on Broccoli's shoulder and said: 'She's always had it in her. It had to come out sometime.' He didn't say exactly what had always been in her and had to come out. We didn't ask him either. He helped Elvira with her coat.

'Old Eckstein was quite taken with you,' he said to Elvira.

At the front door of Berk's building, we stopped. No one wanted to be the one to decide where we were going to eat.

'I know a little bar that serves food,' Mr Berk said at last. 'Cheap, but still edible.'

The bar was next to the Rialto theatre. We stopped in front to see what was playing.

'We should start looking like Marlon Brando,' Broccoli said, while we were perusing the pictures under the marquee.

'Yes,' I said, 'we should try to do that.'

Berk and Elvira were already in front of the bar, looking at the menu in the window.

'What kind of coat is that she's wearing?' Broccoli said. 'Look at it, it looks like it's made of feathers.' Both of us looked at Elvira's coat. It was new.

'You're right,' I said, 'it looks like feathers.'

'That's taking things too far,' Broccoli said. 'Feathers. I bet that was the neurologist's idea. A coat made of feathers. Neurologists are all raving lunatics.'

Once we were in the bar, Broccoli asked: 'Did the neurologist give you that coat?'

She laughed. 'No,' she said, 'I bought it for myself.'

'But it's made of feathers,' Broccoli said.

'Not real ones.'

Berk leaned over for a closer look. He even stuck his nose in the coat and sniffed. 'No,' he said, 'they look like feathers, but they're not.'

'Your Argentine boyfriend dealt in feathers, didn't he?' I said.

'No,' she said, 'he dealt in fur.'

Berk ordered wine. He was in unusually high spirits.

'We've decided to look like Marlon Brando,' I told them.

'Then let's drink to Marlon Brando,' Elvira said.

We all raised our glasses. 'To Marlon Brando,' we said.

'The young Brando, or the old Brando?' Berk asked.

'Both,' Broccoli said. 'It's our key focus at the moment. It's still a secret, but we can tell the two of you. Operation Brando is the name of a hitherto top-secret project. It has absolute priority. If we succeed, we'll be heroes. If not, we will know the meaning of humility for the rest of our lives.'

'Will there be any cosmetic surgery involved?' Elvira asked.

'At this stage, we rule nothing out,' Broccoli said. 'In any case, our hair needs to get thinner.'

'That's because we're placing a bit more emphasis on the older Brando,' I explained.

'We've already been in contact with a hair specialist,' Broccoli went on. 'He's prescribed a hormone treatment that will make our hair thinner and allow it to take on precisely Brando's colour.'

'The Brando of *Last Tango in Paris*,' I said, 'that's the Brando we're shooting for.'

'But it has to remain an absolute secret; if the press gets wind of this, we're ruined,' Broccoli said.

'You can count on me,' Berk said.

'Me too,' Elvira said.

'It's a worldwide secret organisation. All over the world, people are in the process of becoming Marlon Brando, or they already are. But they're keeping it a secret until the time is ripe.'

'And how do all of you stay in contact?' Elvira asked.

'With our shoes,' Broccoli said. 'Once you succeed in joining our organisation, you receive a shoe with a telephone in it. That way we can stay in touch at all times. It will be a revolution, comparable to the French and Russian ones. But our programme is simpler, that's our strength. This world needs more Marlon Brandos. That's all.'

'And you call each other with your shoes?' Elvira asked.

'Yes,' Broccoli said. 'Our shoes are telephones. But once again, absolute secrecy is required. Otherwise we will retaliate. Our organisation is hard, but fair.'

The soup came. I looked at Elvira and I believed everything we had told her. She stirred her soup.

'I've got such a craving for snails,' she said. 'Do you think they serve snails here? In Argentina I ate snails all the time. Do you eat snails here too?'

Berk shook his head.

In the middle of dinner Broccoli suddenly took off his shoe

and held it to his ear. 'Hello,' he said, 'this is Brando 4. Could I speak to Brando 8?'

Elvira took her shoe off, held it to her ear and said: 'This is Brando 8, come in, Brando 4.'

'No,' Broccoli said, 'you're not Brando 8, you're Brando 12.'

Elvira laughed so hard that her shoe fell in her soup. It splattered all over the place.

'What should I do?' Elvira yelled. 'What should I do?'

'Have the waiter fish it out,' Berk said. Then he started laughing himself, really hard. We'd never seen him laugh like that before. 'Waiter, there's a shoe in my soup,' he kept saying. Finally, we went to pieces too, and I had to think about Elvira, how we'd been lying on her bed and how she'd asked me: 'So, are you happy now?'

The other customers were looking at us, but we didn't care.

Finally, the waiter came over. 'I see there's a shoe in your soup,' he said.

'Yes,' Elvira said, 'you're quite right.'

'Shall I remove it?'

'If you'd be so kind,' Elvira said.

Elvira's shoe came back with the main course.

'It's clean,' she said, 'but it still smells like fish soup.'

A few weeks later, when I was alone with her, she suddenly took off her shoe and said: 'Here, smell it, it still smells like fish soup.'

'That's not fish soup,' I said, 'those are your foot juices.'

'My feet don't smell like fish soup,' she said. 'What a thing to say. Here, smell this shoe, does it smell like fish soup? Now smell this one, fish soup, right?'

The other shoe didn't smell too great either, but I had to admit that it didn't smell like fish soup.

'Now let me smell your shoes,' Elvira said.

'No way,' I said, 'I'm not going to do that. My shoes didn't fall in the fish soup. And I don't let just anyone smell my shoes. I have my limits.'

'You're going to let me smell your shoes,' Elvira said, 'or I'll never see you again.' I let her smell just one shoe. She put her nose all the way down in it. 'I love real human smells,' she said. 'At least then you know you're alive.'

'But you know that anyway,' I said. Elvira thought I was missing the point entirely.

When I think about Elvira these days, I often think about her feet and whether they didn't smell just a little like fish soup.

'The house will probably be sold this week,' Berk said when he'd finished howling over Elvira's shoe. 'Mrs Meerschwam started emptying the place today. She's moaning and groaning something fierce. If you don't want your things to fall into her hands, you'd better be quick.'

Broccoli nodded.

'Is your house big enough to store a few things?' Berk asked.

'My house is almost empty,' Elvira said. 'I've sold everything.'

'I never did understand why people surround themselves with furniture,' Berk said. I thought about his attic room and the sausage in the bookcase.

The waiter brought our cognac.

'Well then, to Eckstein,' Berk said. He'd taken off his jacket.

'To Operation Brando,' Broccoli said. 'I've dedicated my life to this operation. From this evening on, we are co-conspirators. If you betray our confidence, the organisation will find you, no matter how far you run.'

'Precisely,' Berk said, 'quite right.' And Elvira said: 'To the conspiracy. May it never be betrayed.'

'I met your father on a trash can,' Berk said. His glass was empty and he'd loosened the top few buttons of his shirt. He smelled a little bit like the Hungarian salami he'd had us take a whiff of earlier. 'I always used to sit on the trash can in front of my house. Your father walked past all the time, because we lived in the same neighbourhood. Then one evening he stopped and said: "Why are you always sitting on that trash can?" "I'm waiting for my daughter," I told him. "I can't relax up there until she gets home."

'We talked for a while, and finally I invited him up. I could tell he didn't feel like sitting on the trash can. I lived where I live now. We walked up all those stairs. He obviously wasn't used to that. When we finally got there, he asked me: "So what do you do for a living?"

"'I'm a bookkeeper, a freelance bookkeeper. I work at home," I told him.

"'Maybe you could do some work for me," he said. I made him some coffee. I used to talk to people all the time while I was sitting on the trash can, but no one had ever wanted to come up before.

"'So where's this daughter of yours?" he asked me.

"'She'll be here," I said. "She'll be along. She's not very punctual." That evening the two of us waited until my daughter came home. My daughter was very pretty, but all fathers say that, I know. Eckstein thought she was pretty too. I could tell right away.

"'Could I take her to the Lido sometime?" he asked me.

"'Don't ask me," I said.

'They started seeing each other regularly, I believe. I never asked about it. After all, by that time I was working for Eckstein. First from my house, later at his. He'd fixed up a room for me.

'One afternoon I came home from the supermarket. The neighbour lady stopped me at the corner. "Oh, Mr Berk," she said, "don't go down there, it's awful, don't go any further." She tried to stop me, but I got around her. She ran after me. "Listen to me first," she said. Then I saw my daughter. She was lying at more or less the same spot where I always waited for her. All she was wearing was a dress. I took off my coat and put it over her, because it was cold that day. There were people standing around us, but I didn't see them. I took her head in my hands. "Say something," I said, "please, just say something." But she didn't say anything.

'"She jumped," the neighbour lady said. "I heard it. At first I thought someone had thrown a garbage bag out on the street. I ran downstairs right away."

'Then the police came. "I can't tell you what happened," I said. "You'll have to ask my daughter."

'"Your daughter won't be telling us anything," they said. They had to do tests on her first, which is why it took a week before she could be buried. I didn't know who her friends were, so I didn't invite anyone. Eckstein was the only one who came, on a motorcycle. "Hop on the back," he said. We were already late, so he drove like a maniac. I was afraid we'd get to the cemetery too late, but we were right on time. At first the watchman didn't want to let us in on that motorcycle, but Eckstein yelled, "This is an emergency!" and drove right past him. When we got to the grave I was so confused that I forgot to take off my helmet. Good thing too, because I hadn't brought my yarmulke. The grave-digger ticked his finger against his forehead a few times. At first I thought that was part of the ceremony, but he was referring to my helmet. I was going to take it off, but Eckstein hissed: "We have to leave them on, otherwise we'll be bareheaded, that's not allowed here." So we just stood there with our helmets on.

'The rabbi asked if we wanted to say a few words.

'"No," I said, "you do it. That's what you went to school for, isn't it?"

'I never spoke another word to Eckstein about my daughter. The year after that he got married, and he asked me to be his witness. The only thing was, he never wanted to come up to my attic room any more.

'After that, I stopped seeing most people, because there was no reason for me to sit out on the trash can any more.' He stood up.

'I've got a lot to do,' he said. 'I have to see to business.' He laid some money on the table and just walked away, as though he'd suddenly realised what a hurry he was in.

We ran out after him.

A LETTER FROM MRS MEERSCHWAM

*W*e followed Berk to his front door. Maybe we were expecting him to offer us another slice of his Hungarian salami. But all he said was: 'I've got a lot to do. It was a wonderful evening.'

For just a second, he laid his hand on Broccoli's head. 'I hope they don't go to Mexico; the heat wouldn't be good for your father.'

'No,' Broccoli said, 'not for my father.'

Berk shook Elvira's hand. 'Get in touch with me soon, then we can finish up our business.'

When he was gone, I asked her: 'What kind of business is that?'

'Nothing important,' Elvira said. 'In fact, it's completely unimportant.'

I thought about Operation Brando. For the first time it seemed I had a clearly defined goal in life. When people asked about my plans for the future, I'd no longer be at a loss.

But no matter what happened, we'd never end up like our parents. Hanging around the bar at the racquet club, waiting for the wind to die down. And we would never take a suitcase full of cutlery with us on a trip. Operation Brando ruled out all that.

Broccoli wanted to go to the Bernard Zweerskade. Most of the furniture had already been removed. On the kitchen table we found a letter from Mrs Meerschwam.

Michaël!
Your room is a pigsty! Even your father's room was never such a pigsty as yours is at this moment. I have a bad back, but please don't leave your parents in the lurch at a time like this. After all, we're not alone in this world, even though you probably think differently. If your room isn't cleared out by Tuesday, I'm going to put it all out with the garbage. I've already called the Salvation Army.
Frida Meerschwam.

Broccoli folded the note carefully and put it in his back pocket. 'Letters from Frida Meerschwam are a rare item,' he explained, 'very rare.'
We walked through the house like prospective buyers. There were still all kinds of cans in the living room, but the furniture was gone. So were the jars of apple sauce. It looked weird: an empty room with only cans in it. Broccoli's room hadn't changed.
'Mrs Meerschwam,' Broccoli said, 'carries a horrible secret around with her.'
'Oh yeah?' I said.
'Everyone carries horrible secrets around with them,' Elvira said.
'Mrs Meerschwam's secret is unusually horrible. Do you want to hear about it?'
We nodded.
'Mrs Meerschwam has rabbit blood on her hands. When I was

six, my parents bought me a rabbit, so I wouldn't be alone. I was crazy about that rabbit, and the rabbit was crazy about me. It was what they call a selfless love. Mrs Meerschwam imagined she was finding rabbit hairs everywhere, and that the rabbit made her sneeze. One morning, with the aid of the vacuum cleaner, she snuffed my rabbit. When I came home from school, my rabbit was in a plastic bag. I wasn't allowed to look. I looked, of course. From that moment on I knew that deep inside Mrs Meerschwam a monster lurked, a monster whose aggression was focused primarily on helpless creatures, like rabbits. I thought you two should know.'

'Are you going to move tonight?' Elvira asked.

'How do you know she did it with the vacuum cleaner?' I asked.

'I don't want to talk about it,' Broccoli said. 'I'm not some creepy little kid who goes around drooling over grisly details.' Broccoli looked around. 'Yes, I'm going to move out tonight.'

'So who's actually moving in?'

'I don't know; Berk's arranging everything,' Broccoli said. He put some things in a bag, but then took them out and replaced them with other things. A white bathrobe, a pair of jeans, a badminton racket, an empty pocket diary from 1974.

Elvira lay down on the bed.

'So you're never coming back here?' she asked.

'I don't think so,' Broccoli said. 'The place is going to be sold. That's why Mrs Meerschwam called the Salvation Army. But, strictly between us, Mrs Meerschwam calls the Salvation Army every spring. If I hadn't been here the house would have been empty long ago. I've protected my parents from many a disaster, but I don't think they realise that.'

'But why does she call the Salvation Army?' I asked.

Broccoli was sitting down, but now he sprang up in a rage.

'Why? Because she's not in her right mind, don't you understand anything? What person in their right mind would attack an innocent rabbit with a vacuum cleaner? What person in their right mind calls the Salvation Army every spring to clear out the homes of innocent people? She called the Gospel of Light Mission, the Red Cross, the charity organisation of the Liberal Jewish Community. And now that we're on the subject, what normal person would complain about little red berries in the garden, as if those red berries were doing something awful to her? And who eats a whole box of bonbons every day? Do you know anyone who eats a box of bonbons every day, and who's also capable of spending three hours going on about little red berries in the garden? Do you? Answer me!'

I had to admit that I knew no one like that.

Behind a box, Broccoli found four crushed lychee nuts. He showed them to us.

'Will you always live with me?' Elvira asked.

'I don't know,' Broccoli said absent-mindedly. 'I don't know.'

She tossed him the husk of a lychee nut. 'What else did your father say to you on the phone?'

'Oh, just things in general,' he said. 'Nothing special. Advice, general advice, an old man's lessons in life.' His bag was full now.

'What about the rest?' Elvira asked, looking around.

'That will come later,' he said. 'Most of it's junk anyway.'

I remembered how Elvira had looked in her sleep that night I'd pulled the condom out of her. And how that one morning she'd told us about wanting to be a saint when she was eight. And I wondered whether I would ever have the nerve to ask her: 'Why once? Why not sixty-eight times, or never, or four hundred and eighteen times? And why a saint?'

It was too late to catch a tram, and Broccoli didn't feel like taking a taxi. 'Let's walk,' he said, 'it's a lovely night.'

When we got to the Leidsestraat, Broccoli said: 'Look, there's Lopatin.' Lopatin was standing at the window of the Bruna bookshop. We recognised him right away: his jeans that were always sagging off his butt, his black shoes without laces, his moustache, his bald spot. We started to walk on, but he'd already seen us.

'I don't really want to talk to him,' Elvira whispered.

He came up behind us. ''t Haantje is closed,' he shouted. ''t Haantje is closed down.'

We stopped.

'It'll open again,' Broccoli said.

'No,' Lopatin said, 'it's been closed for weeks.'

'So where do you eat breakfast these days?' I asked.

'Here and there,' he said. He pointed to the Febo snack bar up the street and to an ice-cream parlour. He pulled a little yellow bottle from his coat pocket. 'They've given me new medication.'

'That's great,' Broccoli said.

'But how can I look at Mimi now? 't Haantje is closed.'

'They'll open a new Haantje,' Broccoli said, but Lopatin shook his head.

'There isn't going to be any new Haantje. They started fighting on a Saturday afternoon. I was sitting where I always sit, and there were three ladies there from Twente, from out of town. Then they started punching each other. The owner and his son-in-law.

'"Stop abusing my daughter," the owner yelled. And the son-in-law screamed: "You crook, you old penny-pincher."

'Everything was flying all over the place: egg salad, cheese, buns, a Thermos bottle. The ladies from Twente started screaming like stuck pigs. I can't take that much noise.

'Mimi ran out in the street and yelled: "Help, somebody, they'll kill each other!"

'No one tried to help. Instead, the man who lives across the street yelled: "Your sandwiches taste like window putty!"

'"But they're killing each other," Mimi screamed.

'The ladies from Twente ran away without paying. Then the owner came outside. He was covered in blood and egg salad. There was a fork sticking out of his arm.

'"It was about time," the man from across the street said.

'Then the police showed up. Everyone had to get in the van. I did too. The owner still had that fork sticking in his arm.

'I said: "I can't go along, I have to lick envelopes at the bank. It's my profession, it's what I get paid for."

'"Then they'll have to find somebody else to lick envelopes today," the policeman said.

''t Haantje has been closed ever since.'

Elvira pulled us along after her.

''t Haantje will open again,' Broccoli shouted as we moved away. Lopatin shook his head.

'No,' he said, ''t Haantje is gone. Mimi is gone, you guys are gone, the only thing left is the envelopes.' Then he went back to the window of the Bruna. I suddenly remembered him telling us that he always took *Playboy* to bed with him.

GALANI, THE FUR KING

'*W*elcome to your new home,' Elvira said.

We could hear water dripping on the kitchen floor, but we ignored it.

Broccoli put his bag in a corner. There were more bags there, and baskets and backpacks. It was the kind of place where you lived out of a suitcase.

Elvira lay down on the bed right away, her hands clasped behind her head. Hadn't she once said that, of all attitudes needed to get through life, lying was by far the most pleasant?

I sat down on a suitcase. We hadn't turned on the lights, there was enough light from the street. There were no curtains left in the house. Taken away. Or sold. Or torn down in a fit of rage.

'I used to work in a restaurant that seated two hundred people,' Elvira said, her eyes fixed on the ceiling like she was trying to keep out the leak. 'The owner was Chinese. He had seven restaurants. After three weeks he gave me my own section to wait on. And after a while I noticed that some people always sat in my section. That's how I met Galani.'

I looked at Broccoli. He was asleep.

'He used to come in alone and read the paper while he ate. One day I started talking to him. I don't remember what I said, something trivial, like why he came in there every day. I don't know why I started talking to him either. I must have been bored.

'"Because I like the food," he said.

'"You never talk to anyone," I said.

'He put down his fork. "I don't believe people wait on tables because they're in need of conversation," he said. I thought that was a strange thing to say.

'The next day I asked him what he did for a living. I thought he was kind of nice.

'"I work at home," he said. "I sit around in fur all day."

'"What do you mean, sit around in fur?" I asked.

'"I deal in fur coats," he said. "If you see a fur coat in this town, there's a good chance that it came from me." He laid his business card on the table. "Most people call me by my surname."

'I refilled his glass, I think. In any case, I tried to make it look like I was hard at work.

'"You don't say much," I said.

'"Forty-seven-year-olds who act like they're still eighteen are pitiable at best," Galani said. "Besides, I like people who don't say much."

'"Why's that?"

'"When you sit around in fur all day, you have plenty of time to think."

'"And what have you come up with?" I asked. I acted like I was wiping his table. The boss kept a really close eye on the waitresses. I thought the things he said were sort of funny, not like most people who came in.

'"That it's important to die on time," Galani said, "not too early and not too late. That's how it is with everything. When something comes along too early, it's no use to you; things that come too late are no use either. Things should come on time. Maybe that's why I appreciate people who don't say much. They can't come along too late or too early. For them, there's always a table waiting."

'I remember that making a big impression on me, because I told a girlfriend who worked at the restaurant about it too.

'After that, I didn't talk to Galani for a week, even though he kept coming in every day.

'One Friday, when it was very busy – Friday was always the busiest day – he said: "I have to go to Los Angeles for a few days, I have a big customer there. You can come along, if you like. I know that sounds funny, but I don't know how else to put it. If I could express myself better, I probably wouldn't have started dealing in fur coats."

'"I'm sorry," I said, "I can't. I hope you're not disappointed."

'"Of course I'm disappointed," Galani said. "People who are no longer capable of disappointment have turned to stone. I hope to postpone the onset of my own petrification for a few years. But I hope to see you when I get back."

'After he came back from Los Angeles, he told me he was getting sick of fur coats. He wanted to do something different. I asked him what, but he didn't know. A few days later he said he was tired of all the chatter.

'"What chatter?" I asked him. He sat in the same corner every day, and he almost always ordered the same thing.

'"The chattering of people who buy fur coats," he said. "And often as not, they don't come by themselves. They bring their whole family along. And they chatter something unbelievable."

'Another girl who waited on tables told me: "That's Galani, the fur-coat dealer, the one you were talking to."

'"How do you know him?" I asked.

'"Everyone knows him," she said. "He's notorious." But she wouldn't tell me why.

'One evening Galani told me he was going to start producing movies. I thought he was joking, but he said: "First, I was the biggest furrier in my neighbourhood, then I became the biggest furrier in town. Now I'm the biggest furrier in the country. So what am I supposed to do: become the biggest furrier in the world? Then I'd have to listen to even more people chattering away about fur or about their family or their children. Everything that can be said about fur I've already said at least a hundred times. Now I want to say something that can only be said in movies."

'"And what exactly is that, Galani?" I asked him. But he stared at his plate as if he'd forgotten I was standing next to him.

'After that I didn't see him for a few weeks. I thought I'd never see him again, until suddenly one evening there he was, at his regular table near the window, with his newspaper.

'He shook my hand, which he'd never done before.

'"I've sold everything," he said, "everything. I'm going to produce movies."

'I congratulated him, but I didn't dare to ask what kind of movies he was going to produce, because I was afraid he'd start staring at his plate again, or at his glass. And forget I was standing next to him.

'Then he said he wanted me to play the lead. I started laughing. "I'm going to study English," I told him. But he said: "No, as a producer I've got an eye for these things. You have to play the lead."

'We agreed to meet the next day, in a big café downtown. He had all kinds of papers with him, and he spread them out on the table. He started explaining things to me, but I couldn't follow him. Finally, he swept all the papers off the table and said: "All my life I've been trying as hard as I can just to feel something."

'I don't think I understood him then. I must have given him a pretty blank look, but that didn't keep him from going on.

'"Do you have any idea what it's like to try to feel something and nothing happens? It's like being in endless labour, and the baby never comes. And no one can tell by looking at you. In fact, people are always inviting me to parties. 'There's Galani the furrier,' people whisper."

'He asked if I knew what it was like to be around people and have them treat you like the heir apparent. And when all you could think was: who are these people, what do they want from me, why do they think I like to talk about fur, why do they think I have nothing to say except what can be said about fur?

'Galani sometimes spent all evening talking to women; some of them thought he was in love with them. "You feel something for me, don't you, Galani" they'd say. But Galani told them he felt something for fur and for money, and nothing else.

'At a certain point he considered committing a murder, just to feel something. But his friends talked him out of it.

'Then he started organising orgies. First at night, then after office hours, finally even during office hours. Just to feel something. He didn't care if people noticed, if the neighbours started whispering behind his back. Ten, twenty girls. Young and beautiful. Sometimes he was so desperate that he'd tell them: "If you've got a dog, bring it with you next time."

'His secretary said: "What are people going to say? 'Galani, the fur king, holds orgies during lunch hour.' Do you think they're going to buy fur coats from someone who holds orgies? You think they won't go to the competition? You're ruining yourself."

'"I don't care," Galani said, "I want to feel something. I finally want to feel something."

'After three months he'd had his fill of orgies. They started boring him. A few years later there were still people who'd drop by his office at lunch hour, because they'd heard about the orgies. He'd tell them: "I'm afraid you're too late."

'A friend told him he should go to Tibet; then he'd be sure to feel something. He spent three months there, but he didn't feel a thing. And as if that wasn't bad enough, the food was lousy and he had to squat along the path to do his duty. That wasn't what he meant by feeling something.

'He told me all this while we were in that café. And you know what I thought? That people had whispered behind my back as well, that people always found something to whisper about.

'"And now," I asked him, "now that you've sold all your furs, do you feel something?"

'He started staring into space again, for what seemed like five minutes. I thought he'd forgotten about me again. But suddenly he whispered: "I want to say something that can only be said in movies, and you have to say it for me."

'"That's impossible," I told him. "I can't say it for you. We all have mouths of our own to speak with."

'He grabbed my hand and said: "Don't you see? I can't do it, my mouth is a barren desert." Then he opened his mouth wide. I'd never seen so many gold teeth in one place. His mouth was like a jeweller's window.

'He got up. I went after him. I had to run to keep up, that's how fast he went. Finally, we stopped in front of a warehouse.

'"Here," he said, "I bought this yesterday. This is going to be the studio. Galani Studios." He was beaming.

'That was when I decided to become an actress. My only thought at first was that it would beat waiting tables in that Chinese restaurant.

'A few weeks later I quit my job. I started answering the phone in Galani's office, amid the remainders of fur. Not that many people called.

'Galani himself was on the phone all the time. Sometimes he tried to read a script, but he couldn't concentrate. "You read it," he'd say. "You read it."

'Then he'd pace around his office or lie on his black leather couch. He kept mumbling: "They can't stand it that Galani the furrier has turned into Galani the movie producer, that's what they can't stand."

'"Who?" I asked him. "Who can't stand it?"

'He led me over to the window. His window looked out on a square. "All of them," he said. "All of them."

'One morning he decided to buy a pistol. He wanted me to go with him. "Why do you need a gun?" I asked.

"'I don't want them to say to you later: 'That friend of yours, Galani, was a coward.'"

"'But who would say that?" I asked him. He shook his head, like he thought I should know better.

'I picked out a script. It wasn't good, but it was the best one in the pile. Galani kept saying: "If you like it, it's OK."

'He started calling actors and camera people and directors. When the phone rang, though, it was usually people looking for fur coats. I had to tell them we didn't sell fur any more.

'A few months before the shooting was supposed to start, I came into the office just before lunch, a little earlier than planned. The first thing I saw was Galani, naked, with a dog's leash around his neck. Then I saw the naked women. The sun was coming through the window, so they were just silhouettes. I turned to leave, but Galani was too fast for me. He pushed me up against the wall. "Don't go," he whispered, "please don't go away."

"'I'm going," I said, "and I'm never coming back."

'He fell to his knees and whispered: "All I'm trying to do is feel something, don't you understand? I'm just trying to feel something." He stood up again.

"'Open the door and let me in," he begged.

"'I've already let you in," I said.

"'Not far enough," he said. "What's wrong, do I disgust you?"

"'It's not so much you," I said. "It's more like people in general."

"'Men and women?"

"'I think so," I said.

"'So who doesn't disgust you?"

"'I used to have a dog," I said. "It died of old age. It didn't disgust me."

"'I'll be your dog," Galani said, "let me bark for you." He started barking. I held my hands over my ears so I wouldn't hear it, but I heard it anyway. The naked women were climbing into their clothes. Galani crawled around on all fours and barked at them. Some of the women were afraid of him. They ran out of the room half-naked. And he just kept barking with that leash around his neck.

'Finally, we were alone. He took off the leash. It was the first time I'd ever seen him naked. He'd been naked the whole time, but I really only noticed it when he took off the leash. He leaned on the table and panted.

'"What do you think of my bark?" he asked.

'I probably should have walked away right then and left the whole movie thing behind. But I stayed. I thought: anything's better than waiting on tables in that Chinese place.

'Galani got dressed. He always wore nice suits. Then he took me by the arm. "We're going out to lunch," he said.

'During lunch, he raved about the movie we were going to make. We were sitting in the garden at a French restaurant. He knew the owner and the waiters and waitresses; he shook everyone's hand. We never said another word about what had happened that afternoon in his office.

'In the next few weeks the people who were going to work on the movie came by to sign their contracts. He offered them incredible sums of money. He said: "My theory, Elvira, is that the more money I spend, the more I make." He never took me to the window again to show me that the world couldn't stand Galani the furrier turning into Galani the producer. We drank champagne almost all day. After a while, I couldn't stand the sight of champagne.

'"Why does it always have to be champagne?" I asked him. Galani hesitated, as if he wasn't sure himself.

'"So no one can ever say I didn't give you the best of the best," he said then.

'We weren't lovers, but I loved him. Well, maybe love is too big a word; I was fond of him. He was a strange man. Sometimes I even told him that. "You're a strange man." He'd just laugh.

'The other girls I knew thought my life was surreal, but it had been surreal from the moment I met my parents. Nothing I'd done in the past had been much different from what I was doing

then. Not asking too many questions, and not being too surprised.
Trying to take everything as it comes, as if it couldn't have
happened any way but the way it happened.'

'Galani took me to a wedding. It was a month before the shooting was supposed to start. I didn't even know who was getting
married. It was somewhere in the countryside. He was going to
fly out there, and he really wanted me to go. So I went.

'There must have been three or four hundred guests. Anyway,
it was a huge hotel. There were rooms reserved for all those
guests. We danced the whole evening. Galani was a very good
dancer, which I hadn't expected. I can't remember what we were
drinking. At the end I think it was a mixture of champagne and
brandy, or champagne and cognac. It was in tiny little bottles.
Galani said: "One vial of this is enough to knock two people off
their feet."

'At a certain point Galani and I started kissing. "Give them a
bit, but don't give them everything", was what my best friend
always used to tell me, that girl who started dancing for money
later on. That's always been my policy too. Besides, I was in the
mood. I can't remember why. What puts you in the mood for
something like that?

'At six in the morning most of the guests went to their rooms.
We had rooms next to each other. Galani wanted to have a drink
with me from the minibar in my room.

'"Just one," I told him. Then he tried to take off my clothes.

'"This wasn't part of the deal, Galani," I said, "this wasn't part
of the deal," and I pushed him away.

'He hit me in the face. He must have bloodied my nose, because
I tasted blood. I was so shocked that I started laughing. It was
absurd. It was really laughable. "Galani," I said. Then he hit me
again.

'He threw me on the bed. He started choking me with one
hand. He tried to force my legs apart with his knees. I was so
drunk that I had almost no strength left. There was music coming

from downstairs, the party was still going. I remember thinking: if I scream, it will only make things worse, and no one will hear me anyway. When I looked to one side I could see the clock radio on the nightstand. It was already getting light.

'He started groping around between my legs, but the material wouldn't rip. It seemed to take hours. I thought: let the material rip, then it will all be over that much sooner. I thought: weird that such thin cotton material can be so tough. After that, the only thing I thought was: I'm going to have a baby, Christ, I'm going to have a baby, and I started crying.

'When it was over he rolled off me and fell asleep almost right away. I walked through the hotel corridors. I was still crying; then I noticed that I was half-naked.

'His room was locked, so I lay down next to my bed. He still had his shoes on. Later that morning he went to his own room, and I was able to lie on my bed.'

'We saw each other that afternoon in the breakfast room. Everyone was still drunk, I think, except for the waiters.

'It was a lovely day. The sun was shining through the windows, lovely spring sunlight. We drank tea from chic cups, hotel porcelain. Even the spoons had the hotel monogram on them. All I wanted was a slice of watermelon.

'We didn't say a word. But while we were having dessert, Galani finally said: "I'm not worthy of you; you deserve better."

'"What a bunch of crap," I said. "That's such a load of crap." When people say "I'm not worthy of you", I've always thought that's the biggest load of crap in the world.

'He poked at his fruit salad without actually getting any on his fork.

'"I loved you in my own way," I wanted to say, but you don't say things like that.

'"I'm going to make this movie for you," Galani said. "I want to say something you can only say in movies."

'"So why don't you just say it?" I asked him.

'"Because I can't," Galani said quietly. "I just can't."

'I suddenly had this image of him wearing that leash, and I found him ridiculous. From that moment on, I always saw him with that leash on, and I always found him ridiculous.

'He turned to the waiter to order a bottle of champagne. "Not for me," I said. All that champagne was making me sick. But he said: "Just drink."

'That afternoon we flew back to Buenos Aires. The shooting started a month later. Every day Galani read pages from the script, but then he threw them away or started writing things of his own. Especially when it came to the lines I had to say. He must have added three lines to every one in the script.

'A girlfriend of mine who was still waiting on tables at the Chinese place said: "Shouldn't you report it to the police?"

'"Report what?" I asked her. I had to laugh. "What kind of world do you live in?"

'Galani never touched me again. Well, maybe my hands a few times. And my hair. He used to caress my hair a lot, with his fingers spread, like his hand was a comb.

'I still answered the phone for him. "The furrier has gone out of business," I was supposed to say. "We make movies these days, ma'am, feature films." Galani's desk was across the room. It was a huge room. The building had once been a warehouse. He got into the habit of watching me through binoculars. Sometimes for half an hour at a time. It made me nervous at first, but after a while I got used to that too.

'"Where did you get those binoculars?" I asked him.

'"I used to hunt birds," he said.

'"When was that?"

'"Before," Galani said. "A long time ago."'

'He always wore black shoes, and he read three newspapers a day, but only the obituaries.

'"What do you think you're going to find there?" I asked him.

'"Names," he said.

'"Names?" I didn't get it.

'"You need a good stage name," Galani said.

'"And you think you're going to find it there?"

'"Sure," he said. "Where else?"

'Sometimes he'd show me a name.

'"You can't do that," I said. "That woman really existed, her family is still mourning for her."

'"So what?" Galani growled. "Now she can exist a little longer. People are so ungrateful."

'Finding a stage name for me seemed more important to him than the movie itself. It drove him crazy. Sometimes he'd look up from his paper and say: "How can they die with names like these?"

'When the shooting started he was still looking for my stage name. But there was something wrong with every name he found. One was too long, the other too short. "It has to be something they'll remember," Galani said. "See it once and never forget."

'He'd calculated that the shooting would take forty-five days, and for every day he'd ordered a hundred and fifty bottles of champagne. Our office started looking like a champagne cellar. With a lone fur coat here and there. Probably an outsize that the man who bought remainders wouldn't take.

'I didn't know much about making movies, but I knew they didn't serve champagne every day.

'"Why are you doing that?" I asked him.

'"I don't want them to say later on: that Galani didn't treat us right. That Galani milked us for all we were worth. I want to give them the best of the best. Even the best of the best isn't good enough."

'We were tripping over crates of champagne. When the director Galani had finally found came in to sign his contract, he asked: "What are all these crates doing here? Is this an office or a warehouse?"

'Galani just beamed. "You and I," he said, stepping over crates and walking up to the director, "you and I are going to say something that can only be said in movies." Galani climbed up on to a couple of crates, pried open one of them and showed the director what was in it. "This calls for a celebration," he shouted.

'I think the director felt like running away. But the contract Galani was waving at him, and the advance Galani was offering, must have helped him change his mind.

'We lived in trailers most of the time we were on location. At first we'd stayed at a hotel, but they kicked us out pretty fast. One of the trailers was completely filled with champagne. Galani was the only one with a key.

'Once the actual shooting started, he began losing interest in the movie. A newspaper sent some people out to interview him, and he just kept telling them that he wanted to say something that could only be said in movies. But he couldn't remember the name of the man who wrote the screenplay. I couldn't either, actually. I sat next to Galani during the interview. When they started talking about his past as a furrier, Galani chased them away. "They're just jealous," he said.

'"No one's jealous," I said.

'"That's even worse," he said. "Why shouldn't they be jealous?"

'Sometimes he'd lock himself in the champagne trailer for days on end. He never said anything about the movie. A few times, though, he told the director: "You're doing it all wrong."

'They would have started punching if we hadn't held them back. "Don't ever touch my stomach," the director shouted. And Galani shouted back: "I'd die before I'd touch your stomach." From that day on, the looks they gave each other kept getting dirtier.

'I didn't sleep in Galani's trailer, but sometimes the director would ask me: "How do you put up with him?"

'One evening I was in Galani's trailer. My duties included something that was supposed to pass for bookkeeping. Other people thought it was strange that the leading lady was also the bookkeeper, but I didn't mind. There were clothes and newspapers lying all over the trailer. There was a plastic bag full of dirty socks and underpants. Hanging over the back of a chair were three identical shirts and three identical T-shirts.

'I was adding up figures at a little table covered with plastic cups and empty bottles. Galani was sitting on his bed. All he had on was a pair of red underpants. He was balding, his eyes were distorted by his thick glasses, his legs were short and his belly hung down over those red underpants. His whole body was covered in sweat. I never knew champagne could make you sweat like that. Then he asked me to marry him. I looked up from the books.

'"I used to be a good-looking fellow," he said. "I can show you some pictures." He made it sound as if the twenty or thirty years that lay between him and that good-looking fellow were nothing but a minor detail. As easy to step over as a puddle on a rainy sidewalk. There was no reason for it to get in the way of our marriage.

'"They used to pick me up off the street, the women," he said. "That's how good-looking I was."

'"Most men get better looking as they grow older," I said.

'"Not me," Galani said. "I'm the exception." He picked up a brush and started wiping back the few hairs he had left. His belly heaved up and down like a giant balloon someone kept pumping up and deflating. On the set they called him "King Kong". But that was an exaggeration.

'He took my hand. "Marry me," he said again.

'"No way," I said, but almost too quietly to hear.

'"Do you want to see the pictures?" he asked, as though he hadn't heard. "From back when I was in the army?"

'I shook my head.

'He let go of my hand and plopped back on the bed. "I've never slept with a woman under thirty-five," he said. I didn't know whether it was a statement or a confession. It didn't seem like he'd said it to impress me. But then it wasn't much of anything to be impressed by.

'"Would you like some champagne?"

'I shook my head. I was working on a long sum, and champagne made me want to barf.'

'When the shooting was halfway finished, the money ran out. Galani threw a party. It wasn't really a party, it was more like a mop-up for what was left of the champagne. He wanted to play blackjack. First, he bet the rest of the champagne, then his watch, then he tried to bet me.

'I walked away, but he came after me. The trailers were on this sandy lot. "Marry me," he yelled. He tripped and fell in a pothole, but he got back up. "Marry me," he yelled again.

'You could hear the music playing in the distance. Later, people asked me: "Why did you stay with him so long?" But I didn't know. How can you know something like that?

'By the time he finally caught up with me, he'd fallen three times. He had sand all over him. "Look," he said, pointing to the trailers and the truck full of equipment, "this was all in my mind, but now it's real. Galani makes it real. Galani turns ideas into reality."

'"This was the last day," I told him. "It's all over."

'"No, it's just the beginning," Galani said, "it's only the beginning. We're going to shoot the rest of the script on an island in the Caribbean."

'He tried to kiss me, but I stepped back. I remembered him sitting across from me that day in the hotel, and how he'd said: "You deserve better." And how he'd tried to spear the fruit salad with his fork. He looked good, especially when you consider that he'd been drinking for twelve hours straight. I didn't want to remember him with the leash around his neck. He was a strange man. I never really thought anyone was a strange man again after that, I've never said to anyone else: "You're a strange man."

'"Marry me," he said. "I'm sick."

'"I'm going back to waiting on tables," I said.

'He was standing in front of me. Even his hair was full of sand.

'"King Kong," I said. I meant it nicely. I've always liked monkeys.

'He started laughing. "King Kong wants to marry you," he said.

'I went with him to his trailer. He had fruit salad. He wanted to stay healthy, and he thought eating lots of fruit salad would help. To make him feel better, I ate some of the fruit salad and had a drink. We were down to the last few bottles of champagne.

'"At least I won't have to drag them all back with me," he said.

'We sat on his bed. I kept eating fruit salad, more from nerves than because I was really hungry. We talked, I don't remember what about. I think it was about my stage name. When I left, we kissed. "Even my mouth is full of sand," Galani said.

'The next morning the director gave me a lift to Buenos Aires. "The nightmare is finally over," he said.

'That same evening I went back to work for the old Chinaman. He received me like a lost daughter.'

I'd never heard Elvira talk like that. It was as though she'd been telling it all to herself, so she'd remember it better. That Broccoli and I were in the room was more or less a coincidence.

'It's time for me to go home,' I said.

'That's OK,' Elvira said. She was lying on the bed in the same position she'd been in two hours earlier. I bent over and kissed her on the chin. That seemed like a neutral spot to me. The way I bent over her made it seem like saying goodbye to someone who was ill.

Broccoli was awake now. 'Are you leaving?' he asked.

'Yes,' I said.

'Don't forget,' Broccoli shouted after me, 'Operation Brando takes full precedence.'

THE HOOK

A woman in a white bathrobe opened the door. Her face had these deep lines in it.

'I'm here for the audition,' I said. She led me along without saying a word. In front of the mirror in the hall she stopped to fix her hair and pull a pack of cigarettes out of a little black bag. She lit one in a hurry. I noticed her hands were shaking. 'My husband will come for you in a minute,' she said. 'Follow me.'

It was a normal house somewhere in Amsterdam-West. I was surprised that auditions were being organised in people's homes these days, especially because this house already seemed too full.

I went with her to the living room. I was holding a picture of myself and the ad for the audition I had come for. I had my résumé typed out on a little piece of paper. Almost all of it was made up, but I was sure no one would ever find out.

She sat down across from me in an old armchair most people would have put out with the trash.

'Would you like some tea?' she asked.

'Just water,' I said.

When she sat down again, she pulled the tails of her bathrobe over her knees. In another room, someone screamed.

'My husband would rather be safe than sorry,' she said. She had a husky voice.

'I realise that,' I said. There were five cookies on a dish on the coffee table. She'd already told me to help myself.

Elvira and Broccoli had stayed home. Broccoli had looked at the advertisement and said: 'That man isn't worthy to tie Elvira's shoelaces, let alone have her audition for him.' The ad was from the classified section of *De Volkskrant*, musicians and artists wanted. I'd been poring over those ads for months. Sometimes it made me feel like one of those people who study the financial pages every day without owning a single share.

I went because I remembered my father saying that, if you failed to make your dreams come true, you had only yourself to blame. When he said that to me, he advised me to start off small, by getting a diploma. 'A typing diploma or something,' he said.

The woman leaned forward and picked up my picture from the coffee table. After she'd looked at it for a while, she said: 'You're still young, but your handwriting is quite arousing.' I'd written my name and address on the back of the photo.

'Oh yeah?' I said.

'Oh yeah,' she said.

Suddenly there was another scream from the back room, but this time it sounded different. This time it sounded like two people screaming.

Behind the woman was a bricked-up fireplace with a painting above it. The woman in the painting looked a lot like the woman across from me. Only the woman in the painting was half-naked, and a mermaid from the waist down.

I didn't dare to look at it too long, because I was afraid she'd ask me whether I liked it. And if I said yes, whether I'd be interested in having it for a very nice price. I'd had things like that happen to me before.

The door opened and a man with grey hair and a moustache came out. He was wearing a leather jacket. I thought I'd seen him on television, but it was probably my imagination. He had a nervous look in his eye and rushed right past us. While he was buttoning his leather jacket, he mumbled: 'The next one can go in.'

'Wait, I'll show you to the door,' the woman said. But he was too fast for her; we heard the front door slam before she could even get up.

I stood up. There was no one else, so I must have been next. I picked my picture and my résumé up off the table.

'My husband would rather be safe than sorry,' the woman said again.

I opened the door. The room was empty, except for a wooden desk. At the desk sat a man in a black, fairly worn-out suit. I thought he said his name was 'Johan', but I wasn't sure and I didn't feel like asking him to repeat it.

'I'm setting up a new theatre group,' was the first thing he said, waving to me to take a seat. After those first words he launched into something that sounded like a fire-and-brimstone sermon against society in general and theatre in particular. One phrase that kept coming back was: 'They make it easy for themselves, but if you want to do theatre you can't make it easy for yourself, that's the essence of true theatre.' Sometimes he paused to catch his breath, and I made use of that to nod at what he said or whisper a hoarse: 'Yes, how true.' But usually he didn't even give me time to do that.

After twenty minutes he stopped talking and pulled a Polaroid camera from the desk. 'I have to take a picture of you,' he said, 'otherwise I won't remember who you are.' He turned a lamp on my face. 'Relax,' he shouted, 'just relax.' Then he took the picture.

His wife came in. 'Is everything OK?' she asked.

'Great,' her husband said, flapping the photo to make it dry faster. When she'd left, he said: 'That's Bianca. She'll be responsible for the sets, the whole decor, stationery, everything. So people can pick us out of the crowd.'

He stared at the photo, as if there was more to see than there was on my own face, which was only about eighteen inches away from him.

'Great,' he said. 'So let's hear your monologue.'

I stood up and started my monologue. It was a monologue from a Greek tragedy. The same one I did at the Maastricht Theatre School.

Halfway through, he stopped me. 'Great,' he said, 'very nice, very nice.' He came out from behind his desk. I saw he was wearing pointy black shoes. 'I'm going to tell you,' he said, 'about the hook we're going to hang this piece on.' He still hadn't told me which play I was auditioning for, but at least now I knew there was going to be a hook to hang it on.

'The hook is loss,' he said, 'the whole thing reeks of loss. Everyone in it is at a complete loss. So the hook we're hanging it on is loss. Not our petty little individual loss. No, universal loss. We have to pass through our petty little loss before we can get to the great big loss. You know the kind of loss I'm talking about?'

He lit a cigarette and I said that anyone in their right mind would have to agree with him. It came out kind of hoarse again, but that's because he was standing so close.

He inhaled deep and long, ran his hand over his stubbly cheeks, looked at me and said gravely: 'Why and what for, those are the key questions.' He took a couple of steps towards me. 'Why and what for, those are the key questions.'

'Right,' I said, 'that's the key.'

Then he went back to his desk and pulled out an acting copy of *The Three Sisters* by Chekhov. Slowly he whispered: 'If only we knew, if only we knew.'

I finally knew which play he was talking about.

He came back around the desk, put his hand on my shoulder and said: 'Give us some pain.' Like he was ordering a beer in a café.

I took a step back.

'Despair,' he clarified, 'just scream it out.'

I started screaming. We were in a normal house, in a row of houses, so I was afraid the neighbours were really going to call the police this time. But the audition came first.

'Fall on the floor,' Johan shouted.

I fell and pounded my fists on the floor, which Johan liked a lot. He knelt down beside me and put his ear close to my mouth. 'Here comes the despair,' he screamed, louder than I did, 'here comes the despair.'

Finally, I was allowed to stop screaming.

'That was very good,' he said. 'That was very good.' He wiped his hands on his trousers.

'Why and what for,' he said again, 'those are the key questions every actor, every artist, has to ask himself.'

He lay down on the floor and lit a cigarette.

'Hand me that drawing on the desk,' he said.

I picked up the drawing he was pointing at. It was a drawing of all kinds of socks. A huge pile of socks.

'That's the decor,' he said. Without taking the cigarette out of his mouth, he took the drawing and looked at it for a long time. 'Do you get it,' he said finally, 'the pile of socks, what's lost, the universal loss?'

'Yes,' I said, 'I get it.'

He lay there on the floor for about ten minutes without saying a word, then he said: 'The audition is over.' I thought about Elvira, how she lay on the bed and talked about Galani, making it seem like we weren't even there, while the leak in the kitchen just kept getting worse.

A girl was sitting in the living room. She had a lot of make-up on, but you could tell right away she was sick.

'Wait, I'll show you to the door,' said the woman in the white bathrobe.

SALAMI THIEF

*H*e was lying on the bed. The neighbour lady had found
him on the doormat in front of his attic apartment. 'What
are you doing?' she'd asked him. Mr Berk had told her she'd find
out soon enough.

I looked around. The Hungarian salami was still drying in the
bookcase.

Berk was wearing his shirt and pants, and he had his socks on
too. The neighbour had taken off his shoes. When he saw
Broccoli, he said: 'She wants to start a hotel in Mexico.'

'It will all turn out fine,' Broccoli said.

'I think he's got pneumonia,' the neighbour lady said. She was
wearing so much perfume that the smell of it had mingled with
the salami.

When Berk heard the word 'pneumonia', he opened his eyes
again and said: 'Your parents called. Your mother thinks they'll
end up in prison. She wants to start a hotel in Mexico. Mexico;
God only knows why Mexico. Your father can't stand the heat.

He's told your mother that as far as he's concerned she can go hang herself in Mexico, along with her cutlery.'

'We went to Mexico on vacation once,' the lady from downstairs said. 'What a wonderful country.'

Suddenly Berk sat up. His head was resting on his shoulders like a wooden block at the top of a tower that could topple over any moment. He pointed to the neighbour lady. 'Did she take some of my salami?'

No one answered. His neighbour took a few steps back.

'She ate some of my salami, that dirty salami thief!' he shouted. Then he fell back on his pillow.

'Saints preserve us,' the neighbour said. She made the sign of the cross. Then she said quietly: 'When he was young, I wanted to marry him.'

Elvira had taken one of the folding chairs. She was looking at me.

'He's lived here so long,' the neighbour lady said, 'and he's never even had the painters in.'

Berk sat up again. 'She can't taste the difference between packaged bologna and this salami, she can't even taste it, the dirty salami thief.'

When she heard him say 'salami thief' again, the neighbour lady genuflected anew.

'I'll call the hospital,' she said. 'I can't care for him here, my husband wouldn't like that either.'

Berk's eyes were red around the edges. 'I don't need a hospital,' he said. 'I want my salami back. Do you people have any idea how much trouble it was to get that salami?'

The neighbour lady called the hospital. When she asked them to send an ambulance, Berk shouted that he wasn't planning to waste away in some hospital, that if she thought he was going to waste away in a hospital she had another thing coming.

The neighbour lady seemed relieved to see us. She rattled on and on. About how she knew a painter who would do Berk's whole house for a song, now that he was going to the hospital anyway. It would freshen things up for when he came home. Broccoli asked Berk whether the house on the Bernard Zweerskade had already been sold, and whether his parents were still in Zurich or back in Lenzerheide, but the only sound coming from Berk's mouth was this rattling.

The neighbour lady only stopped talking when the ambulance people arrived. There were two of them, a man and a woman. The woman asked if we were family.

We looked for Berk's identification, or some proof that he was insured, but we couldn't find it. Finally, they said they'd take him anyway.

As they were lifting him on to the stretcher, Berk opened his eyes again. 'Oh my God, a *schwarze*,' he said. 'Is she going to eat my salami too?' He pointed at the woman from the ambulance.

'Just close your eyes and go back to sleep,' the woman said.

But Berk shouted: 'Not on your life!' Then he pointed at me and said: 'Get me that salami. There'll be nothing left of it other-wise. And they can't even tell the difference between salami and packaged bologna.'

I went to the bookcase and brought him the salami. He slid it under the blankets and went back to sleep.

The ambulance crew didn't seem to mind taking a salami to the hospital. They carried him down the steps without a word. We followed them.

'Will you stay with me?' Elvira asked suddenly. 'And if I go away, will you wait for me?'

'Yes,' I said.

'Even if it takes twenty years?'

'Even if it takes twenty years.'

Outside, the sun was shining, but there wasn't much strength to it any more. Broccoli went along to the hospital.

'Such a friendly man,' the neighbour lady said, 'but when we gave parties he never came. Strange, isn't it?' Then she turned and went back inside.

Elvira and I had agreed to wait for Broccoli at Henry Smith's.

She said: 'Before I left for Amsterdam, Galani gave me Eckstein's number. He said: "If you ever get into trouble, call him and mention my name. We've known each other for a long time."

I wasn't really listening. Later, I met people who told me their whole life's story in less than two hours. We'd sit across from each other, and all I'd have to do was look at them and the air would start running out of them like a balloon. I don't know whether you could call that a talent.

Sometimes, when someone's sitting across from me in a restaurant and telling me their whole life's story and I don't have to do much more than look at them and keep my mouth shut, I think about Elvira and the night she told me that people had whispered about her too.

One time I asked her: 'Elvira, what was it people whispered about you?'

'The most terrible things,' she said. 'And you know what's weird? It was all true.' Then she looked at me and laughed. She had a sadder laugh than anyone I've ever known. Elvira could laugh so sadly, it sent shivers down your spine. And when she was finished laughing, she looked at her legs and said: 'Pull up my socks again, would you? I have such bad luck with socks.'

One ice-cold afternoon we buried Elvira's busted socks at the sock cemetery, three kilometres south of Katwijk aan Zee. It was a solemn occasion. There was a procession, the socks lay on a silver tray (requisitioned from the Bernard Zweerskade) and Broccoli made a short speech.

The next morning Frohlich called my parents' house. He had another role for me. Apparently they'd liked the way I'd been thrown down the stairs in The Butcher's Wife.

This time it was for a popular Dutch broadcasting company. A minor role in a TV series that was supposed to not only encourage people to lead a healthy life, but also to entertain them. I was going to play a boy who couldn't resist the temptation of smoking. My father would be played by the great comedian Peter

Bergsteen. My mother was also an actress of some standing, Katja Stokvis.

'OK, it's only for the TROS,' Broccoli had said, 'but the point is to be discovered.' Elvira kissed me. She was awfully happy that day. 'We're going to see you on TV,' she said. That made her laugh so hard that she had to spit out the pistachio she'd just put in her mouth. And Broccoli yelled: 'Burying socks brings luck, we should do it more often.'

A meeting had been organised at one of the TV studios in Aalsmeer. When I came in, Bergsteen and Stokvis were already sitting at a table, drinking coffee. Bergsteen was a lot shorter than he looked on TV, and he was fat too. Katja Stokvis wasn't fat at all. She was slim as a willow and had huge blue eyes.

'So you're my son,' Bergsteen said, and held out a hand that was barely open. 'And I didn't even have to work for it.' Just to be sure everyone had heard, Bergsteen said it again: 'He's my son and I didn't even have to work for it.' Everyone started laughing. I laughed too, of course.

Katja Stokvis said to me: 'Speak loudly, or I won't hear you. I'm still wearing earplugs.'

Then the director came in. His name was Sebastiaan Geuzing, and he was very famous too. In fact, I was surrounded by famous people, just the way Broccoli said I should be. Geuzing had a handsome, rugged face. Oblong and brown, with little tufts of hair on top. He was carrying one of those underarm portfolios, the kind teachers use.

He sat down, pulled the script out of his portfolio and started reading out loud. I think it was the first time he'd ever read it. When he got to the bottom of the first page, he looked at us. 'We're going to have to get cracking,' he said quietly. 'We definitely have to get cracking.'

Then Geuzing turned to me and said: 'What did you say your name was again?'

In the long run, I never played in that series. The more they thought about it, the less they thought I was suited to play

Bergsteen's son. It was already in the air that day; while Geuzing was flipping through the script he suddenly he asked me: 'Do you even smoke?'

After they threw me out of the series, I never heard from Frohlich again. I went to his house in tears to tell him that they'd thrown me out of the series. I made sure the tears were dried, of course, before I rang the bell, but Mr Frohlich had no time to let me in.

'You'll make it,' he said through the intercom. 'You'll make it, and you don't need my help to do it, sweetheart.'

To comfort me, Broccoli and Elvira took me out to dinner that night at the Hotel American. They were all dressed up.

'When the time comes,' Broccoli said, 'Operation Brando will inflict terrible punishment on Henry Frohlich. Don't you worry about that. For starters, we're going to set Mrs Meerschwam on him.'

Elvira and I applauded. And Elvira took off her shoe and pounded it on the table. 'Ronald Reagan did that once,' she said, after a waiter had bustled up to our table and shouted: 'I'm afraid I'll have to ask you not to do that!'

'Excuse my saying so, Elvira,' Broccoli said, 'but that was a Russian. Ronald Reagan never pounded his shoe on the table, at least not in public. Isn't that right, my good man?'

Broccoli had started calling all waiters 'my good man'. Sometimes he even said 'my good man' to people who weren't waiters.

That evening Elvira confessed to us that she was an excellent flamenco dancer.

'Dance for us then,' Broccoli said.

Elvira shook her head. 'I don't do the flamenco any more.'

When I'm in restaurants these days, I often think of Broccoli and Elvira. I don't believe in destiny, but if we'd had a destiny it would have been to sit in restaurants. Sometimes, when we'd spent another four hours sitting in a restaurant, Broccoli would say: 'My, aren't we bourgeois today.' Then he'd look at us with one of those sly smiles and say: 'No one in Amsterdam is as bourgeois as we are today. If the revolution comes now, they'll hang us from a lamp-post, or from the national monument on the Dam.'

I stole the phrase 'aren't we bourgeois today' from him, and I use it on occasion, but it never works for me quite the way it did for him. I've got charm, they say, but not like Broccoli's. A charm which he himself, by the way, spoke of as 'devilish'. He would speak of it to anyone who would listen, but preferably to people he'd met only three minutes earlier. 'I must warn you,' he'd say then, 'my charm is devilish.'

Later, he began doubting it. He'd look at me and say: 'Do you really think my charm is devilish?'

MME BERCOWICZ

*T*he little apartment was cold as ice. She was wearing a knitted vest in every colour of the rainbow, and she had lank grey hair that fell down over her eyes. We kept calling her 'Mme Berk' by mistake, and she'd jump up in annoyance. 'Bercowicz is my name,' she shouted. 'That my brother, the unlucky soul, changed his name is bad enough as it is.'

Broccoli and I had been sitting with her on the couch for half an hour when she said: 'There's nothing in the house, maybe we should go to the delicatessen. You boys would probably like a beer.'

We admitted to a fondness for beer. As we were helping her with her coat, she told us she had a strong dislike for the neighbour lady. 'All the old biddy talks about is cancer and grandchildren. I've been spared both cancer and grandchildren until now, so please let's change the subject.'

At the deli we were going to buy a six-pack of beer, but she said: 'No, three's enough. Otherwise I won't have anything left for breakfast.'

Broccoli offered to pay for everything. At first she refused, but then she changed her mind and went off looking for a bag of potato chips. It took her ten minutes. For every bag she picked up, she knew the price she'd pay in a normal supermarket. 'What a gyp joint,' she mumbled.

Finally, we succeeded in taking three cans of beer and a bag of chips back to her house. 'My house is much better than a café, isn't it?' she said. She never stopped talking. Her dentures seemed a little too big for her mouth. Occasionally, she interrupted herself by saying: 'So tell me about yourselves.'

When we got back to her house she put the cans of beer in the fridge. 'Just to cool them down a bit,' she said. We were too embarrassed to tell her that they were already cold. She took the bag of chips and slipped it into a cupboard.

We sat down on the couch again. She spent the next fifteen minutes hustling back and forth between the kitchen and the living room, with cups and spoons that remained untouched on the table in front of us for the rest of the evening. While she was in the kitchen she kept talking, even though there was no way we could make out what she was saying at that distance, probably because of those ill-fitting dentures.

At a certain point she came back from the kitchen with a photograph instead of a spoon. 'Isn't she a beauty?' she said.

'Who is it?' I asked.

'My mother,' she said. 'When we had guests for dinner, my mother would always say she'd already eaten, but as soon as they'd left she'd lick their plates clean. My father was a waiter. When my mother didn't have enough food for him at home, he'd lick the plates in the restaurant too. He prided himself on being able to lick plates so fast that no one noticed. After all, restaurants are full of people who'd like to lick the plates.'

'Yes, of course,' Broccoli said.

'Oh, wait a minute, the beer,' Mme Bercowicz said, 'I've completely forgotten the beer.' She trotted into the kitchen, but didn't come back with the beer. Instead, she came back with two beer glasses, which stood untouched on the table in front of us for the rest of the evening as well.

'So you know my brother?' she said, once she was finally seated across from us.

'That's why we're here, Mme Berk,' Broccoli said.

'Bercowicz,' she shouted. 'My father was a miller. He only became a waiter when they got here, because my mother said he should. She said: "If you get a job in a restaurant, you can bring home leftovers." But he never came back with anything more than a potato skin.'

She got up. 'Come with me,' she said. We followed her to the bedroom. It may have been even colder there than it was in the living room. There were boxes of papers everywhere.

'I'm working on a book,' she said. She walked back and forth between all the boxes. I noticed that each box had a big number on the side to show what version was in it. There were at least twenty of them.

'It's about Rachel,' she said. 'Do you know who that is?'

We shook our heads.

She pulled a badly thumbed book from under her bed. It looked like a Bible. She brushed the wispy hairs away from her eyes. 'The great Rachel,' she whispered, 'the French actress. She had so many lovers. A different lover every day of her life. And she wasn't pretty. She decided to be pretty. I have some boiled prunes with whipped cream, could I offer you some?'

'No,' I said, 'thank you.' It must have been comforting to think that you could decide to become pretty from one day to the next.

Mme Bercowicz shuffled around amid the boxes, looking for her latest version. She wanted to read us a few pages out loud.

'We actually came here for your brother,' Broccoli said.

'My brother,' she said loudly, opening one box after the other, 'my brother has never shown any interest in things of this sort. "Berk" he calls himself. Phooey! That's not a name, that's an insult.' She spat, or seemed to, but maybe she just couldn't retain her saliva.

'Here,' she said. She'd found what she was looking for. The paper trembled in her hand. 'This is where they auction off Rachel's wardrobe.'

She led us back to the living room. The empty beer glasses were still on the coffee table. In one corner of the room was a piano, which I noticed then was also covered in boxes of manuscript.

She was about to read to us from her own work, but then, as if something had suddenly occurred to her, she put down the pages and leaned over to us as far as she could. We'd just settled down on the couch again.

'Did you boys know . . .' she said. It sounded like she was about to make a key confession. Maybe she was finally going to tell us why she and her brother hadn't spoken for thirty years. 'Did you know,' she said again, 'that I have a better voice than Marilyn Monroe?'

She leaned back in her chair. 'Marilyn Monroe,' she said, 'couldn't hold a note. She wasn't much of an actress either, if you ask me, but that's another story. Phooey.' It looked like she was spitting again. 'I heard her sing once. On Kennedy's birthday. On television. "Happy birthday, Mr President." It was awful.'

She started singing. '*Happy birthday, Mr President.*'

When she was finished, she said: 'I don't have much of a voice either, but at least it's better than Marilyn Monroe's.'

'About your brother,' Broccoli began again.

'He can't sing either,' Mme Bercowicz yelled, 'but he thinks he can. So let him think.'

She went back to the kitchen and returned with the bag of chips. 'I only eat one meal a day,' she said.

She picked up the pages of her book, flipped through them and said: 'It may not be great literature, but it's better than the rest of the trash that's being written. I want people to know that someone like Rachel existed, do you understand?'

She emptied the entire bag of chips on to a plate.

'The real reason we came,' Broccoli said, 'is because your

brother worked for my father for years. He's in the hospital now, and he's delirious. We couldn't find any papers in his apartment. Would you happen to know if he has any papers or notes, and where we might be able to find them?'

She looked at us. 'No idea,' she said. She stuffed a few potato chips in her mouth. The crumbs stuck to her lips. 'He's been delirious all his life.'

Then she showed us to the door.

'I'd like you to come to dinner sometime soon,' she said. 'I'm a bit clairvoyant, and I sense that you two are a good team.'

'Thank you,' I said.

She reached out and touched my curls. 'God, am I jealous,' she mumbled. Then she took my hand and laid it on her own hair. It felt like hay with a lot of oil dumped on it.

'Perhaps you could go with us to the hospital some time,' Broccoli said. 'Maybe you could get some sense out of him.'

She found a scrap of paper and wrote down her name and telephone number. The word 'Bercowicz' was underlined three times.

We were already out in the hall. 'I forgot all about the beer,' she said. 'Do you boys want to take it with you?'

'Keep it,' Broccoli said.

'I won't drink it,' she promised.

'You can drink it,' Broccoli said, 'as long as you drink to us.'

JEWS FOR JESUS

*T*wo nurses were busy sticking a needle in his penis. It was cold outside, but the hospital had a kind of jungle heat. Maybe that's why the nurses hadn't closed the curtain around Berk's bed. Or maybe it was because they thought no one would be even slightly interested in Mr Berk's penis. In the bed across from him was a man with a broken hip. He had eight children, two of them mentally handicapped. It was visiting hour.

'Are you family?' the one nurse asked.

'No,' I said, 'I'm an acquaintance.'

I'd come to visit him by myself. Broccoli and Elvira were busy rehearsing the *Macbeth* monologues.

'So, now you should be able to pee better,' the other nurse said once the needle was finally stuck in Mr Berk's weenie. It wasn't a pretty sight, a needle sticking in a weenie like that, so she pulled a sheet over his lap. Berk was sitting in a chair. He didn't look happy, but then he didn't look unhappy either. He looked like someone who, despite his years, still hadn't ceased to be amazed at everything that happened to him. But that amazement had become so vast that he no longer had the words to share it with anyone else.

He sat next to me for half an hour without saying a thing. Then, when visiting hours were almost over, he suddenly said: 'They took my salami.' He pointed at the man in the bed next to his, as if to say that he was the one who'd eaten his salami.

I tried to encourage him to tell me more about the theft, although I'd come for something completely different. But he didn't say another word.

She came into the room like someone who'd forgotten something important. She hadn't changed a bit since the time we'd visited her apartment. The same vest, the same hairdo, even the same smell, I noticed then. Mr Berk's sister was one of those people who smell like vegetable soup.

She hugged him. 'Don't you recognise me?' she asked.

'Of course I do,' he said. 'I'm not crazy.'

She pulled the sheet off his lap. 'What's that?' she asked, pointing at the needle.

'If I knew that I'd be a doctor,' Mr Berk said.

A nurse came in carrying a bowl of greyish pudding on a tray. 'Your dinner, Mr Berk,' she said cheerily.

'Bercowicz,' Mr Berk's sister said. 'Berk is something else.'

'He came in here as Berk,' the nurse said, 'and besides, visiting hours are over.'

'He came into the world as Bercowicz,' his sister said, 'and when you're born a Bercowicz, you stay a Bercowicz.'

I had the feeling his sister was about to jump on him, but Berk lifted his hand and said: 'I wrote a letter to the Queen. I want to change my name to B. And I want all of you to call me Mr B.' Then he pointed at the man with the broken hip. 'Those people ate my salami,' he whispered desperately.

Mme Bercowicz shouted: 'If they put Berk on your tombstone, you won't be seeing me at your funeral.'

'Fine by me,' Berk said.

'The sheet has to stay on your lap,' the nurse said, 'it's distasteful for the other patients.'

'I took it off,' Mme Bercowicz said. 'What *is* that doohickey?'

'Your husband needs it,' the nurse said.

'He's not my husband, he's my brother.'

'Well, whatever he is, he needs it.'

I put on my coat. 'Mr Berk,' I whispered in his ear, 'how did Mr Eckstein meet Elvira?'

His head had been hanging down the whole time, chin resting on his chest. Now he lifted it and looked at me. His eyes were suddenly alive again. 'You think he ever told me anything? God only knows where he met her. Probably at the Victoria Hotel. That's where he meets everyone, isn't it? Nuts in the noggin, all of them.' And he rapped his knuckles against his forehead.

After he was released from the hospital, Mme Bercowicz made her brother move in with her. He protested loudly, but it was no use.

'She's a vegetarian. She never let me eat salami before,' he told them as they were carrying him out of the hospital. 'You think she's changed any?'

No one listened to him. They gave him friendly little pats on the cheek by way of farewell.

Mme Bercowicz slept on the couch and Berk had to sleep in her bed, amid the twenty drafts of her book. Broccoli called him up right away, but all Berk said was that he felt like a goose being fattened for its liver.

That same evening, Broccoli called the hotel in Lenzerheide – the receptionist told him his parents had left a few days earlier. She couldn't say whether they'd actually gone to Mexico. Broccoli called a few other people in Switzerland, but they couldn't tell him where his parents had gone.

'Don't worry,' he said to me. 'They do this sometimes. They disappear for a while, then they show up again, brown as berries.'

Right after that, he called Mme Bercowicz. She'd bought an answering machine. 'Listen to this,' Broccoli said to us.

Elvira and I had to listen to Mme Bercowicz's message. It went like this: 'This is Bercowicz's answering machine. Leave a message after the signal. It would quite nice if you actually did that, because listening to an empty tape is extremely annoying. End of message.'

Broccoli left five messages on her machine, but she didn't call back.

When Mme Bercowicz finally called, we were busy helping Elvira into her jeans. We'd had to do that pretty often lately. Elvira said she was getting fatter, but you couldn't see it; we maintained that her jeans had shrunk in the wash. We stood on each side of her, then picked her up by the jeans in the hope that her legs would slide into place. Sometimes it worked, but sometimes we also heard this loud cracking sound.

Mme Bercowicz invited us over for dinner. Broccoli thought it was a good idea. He was anxious to talk to Mr Berk. After all, he hadn't heard from his parents since they'd left. But, more importantly, I believe he had also exhausted his financial reserves.

Mr Berk was sitting in front of the television. He hadn't shaved. When he saw us he mumbled something, but we had to lean down in front of his mouth to understand him. 'Go away,' was what he was saying.

When we were seated at the table, Mme Bercowicz had to call her brother three times before he made a move to get up. On the way to the table he lost a slipper. It was a lady's slipper.

Mme Bercowicz served lentil soup. We whispered to each other that lentil soup this disgusting probably only came along once every hundred years.

There was no need to hold up our end of the conversation; Mme Bercowicz did all the talking. There was Vivaldi coming from the cassette recorder. I didn't know it was Vivaldi, but Mme

Bercowicz said: 'I could listen to Vivaldi all day.' The music was on so loud that we had to shout at the top of our lungs.

When Mme Bercowicz finished her soup first, Berk said. 'I want to confess.'

Mme Bercowicz dished herself up a second helping, so vigorously that soup spattered all over the place. Then she said: 'He wants to get converted, the idiot.'

'I already *am* converted,' Mr Berk said calmly. 'But now I want to go to confession.'

Broccoli put his spoon down on the table. He'd already done that a few times, but this time it looked definitive. 'Are you serious?' he asked. 'Do you really want to go to confession?'

'Yes,' Berk said. 'They tell me you feel like a different person afterwards.'

'But how would you get to a church?' Broccoli asked.

'I want someone to come here,' Berk said.

'I won't have them in my house,' Mme Bercowicz said loudly. 'My niece is like that too, and I won't let her through that door.'

Elvira said she'd stopped going to confession when she was eleven, and she assured Mr Berk that it didn't make you a different person.

Mr Berk insisted, though, and added that the person who'd made this soup had something to confess as well.

'Oh, great,' his sister said, 'it's not enough for you to call yourself Berk, now you have to make fun of my soup and get yourself converted.'

'No, that's right, it's not enough,' Berk said. He shuffled back to his chair in front of the television. Now he'd lost the second slipper as well. He was wearing green socks with holes in them.

Broccoli asked him a few times if he knew where his father's papers were. All Berk said was that he knew he was talking gibberish, but we shouldn't forget that that was how Jesus had gotten started.

Every time Broccoli's father was mentioned, I looked at Elvira. As usual, her face betrayed only that she was pretty and extremely good at smiling absently. She was a real expert at that, the absent smile.

Two days later, we heard that Berk was back in the hospital. This time he was in a ward with a man who had no nose.

Eight people were standing around his bed when we got there. Two of them were taking notes the whole time. The oldest, a man with glasses and neatly combed hair, told us that Berk had a collapsed lung, but that he would probably pull through. 'A collapsed lung like this usually collapses back out again,' he said, 'to put it in layman's terms.'

He also asked if we were family. 'No, we're not,' Broccoli said, 'but there's a very good chance that Mr Berk knows the whereabouts of my parents, or is in any event aware of a number of things I'm not aware of. Whether the house has been sold, for example.'

'Aha,' the doctor said. He took a few steps back, looked at the patient again and then said, for the second time: 'Aha.'

Mme Bercowicz came in right then. She had a dark-haired lady with her whom she introduced as her niece. Later, I heard that her niece belonged to an organisation called 'Jews for Jesus'. She was married to a man who was so handicapped that all he could do was nod his head, and even then only on a good day. Mme Bercowicz pushed the doctors aside and shouted in Mr Berk's ear: 'It's me. Your niece has come over from Scotland to pray for you.'

We saw Mr Berk try to lift his head from the pillow and fail. Then he made some movements with his hand, but it was strapped to a wooden plank all the way up to the elbow.

'Mme Berk,' said one of the men who'd been taking notes the whole time, 'your brother needs his rest.'

'Bercowicz,' Mme Bercowicz roared. 'I won't stand here and be insulted.'

The doctor didn't seem to get it. He said: 'No, of course, I wouldn't do that.' And his colleague chimed in: 'If you feel the need for a social worker . . .'

The niece took this opportunity to crowd her way up to the bed. She picked up the hand with the plank and said: 'I prayed for you all the way over here, Uncle Ludwig.'

Mr Berk lifted his head again. Slime came out of his mouth, and then about ninety seconds of incoherent noise. But finally we could all make it out clearly: 'You shouldn't have.'

Everyone, including the doctors who were still in the room, turned to Mr Berk's bed as if something highly unusual had happened. An oxygen unit began beeping, but none of the doctors seemed interested. It was like a persistent car alarm that no one noticed any more. No one except for Mr Berk's niece, who shouted: 'Help him, please, please help him.' She started pounding on the oxygen unit with both hands, which only made it beep more loudly.

One of the doctors came over to her and said: 'These machines are sometimes a bit off, don't let it upset you.'

But she did get upset. She got awfully upset. She crossed herself a few times and then began making the sign of the cross over Mr Berk, singing hymns in English the whole time. Mr Berk tried to pull his hand away, but she had him in an iron grip. Meanwhile, Mme Bercowicz was explaining to the doctors that her name was Bercowicz, and that Berk's name was actually a misunderstanding. 'Even she,' she said, pointing at her niece, 'even she, who thinks Jesus is her saviour, still calls herself Bercowicz.'

'That has nothing to do with the matter at hand,' we heard the doctor say.

'This is getting us nowhere,' Broccoli said. I followed him out of the room. At least twice a day on average, my parents accused me of following him around like a puppy instead of thinking about my own future. Maybe they were right, but I didn't care. If my life ever turns out like it should, that will be thanks in part to Broccoli. Some people bind themselves to other people with all kinds of ceremonies and showers and smorgasbords. I had bound myself to him casually and without thinking about it, but the bond was no less binding for that. Even if only because I knew that he, and no one but him, bound me to Elvira.

'Elvira told me that Galani gave her your father's number,' I said as casually as possible.

'Oh yeah, did she tell you that?' Broccoli said. He looked at me so sarcastically that I didn't dare to say anything else.

A bald man was doing needlework in the corridor. He didn't look up when we sat down beside him.

Part Five

VILLA VILLEKULLA

*T*he day Mr Berk's other lung collapsed and he was taken to intensive care, I was picked for a role in a children's play. The play was going to be held in a museum. The idea was to allow children to become acquainted with art in a playful manner. The Villa Villekulla Children's Theatre wanted to hire me for two months. They were paying minimum wage, plus five guilders and fifty cents a day for expenses.

When my father heard that I was actually going to make money doing this, he was probably even happier than I was. 'This is a great day for you,' he said, 'but it's not a solution. In two months you'll be an unemployed slob again.'

'Don't expect great things,' the girl from Villa Villekulla told me. 'The play you're in lasts about eight minutes.'

Broccoli kept calling hotels in Zurich and Lenzerheide every day in search of his parents, but they were nowhere to be found. When he heard that I had a job with Villa Villekulla, he hugged me and vowed not to call a single Swiss hotel all day. To celebrate the good news, Broccoli bought me foie gras.

That evening Elvira, Broccoli and I ate foie gras.

'I've never heard of Villa Villekulla,' Elvira said.

'Neither have I,' Broccoli said, 'but that's beside the point. I called Mrs Meerschwam to tell her you'd be on TV soon.'

'But it's not going to be on TV.'

'How do you know?' Broccoli snapped. 'Did they tell you it would never be on TV?'

'No, not in so many words.'

'So how's Mrs Meerschwam doing?' Elvira asked.

'Wonderfully,' Broccoli said. 'She's almost got the house cleared out, soon there will be nothing left of the Bernard Zweerskade.' He opened one of the suitcases on the floor and pulled out a bathrobe. It was white, and it had the word 'Hilton' embroidered on it.

'I'm not so fond of foie gras,' Elvira said.

'Neither am I,' Broccoli said, 'but you have to try everything in life. That also goes for foie gras.'

We went outside and tried to palm off the foie gras on a few tramps, but in the semi-darkness it looked just like cat food. That's probably why we couldn't get rid of it.

The next morning I had to report to the offices of Villa Villekulla for a production meeting. The other actors and actresses were there, and I also met the artistic director of Villa Villekulla. She had long white hair and big glasses, and throughout most of the meeting she sat with her thumb in her mouth.

The meeting was about the lunch allowance we'd be getting during the rehearsals. Or, more accurately, about whether the allowance would be paid in kind or in cash.

A young actress who occupied a twilight area between male and female kept saying: 'Chicken curry upsets my stomach. When we did Brecht I lived on chicken curry, and I'm never going to do that again.'

A man with lots of pomade in his hair and wearing what looked to me like whiteface exclaimed: 'I'm not really an actor at all. I came here from an employment project. In fact, I'm originally a pianist.'

The artistic director pulled her thumb out of her mouth and said: 'No, Henk, you've got what it takes, we've already discussed this at some length.'

He nodded sadly a few times, then said: 'Yeah, that's what they all say.'

The production manager, a man somewhere in his forties, rapped on the table and said: 'OK, let's take a vote. Will everyone in favour of the lunch allowance being paid in kind please raise their hand?'

Henk said: 'I withhold my vote. I never eat lunch anyway.'

'You can't do that,' the production manager said. 'Everyone has to raise their hand at least once, otherwise we get an even number, then the votes will be tied and we'll still be here tomorrow.'

'Let's try it another way,' the artistic director said. 'Who's vegetarian?'

'I'm not a vegetarian,' Henk said, 'I just don't eat eggs. It's not because I don't want to, but the doctor won't let me.'

'I don't eat turkey,' said one actor who'd been playing with his sunglasses the whole time.

A very old man said: 'I'll eat anything.'

'All right then,' the artistic director said. Then she turned to the production manager: 'Marcel, maybe you could put together a list of what everyone doesn't eat, because I think we should pay the lunch allowance in kind.'

'No,' the chicken-curry girl cried, 'please, not in kind.'

The man with the sunglasses shouted: 'How am I supposed to know what I won't want to eat in two months' time?'

A few of the others agreed with him. The production manager pounded on the table. 'We're talking about food you don't eat as a matter of principle, or that the doctor says you can't eat, like Henk and his eggs.'

'I'll pack my own lunch,' Henk said.

'Yeah, if this is how it has to go, then keep your allowance,' the chicken-curry girl said.

'Quiet,' the production manager shouted. 'Let's get the ball rolling. I want everyone to tell me what it is they morally object to eating. Or what they don't eat for reasons of health. Is that clear?'

'Only chickens' eggs,' Henk said. 'Eggs from a quail, for example, are no problem.'

'What do you think?' the chicken-curry girl said. 'Do you think they're going to serve us quails' eggs?'

'I have diabetes,' the very old man said, 'a light form of it, sure, but it's still diabetes.' Besides being an actor, he also gave Gestalt therapy in his spare time. He was a little deaf, so we had to scream at him.

'That's what you get from an irregular diet,' the man with the sunglasses said.

'That's ridiculous,' the chicken-curry girl said. 'My grandmother has it too, and she's eaten regularly all her life. It's hereditary.'

'Quiet,' the artistic director shouted, 'quiet! Everyone listen to Marcel. Marcel, go ahead.'

'Quiet,' the production manager shouted, 'quiet now, otherwise we'll still be here tomorrow. Ewald Stanislas Krieg, which one of you is that?'

Everyone started looking around.

'Here, that's me.' Now everyone was looking at me.

'So what do you want to be called?' the production manager asked.

'David,' I said. That was my stock answer.

The production manager stared at his list. He turned it over, then stared at it again. Then he started shuffling through a pile of papers.

'Is this going to take long?' the man with diabetes asked. 'I have an important appointment. I'm going to a movie.'

'If there's someone who has to go to the toilet real bad, would they please do that?' the man with the sunglasses shouted.

'It stinks in here,' the chicken-curry girl whispered.

I felt my face turn red. Even though, as far as I could tell, I didn't stink at all. But I did have to admit that the little meeting room did stink rather badly.

'One last time,' the man with the sunglasses yelled, 'if someone has to go to the toilet real bad, let them do it now. Otherwise I'm going out to the hall.'

'Quiet,' the production manager screamed. 'Everyone stays put, and everyone stays quiet. Quiet. It says here that your name is Ewald Stanislas Krieg. Are you telling me your name is also David?'

I heard some other people mumbling my name. 'Ewald Stanislas Krieg.'

'No, my name isn't David, but you can call me that if it makes things any easier.'

'Quiet,' the production manager shouted, 'or we'll never get out of here. The easiest thing by far is to call everyone by the name he or she was given at birth. Do people call you Ewald or Stanislas?'

'Or Krieg?' asked the man who'd said that anyone who had to go to the toilet badly should do so.

'Ewald.'

'Ewald,' the production manager said. 'What is it you don't eat?'

Everyone was looking at me, I felt like a contestant on one of those quiz shows. Right then a woman in a long blue coat came in. She had blonde hair down to her shoulders.

'This is Frederika Steinman,' the artistic director said, 'she's acting with us as well.'

We all knew her name, and those of us who'd seen her in the movies knew her face as well. Henk and I were from a project for the chronically unemployed, we'd probably been taken on keep the costs down. For the rest, there were a few unknown actors from the children's theatre circuit, and then there was Frederika Steinman, the great Frederika Steinman. If the word 'star' could be applied to anyone in Holland, it was Frederika Steinman. I wondered how the hell she'd ever ended up at Villa Villekulla.

She shook hands with everyone, then sat down at one end of the table, next to Henk. She was wearing a cap made of fur or imitation fur. She took it off and shook her blonde hair a few times. A few wisps hit Henk in the face. There was an uneasy silence. Some of the actors were crunching their plastic coffee cups. The artistic director had even taken her thumb out of her mouth.

'Excuse me,' Frederika said to Henk.

'Oh, that's all right,' Henk said. He was trying not to look at Frederika. 'I've had hair in my face before.' From Henk's few comments I'd figured out that he didn't like women, but he didn't like men much either. All his affection was directed at his two German shepherds, who it pained him deeply to leave alone.

'We were at Ewald Stanislas Krieg,' the stage manager said. 'For those who just arrived: Ewald Stanislas would like to be called Ewald. Ewald, what is it you don't eat?' He was holding his pen at ready.

'Could we open a window?' Frederika asked. 'It's a bit stuffy in here.'

Under the directorship of Richard Zwarthuis, I spent the next four weeks rehearsing a play about a firebird, and about a boy who was in love with that firebird. I played the boy. The lines I was supposed to say were unclear to me when I first read them, and they remained unclear right up through the final performance – although I managed to keep that hidden. Six of these little plays were to be performed simultaneously in the museum, none of them lasting longer than ten minutes, and all done by a different director.

After the premiere, a few people came up to me and said: 'You can't act, but you know what you're saying, and that's something you can't say for a lot of actors.'

One afternoon, the playwright came to watch. She said she thought it was wonderful.

'And what do you think of my script?' she asked.

Of course I didn't tell her that I couldn't make head nor tail of it, and that I seriously doubted if seven-year-olds could either, but she was probably more familiar with the childish mind than I was. 'Unique,' I mumbled.

The firebird was played by a young woman named Hilde. She had gone to the Maastricht Theatre School, and during rehearsal breaks she often talked about how she'd had to choose between her career and her children, and what a hard choice that was. I agreed with her. Then she'd sigh deeply. My God, that woman could sigh deeply. She sighed deeply after everything she did. She wore tight leather pants almost all the time. Late one afternoon – as we were waiting for the director to show up – she told me that the best sex you could have was with people you didn't love. And she sensed that I felt the very same way.

Rehearsals were at the Sleep-in. At first, Zwarthuis thought it was best for us to do our lines while lying in a filled bathtub. He obviously couldn't figure out the script either. That wasn't really his fault. I've never met anyone who did understand it. Finally, he decided we should do our lines standing up, but without moving.

The Gulf War had just broken out. Some of the actors walked around all day with a transistor radio held to their ear. Hilde shouted: 'What's the point of all this, now that the Gulf War has broken out?'

The premiere would be held at the Fodor Museum in Amsterdam. Three days beforehand, we moved from the Sleep-in to the Fodor. One of the rooms had been vacated and turned into a dressing room. That was where I saw Frederika Steinman again. She was playing a punk girl.

She changed into her costume next to me, after Zwarthuis had introduced us by saying: 'Frederika, this is one of your colleagues.'

'I know,' she said. 'You're Ewald, aren't you?' We shook hands.

The boy who loved the firebird wore a tuxedo. They'd bought a tuxedo especially for me at a store on the Kalverstraat. They'd also bought me a pair of patent leather shoes. The girl who did the costumes was heavily pregnant, but she insisted on going into the changing booth with me there in that shop on the Kalverstraat. There was almost no room for me to try on my clothes.

I wore white underpants from the Hema that Broccoli said looked like underpants from long before the Second World War. My father also wore underpants like that. Broccoli wore boxer shorts. Elvira said almost all her lingerie had been bought at airports.

I couldn't tell you what kind of underwear Frederika Steinman wore. I could have taken a look, but I didn't, because I felt that wasn't done. I think differently now. People don't really change. Details change.

One hour before the premiere, Hilde, Zwarthuis and I were sitting in the locked room at the Fodor where Hilde and I would be playing the firebird and the young man. There was blue ceramic artwork on the walls. The art was supposed to have something to do with the lines we'd be saying.

Hilde was walking around, rehearsing her part. She walked over to me once to straighten my bow tie and brush a few curls from my face with a wet finger. 'Otherwise no one can see your eyes,' she said.

I did my best to feel like I was in love with the firebird, but I wasn't even fond of the firebird. All I felt was fear, not of the firebird, but of the hundred-odd people who would soon come pouring into the room to look at the blue artwork on the walls, at Hilde and at me.

Soon enough they would discover that, no matter what the programme said, there was no firebird and no young man in love with the firebird. That would be the first debunking. The second would follow on the heels of the first. They would discover that I was not an actor. My registration form at the employment office, the photos I'd had taken and all my big talk couldn't help me then. At best they would think: he can't help it, he's from an unemployment project.

Elvira and Broccoli would be there. I'd advised my parents not to come. Not so much for their sake as for mine. I was ashamed of my parents. A shame almost as great as my fear of the people who'd be coming in ten minutes to look at the firebird and the doting young man.

The firebird wore a petticoat. One minute before the crowd arrived, she asked me to check her zipper.

There was no stage lighting, only the lamps that were always on in the museum. I could see everyone coming in. They barely looked at us or at the blue artwork. It looked more like they were wondering: how did we end up here? I saw Broccoli and Elvira. She was wearing her boa constrictor. I saw Frederika Steinman. She had just come off stage and still had her costume on.

A few seconds after I started doing my lines, I heard a woman say: 'That seat is taken.' And a few moments later: 'OK, sit there, but I'm telling you, my husband will be back from the men's room any minute.' She said it in a whisper, but everyone was looking at the fat woman. Like me, they knew that the fat woman was infinitely more interesting than any conversation between the firebird and the young man. But no one heckled me, and no one yelled 'boo' when it was over. They all applauded politely. Some of them even complimented me afterwards. One man kissed me and said: 'Fantastic, really fantastic, but what was it all about?'

Downstairs was a cold buffet with champagne, but only the fittest could get to it.

I found Broccoli and Elvira amid all the hubbub. Elvira grabbed me by the scruff of the neck and said: 'That tuxedo looks good on you, you look like some little livery boy.' Did she actually use the term 'livery boy'? Or was it something else? In any case, it was something that had fallen into disuse a long time ago.

I caught sight of the artistic director. She waved to me. 'Hurrah!' she shouted.

'Hurrah!' I shouted back.

'Let's get out of here,' Broccoli said.

'I still have to change,' I said. I climbed the stairs to the dressing room. There were flowers everywhere. Some of them had already been trampled. Frederika Steinman was busy putting on her shoes. Those army boot things. She was eating an apple.

'Would you like one?' she asked. She opened her bag.

'Yes, please,' I said. Then I got dressed as fast as I could.

'It reminded me a bit of the FNV movie,' Broccoli said once we were at Elvira's place.

'No,' Elvira said. 'The FNV movie was worse.' She'd sold her table, to Broccoli's great chagrin. She sold everything.

The phone rang.

'You answer it,' Elvira said to me.

It was Elvira's mother. She enquired at length about my health, and told me she was still painting flying females.

FREDERIKA STEINMAN

*T*hree times a day I played the young lover, for children between the ages of six and twelve. They didn't come in by accident or in any way of their own accord. The schools dragged them in.

I had to look at the firebird in an extremely loving way, and on several occasions it had struck me that there was moss growing on the firebird's front teeth. A patch of moss, I don't know how else to describe it. Maybe Hilde didn't have time to brush her teeth. That's possible. There were days when she didn't have moss on her teeth, but those were rare. Joseph Heller once wrote that it's difficult to respect a supreme being who would include tooth decay in his divine creation. As far as I was concerned, Hilde was living proof of that.

I spent the time between shows reading in the Fodor, or walking the halls and looking at art I'd already looked at a hundred times. Sometimes I talked with my colleagues; there was, however, still the distinct possibility that someday I would be unmasked, so I usually kept my mouth shut.

I didn't see much of Broccoli in those weeks. He spent every morning at Berk's bedside, and every afternoon calling Swiss hotels. In between times, he rehearsed with Elvira, or walked through town with her.

At lunchtime they handed out sandwiches that reminded me most of a bouquet garni. The actress who occupied the shadowy zone between the sexes was on a diet, and ate only bananas. They'd passed out a ditto sheet urging us to eat lunch together, but what actually happened was that we all ate our sandwiches alone in some corner of the room where we performed our plays.

A few times I was unable to finish my sandwich on time, and in my haste left it lying on one of the stools. Whenever a child sat on one of my sandwiches, a huge ruckus would break out. Only one of the children had actually sat on a cheese sandwich, but it resulted in mass screaming on the part of the whole class. The first time it happened I just went on saying my lines, even though I couldn't understand a word of what the firebird was saying above all the screeching. I figured: when we get to the end, the play's over. But after a few days I received orders to step out of my role when such calamities took place. I was to go to the teacher and tell him or her that we would only continue once the children were quiet.

I could see why the kids screamed like that. This kind of introduction to art and theatre couldn't be much fun. I don't know how they managed to do it, but some of those kids sat down so hard on the sandwiches I'd left lying around that they had to be scraped off the back of their pants.

When a disaster like that happened, I felt like a priest. I'd take a few steps forward, spread my arms and cry: 'Kids, kids, we'll only go on with the play when your teacher has quieted you down.'

An actor, who was playing a farmer sitting on a mountain of cabbage a few doors down, told me I was lucky I didn't have to perform for high school kids. 'If you knew what I've been through . . .' he said.

'Tell me,' I said.

But he didn't want to dredge up the details.

The oldest actor, the deaf one, had his eye on Frederika Steinman. He'd already tried a few times to get her to go into Gestalt therapy. 'It's awfully nice of you to offer,' she said, 'but no, thank you very much.'

Frederika Steinman kept a journal, and she often wrote in it while she was in the dressing room. She had this pained expression on her face while she wrote. That made her even prettier, I thought.

One evening, as I was hanging up my tuxedo, which had started to stink slightly by then, Frederika said: 'We're all going out to dinner, are you coming along?'

'I'd like that,' I said. Actually, I'd agreed to meet Broccoli and Elvira, but I called to say I couldn't make it.

We went to Panini. The actress who was dieting didn't go along, and Henk, the former pianist, got sick halfway there, but otherwise the evening was a success.

There were seven of us, so after dinner we spent at least fifteen minutes figuring out how to split the bill. When the coffee came Frederika Steinman suddenly asked me: 'Do you write poetry as well, Ewald?'

I decided then and there that she had the gift of prophecy, or that she was at least a little clairvoyant, like Mr Berk's sister.

'How did you know?' I asked.

She looked at me without a word, and her eyes, which were none too small to begin with, grew even bigger.

In the days that followed, Frederika Steinman often came and sat beside me as I perched on my stool in the room with blue artwork, waiting to play the young lover. She wouldn't say a word. She'd just sit there. Or she'd walk around the room, rehearsing her lines. Or walk around and chew gum. Frederika Steinman went through huge quantities of chewing gum every day. I've never seen anyone chew gum the way she did.

Hilde, the firebird, always went to a café between performances to smoke. You weren't allowed to smoke in the museum,
otherwise the alarm would go off.

During the performances I noticed that it was mostly the teachers who yawned. One time I even had to wake a teacher after
the play was finished. 'It's over,' I said, 'your class has already
gone to the next room.'

'Oh my God, thanks,' he said.

Most of the children seemed flabbergasted by what they saw.
Some of them looked like they felt sorry for us, but maybe that
was my imagination.

One morning I saw Broccoli sitting among the children.

'I finally talked to my mother,' he told me after the show.
'They're in Rabat. She still wants to start a hotel in Mexico. Now
she thinks the Swiss tax service is going to come after her too.'

'Where's Rabat again?'

'In Morocco.'

'And what about Mr Berk?'

'No change.'

Broccoli looked bad. Neither of us were looking much like
Marlon Brando. We had a long way to go before we'd start looking like Marlon Brando. I hoped we'd get there before we died.

'Elvira wants to know when you're coming by,' he said. Then
he walked away. But an hour later he was back.

'I've been thinking about it, and I really think I should start
a newspaper. A daily, unlike any other daily.' Then he left again.
From the back he was starting to look like his father.

That was the same day Frederika Steinman asked me: 'Could
I read a few of your poems some time?' I did my best to look at
her. You can't always look the other way when people talk to you.
She had freckles.

'OK,' I said.

With Broccoli's help, I'd published a book of my own poetry
which I called *The Machiavellian*. I'd heard of Machiavelli, and I

considered myself a Machiavellian. Sly, smart and tough as door-nails.

At Broccoli's recommendation, we'd held the launch at a launderette. Not that there was any direct connection between my poetry and the launderette, but that was a minor detail. I recited the poems, and about a dozen people sat there staring at the washing machines. It was Broccoli's idea to turn on all the washers during the final cycle. We'd agreed to pay the lady who owned the launderette two hundred guilders, but when the launch was over she said: 'Aw, make it a hundred.'

Sales didn't go too well, so I'd distributed most of the copies door-to-door in my own neighbourhood. The way the free local paper was brought around, just by shoving it through the letter box. I'd written my phone number in the books, but no one ever called me. Broccoli said: 'Don't worry about it. Just wait until people find out about Operation Brando.'

The next day I brought in a copy of *The Machiavellian* for Frederika Steinman. Instead of writing in her journal, she sat in the dressing room reading my book. It made me uncomfortable.

During lunch – I was at the café with the smoking actors and actresses – she suddenly sat down beside me. I still had on my tuxedo, even though they'd handed out another ditto expressly forbidding us to wear our costumes outside the museum.

'Would you write a monologue for me?' Frederika Steinman asked. Again I saw those freckles and those big blue eyes.

'A monologue?' I didn't get it. We barely knew each other. And I was wearing that stinking tuxedo.

'I feel we have something in common,' she said. Then she took my book out of her bag and pushed a pen into my hand.

'Sign it, here,' she whispered, holding open the cover.

My God, I thought, the great Frederika Steinman is asking me, a skinny nineteen-year-old with a bad complexion and a haircut like a poodle, to write her a monologue. Maybe Broccoli was right, maybe I really have become a genius. Maybe that's what happens when you're the secretary of the Association for Geniuses.

I signed the book. It felt like I was signing my own death warrant. I don't really have a signature of my own. I've tried out about twenty of them. These days I just draw a line with a loop around it.

'Would you consider it?' she asked. I racked my brains to figure out what Frederika Steinman and I could have in common. But I couldn't come up with anything. She was a celebrated actress at the height of her career, and I was a young man who planned to start looking like Marlon Brando, but who so far had about as much in common with Marlon Brando as he did with a watermelon. That I was the secretary of the Association for Geniuses, an association whose members planned to become world-famous, was something I'd be better off not telling Frederika Steinman. Better to say nothing about Broccoli and Elvira either.

'Sure,' I said, 'I'd like to, but . . .'

'I see myself sitting naked on a black cube,' she said.

'Oh, yeah,' I said. My mouth was dry. Naked on a black cube, I thought, and suddenly it came to me in a flash. This woman goes through hell every day. When she said that she wanted to sit naked on top of a black cube, her expression was just like that. Like a woman who goes through hell every day. I knew faces like that.

'That's the image I've been seeing for a long time now, almost two years. And you have to write the text to go along with it.'

I could produce nothing more than a murmur of consent.

Then the old actor butted in. 'Next month I'm starting a new class in Gestalt therapy, so if anyone's interested . . .'

'Enough already with the Gestalt therapy,' Henk said. He was looking sadder by the day. He probably missed his German shepherds.

'Maybe we should do it on the beach,' Frederika Steinman said as we were walking back to the museum.

'Yeah,' I said. 'On the beach.'

■ ■ ■

We agreed to meet at Café Scheltema. Frederika was going to tell me about her Dutch Reformed childhood, and about her plan to sit naked atop a black cube. Just by way of background for the monologue I had to write. I'd been sitting there for half an hour when I saw Frederika go by on one of those old-fashioned black bicycles.

Fifteen minutes later she finally walked in. Two British tourists were asleep at the next table. Frederika took off her cap and shook her hair. Then she gave me a kiss. Our noses bumped.

'No sleeping here,' said Frans, the waiter, and he slammed his hand down on the tourists' table. 'This isn't a hotel.'

'Have you eaten already?' Frederika asked. 'I just had some soup.'

'I haven't had anything.'

'Well, would you like something to drink? I'll have a double espresso.'

She slid the cookie off her saucer and took little sips of the espresso. She started telling me about the men who were in love with her or had been. And about her grandmother who had subscribed to the church intercom system. A businessman from New York had asked Frederika to come and live with him. She told me how many orgasms he'd given her. I nodded as though women told me these things every day. The world of multiple orgasms and glorious sex was one in which I had yet to set foot. But I didn't let on, of course. When she said 'Fourteen times', I said: 'I see.'

She looked at me searchingly. 'I lived in Kampen for a while,' she said. 'Have you ever been there?'

'Once, with my father, when I was about seven. He always took me to places like that to go for walks.'

That evening, I didn't have to do a thing but listen to Frederika Steinman.

Every once in a while, Frans came by and slammed his hand down on the tourists' table.

At ten-thirty, Frederika got up. She put her cap on. 'Was this of any use to you?' she asked.

'Oh, absolutely,' I said. 'All your men are now inside my head.' We kissed. This time I made sure our noses didn't bump.

Broccoli found out that the house on the Bernard Zweerskade had been sold. Mrs Meerschwam had called the Salvation Army, and this time they'd actually come, along with the Help for the Homeless Project. Broccoli had told Mrs Meerschwam: 'Elvira Lopez is the one who needs the Help for the Homeless Project, but do you think they ever come by with a table or chair?'

A few days later Broccoli went by and met the new owners. A young couple with four guard dogs. That same day he took forty cans of preserves that were still in the cellar to Elvira's place.

While Mrs Meerschwam was cleaning the toaster she'd found the remains of a few mice. She refused to set foot again in the house on the Bernard Zweerskade.

One evening I went with Elvira and Broccoli to visit Mr Berk. I hadn't seen him for a long time. He had a room of his own now. Most of the time we were there, he slept. When he finally woke up, he asked: 'What have you people done with my salami?'

Mme Bercowicz was there too. She'd brought a bag of groceries and a letter from Broccoli's father. She hung it on the wall above her brother's head, because she said there was no use reading it out loud to him.

Berk lay pressed up against the railing of his bed, the way monkeys cling to their cages at the zoo. His eyes were open, but he didn't seem to hear anything. We shook hands with him through the railing, which they'd raised a little after he'd fallen out of bed a few times. One of his eyes was sort of turned up in his head.

Broccoli read his father's letter out loud. It was postmarked Zurich. Mr Eckstein said he was sorry he couldn't come to Amsterdam. He was pleased to hear that everything had been arranged with the house, and said he had no more strength to battle with his wife and would therefore be leaving for Mexico soon. The last few lines were about some Russian farmer sitting under a tree, waiting for his end to come. Eckstein wrote that he hoped to die that way, too, but that it was probably too hot in Mexico to sit under trees.

A nurse came in and put a pair of pantyhose on Mr Berk because, as she explained, he kicked off his blankets at night. While she was pulling on the pantyhose, he looked at us with big eyes.

Elvira asked where I'd been all this time. And if there was any way we could go out to dinner again soon. She felt like dropping another shoe in her soup.

After the final performance, Villa Villekulla threw a party. All the directors were invited, and the artistic director announced that she was pregnant. Everyone seemed to be getting pregnant. The costume designer was due any moment, one of the actresses was in her third month, another was in her fourth. They were getting pregnant like it was going out of style.

We were sitting around two long tables at Het Karbeel on the Warmoestraat, eating cheese fondue. Everyone seemed relieved it was over, especially Henk. Frederika Steinman was at the other table. I looked at her and saw how she occasionally dipped a chunk of bread in the fondue with great deliberation. She wasn't much of an eater. She was telling the others about a movie she'd be playing in soon.

At eleven-thirty, the people with children started to leave. Henk got up too. 'I have to get back to my dogs,' he said. He waved to us without saying goodbye to anyone in particular. The actress-mothers kissed us heartily. 'You were fantastic,' they said. They'd had so much to drink that they didn't notice the crusted fondue on their lips. Hilde, the firebird, left as well. 'Good luck,' she said. I knew she hated Frederika Steinman. Frederika Steinman had no husband, no children, no babysitter, and no moss growing on her teeth.

■ ■ ■

The little group that was left over finally went to a bar on the Nes. The actor who did Gestalt therapy went along too. He kept talking the whole way, without noticing that no one was walking beside him. Frederika's lock was broken, so she took her bicycle into the bar. I'm sure it was strictly forbidden to take bicycles into bars, but when Frederika walked in with hers no one said a thing.

Frederika acted like I was a total stranger. I got into a long conversation with the Gestalt actor. He belonged to the actors' union, and he was telling me about all the good reasons to join up.

At two-thirty, the Gestalt actor finally went home. He forgot to pay his part, but I was too happy he was leaving to feel much like reminding him.

Then I was alone with Frederika and a man who wrote children's plays. He was only thirty, but he was already balding. The writer sat down next to me and whispered: 'Music is the highest form of art. All art strives to be music.'

I had to agree with that, the way I agreed with everything.

Then the Gestalt actor came back in. 'Oh, wait, I've already been here,' he said, and left again.

'I'm going to visit my lover in Israel next month,' Frederika told me while the writer was off in the men's room.

'Does your lover live in Israel?' I asked.

'Yes,' she said dreamily.

'That's funny,' I said, 'my sister lives in Israel. I'm going to visit her at the end of March.' I said it without thinking. All important things are said without thinking. How else could you say them?

Frederika grabbed my arm. 'Then we can meet there,' she said.

'Yes,' I said, 'we could do that.'

She pulled her diary out of her handbag.

'Here,' she said. 'Read this. But only this page.'

I read it. It was about love. I figured. About sex too. But then very poetic. I was afraid I was going to blush and that she'd notice, so I stopped reading.

The writer came back from the men's room. 'All art strives to be music,' he said. He looked Frederika in the eye and kissed her on the lips.

Frederika's bicycle was between me and Frederika.

'We had something together once, a long time ago,' she told me later, 'but he went crazy. He started thinking he was an angel. So I left him.'

When she left I shook her hand.

TEL AVIV, RECHOV HA'AVODA

*D*ear Broccoli and Elvira,
    By the time you read this I will be in Israel. At my
sister's. My parents think it was a burning desire to see my
sister that drove me to Israel, but in fact it was Frederika
Steinman. She's an actress, and she's famous. Maybe you
two have heard of her. Her grandmother had (or has) a
subscription to the church intercom service.

She wants me to write a monologue for her. Not her
grandmother, Frederika. God knows why. She has an Israeli
lover. I've been invited to visit her at her lover's place.
Some invitations should definitely be accepted, I'm sure you
two will agree with me on that.

I'll be back in ten days, in plenty of time to see Elvira as
Lady Macbeth.

Every morning I do the exercises people have to do to
look like Marlon Brando, but progress is slow. How are you
two coming along? My mother sings every morning for ten

minutes to expand her lung capacity. If I think of all the exercises people do in the morning, the Marlon Brando exercises seem by far the most pleasant, and probably the most productive.

Give my heartfelt regards to Mr Berk. I think of him often. But that's probably not enough.

Promise to wait for me before opening another can of foie gras?

Fondly,

Ewald S. Krieg

On the phone Frederika said she was very happy, and that I should come by for dinner. Her lover was apparently an excellent cook.

I arrived fifteen minutes early at the Rechov Ha'Avoda in Tel Aviv. I walked up a flight of stairs. There was no bell and the door was open, so I just walked in.

A fat woman was down on her knees scrubbing the kitchen floor, with five kids running around her. 'Excuse me,' I said. I showed her the scrap of paper with the name of Frederika's lover. She pointed to indicate that I should try upstairs.

The door there was open too. Frederika was in the kitchen. She was standing at the stove, poking a fork into a piece of meat. She was wearing a light-blue summer dress. She hugged me. And said again that she was very happy. That she'd never been happier, and that it had always been her parents' dream to see the Holy Land as well. She turned down the heat under the pan and we sat at the kitchen table.

'Wow, it's weird seeing you here,' she said.

'Yeah,' I said, 'really weird.'

Then her lover came in. He was tall, balding too, and he had a little beard like Lenin's. The first thing he said was: 'No curry powder, sold out everywhere.' Then he hugged me and said something along the lines of: 'My house is your house, my food is your food, my blanket is your blanket.' He didn't quite say: 'My woman is your woman.' But that seemed to me an implicit part of the package deal he apparently offered all his guests.

We ate lamb. Frederika told him I was going to write a monologue for her about a naked woman sitting on a black cube.

'Fantastic,' her lover said, 'that's fantastic.'

During dinner, Frederika showed me her publicity folder. In some of the photos she was wearing an evening dress and had a huge glass goblet in her hand. A man in a tuxedo was standing beside her, with his arm around her.

Her lover's name was Jonathan. He told me that he originally came from Argentina, and that he'd been living in Tel Aviv for twenty years but had kept his Argentine passport, just to be sure. He said: 'After this war, I want to enjoy every moment of my life.' He was referring to the Gulf War.

'Yes,' I said, 'you see, the way I look at it, you go to the market and see beautiful tomatoes. You buy them, but when you get home the tomatoes are rotten, mouldy, full of worms. And life is even worse; life has no tomatoes.'

'You don't know what happiness is,' Jonathan said.

'I know,' I said, 'I know very well, but I don't like the way it tastes.'

'Let's go to Jaffo and dance,' Frederika suggested. She went to change her clothes.

We took a taxi to a discotheque where we drank anise cocktails. I sat on a bench along the wall with Frederika's bag on my lap. She had a big bag, because she'd wanted to take all her publicity folders with her. She danced wildly. Not only with Jonathan, but also with lots of other men.

When we parted ways at four o'clock, I asked Jonathan if by any chance, when he was still living in Buenos Aires, he'd known a girl by the name of Elvira Lopez.

He looked at me in shock, but then his face resumed its old cheerful expression.

'Oh yes,' he said, 'very well. We worked together once. Beautiful girl.'

'See you in Holland,' I said to Frederika.

She kissed me. 'Start writing,' she shouted after me.

I took a room in a little hotel by the beach, right next to a brothel. My sister lived in Gaza, but it was impossible to get from Tel Aviv to Gaza by public transport in the middle of the night. My sister adhered to the idea of a Greater Israel. People sometimes asked me what idea I adhered to. I never told anyone that I adhered to the Greater Marlon Brando idea. To whom could you tell that?

The taxi driver tried to sell me a tape player. The anise cocktails had made me so nauseous that I just bought it.

MY WIFE WILL SMELL IT ANYWAY

*B*roccoli met me at the airport. Mr Berk had died and been buried. Berk's niece had gone back to Scotland right after the funeral, to devote herself entirely to her handicapped husband and the veneration of Jesus. Mme Bercowicz was busy finding out if there wasn't some way to actually have 'Bercowicz' put on the headstone.

Two men had carried Mr Berk to his grave in a prayer shawl. Broccoli said it had looked like they were toting a roll of carpet. Some other man had rattled his way through the prayers. Afterwards he came up to Mme Bercowicz and said: 'Sorry about that, but I have the flu.'

Broccoli's parents had written a letter to Mme Bercowicz.

'I'm sure you understand why we can't be present.' Mr Eckstein had written. *'At two points in my life, your brother helped me when no one else would. What's more, he taught me that silence is truly the supreme virtue. And he also taught me that other great truth in life: run, run, run, as fast as your legs will carry you, and then some. He*

*was the last living person I knew from a given period in my life. I'm
starting to feel like a museum piece.'*

We took the train from Schiphol to the south side of
Amsterdam. Broccoli carried my suitcase. He didn't ask about
Frederika Steinman. He did say that he'd finally signed the
contract with Mr Lebbing, and that the premiere of *Macbeth*
would be held in Lebbing's shed in May. He was less excited
about it than I'd ever seen him.

'Elvira sends her greetings,' he said when we got out at
Amsterdam South Station. 'She asked me to kiss you.' He kissed
me. I looked the other way so as not to see his teasing look.

I walked to my parents' house. Broccoli took the number five
tram to Elvira's.

I had to wait three weeks for Frederika to come back from Israel.
Then I waited another week. Finally, I called her. The message
in English on her answering machine said that this was Frederika
Steinman's number, and that I could contact her agent in
London or her agent in Paris. I left a message saying that I
preferred to contact her in person about the monologue I was
going to write.

A week later she called back.

We made a date for lunch at Keyzer. That was my idea. I'd
had meetings there before that had proven completely fruitless.
That's precisely why I was stuck on the place. The way someone
who's lost twenty times at roulette keeps sticking to red.

Inside Keyzer, I saw my old Latin teacher. We nodded to each
other. I hoped she'd recognise Frederika Steinman. When
Frederika finally walked into Keyzer – half an hour late – no one
recognised her, not even my old Latin teacher.

When we kissed I knocked over the sugar bowl. Then she
hung up her coat and disappeared into the ladies' room for at
least fifteen minutes.

When she was finally back across from me, she said: 'I just
got in from Rome. They've offered me a role. They're going to

film Oberski. You know that book? I may be playing the girlfriend. Really fantastic. There's this beautiful scene in it, right
after they're liberated, where she takes a bath with that boy. If I
do it, I want to make that a real water ballet.'
    'A water ballet?'
    'A party,' Frederika said.
    'Well it's not my movie, but if they've just been liberated, don't
they have anything better to do than throw parties?'

Ten days later Frederika invited me to visit her little canalside
apartment.
    'Does it get any more Amsterdam than this?' Frederika asked.
    I shook my head.
    'Cup of soup?' she asked.
    'Yes,' I said, 'that would be nice.'
    We sat across from each other and spooned at our soup. Every
once in a while she looked at me and nodded encouragingly.
When she got up to go to the bathroom, she turned the music
up loud.
    I'd already started on the monologue a few times, but I didn't
know how you went about something like that, writing a monologue for Frederika Steinman. The title I'd chosen was A Couple
of Words She Said By Way of Greeting. In retrospect, that didn't
seem like such a great title for a monologue.
    When I'd finished my soup, she put the pan in the fridge.
'That's for tomorrow,' she said. While she was rummaging around
in the kitchen, I imagined Frederika Steinman calling me up on
to the stage in my tuxedo, to receive an ovation for A Couple of
Words She Said By Way of Greeting.
    'This Johan,' she said, 'have I ever told you about him?'
    'No,' I said, 'I don't think you've ever mentioned the name
Johan. Jonathan though, that's your lover's name.'
    'Yes,' she said, 'Jonathan is my lover, but Johan was my first
boyfriend. I met him at one of those camps, a summer camp.
Later, when I was twenty-six, I ran into him again at the disco.

In the village where my parents lived.

'I asked him; "Are you happy?"

'"What do you mean?" he said.

'I said: "Just that. Are you happy?"

'We danced all evening, he didn't want to go home. He said: "When I'm in bed with my wife, all she does is stare at the ceiling."

'We went out for a drive in my father's station wagon. We found a quiet place and made love for two hours in the back. At a certain point, it was almost four o'clock, and I had to go home. I wanted to drop him off, but he said: "No, I'm not going home. My wife will smell it anyway."

'When we said goodbye, he said: "You've made a dream come true, I've finally been kidnapped by a woman."'

'That's a wonderful story,' I said. 'Only I don't know if that's my big fantasy. Being kidnapped by a woman, I mean.'

'I always wonder what he thinks when he sees my name in the paper.'

Frederika offered me a bonbon, but I said no thanks.

Before she showed me to the door, she said: 'My very first sweetheart was Moluccan, he's the one who shot the pastor.'

Afterwards, I wandered through the city in a daze. It was warm, I had my jacket over my arm. I kept thinking about what that Johan had said. 'I'm not going home. My wife will smell it anyway.' As far as I was concerned, Frederika's entire monologue could consist of those two lines.

Dear Ewald,

In some strange way, a friendship has grown up between us, and I hope you can validate that. For that very reason, I am afraid the trust between us could be violated. I believe you understand that very well. You of all people. Our project must go on, now more than ever. Encircle my stories with love, and you will receive my love.

Enclosed here you will find a postcard of a painting by

Edvard Munch. It says more than a thousand words. About me as well.

I'll see you next Tuesday at six-thirty, in front of Tuschinski.

Love,
Frederika

In the envelope was a card showing *Puberty* by Edvard Munch. All that was written on the back was her name: Frederika. That card stayed on my desk for years, until it got lost during a move.

At the Tuschinski theatre we saw *The Indecent Woman*. After twenty minutes, Frederika stood up and walked out. I went after her. It was the first time I'd ever walked out of a movie.

'What an embarrassing display,' Frederika said as she unlocked her bike. 'I'm so glad I turned down that role.'

'Embarrassing,' I said, 'extremely embarrassing.'

We went to eat something at the Film Museum. All she wanted was a salad. 'The food here is lovely,' she said. 'So what about your life? Tell me.'

'Me? Oh. All I do is—'

'No,' she said, 'I couldn't live on desire alone. I need contact.'

She didn't feel like having a drink either. She had to get home. I walked with her part of the way, as far as the Leidse Bosjes. She told me that when her parents found out that her sweetheart had shot that pastor, her father had made her kneel down beside him and beg the Lord for forgiveness.

At the gates of the Vondelpark, she asked me: 'Do you know the whore of Jericho?'

'Not off the top of my head,' I said.

'I have to go,' she said. She stared at me earnestly and, with a pensive look in her eye, said: 'You are a soul on fire.'

I couldn't think of anything better to say than 'Thank you'. I kissed her hand. Then she cycled off.

MOSQUITO LARVAE

I placed a classified ad in the *NRC/Handelsblad*: 'Writer seeks office/pied-à-terre.' Now that I was writing a mono- logue for Frederika Steinman, I needed a place to receive her.

Two people reacted to the ad, a man and a woman. I went to the woman first. She lived on the Reijnier Vinkeleskade. She came to the door in a dress and bedroom slippers. There was a racing bike in the hallway. She showed me to the living room, where she introduced herself as Hanne and said she suffered from excruciating headaches.

'I'm very sorry to hear that,' I said.

'That's why I don't want students in my attic room, only quiet people, like writers.'

I nodded, just to underscore the fact that I was very quiet. She went into the kitchen and came back with a tray with two cups of coffee on it. She wasn't wearing pantyhose. I could see the hair on her legs.

'I used to be a lab assistant,' Hanne said, 'but the headaches keep me from going out these days.'

She sat down beside me and dropped three sweeteners in her coffee. Then she looked at me. 'So you're a writer?' she said.

I pulled a copy of The Machiavellian from under my coat. It was the only proof I had that my ad was telling the truth.

She looked at the cover, put the book down and said: 'I had a boyfriend, a neurologist. He was Jewish, but it didn't work out.'

'I'm sorry to hear that.'

'You're Jewish, aren't you?'

'Yes, but I'm not a neurologist.'

We went upstairs to the attic room she wanted to rent. It was full of boxes of clothes, and there was a little window with all kinds of flies stuck to it.

'The Salvation Army is coming by soon to take this away,' Hanne said. 'Then you'll have all the room you need.'

Suddenly, I couldn't stop thinking about Mrs Meerschwam. I was sure that Hanne and Mrs Meerschwam had a psychic link. I took another good look around. Even with all the boxes gone, the attic would still have been full with two people in it. It didn't seem like the kind of place I could receive Frederika Steinman. This was not the place to receive people who were planning to become world-famous actresses.

Hanne walked me to the front door and said: 'Come by again some time, we can talk.'

Frank Rapp was busy feeding mosquito larvae to his tadpoles. It was an activity which seemed to give him pleasure. The mosquito larvae were in a sandwich bag, and he scooped them out carefully with a fork. He wanted me to come over and see how the tadpoles ate the mosquito larvae.

Rapp was wearing bedroom slippers and a bathrobe that fell open now and then. Later, I found out that he spent his days in a bathrobe. He only got dressed when he had to go to the doctor or to a funeral. Someone once told me: 'Everything we do is done out of protest, or the desire for a better life.' But maybe I read that somewhere.

It was four-thirty on a Wednesday afternoon. Mr Rapp lived on the Jacob Obrechtstraat, and he too had office space to let. For the last hour he'd been telling me stories about his life. I didn't have to do anything but nod once in a while. We drank sherry from one of the four big carafes on his side table. He didn't ask what I'd written. That was a relief. All he said was: 'Someone should write my story, I've been published in *De Gids*.'

Between anecdotes he got up and shuffled out on to the balcony to feed nuts to the birds. He seemed like a nature lover. His furnishings consisted largely of plants and newspapers. There were also a few books and a bit of furniture, of course, but they were completely buried under plants and newspapers. He smoked cigarettes, which he broke in two and stuck in a holder.

Finally, he showed me the room in the basement. It was dark. In the middle was a gigantic conference table, with two huge wooden chairs on both sides that looked like thrones. Around the table were wooden statues. The glassed-in porch at the back contained a desk and three wooden Christ figures, once again amid a collection of plants.

'Three South American artists used to work here, but they hanged themselves,' Mr Rapp said. 'So it's been empty for a while.' I nodded and said that was no problem.

The room reminded me of the Führerbunker. Of course, I'd never been in the Führerbunker, but a Führerbunker seemed like an excellent place to write a monologue for Frederika Steinman.

Beyond the porch was a huge overgrown garden with a pond. This looked like the kind of place to receive Frederika Steinman. 'I'll take it,' I said.

Rapp took a few steps in my direction. 'I'm not asking much for it,' he said, 'but of course you'll have to bring me some juice oranges now and then.' His dentures didn't fit well. He had to keep pushing them back into place with his tongue. 'And a few mosquito larvae. But not the frozen ones, they have to be fresh.'

That evening I called Broccoli. 'I've rented the Führerbunker,' I told him.

'Good,' he said, 'very good, a Führerbunker is exactly what Operation Brando needs.'

'You have to splatter that Dutch Reformed pain all over the paper,' Broccoli said. I'd finally told him about Frederika Steinman and the monologue I was going to write for her.

Broccoli, Elvira and I were sitting on a bench in the Sarphatipark. We were on our way to the Albert Cuyp market, where Elvira wanted to buy fish.

'But what do I know about Dutch Reformed pain?'

'You should read the New Testament,' Elvira said.

'Dutch Reformed pain is immense,' Broccoli said, 'I've read books about it.'

According to Broccoli, Kampen was the Mecca of Dutch Reformed pain, and Dutch Reformed women. I would have been glad to emigrate to Kampen for Frederika Steinman, if that was where I could make Dutch Reformed pain my own.

I was very flattered that Frederika thought I was a burning soul, but I'd also listened to her carefully and knew that she considered herself a burning soul as well. I'd heard stories about burning people, but the world of burning souls was a new one to me.

Broccoli went into the post office to make a call. Elvira spent a long time picking out a fish. The fishmonger didn't mind, because he loved Elvira, or acted like he did.

'Is it important to you, this monologue?' she asked.

I said: 'Yes.'

'And Frederika Steinman?'

'Well,' I said. Then, 'Aw.' And after that: 'I don't know.' But by then so much time had gone by that she seemed to have forgotten what the question was.

Finally, she pointed to a cod fillet.

'When did you actually meet Broccoli's father?' I asked while extracting a piece of used chewing gum from its wrapper.

'A long time ago,' she said. 'So long that I can't remember any more. You start forgetting a lot of things as you get older.'

She paid for the cod fillet. I thought about Frederika Steinman and the Dutch Reformed pain I was going to splatter all over the paper. Elvira looked at me. 'You bought yourself a new pair of pants, didn't you?'

I nodded.

'They cheated you. Your butt is much too small for those pants. From the back you look like some grandpa.'

'Grandpa?'

'A grandpa with baggy trousers,' she said. 'One of those old men who have to hitch up their pants all the time, so they wear suspenders, that's the kind of pants you've got on. Next time you buy pants, take me along. Or Frederika Steinman, of course.'

Then she went into the post office to find Broccoli.

REFORMED PAIN

'I've been talking all afternoon, I can't talk any more,' Frederika Steinman said. We were in the first-class restaurant at Centraal Station. I remembered sitting in that very same restaurant with Broccoli and Elvira, eating pistachios.

She had her hat on. And she didn't take it off either. She'd been discussing a movie with a director. I didn't know you had to talk so much about these things.

'Maybe we shouldn't do the monologue on the beach,' Frederika said.

'No, not on the beach.'

She looked at me silently. She was in deep earnest.

'Frederika,' she said, 'like some cow.'

'What?' I said.

'Well, Frederika,' she said, 'that's a cow's name.'

'Naw,' I said, 'it's not that bad. They give cows the weirdest names. Besides, Ewald isn't such a great name either.'

'No,' she said, 'they'd never name a cow Ewald, never.'

She stared sombrely into space. 'I want to act again,' she said.
'I can't stand this waiting.'

'I can't stand waiting either.'

As soon as I'd written the monologue for Frederika I could
stop trying to become an actor. No one believed in it anyway,
except for Broccoli and Elvira. And no one ever *had* believed in
it. I would write monologues for actresses and splatter the
Reformed pain and Catholic pain and Jewish pain all over the
page. It would look almost like a profession. People would respect
me, or pretend to. That was already getting somewhere.

'That boy, you know,' Frederika mused. 'I didn't know anything
back then, but he gave me some advice: never eat dry rusks
before kissing someone.'

'That's good advice,' I whispered.

She got up. She wanted to go eat somewhere. I followed her.
I thought about Elvira and imagined that I didn't matter to her,
and not only to her, but to no one. It was a pleasant thought. It
relieved me of all responsibility, and also of all thoughts having
to do with Operation Brando. I didn't dare to tell Frederika about
Operation Brando. I'd tried to once, but quickly realised that I'd
better keep it to myself.

'I just wish my parents could pray for me to be offered a role.'
Frederika was walking her bike. I didn't have a bike. That's why
she had to walk. She didn't want to take me on the back.

'Yeah,' I said.

'They pray all the time anyway.'

'You have that sometimes,' I said. 'My sister's the same way.'

She took me to a Pakistani restaurant she knew quite well. It
was really cheap, she said, but the food wasn't disgusting. Again
I thought about Elvira and how we'd found cat hair at the bottom
of our trays of egg foo young. How she'd sat on the toilet right
after we found the cat hair, and how, half an hour later, she'd
jerked us off while half-eaten trays of egg foo young were still
lying all over the house.

I watched Frederika eat her Pakistani food, and I admired her for knowing what she wanted, and for being willing to give up everything for that one ideal: becoming a world-famous actress.

'Don't eat too many dry rusks, hear?' I said to Frederika once we were out on the street.

'No,' she said, 'same to you.'

The monologue wasn't really coming along. Dutch Reformed pain was still too foreign to me. Broccoli had bought me a copy of the New Testament, but that didn't help much either. Every once in a while, though, I did start thinking I was Jesus. Maybe I should just have asked Frederika: 'Why do you want to sit naked on top of a black cube? And if you do have to sit naked on top of a black cube, why do I have to write a text to go along with it? Wouldn't it be better to just sit there and say nothing? On top of that black cube?'

But I thought questions like that were unseemly. I thought my intelligence was too limited to grasp the hidden meaning of a naked woman atop a black cube. And if it wasn't my lack of intelligence, then it had to be my inexperience. There were whole worlds I knew nothing about, and about which I wanted to know everything. The world, for example, in which you shot a pastor and then got to be Frederika Steinman's sweetheart.

I let Frederika read a page of the monologue.

'It's like a streetcar going by,' she said.

Neither of us said anything for a moment.

'Do you mean that in a positive sense?' I asked.

'Oh yes,' she said.

This conversation took place in Café Luxembourg. It was the same afternoon that she told me we shared a sexual obsession.

Most of my days were spent in the basement room at Mr Rapp's, which I rented for a reasonable monthly sum. The only condition was that he was allowed to walk in at any time. And that I did a little shopping for him. I often bought him nougat. He devoured nougat, huge chunks of it. God only knows how he could do that with his dentures.

Rapp lived on the first floor, and right above my office lived a young man who worked for a big consultancy firm. He made love every Thursday evening to a girl who always left her tennis racket at the bottom of the stairs. After making love they would watch the late news on RTL4.

Downstairs, I was trying to give voice to Frederika Steinman's pain; since that wasn't working, I had all the time in the world to listen to the noises coming from the upstairs apartment. 'Hoo!' my neighbour would shout. 'Hoo!' And, all the way at the end: 'Hooey!' Whatever else happens, I promised myself then, I'm never going to yell 'hoo', and not 'hooey' either.

Sometimes I murmured: 'Frederika Steinman and I share a sexual obsession.' Like a hymn to convince God that the time had come for me to give glorious voice to Dutch Reformed pain.

I hadn't told Broccoli about the sexual obsession. First, I needed to find out exactly which sexual obsession Frederika Steinman and I shared. After all, there were thousands of them.

'I'm going to Athens soon. Konstapoupolos, the director, has asked me to work with him again. He's a very special man. He gives me everything I need. As an actress, that is.'

We were sitting in Mr Rapp's garden. He was watching us from the balcony. It felt like summer. She had broken up with her Israeli lover. She'd gone back to Tel Aviv once, and he'd been waiting at the airport with a ring. She thought that was dumb. Besides, he'd kept falling asleep.

'You should come to Athens too,' she said. 'You could write in my apartment.'

We were eating cherries.

'Yes,' I said, 'that would be nice.' I imagined myself popping off to Athens and writing in her apartment, waiting until she came back from her day on the set with Konstapoupolos. I was even willing to wash her clothes and clean the toilet during the day. And cook her dinner for her at night. I was in the process of becoming worldly. At least, I was doing my best. And once I was good and worldly, nothing would be left of the odour of the ghetto which I thought still clung to me. After all, a voluntary ghetto is a ghetto nonetheless.

'I'll write to you,' Frederika said. Then she got up to leave, because she still had to pack her bags. This time she said nothing about our shared sexual obsession.

As we stepped out the door, I handed her a copy of a booklet I'd written and photocopied myself. It was called *The Frederika Book*. In it, I had tried to accurately summarise our meetings. To make up for the fact that the monologue, which should have been ready long ago, still wasn't finished. And maybe also because I sensed that I would never write the monologue at her apartment in Athens, and that I would never, ever stand beside her on stage to receive a Golden Bear or a Golden Lion or whatever they call those things. That the only thing that would come of our meetings would be my own, hand-copied booklet.

The first sentence of *The Frederika Book* went as follows: 'May I be a memory to you, then you may be one to me as well.'

She flipped through the book and laughed. 'Let's go have dinner,' she said. 'This is definitely a special occasion.'

Sitting at the table, she read the whole book. She wanted us to do the dialogues together out loud. The book consisted mostly of dialogue. It was strange, like we were playing ourselves. Occasionally she grabbed my hand. I was afraid she'd feel how clammy it was, so I kept pulling it back. 'Why do you do that?' she asked.

We had frozen fish fillets at the café. When we were finished, she said she really had to go and pack her bags.

As she climbed on to her bike, she bunched her dress up in her crotch. I guess she was afraid I'd see her knickers. At that moment Frederika Steinman was as desirable to me as Elvira. Maybe even more. I've never completely understood what makes people desirable to each other. Probably there's just desire that needs somewhere to go, like sound, or light, or a bullet.

'I'll write to you,' she said.

IT WILL BE IN THE PAPERS

*E*very day I walked to my post office box to see if a letter had come from Frederika Steinman. I'd rented the post office box a long time ago, to keep people from finding out that I still lived with my parents. Sometimes they asked me: 'Do you live in that post office box?'

And I'd tell them: 'Yes, I do.'

In the two months that Frederika Steinman was in Athens, there was no letter, no plane ticket, no card with her address. Not even a telegram saying 'come here and write'. Frederika was silent. The exhilaration I'd felt when I opened my post office box and found a letter from her remained a one-time thing.

Elvira rehearsed the Lady Macbeth monologues every day. To make an evening-long programme out of it, Broccoli had tossed in a few of Macbeth's monologues as well. 'Who the hell's going to notice?' he said.

I asked Elvira if she knew an actor from Buenos Aires by the name of Jonathan. 'No,' she said, 'I've forgotten almost everything about Buenos Aires.' It was in the middle of the night. She had her slippers on and was eating a croissant she'd bought at the all-night deli.

Elvira didn't have a bathtub in her house on the Tweede Tuindwarsstraat, only a shower built into a kind of closet. Elvira loved to take baths, especially bubble baths. Once every two weeks Broccoli rented her a room at the Victoria Hotel, so she could take a bath. The days of taking baths at the Bernard Zweerskade were over.

Broccoli told me his parents had left Rabat and were on their way to Mexico. Every once in a while, Mrs Meerschwam called to ask where her money was.

Elvira often looked at me laughingly and asked: 'Are you still working on becoming Marlon Brando?' One time, when we were buying soft ice at the Febo, she asked me: 'Is Frederika Steinman trying to become Marlon Brando too?'

Two months later, Frederika called. 'I'm back from Athens,' she said. 'We have to get together.'

'Yes,' I said, 'we have to do that.'

She was waiting at the tables in front of Café Scheltema. She was wearing sunglasses. She'd had a fantastic time.

'It was a real eye-opener,' she said. 'Konstapoupolos took me by the hand and said: "You can do it, Frederika, you can do so much."'

'That sounds good,' I said.

'Yes,' she said, 'and it's true. I can do so much. I'm drowning in my own talent.'

I nodded, quite seriously. Because she was quite serious too.

Then she took off her sunglasses and said: 'And now about that booklet.'

'What booklet?' I asked.

'That Frederika book, the one you made for me. Looking

back on it, I'm not so happy about that.'

I tried to say 'oh yeah?' as casually as possible. I don't think I succeeded very well.

'It's something that should have stayed between you and me.' As she spoke the words 'you and me', she brought her face up close to mine. I held my breath because I was afraid I stank. I've had that at the weirdest moments in my life. Usually right in the middle of a conversation. People get angry. They think it's rude. That I suddenly just stop talking. But it's the exact opposite of rudeness. I don't want to be smelled. At a certain point, I got into the habit of looking at the ground when I talked to people.

'It *has* stayed between you and me,' I said, once I'd leaned back in my chair.

'I saw that you made twenty-seven copies of it,' she said. 'It says so in the colophon.' She was playing with her sunglasses. 'I'm afraid it will be made public. I'm not exactly unknown.'

'No,' I said, 'you're not exactly unknown.'

'I want to have all the copies, and I'm prepared to pay for them.'

'But I don't have all of them any more. I gave a few away, or sold them to cover the cost of the photocopies.'

'I must have them,' she said, 'so buy them back. The contents must not be made public.'

'But there's nothing in it. Only what we said to each other. So what did we say to each other?'

I tried to remember exactly what was in *The Frederika Book*. What had we said to each other anyway? 'Your name isn't even in it. Only your first name. There are thousands of people called Frederika.'

'They'll recognise me,' she said, 'you don't know how people are. It will be in the papers.' She had a panicky look in her eye.

'So what? What did you say? That you shouldn't eat dry rusks before kissing someone? Who could be offended by that? Frederika Steinman doesn't eat dry rusks before kissing. Millions of people don't eat dry rusks before kissing. The gossip columns aren't exactly going to pounce on that.'

'You don't know how people are,' she said again. She was staring into space, looking angry.

I finally had to promise that I would try to get back all the copies, but I said I couldn't guarantee anything.

'What are you going to do with them?' I asked.

'I don't know yet,' she said, 'probably burn them.'

I didn't say a word. We watched the people getting off the tram. Then Frederika said: 'I just came from Mr Frohlich. Do you know him?'

I remembered my visit to Mr Frohlich, along with Broccoli, and how he'd run his hand over my cheek and said 'soft'. 'Yes,' I said.

'He told me: "Frederika, you're such a great actress, why do you turn down all these roles?"'

She stirred her coffee in silence for a moment, then said quite cheerily: 'I don't want to play in anything that's beneath me.'

I said I could easily understand that.

'So how's the monologue coming along?'

'Good. Very good. It's almost finished.'

It was about a woman who committed suicide because she thought she was the whore of Jericho. It was set in a beach house. It was still lacking something.

She put on her sunglasses and pushed back her chair. 'Let's go inside, I see someone I don't want to talk to.' She grabbed me by the hand and pulled me inside.

'Too warm outside for the ladies?' the waiter asked.

We found a table in the darkest corner of the café.

'I'm leaving again in two weeks,' Frederika whispered. 'I'm going to the Venice festival. They're showing my French movie.'

'Aha,' I said, and the whole time I kept thinking: Frederika Steinman is worldly, Frederika Steinman is worldly. Wherever she comes from, she doesn't reek of the prematurely afflicted. She's not a walking fount of misfortune.

'Let's fix a date before then for me to pick up the booklets.'
'Yes,' I said, 'let's do that.'

She was sitting at a table outside Keyzer, with her sister-in-law.
This time Frederika Steinman didn't take off her sunglasses.
Frederika's sister-in-law told me she was a nurse. I had eighteen
copies of *The Frederika Book* with me, in a plastic bag.
'I can't locate the others,' I said. 'And I need two hundred
guilders to sort of cover the costs.'
She pulled out her pocketbook and handed me two hundred-
guilder notes. 'Then this is another case closed,' she said.
'That's right,' I said.
'What you did wasn't *comme il faut*,' she said.
I think '*comme il faut*' is such a lovely phrase. Later, I heard
other people use it a few times. It's a real beauty.
The sister-in-law watched closely as I put away the hundreds.
Frederika said she wasn't planning to just toss the booklets
in the trash. She was afraid someone would read them then
anyway. They would have to be burned, and the ashes could
go in the recycled-paper bin. She looked at me with her big
blue eyes, which were practically invisible behind those
sunglasses. There was absolutely no reason to assume she wasn't
serious.
So what I said was: 'Yes, burning them would probably be the
best.'
Mr Berk had once said that in most cases he preferred to be
silent, because people usually misunderstood him anyway. Now
I knew what he meant. Anything I said to Frederika would have
been futile. She wanted to burn the booklets because she was
afraid people would think that the real Frederika, just like the
Frederika on paper, had said: 'Never eat dry rusks before you kiss
someone.'
So the three of us sat outside Keyzer and talked about how
badly nurses were paid these days. The sister-in-law was wearing
a see-through blouse. Not a pretty picture.

After half an hour, Frederika said: 'We have to be going. Call me when you've got the monologue finished.'

I nodded.

The sister-in-law put a ten-guilder note on the table. 'For the coffee,' she said.

DEAR FREDERIKA

*D*ear Frederika,
　　　After our cosy encounter in front of Keyzer and the pleasant meeting with your sister-in-law, I felt it was time to drop you a line.

I don't think there ever will be a definitive version of the monologue I was supposed to write for you. I have no desire to write monologues for someone who burns the booklets I made for her.

Excuse my saying so, but your sense of humour is a bit too Reformed for me. Undoubtedly you are the pathetic product of your upbringing, and that should excuse you. But a few too many people hide behind their pitiful upbringings, and therefore you are not excused. Even if you imagine a thousand times over that you're the whore of Jericho. Please allow me to disillusion you: you are not the whore of Jericho.

In a letter, you once promised that I would receive your

love. I realise now that I should not have taken that as a promise, but as a threat.

I've done my best to splatter your Dutch Reformed pain across the page. It was the first time I've ever tried something like that, and the last. Pain should remain pain. Pain can't be for splattering across paper. Although that is undoubtedly an extremely God-fearing and Reformed thing to do. The splattering of pain across paper, that is.

I would have liked to write at much greater length, but I'll leave it at this. Please know that there is always one comfort: if you don't become a world-famous actress, you can always – like your beloved grandmother – subscribe to the church intercom service.

None of this can detract from my pleasure at having met you.

Write back. I haven't done my best to insult you for nothing.

Ewald

I walked from the kitchen out on to Mr Rapp's porch, then back again. What I wanted most was to write her five more letters that same evening, but I knew that wouldn't say much for my dignity. I sat down in a chair with a view of the three wooden Christ figures. I remembered Frederika telling me that her life was one great search for passion. You couldn't say that about mine. Distance and passion don't really mix. On the other hand, distance can prove quite useful when it comes to staying alive. There's good reason for them to say that true passion is destructive. Without deceit, there can be no passion; so in the long run, passion must be destructive as well.

I thought about how Frederika and I had sat waiting in the Fodor Museum; it seemed like that was the only reason for us to have been there at all. To wait. Until the next class came stumbling in, with children who looked like they were going to a funeral. Or worse. To a public execution.

IT'S RAINING MEN, HALLELUJAH

*A*t seven o'clock on a Tuesday morning, I left my parents' house with one suitcase. I'd asked Broccoli if I could sleep at Elvira's. The days I would spend on Frank Rapp's porch. If anyone asked what I was doing, I would tell them I was working on a monologue for Frederika Steinman. Even though I knew that monologue would never come, and if it did it would be tucked away in the same drawer where I kept the four remaining copies of *The Frederika Book*.

I stuck close to the housefronts. I was afraid someone would see me, although there was absolutely no reason for anyone to look at me. Still, I had the feeling I was being watched.

I was wearing my duffel coat. It was raining, so I had the hood up. I hadn't told my parents I was leaving. They would never be able to take it if I left.

On the Apollolaan I suddenly heard someone shouting: 'Ewald Krieg, yoo-hoo, Ewald Krieg.' I turned around. A little man was running after me. I only recognised him once he was standing right in front of me. It was the pack-mule, Mr Meerschwam.

'You're Ewald Krieg, aren't you?' he asked.

'Yes,' I said, 'I am.'

'I'm Mr Meerschwam. Remember me?'

I turned and walked on, but he stayed right behind me.

'How are Mr and Mrs Eckstein? We never hear from them.' He kept looking around, as if someone might be listening. 'Are they coming back?'

'I have no idea,' I said.

'They're such fine people. These days I do a lot of driving for an old woman, but it's not the same.'

I walked as fast as I could in the direction of the De Lairessestraat.

'We hear such peculiar things about the Eckstein family,' he whispered, 'not that we attach any importance to them. Do you hear peculiar things too?'

'No, I hear nothing peculiar.' I was close to the Hilton now, and he was still following me.

'Strange, because almost everyone I've talked to has heard peculiar things about the Ecksteins. That they've fled to Mexico and changed their names. That's pretty peculiar, don't you think?'

'I don't know a thing. Believe me, I don't know a thing about it.'

'Well, people are saying the most peculiar things about the Ecksteins these days,' he went on, completely unfazed. 'That's what you get. You're barely out the door and people start saying the most peculiar things about you. Well, I hope I'm spared that.'

'So do I.'

'You know what they're also saying? That he sold houses that didn't even exist, and businesses that still had to be incorporated. Which is why he's fled to Mexico and assumed another name. That's what people are saying. Not that my wife and I put any stock in it. But still . . .'

'I don't know a thing. Believe me, I don't know a thing about it.'

'Right after the war Eckstein got into flour. When no one else had flour, he did. Some people even say he was a Russian spy. Imagine that, me with a Russian spy in my car. Imagine. But you don't know anything about it? You used to go over there all the time. My wife saw you there regularly.'

I shook my head.

'Funny, because people say you still see young Eckstein all the time. Doesn't he know anything about it?'

I shook my head again. My suitcase was feeling heavier by the minute.

'And Berk is dead,' Meerschwam whispered. 'It must have been a terrible way to go. The kind of thing you wouldn't wish on your worst enemy. Not even on a strange man like Berk, just between us.'

'Yes,' I said. I was walking as fast as I could, but the suitcase must have weighed fifty pounds.

'You know what they say about poor Mr Berk? That he went to the whores. Well, just between us, that's no real news. My wife and I have known that for years. Everyone knew it, but we never said anything about it. People say Berk died of that terrible venereal disease – I don't even want to mention the name. Well, what do you expect when you go to the whores all the time? That's how I look at it. What goes up, must come down.'

'It was pneumonia,' I said.

The pack-mule shook his head.

'So they never said anything to make you think Eckstein was up to something funny? Strange. Because everyone's talking about it. Absolutely everyone. Listen, not that I put any stock in it, but let's face it, he *was* awfully rich. He's welcome to it, it's not that, but he *was* awfully rich. My wife says: "Tomorrow it will be in the paper and they'll come knocking at our door, mark my words." That's why it's a bit of a bother for us. The Ecksteins were always very generous, but we don't want any trouble.'

I'd reached the Willemsparkweg and decided to wait there for the number two tram.

'Can I buy you a cup of coffee?' the pack-mule asked.

'No,' I said, 'thank you. I'm in a hurry.'

'What's in the suitcase?'

'Clothes,' I said.

'Clothes,' he echoed. 'So you're leaving as well.' Then he whispered in my ear: 'Are you afraid they'll come knocking at your door too?'

When I finally got to Elvira's, Broccoli said I looked like an ornamental gnome with a red nose. I looked in the mirror, and I have to admit it was an accurate description. I said nothing about my encounter with Mr Meerschwam.

Elvira was sitting on the bed. She was writing in her notepad. She told me she'd stopped taking acting lessons, because they weren't teaching her anything. I sat down next to her. She stopped writing.

'Don't you have to go see Frederika Steinman?'

That evening we ate borscht at Mme Bercowicz's. She'd lost her court case; her brother's headstone would have 'Berk' on it. She'd already announced her intention to boycott the stone and place another one beside it with her own hands. The owner of the cemetery had written to say that her emotions were understandable, but that the dead deserve peace and respect. Mme Bercowicz had written him a little note back: 'You're mistaken. The living deserve peace. To say nothing of respect.'

Like last time, she'd asked Broccoli to bring beer, and just like last time the bottles disappeared into her refrigerator and didn't come out for the rest of the evening.

While we were eating, Broccoli asked if she'd found any papers in her brother's attic that might have something to do with his parents.

She hadn't found a thing. Only two huge salamis at the back

of the closet. Her brother had stowed them away like hidden treasure, she said, and she tried to give us one as a present. We didn't feel we could accept a present like that.

The borscht wasn't as bad as the soup she'd made last time. When our bowls were empty, she took us into the bedroom. There were now three new versions of her book. It had become completely impossible to move around.

She took the latest version out of a cardboard box and began reading aloud. After half a page she stopped. She looked at us and asked if we'd ever heard Marilyn Monroe sing. A little later she led us back to the living room. 'Is it too cold in here for you?' she asked. Her house was cold as ice, but we didn't tell her that.

I went to the toilet. There was a pool of water in her bathtub, with about twenty pairs of knickers floating in it. When I came back I heard Broccoli inviting Mme Bercowicz to Elvira's *Macbeth*.

Mr Lebbing was pacing back and forth, rubbing his hands together. 'We'll pack them in,' he kept saying. Then he'd disappear into the makeshift dressing room where Broccoli and Elvira were sitting. He said it to me too: 'We'll pack them in, you wait and see.'

The play was supposed to start at eight-thirty, but Broccoli insisted that we wait another half-hour. Except for Lopatin and myself, no one had showed up.

Broccoli had placed ads in *Het Parool*, *Trouw* and *De Volkskrant*: 'Elvira Lopez plays Lady Macbeth.' It hadn't helped.

Half the performance was impossible to understand because of Elvira's heavy accent. What's more, they'd chosen a very formal translation, and then pasted together all those monologues, so you couldn't make head nor tail of it. In fact, it wasn't really a performance at all. It was more like a religious rite.

Elvira was wearing an evening dress. Broccoli had on a tuxedo. He was sitting in the front row. He'd rented sixty folding chairs from a church. Mr Lebbing sat behind him. And Lopatin and I were right in the middle.

When it was over, Mr Lebbing shouted: 'You've got what it takes, hey, you've got it.' And he threw his arms around Elvira. He still had that grey beard. His wife was in bed with a migraine, he said, but sent her regards to all of us.

Elvira seemed relieved that the whole thing was over. 'At least I got a nice dress out of it,' she said.

Lopatin had been counting on chocolate cake. When it turned out there wasn't any, he just disappeared.

'Shall I get some cheese out of the fridge?' Mr Lebbing asked.

'No,' Broccoli said, 'that's not necessary. I'll come by tomorrow to pick up the folding chairs.'

Mr Lebbing shook Broccoli's hand long and hard. 'We should work together more often, buddy,' he said.

At Elvira's house we drank champagne with cognac in it. Elvira said the person who'd invented that concoction should be put behind bars. Actually, I had to agree with her. But we kept drinking it so Broccoli's feelings wouldn't be hurt. You had to shake it well, he said, to make it fizz. He slammed the glasses down on the table to mix the stuff.

According to Broccoli, the time had come for Elvira to go to Hollywood. She'd outgrown Holland.

Elvira didn't say anything. She just put on some music. Between numbers, she whispered that she'd once liked nothing better than sitting on the back of a motorcycle. That she'd sat on the back of motorcycles for days on end, and that, looking back on it, it was one of the finest things she'd ever done.

'You can sit on the back of a motorcycle in Hollywood all you want,' Broccoli shouted. Then he said pensively: 'Mme Bercowicz didn't show up, I was really counting on her.'

Elvira danced for us, and Broccoli kept saying that she should go to Hollywood, that we should all go to Hollywood. Meanwhile, he kept mixing enough cognac and champagne to supply an orphanage.

When Broccoli got tired of mixing, he started calling travel agencies, even though it was the middle of the night. A few times we heard him say: 'But if you're not a travel agency, what are you?'

Finally, he gave up. Then he started doing a striptease. First his bow tie, then his patent leather shoes. We put on 'It's Raining Men, Hallelujah'. And we kept playing it over and over. I bet we must have played it a hundred times that night.

Broccoli started in on his shirt. 'You should go into nude dancing, Broccoli,' Elvira said, and she began mixing cognac and champagne herself.

'That's right,' Broccoli said, 'in Hollywood we'll be the three Dutch nudies. We'll be a huge hit. No party will be complete without us. And when they're handing out Oscars, the three Dutch nudies will dance at intermission.'

When Broccoli was down to his pants, Elvira said: 'Now it's your turn.'

'It's Raining Men' was still on. I started with my shoes. I used my left hand to swing the laces around, the way I'd seen Broccoli do. With my right hand, I massaged my crotch and jumped around at the same time. I figured that's what nude dancers did. Between jumps, Broccoli brought me cognac, because the champagne was finished. While I was working on my shirt, Elvira suddenly said: 'Do you hear that?'

We turned off the music. Now we could hear it clearly. The downstairs neighbour was pounding on the ceiling with a broomstick or something. That put a premature end to my nude dance.

A little later we noticed that the pounding wasn't coming from downstairs, but from the door. Broccoli looked through the peephole, came back and said the downstairs neighbour was pounding on the door with a mop. We all went to look. He was right. The neighbour was pounding on the door with a mop handle.

'Don't open it,' Elvira said.

'It's all over,' Broccoli shouted through the door. 'We're just three Dutch nudies bound for Hollywood.'

WE'VE GOT TO GET OUT OF HERE

*T*wo days after Broccoli decided we should go to Hollywood as nude dancers, he told us his money was finished. At least that's what Mr Tuinier at the Amro Bank had said.

'To cover the deficit I even had to sell all your stocks and bonds,' Tuinier had told him.

'Now I have to go to Zurich,' Broccoli said. I suddenly remembered Broccoli's father saying that his son would be the last Eckstein with a bank account in Zurich.

Lucky for him that his parents had left Switzerland. They'd also left Mexico. They were in Venezuela now. There they'd have time to think about their final destination.

Broccoli would take the night train to Zurich and come back a day later. He didn't invite us to go along.

That night Elvira slept on the bed, and I slept on a mattress Broccoli had bought somewhere on the cheap. She said Broccoli was serious about going to America, and she'd probably go with him.

'What are you going to do there?' I asked.

All she said was that you had to do whatever necessary to make sure life didn't get boring. That some day I would find that out for myself. That in the end almost nothing mattered; not whether you became sort of famous, or not at all, or even extremely so, and not whether you had a bank account in Zurich, or no bank account whatsoever. At a certain point nothing really mattered much any more, as long as you made sure life didn't get boring.

I asked her what the best way was to make sure of that.

'Sit on the back of a motorcycle,' she answered. 'Sit on the back of a motorcycle for days on end.'

When I tried to kiss her, she pushed me away. Now I knew for sure that I'd never ask her: 'Why once, why not sixty times, or never? Why once?'

The next morning the phone woke me. Elvira slept right through it, so I answered. I was expecting it to be Broccoli, but it was Mr Meerschwam. He wanted to talk to Broccoli. When he heard that Broccoli wasn't there, he asked me to pass along a message: there were bills to be paid. And his wife had called a few times already.

How the hell did he get this number? I wondered.

'Who was that?' Elvira asked.

'Wrong number,' I said, 'some prankster.'

I suggested going out for breakfast. 'Let me sleep,' Elvira said, 'please, just let me sleep. You go out for breakfast.'

Now that Broccoli's money was finished, I had to come up with other funding. I started stealing from my parents. Small amounts, so they wouldn't notice.

A rabbi came to visit me at Mr Rapp's. I hadn't seen him for a long time, so I thought his visit had something to do with my thievery. He spoke broken English. Or maybe it was broken Dutch. In the synagogue he held long speeches in which he tried to explain God's actions as best he could. He also sketched the standards to which the Jews had to live up if the Messiah was ever to come. He had twelve children he couldn't feed himself, so other Jews had to support him. My mother had brought him a basket of food once, but he hadn't accepted that.

Now he was sitting next to me on Mr Rapp's sun porch. He was a bit startled by the three wooden Christ figures, but when I told him someone else had made them he breathed a sigh of relief.

'Jesus was a Jewish peasant,' he said.

'Yes,' I said.

'He was confused mentally,' the rabbi said, 'and the Jewish community was divided. That's why they couldn't help him. You're a little confused too, and we'd like to help you.'

The rabbi was the first person to establish a direct link between Jesus and myself. Afterwards, other people established that link as well. There were periods in my life when I saw myself as the liberator of Jerusalem, dressed in a blue velvet suit and sitting on a donkey. I was awfully pretty. I didn't wear glasses. My body was no longer skinny, and I'd stopped biting my nails. I excelled in the martial arts. I say this without a trace of arrogance, because there have simply been periods in my life when I thought of myself that way. There was also no trace of bad breath that could be smelled by others.

I told him I didn't need help. The rabbi didn't want anything to eat or drink. He said my mother had given him my address.

'You're a Jew,' he said, 'you can't escape from that, even if you surround yourself with twenty graven images.' He talked about how Abraham had dealt with idolatry. How he had said: 'They have ears, but they hear not, mouths but they will not speak, eyes but they cannot see.' And how Abraham had then smashed the graven images into a thousand pieces. It seemed quite plausible to me that God had ears but didn't hear, eyes but could not see. But of course I didn't tell the rabbi that.

'I don't want to escape from anything', I said. But that's probably exactly what I wanted to do. Escape from everything, escape from life itself.

The rabbi suggested giving me Torah lessons, to lead me back to the source. He didn't want any money for it. It was an honour to bring someone back to the fold. I thought about Elvira, and how we had decided to go to Hollywood as nude dancers. I promised him I'd think about it.

'Don't forget,' the rabbi said, 'how Abraham trusted in God when he climbed the mountain with Isaac. Up to the very last moment he trusted in God, to the very last moment.'

The rabbi said I should do that as well. But was I Abraham or was I Isaac? And where was the knife? Before he left, he gave me a prayer book as a present.

Broccoli came back from Switzerland with ten thousand Swiss francs. 'That's all there was,' he said.

At a pizzeria close to Mr Rapp's he announced that I should no longer call him Broccoli, but Michaël Eckstein, and that he and Elvira were going to America together.

'Why America?' I asked him.

'This is no place for Elvira,' Broccoli said. 'How many people saw her play Lady Macbeth? Two. How many people know what she can do?' He told me he was going to produce movies for Elvira to play in. He would become the Louis B. Mayer of the twenty-first century. He'd be as big as the Warner Brothers, probably even bigger.

'Can't you see it?' he said. '"Michaël Eckstein presents".'

I nodded.

'And don't forget,' he said, 'that we haven't had a femme fatale since Marlene Dietrich. But now we have Elvira.'

'Yes,' I said, 'now we have Elvira.'

'We've got Fort Knox here, don't you see that? Only they haven't seen it yet, they just haven't seen it.'

'Why can't I call you Broccoli any more?'

'The Association for Geniuses has been disbanded,' he said. 'The time isn't ripe for geniuses, and especially not for associations for geniuses. Operation Brando is the only thing that matters.'

Later that day he ran down the Beethovenstraat. I had trouble keeping up with him. He asked if I wanted to go to America too, but I hesitated. I thought I should stay in Amsterdam, on Frank Rapp's sun porch, to write monologues for Frederika Steinman. Whether she ever performed them made no difference to me.

We came to the house on the Bernard Zweerskade. There was a big fence around it now. You couldn't see the garden any more.

'Look,' he said, 'there's nothing left here for me.' He grabbed me by the shoulder. 'I have to go to Hollywood. If I don't go to Hollywood, my whole life will have been in vain. "Michaël Eckstein presents", can't you see it?'

Once again I told him I could see it.

'I'm leaving early next week, there's no time left.'

'Why isn't there any time left?' I asked him. 'Hollywood's not going anywhere.'

'It *is* going somewhere,' he said. 'Don't you think the world will see that we haven't had a femme fatale since Marlene Dietrich, but that now we have Elvira Lopez? We'll become an unbeatable trinity. I produce the films, you write them and Elvira acts in them. Unbeatable, I kid you not.' He had that look in his eye again, the one I'd first seen on the platform in Paris.

'Mr Meerschwam is looking for you.'

'How do you know?'

'He called Elvira's house.'

'I knew it,' he said. 'I knew it. They hate geniuses. Mr Meerschwam, his wife, the baker, Elvira's landlord, Albert Heijn, Henry Frohlich, the Bijenkorf, the Dutch Railways, my tailor: they all hate geniuses. That's why we have to get out of here. Out of here, do you hear me, out of here.'

He ran away. But a minute later he came back. 'Am I charismatic?' he asked me. 'A movie producer has to be sort of charismatic.'

THE ECKSTEIN COMPANY

*W*e were sitting on the floor, playing chess. One rook was missing. We used a piece of chewing gum instead. We were waiting for Broccoli. He was still at the travel agency.

I'd already asked her a few times if she liked the idea of going to America.

'Yes,' she'd said, 'a lot.'

Broccoli had told her that I wasn't going with. But she never said anything about it. And she never asked why. I wouldn't have known what to say if she had. That I was scared? That I thought I wouldn't be able to adjust? That I'd rather stay in the Führerbunker?

Elvira won.

'One more game?' I asked.

She said she couldn't concentrate. 'I need to get some sleep,' she said, 'I'm going back to sleep.'

'Remember how you told me you liked sperm in your hair, that stuck in your hair so you had to wash it three times to get it out?'

'Yes,' she said, 'I remember everything.' Then she closed her eyes. But I didn't want her to close her eyes, I wanted her to do anything but close her eyes, so I asked her: 'Remember how you told me you loved sperm that burned in your intestines like chilli peppers?'

But no matter what I said, no matter what I promised, no matter how crazy I acted, she wouldn't open her eyes.

Broccoli came home at seven. He had the plane tickets. Elvira was still asleep. They would go to New York first, then on to Hollywood. Broccoli had bought himself a hat. A cream-coloured hat.

'Are you sure?' he asked, waving the tickets under my nose.

If I'd said 'OK, I'm going with you', he actually would have bought me a ticket. All I had to do was nod. Maybe only move my lips. Maybe all I had to do was blink, but I didn't do anything.

'Broccoli,' I said.

'Stop calling me Broccoli. I'm Michaël Eckstein.' He showed me calling cards with 'Michaël Eckstein, producer' printed on them.

'Where are you two going to stay?' I asked.

'I have a cousin somewhere close to New York. A cousin or second cousin.'

'Does he know you're coming?'

'No, of course not.'

Elvira was awake now. She looked at us in amazement, as if she still couldn't figure out where she was. She was at her most beautiful when she'd just woken up, unwashed, uncombed, smelling of her own sweat.

That evening we were going out to dinner. There wasn't much time before they'd be leaving. 'The farewell dinner has to be a major feast,' Broccoli said.

He wanted to take a shower first. When he came out he was wearing his white bathrobe with 'Hilton' on it, and he refused to take it off.

'We can't go out to dinner like that,' I said. 'They won't let us in. Have you ever seen anyone in a restaurant wearing a bathrobe?'

'I stole this bathrobe from the Hilton with my own two hands, and I'm going out to dinner in it. If I feel like going out to dinner in a bathrobe, then I go to dinner in a bathrobe.'

'You say something,' I said to Elvira.

'No,' she said.

That's how we walked through Amsterdam; Elvira and I in our street clothes, and Broccoli in his white bathrobe, wearing his bedroom slippers and his new hat. He was carrying a leather bag with his new calling cards and a pile of papers.

'A pile of papers,' Broccoli said, 'a movie producer needs a pile of papers. Ever see a producer without a pile of papers?'

People were looking at us. Some of them shouted at us as we went by. 'Lesbians', for example, is one thing we heard them shout a few times. Strangely enough.

'Did Meerschwam call back?' Broccoli wanted to know.

'No,' I said.

'That's what I thought,' he said. 'You see, I unplugged the phone. Genius is in the details.'

'God is in the details,' Elvira said.

'Cruelty is in the details,' I said.

'Everything's in the details,' Broccoli said. 'So let's change the subject.'

'Aren't you cold?' I asked.

'I don't know the meaning of cold,' Broccoli said. 'I served in Korea.'

That's how we walked through Amsterdam; Broccoli with his bathrobe blowing every which way, then Elvira being silent, then me. When we got to Henry Smith's, Elvira suddenly said: 'A kid and two dogs, I could live with that.' She actually said that: 'A kid and two dogs, I could live with that.' We didn't ask her why she said it, or what she meant. Only unpleasant things need a meaning. And the lovely thing about Elvira was this: everything she said was pleasant. If she had something unpleasant to say, she just didn't say it. She'd keep her mouth shut for hours. She simply refused.

At first, they didn't want to give us a table at Henry Smith's, but after a lot of complaining we finally got one in the back, in a darkened corner.

Broccoli kept his hat on during dinner.

'Aren't there all kinds of things we have to arrange?' Elvira asked.

'Of course not,' Broccoli said, 'everything's already arranged. Look at this' – again he showed us his calling cards – '*Eckstein film productions presents: Elvira Lopez in . . .* – does that sound good, or does that sound good?'

We agreed with him that it sounded good, and Broccoli ordered another bottle of champagne. Elvira said we'd never be able to finish it; we were already half drunk, and she wanted to go to sleep. All she wanted to do was sleep. She'd arrived at a period in her life when she woke up and instantly began yearning for sleep. But Broccoli said: 'We have to celebrate the birth of The Eckstein Company. The Eckstein Company will be sort of like Warner Brothers, but then bigger, much bigger.'

A waiter came by and filled our glasses.

'Have a drink with us,' Broccoli said. 'It's on The Eckstein Company. The whole tab's on The Eckstein Company. Tonight The Eckstein Company has something to celebrate.'

The waiter shook his head. 'I'm not allowed to drink on the job,' he said. 'That's not allowed.'

'They hate me,' Broccoli said, 'do you see that? They hate geniuses; that's why we have to get out of here.'

'Come back here,' he shouted to the waiter. 'Please, Mister Waiter, come back here.'

The waiter came back.

'Did you know,' Broccoli said, 'that at the age of eight I played my violin on the rooftop patio? Even when it was eighteen degrees below zero, I played my violin on the patio. The neighbours' children threw rotten apples at me, but I went on playing my violin on the patio. Because I was a wunderkind. Did you know that?'

'No,' the waiter said, 'I didn't know that.' He walked away again.

'Come back,' Broccoli shouted. 'Please, Mister Waiter, come back here. Did you know that my father produced the biggest turds the world has ever seen? And that his turds clogged our toilet? And that's why, at the age of twelve, I already knew more about unplugging toilets than most plumbers know at fifty? I used an electric spring mechanism to deal with my father's turds, because I was a wunderkind. You didn't know that, did you?'

'No,' the waiter said, 'I didn't know that.'

We tried to go on with dinner, but Broccoli yanked the silverware out of our hands. He took one of Elvira's hands and one of mine and said: 'The Eckstein Company will be spoken of in the same breath as Warner Brothers and MGM. The same breath as Walt Disney.'

Elvira laughed. 'Yes,' she said, 'I bet it will.'

'Let us drink to The Eckstein Company.'

'No,' I said. Because I didn't want to drink to The Eckstein Company. I'd risen to my feet.

'Let us drink to sperm that sticks in hair, so badly that it must be washed three times to get it out. Let's drink to sperm in the intestines, that burns like chilli peppers. To sperm in the eyes, that stings like shampoo. Let us drink to all the sperm in the world, may it be good sperm, grade-A quality. Let us drink to that.'

For the first time that evening, Broccoli was still. He looked at me thoughtfully, as if he hadn't expected something like that from me. 'All right then,' he said, 'we drink to sperm.'

And Elvira smiled and said. 'This evening I drink to everything.' Then she took my hand and kissed it. 'That was a lovely speech,' she said.

During dessert Broccoli said he thought the man at the table next to us was Mr Meerschwam in disguise.

'No,' I said, 'that's a really old man, he doesn't even look like Mr Meerschwam. You're mistaken.'

But Broccoli would not be convinced.

Broccoli wouldn't let us finish our dessert either. He paid the waiter and bustled us outside with half a bottle of champagne.

'Now you two have seen with your own eyes,' he said, 'how much they hate geniuses.'

'That's right,' Elvira said, 'they hate geniuses. That's how things are in this world. And there's nothing you can do about it.' Then she hugged Broccoli. It was a very long hug. I think it must have lasted ten minutes. At a certain point his robe fell open.

'Broccoli,' I said, 'you're standing on the street in your underpants. Look out.'

Robe wide open, slippers on his feet, hat on his head and leather bag in hand, Broccoli ran down the street yelling: 'They hate geniuses, you people hate geniuses. That's right, you behind those curtains, come out of your houses and pelt this genius with rotten apples. Because I'm used to it. I've got some rotten apples in my bag too, let's see who can keep it up the longest. And then I'm going to unclog all your toilets, because I was an accomplished plumber by the age of twelve. Pelt me then, you cowards! Are you afraid, you chickenshits, where are you, huh? Where were you when Elvira played Lady Macbeth, where were you then? Were you watching TV? Pelt me, you hear? I want to get pelted.'

Elvira was so drunk that she had to stop every once in a while. When we got to the Stadhouderskade, she lay down on the ground and stayed there for at least ten minutes.

That evening we practised our nude dance act to 'It's Raining Men' one more time. We practised until we couldn't do it any more.

They had three suitcases with them. It was a warm day in June.

'We'll buy the rest when we get there,' Broccoli kept saying.

Elvira was wearing a long dress and sandals. She'd already

given up her apartment. I could put the few pieces of furniture that were left out with the garbage, but I could also keep anything I wanted.

At Schiphol we went to a restaurant that looked out over the planes. 'You have to come real soon,' Broccoli said. He took off his hat and leaned over to me. 'Don't forget that there hasn't been a real femme fatale since Marlene Dietrich,' he whispered. I noticed he was already going bald on the sides.

While Elvira was in the ladies' room, I asked him if he didn't mind paying her way.

'My father wanted it that way,' he said. There was something about the look he gave me that kept me from asking any further. All I said was: 'You never gave her one of those famous cards at Schiller – "*Mr Broccoli has the honour of offering you a drink.*"'

'Sure I did,' he said, 'but then I already knew her. Does it make any difference?'

I hesitated for a moment. 'No,' I said, 'it doesn't make any difference. It makes absolutely no difference.'

When Elvira came back from the ladies' room, she said: 'We have a present for you.'

She gave me a notepad. The cover was made of cork. She said it was from Argentina. 'To start making notes for the movie you're going to write for Elvira,' Broccoli said.

'And not for Frederika Steinman,' Elvira chimed in. It had been a long time since she'd said that name out loud, but from the way she said it I realised it had been on the tip of her tongue pretty often.

We went downstairs. They didn't have any hand luggage.

'Back in a moment,' Broccoli said. 'Be right back.'

He ran off.

'Is he like his father?' I asked.

'He's like Galani,' she said. Then she laughed. 'Weird, huh?'

'And what about me? Am I like Galani?'

She shook her head. 'You're sweet,' she said, 'a sweet coward, a big, sweet coward. Your cowardice may be just a little bigger than your sweetness, but not much.' Then she kissed me on the lips.

'Elvira,' I said.

'No,' she said, 'concentrate. Shut up and concentrate.'

Broccoli came back with drinks and plastic cups.

I went with them almost all the way to customs.

'We'll see each other soon,' Broccoli said, 'real soon.' He was more nervous than ever.

'Don't forget Operation Brando,' Elvira said.

'No,' I said, 'I won't.'

Once they were through customs, Broccoli yelled: 'Call Mme Bercowicz now and then. She may be a genius too.' Then he put on his hat. From a distance you couldn't see anything but that hat.

AWFULLY CLOSE

*T*he next day I went to Elvira's place.

I put the chairs out with the garbage. The bed I had picked up by a scrapyard. I brought the empty bottles to the bottle bank. It took three trips. The telephone had already been disconnected. Amid all the rubbish I found Elvira's red notepad. I took that with me. A letter came too, from Mr Lebbing. A bill for five hundred guilders for sixty folding chairs that had never been picked up. No other mail.

I spent my days on Mr Rapp's sun porch. The hours, days and months lay before me, and I thought: I have to do something constructive. Sometimes I looked at the monologue I'd written for Frederika Steinman, but I didn't like what I saw.

I never called Mme Bercowicz.

That fall I ran into Frederika Steinman again. At De Oranjerie. I was sitting at the bar when I heard someone say: 'You don't recognise me, do you?' I turned around and saw a woman with long hair who I definitely did not recognise.

'Frederika,' she said, stressing each syllable.
'Oh, Frederika,' I said.
She asked how I was.
'Good,' I said, 'and you?'
'Good,' she said. 'Busy, busy, busy.'

That winter a card came from America. It said: *'You're a timorous, frightened little man. I hope you get far. In fact, I expect you to. Michaël E.'* No return address, nothing. It was postmarked Miami.

A few months later I received a note from Elvira. She was living on Sixth Street in New York. Michaël – she called him Michaël now too – had gone on to Los Angeles. She was expecting him to call any moment.

I wrote back a few times. I promised that I would finally buckle down and write that script. But I heard nothing more. The fourth letter I wrote came back, stamped *'address unknown'*.

A couple of weeks later another card came. Broccoli wrote: *'Have you gotten far yet? Michaël E.'* The card was postmarked San Diego.

I went to the Amro Bank on the corner of the Stadionweg and the Beethovenstraat once too. Mr Tuinier had resigned to start a camp site in the south of France. His successor could give me no information, not about Broccoli, and not about his parents either.

Lopatin I ran into once by accident, in front of the Bruna bookstore on the Leidsestraat. His gym shoes had even more holes in them. When I shouted: 'Hey, Lopatin, you haven't changed', his only reaction was to walk away faster. When I went after him, he started running. At the bank where he worked parttime they told me, after a bit of pushing, that he'd stopped licking envelopes months ago. Just like that, from one day to the next.

I walked past the house on the Bernard Zweerskade a few

times too. It had a big fence around it, and an alarm installation. The rhododendrons had been dug up. The neighbours told me that embassy personnel lived there now. They didn't know what country the people were from. India, they thought.

One day, while I was waiting to pick up my order at Van Dam's butcher shop – I'd ordered a soup bone – someone whispered in my ear. 'They're in Venezuela now.' Mr Meerschwam was looking at me with a gleam in his eye. He was looking good.

'My wife's family, they saw them there. He sold houses that didn't exist, cars that still had to be built, businesses that still had to be set up,' Meerschwam said quietly. 'Why else would they stay in Venezuela and never get in touch with anyone? Believe me, it will all be in the papers before long.'

The girl behind the counter handed me my soup bone. I tried to leave, but Meerschwam was standing in my way. 'They didn't pay the last bill we sent them. After thirty years of faithful service, what do you say to that?'

He didn't give me a chance to say anything. He leaned over and whispered in my ear: 'Their boy is in a penitentiary in America. What do you say to that? I heard it from my brother-in-law's son, he goes to school in America. Just a little article in the paper, but when he saw the name Eckstein it rang a bell. It's been in the papers there, so you can bet it will be in the papers here before long. Then they'll come knocking at our door, my wife says, the papers, the radio, the television crews.'

I walked out of the shop, but Meerschwam came after me. 'Cup of coffee?' he shouted. 'Cup o' tea? You'll be interested to hear. Young Eckstein tried to hang himself, but it didn't work. He can't even hang himself properly. What do you say to that? Buy you a drink? It must come as a shock. You were pretty close, weren't you? At least that's what my wife says, you two were awfully close.'

'Thanks a lot,' I said, 'but I really have to go, I have a very urgent engagement.'

■ ■ ■

A few times I practised the nude dance to 'It's Raining Men'. Only when no one could see me, of course. But one time Mr Rapp walked in unannounced. I didn't hear him because he was wearing slippers. When I saw him, I stopped dancing and turned down the music. He didn't ask what I was up to. All he did was ask me not to forget the mosquito larvae.

RECYCLING

I live in New York too these days. I was as good as my word, only with six years' delay. But then what's six years in the course of a human life?

I have satisfactorily completed the 'salesperson in real estate' course. I have a licence. I am a salesperson in real estate. A broker, they call that in Holland, a moneygrubber. It's a fine profession. I show people houses they want to rent. I listen to their wishes. Sometimes I give them advice, or pretend to. It's not a job that requires a lot of thought. I sell service.

My real estate diploma is hanging in my kitchen, right above the stove; I never cook anyway.

I want to tell you a little bit about Gloria, because when I met Gloria I was reminded again of Elvira and Broccoli. I hadn't thought about them for a long time. I hadn't wanted to think about them for a long time. I felt like I'd thought enough about them to last me the rest of my life.

I met Gloria and her girlfriend at a nightclub. We danced, or at least we tried to dance. I tried to dance, and she danced real well. That's actually how it went.

They said: 'Come over for dinner tomorrow, we think you're nice.'

'All right,' said the moneygrubber, 'I think you two are also pretty nice.'

The next day the moneygrubber went to their place. Gloria's girlfriend was named Sonya, she opened the door. She let the moneygrubber listen to a recording of some songs she'd sung herself. 'Don't you think it's pretty?' she asked.

'Real pretty,' the moneygrubber said because he was drunk. Then Gloria came in. One eye was swollen shut.

'Her boyfriend punched her in the eye,' Sonya said, 'but she loves him anyway, can you figure that?'

The moneygrubber thought Gloria's squint made her even lovelier. I'd been invited over to dinner, but they didn't make dinner. They started kissing. At a certain point everyone was naked. The moneygrubber, Sonya, only Gloria was still wearing her panties. 'Take off your panties,' the moneygrubber said, because he believed that fantasies should come true even when you're afraid of them.

'No,' Gloria said, 'I can't do that.'

'Why not?' asked the moneygrubber.

Then Gloria started laughing and said: 'I have a penis.'

At first, the moneygrubber didn't believe her, because she was more beautiful than Sonya. And he ran his hands over her breasts. She said: 'I had shots to get those, but it costs a lot more to have a penis removed. Can't you help me become a complete woman?'

'Do you mind her being a transsexual?' Sonya asked.

The moneygrubber looked at Gloria. He thought she had lovely eyes, and he said: 'God, has this ever been a strange getting-acquainted.' He ran his hand over Gloria's hair.

'You don't mind, do you?' Sonya said. 'You're a gentleman.'

'Yes,' said the moneygrubber, 'I'm a gentleman.' He couldn't help himself, he had to grin, he had to grin broadly.

Finally, we went to eat something at a restaurant that belonged to a Venezuelan who never took off his sunglasses. We drank three bottles of wine and ate greasy little snacks. Gloria drank only water.

Sonya kept saying: 'Don't put your elbows on the table. You'll never become a woman that way.' I had my elbows on the table too, but she must have been talking to Gloria, because I didn't want to become a woman. In fact, I'd never considered it, becoming a woman. But it's something to keep in mind, should things ever get too hot for me.

Gloria said: 'I've been on the street ever since I was twelve.'

'What have you been doing all that time?' I asked.

'You name it,' Gloria said, 'and I've done it.'

The owner brought over some more snacks. '*Bellisima*,' he said to Sonya, '*bellisima*.' Or something like that. He didn't say anything to Gloria, because he didn't like transsexual.

That evening reminded me of Elvira. Not because Elvira was a transsexual. As far as I know she was born a woman, and if she's still alive then she's a woman to this day. There was nothing in the way she acted to indicate that she would rather have been a man. But you can be mistaken. I think it was Gloria's eyes, or something in the way she spoke. Or maybe it was just me that suddenly made me think of Elvira.

'When I met Gloria she was real fat,' Sonya said. 'She was a depressive.'

'Where did you two meet?' I asked.

'On the street,' Gloria said. 'Where else do you meet people? I knew I was a woman from the time I was twelve, but my parents could only love me as a man. That's why they kicked me out of the house.'

We got up and danced, there in that restaurant where the owner never took off his sunglasses. Gloria wanted to dance with me. 'I love you,' she said. Gloria was beautiful.

She smelled sweet, and we didn't step on each other's toes. The tango lessons had been good for something. She said: 'I've stolen, I've let myself be hit, I've let myself be fucked up the ass; you name it, and I've done it. Anyone can survive on the street, but then they have to be willing to survive.'

Elvira always used to say that too: 'You name it.' And then she'd laugh a bit derisively.

You name it.

We danced closely, but I still couldn't tell she had penis. We danced for a long time. When she went to the ladies' room I asked Sonya: 'Is she really a transsexual?'

Sonya said: 'That's what she told me. But I've never seen her naked. You like her, don't you?'

'Yeah,' I said, 'I like her.'

Maybe she'd folded up her penis so you couldn't feel it. That's possible. You can do the weirdest things with penises.

When closing time came and we were standing in front of the restaurant, Sonya said: 'Why don't you come up?'

When we got there, Sonya went to the toilet, but she didn't close the door. I always close the door when I'm sitting on the toilet. And if the door can't close, I don't go to the toilet. I'm very particular about that. Sonya was sitting on the toilet, singing. She sang a song for me. 'Will you produce it for me?' she asked when she was done.

'I'm not a record producer,' I said.

She didn't care. She asked for my phone number. I wouldn't give it to her. Sonya had stuffed some money in my breast pocket to help pay for the wine, but I laid it on the table and said: 'Since I'm not giving you my number, I guess I'll give you this back.'

'Yeah,' Gloria said, 'that's OK.' That's how things go between moneygrubbers. You have the loneliness of the striker before the goal, and you have the loneliness of the moneygrubber.

When we said goodbye, Gloria said again: 'Give me some money, so I can become a complete woman.'

The moneygrubber gave her a hundred dollars.

Then I took a cab. I got a cabby who drove in his sleep, I could see it in the mirror. He had his eyes shut.

'Are you all right?' I asked.

'Yeah,' he said, and drove on. I fell asleep – I do that pretty often in taxis – and I thought about Elvira. Sometimes I snapped out of my sleep, and when I'd see that we were stopped at a green light, I'd tap on the glass and shout: 'Hey, man, are you all right? We're stopped at a green light.' Then he'd drive on, his eyes still shut. He only opened his eyes for a moment when he hit the brakes. It was scary to see, but when I closed my eyes I didn't notice it any more.

Gloria wanted to be an actress, but she only wanted to start auditioning once she was a complete woman. I can imagine that. Things like that don't allow for halfway measures.

Elvira had wanted to be an actress too. She already was one. She lived on Sixth Street. That, at least, was the last address I had.

Of course I went to Sixth Street once, number 206 East, apartment 3. Four French girls were living there. They'd never heard of Elvira Lopez.

'Or wait a minute,' one of them said. 'Wasn't that the girl who used to live here with the photographer?'

'Impossible,' I almost said, but then I realised that Broccoli could have become a photographer.

'Could be,' I said.

'They really trashed the place,' the French girl said.

'Yeah,' the other three chimed in, 'they made a complete mess of it.' If I only knew what the apartment had looked like when they moved in. I told them I was a real estate agent and knew all about houses and how they were left behind.

Acting on advice from a colleague, I called a private detective. 'It's about missing persons,' I told him. We arranged to meet in the detective's car. It was parked at the corner. Five minutes before our meeting, he called to tell me his location and the colour of his car.

He barely looked at me when I slid in beside him. He had a

moustache. I had the feeling our conversation was being recorded. There was a kid's seat in the back. He kept staring straight ahead. I handed over the information. There wasn't much to hand over. Their names. Broccoli's date of birth. The year Elvira was born, and her mother's phone number in Buenos Aires. Elvira had always kept her precise date of birth a secret. She hated birthdays. She was a vehement hater of birthdays. In fact, of all official celebrations.

'Are you sure this information's correct?' the detective asked. His calling card said his name was Steve, and that he specialised in marital problems and missing persons.

'Yes,' I said, 'very sure.'

'And what was your relationship with the missing persons?'

I hesitated. 'A friend,' I said, 'and we were in business together.' It was a pretty skimpy summary, but I didn't feel like going into it any further than that.

'What kind of business?'

Again I hesitated. 'We worked as silent extras in the movies; Dutch-language features, promotional films, trade-union commercials, anti-tobacco spots. That kind of thing.'

He wrote it all down. Without comment.

'Do you still work as an extra?'

'No,' I said, 'I sell service, I'm a dealer in real estate.' I gave him my card. 'How much is this going to cost?'

'Five or six hundred,' Steve said, 'but if they're not in the States any more, it'll be more expensive. Then we'll have to slip the Immigration Service a little for the information we need, that might be a few hundred bucks. But then at least we'll know for sure that they're no longer in America. Would you happen to know if they have a credit card?'

'I'm pretty sure they have a credit card. Doesn't everyone have a credit card these days?'

It was a hot, muggy day. I was sweating hard, even though the air-conditioning was on. When the detective said he'd take my case, and once I'd paid his retainer, we shook hands and he looked at me briefly. Maybe it was my imagination, but I had the impression there was pity in that look.

A few weeks later he called. The number in Buenos Aires I'd given him no longer existed. He wondered whether I had any other numbers in Buenos Aires belonging to the family of Elvira Lopez. I didn't. 'Eckstein's parents live in Venezuela, though,' I said quickly, 'under a false name. That's what people say.'

After that, I never heard anything from the private detective, specialised in marital problems and missing persons. Maybe they weren't missing at all. Maybe it's not up to us humans to decide who's a missing person and who isn't.

Whenever I go to the movies I always stay until the last credits roll off the screen. One day I'm expecting to see: 'Woman in café – Elvira Lopez', or: 'Third pedestrian – Michaël Eckstein'. Or something along the lines of: 'A production of The Eckstein Company.'

Maybe there's no point in staying for the last credits, because maybe Elvira has finally found her stage name. One that really fits. One Galani couldn't have found for her.

Recently I saw a movie with Frederika Steinman in it. That's how I got to see her tits for the first time. Nice tits.

Sometimes, on a Friday afternoon, I read through Elvira's red notepad. It's the only proof I have of her existence.

'*The Meisner Method for Actors.*' That's the first entry.

I don't read it with the idea of still somehow becoming an actor. I am an actor. Anyone who sells service is an actor.

'*Day One,*' she wrote. I don't even know any more what year it was when she wrote that, 1988 or 1989.

'*Listening is the key,*' it says. And below that: '*Definition of acting: the ability to live genuinely under unreal circumstances.*'

'*Day Two. Don't ask questions.*'

'*Day Seven. Don't avoid the obvious. Don't be practical. Forget a little. Don't show your feelings, they can take care of themselves.*'

Between it all a phone number and a name: 'Pretty Face Bo'. And on the next page my own handwriting, in block letters: '*Rolling off a log.*' Elvira has put question marks around it.

And then suddenly, in the middle, Day Two starts all over again: '*Give no information*' is written in big letters.

After the twelfth day, the notes stop. There are a few doodles and the occasional appointment. And a few translations of Dutch words into Spanish. When I look through that notepad I can hear Elvira speak, and I speak back. It's impolite not to speak when spoken to.

Everything they whispered about Elvira was true. She told me so herself. And the whispering about Elvira is still going on. I hear it wherever I go. The whispering about Elvira will never stop. That's what Broccoli promised us, in the fitting room at De Bonneterie.

I have cuts on my weenie. Three in total. They've tried everything. Now they've given me a salve to rub on it every morning. A sort of zinc salve, real greasy in any case. Just to be on the safe side, I wear two pairs of underpants.

The last time I was with a woman was in a hotel on the West Coast, where I was spending my holidays. The sex lasted almost eight minutes. Before and afterwards we spoke at length, and quite pleasantly, about recycling.

Last week I ran into Wolf in a strip joint. He was dancing with a naked fat woman up on stage. His shirt was unbuttoned to the navel, and his tie was hanging down his back. He'd put on more weight. At first I couldn't believe it was really him. What the hell was he doing in New York? When he came down off the stage I shouted 'Wolf!' He turned around, but when he saw me he walked away immediately. I ran after him. I wanted to ask if he'd seen Elvira, if he knew where she was hanging out. When I got out on the street, he was gone.

I think Broccoli and Elvira will come to me of their own accord.

I think I just have to be patient. Maybe they're already close by. Maybe they're already in town.

Broccoli had said: 'Operation Brando countenances no betrayal. Operation Brando is hard, but fair.'

This world needs more Marlon Brandos. There's no denying that.

I think Broccoli's working on it right now. All over the world, people are in the process of turning into Marlon Brando. And Broccoli and Elvira are leading the operation.

You can tell the members by the telephone they carry in their left shoe. Sometimes on the street I see someone messing with his shoe and I think: that's one of them.